# THE BEWITCHING MISS BLAIR

DARCY MCGUIRE

Boldwood

First published in Great Britain in 2026 by Boldwood Books Ltd.

Copyright © Darcy McGuire, 2026

Cover Design by Head Design Ltd

Cover Images: Head Design Ltd and Shutterstock

A CIP catalogue record for this book is available from the British Library.

Paperback ISBN 978-1-80656-305-0

Large Print ISBN 978-1-80656-299-2

Hardback ISBN 978-1-80656-340-1

Trade Paperback ISBN 978-1-80656-326-5

Ebook ISBN 978-1-80656-334-0

Kindle ISBN 978-1-80656-337-1

Audio CD ISBN 978-1-80656-306-7

MP3 CD ISBN 978-1-80656-313-5

Digital audio download ISBN 978-1-80656-304-3

This book is printed on certified sustainable paper. Boldwood Books is dedicated to putting sustainability at the heart of our business. For more information please visit https://www.boldwoodbooks.com/about-us/sustainability/

Boldwood Books Ltd, 23 Bowerdean Street, London, SW6 3TN
www.boldwoodbooks.com

*To the witch in every woman, may she burn bright in the darkest times.*
*And to Derek, my forever.*

# 1

## FEBRUARY 1866

The man's spirit lingered, anguished and alone. Clio Blair could sense his jagged energy, sharp as the metal tang of blood tinging the air.

Viscount Beachley's maids had done their best to clean the entryway. The Aubusson rug where his body had been discovered no longer graced the grand entrance to his resplendent Mayfair mansion. Dark mahogany wall panels had been polished with lemon oil and beeswax. The parquet was scrubbed and swept. Carpets on the stairs winding up to the first floor were brushed to burgundy finery.

But death still settled in the cracks like dust and clung to the shadowy corners as sticky as cobwebs.

She turned a slow circle and waited for her magic to fill in some of the blank spaces in Superintendent Lachlan MacDougal's story. One thing was certain: Uncle Lachlan would be relieved the victim's ghost remained. It was impossible to determine whether a soul would move on or stay. In this case, Viscount Beachley was most assuredly still in his house, in spirit, if not in body. Which meant Clio could help her uncle with the case.

*Lucky me.*

Sir Robin Goodfellow, Clio's feathered familiar, clacked his beak and adjusted his perch on her shoulder. Sleek raven feathers brushed against her cheek as she noted a scuff mark on the wainscoting that lemon oil couldn't remove.

Uncle Lachlan had sent a missive requesting her presence at his office far too early that morning to discuss the case with her in hopes she might accomplish three tasks.

One: determine if Viscount Beachley's spirit had remained earth-bound.

*I can tick that off the list.*

Two: win the trust of the spectre.

*Decidedly more difficult.*

It could take days, weeks, or even months to win over a ghost. Until a spirit trusted her, they would remain hidden. Once she could prove she intended to help, often the ghosts would show themselves, but that didn't come without risk. A corporeal spirit, while not able to harm most of the living, could harm Clio if it wished. She hadn't quite worked out the why of it. She could see them when no one else could, so perhaps that connection allowed them to interact physically with her.

It was why Aunt Rowan hadn't allowed Clio to help Uncle Lachlan until her twenty-first birthday – seven times three – when her magic was fully fledged. Even then, her protective aunt was reluctant. Four years and eight cases later, Clio had managed to help all but one soul make peace with their passing. A particularly vexed marchioness had wanted the impossible: vengeance. That was something Clio could not provide.

Anger was a common emotion among wronged spirits, but when Clio refused to help the dead woman, her rage eclipsed anything Clio had encountered.

She had needed her entire coven – her sister, her cousin, and her aunt – to help cast the binding spell, imprisoning the spirit within a talisman where it could do no harm. Clio could not force a ghost to transition, but she could contain the soul in an object until it was ready to move on. It was akin to holding them in a prison cell with only one key to freedom. Passing from this plane to the next, wherever that might be.

Binding spells were dangerous magic. Taking away any creature's choice was not the craft she and her coven practised unless they must, and as with all power, it required sacrifice. It had taken Clio weeks to feel strong enough to leave her bed after the ordeal, and her right arm and torso bore scars from the battle she waged with the woman. Aunt Rowan strictly forbade her to work with any more ghosts, but her gift was connected to fire, the element that transformed physical objects into heat and smoke. Her witchfire was designed to aid in transition, and she could not turn away from helping those who were trapped in a world where they no longer belonged. It wasn't impossible for a witch to reject her magic, but it was incredibly difficult.

*And incredibly stupid.*

Something Clio was decidedly not. So, she hadn't told Aunt Rowan where she was going that morning when she left the house and drove herself in her smart little cabriolet to 4 Whitehall Place to speak with Uncle Lachlan. Why borrow trouble before she even knew if the ghost lingered?

*But now I know he remains, and he needs my help. I cannot refuse to take this case.*

Which brought her back to Uncle Lachlan's last task.

Three: find the murderer.

*Easy as you like. I'm sure to have this buttoned up by teatime.*

After listening to Uncle Lachlan summarise what Scotland Yard knew about the death of Viscount Beachley, it was clear facts wouldn't be enough to solve his murder. This crime needed more than just investigative skills; it needed a little bit of magic.

Luckily, Clio had both. She would use all of her abilities to help win the ghost's trust and use his eyewitness account to find the culprit who murdered him. Once Viscount Beachley knew his killer would face justice for the heinous deeds committed, she hoped he would transition peacefully. If he had any other unfinished business, she would do her best to help.

Aunt Rowan wouldn't be happy.

*But when is she ever pleased about one of us working with Uncle Lachlan?*

Clio, her sister, and her cousin all lived with Aunt Rowan in a townhouse not far from Viscount Beachley's Mayfair mansion in Grosvenor Square. As the last living matriarch of their family, Aunt Rowan had very particular feelings about her nieces and their activities regarding Superintendent Lachlan MacDougal. He wasn't Clio's real uncle; she didn't have one of those any more. But her family had known him from their childhood in Scotland, and he was the only male Aunt Rowan trusted in London. Even if she hated him in equal measure.

Whatever caused the ire between Aunt Rowan and Uncle Lachlan sparked many a late-night discussion between Clio, her sister Eleanor, and Cousin Helena. But not even their combined magic was strong enough to combat Aunt Rowan's shielding spell on her thoughts regarding Uncle Lachlan.

*Infuriating.*

Clio hated when she couldn't achieve her goal. But delving into family secrets was a problem for a different day. Today, Clio needed to begin winning over the trust of a rather grumpy ghost.

She crouched as Sir Robin flapped his wings and landed gracefully a few feet away, hopping in the adorable way ravens had as he conducted his own explorations. He was awfully good at finding lost things. Especially shiny objects like rings, coins, and necklaces. Occasionally, he found them when they weren't lost at all, but Clio was working with him on his habit of 'borrowing' items.

She tugged off her gloves and tucked them into her pocket, her bare hands hovering over the patch of wood where the rug had been. Sometimes, it helped to touch where the body had lain. The sensory connection could help focus her visions of the past. Wide skirts hindered her movements. Her tight corset constricted her ribs and dug into her full hips as she leaned further forward.

'Blasted fashion,' she muttered to Sir Robin.

'Blasted fashion,' he replied in his uncanny mimic. It was a trait that shocked most people when they first heard him, but ravens were cunning birds, and Sir Robin was especially brilliant.

Clio might hate corsets, but she did love a daring dress. Today's ensemble was fuchsia with bold ebony stripes and black lace trimming. The bright colour brought some much-needed cheer to a dreary, grey February day. It also highlighted her pink cheeks and midnight hair, contrasting nicely with her amber eyes. An enterprising fool recently described their light colour as honeyed gold, earning himself a swift exit from her presence.

'The only gold he's interested in is what's in my pockets. Fortune hunting basta—'

Before she could finish her assessment of the impoverished lordling, the front door crashed open.

Sir Robin cawed in alarm and hopped closer to Clio's skirts.

A large man in a black greatcoat, tall hat, Hessian boots, and dark trousers stood in the doorway. Wind tangled his coat tails, making the fabric twist and swirl behind him like bat wings. His sharp gaze found Clio almost immediately. Black brows pulled low over piercing green eyes. Pointing the silver handle of a beautifully carved walking stick directly at Clio, he could have been a dark angel sent to steal her soul.

'Who the bloody hell are you, and what the bloody hell do you think you are doing here?'

For a surreal moment, Clio froze, her shrewd mind trapped in stasis, her hand still reaching out to touch the floor. A rogue image flashed of the man's face, in a different time. The lines bracketing his lips were gone, his hair cut in a fashionably short style, impeccably combed. His eyes were stricken with grief, his beautiful mouth twisted in pain. Then it was gone, as swiftly as lightning disappearing in a black sky.

*Holy Hecate. What was that?*

Clio had visions of the past, but they were only ever linked to the dead. Never the living. Blinking, she forced herself back to the present and slowly rose. As she did, Sir Robin took the opportunity to flap back onto her shoulder.

'Bastard!' Sir Robin's timing was impeccable as he finished Clio's last sentence.

The man's eyes widened in shock, and she took a measure of satisfaction in unsettling him.

'Did your bird just call me a bastard?'

'Don't be ridiculous.' It wasn't ridiculous at all. She was quite certain that is exactly what Sir Robin had done, and she was inclined to agree. A beautiful bastard, perhaps, but trouble, nonetheless. Unease rippled through her. 'One might ask why *you* are here, and what *you* are doing, though I would never deign to do so in the rude fashion you have demonstrated. Such language, sir, in the presence of a lady. Shocking.' She pressed her lips together, the lie bitter on her tongue. She was many things, but certainly not a lady. Her blood ran as red as any other commoner, even if her bank account was richer than most peers of the realm.

While Aunt Rowan's apothecary shop on Savile Row, All Things Bright and Beautiful – catering solely to the beau monde's most distinguished ladies seeking the elusive recipe for eternal youth –

had made Clio and her family richer than most of their Mayfair neighbours, it hadn't bought them a title. Not that Clio cared. Titles were as useless as suitors. They both required the same thing from women. Submission to rules neither benefitting nor protecting them. A woman was required to sacrifice her land, wealth, and autonomy on the altar of matrimony. A husband could do with them, and her, as he pleased. Hardly a worthy trade in Clio's estimation.

Her mother tried to follow convention, and it ended in her death. She was the one ghost Clio desperately wished to see but never had. Aspen Blair abandoned her daughters in life, and so too did she slip away from them in death. She gave every part of herself to a man, and it killed her.

*No love is worth such a sacrifice.*

In Clio's five and twenty years, she knew several ways to keep herself safe from all manner of danger. Always hang a mirror facing the door, sprinkle each entrance of a home with black salt and sage, and stay far away from handsome men with smouldering eyes and a lying tongue.

*Bollocks to men and their false promises.*

And bollocks to this gentleman who glowered at her like a bull seeing red.

'You are reproving me for base language when that crow on your shoulder just accused me of being a bastard. I've called men out for less,' the man growled, his low voice echoing in the entry.

Clio rolled her eyes as Sir Robin fluffed his feathers. 'Sir Robin Goodfellow is hardly a crow. He's a raven. Any fool can see that. And it would be rather silly to call out a bird, don't you think? He couldn't possibly hold a gun, let alone pull the trigger. Ridiculous notion.'

Lowering his walking stick, the man blinked, no doubt trying to process all that comprised Clio Blair.

*Good luck with that, sir.*

He stepped across the threshold of Viscount Beachley's home. 'A profane raven named Robin. And you call me the fool?'

Clio frowned. Did this man know nothing of literature?

'He's named after the mischievous sprite, Puck, from Shakespeare's play. Surely, you've heard of it, *A Midsummer Night's...* oh, never mind. I doubt you're much of a reader.'

His high cheekbones flushed.

*Dear me, I've managed to embarrass the man. Well done me.*

Recovering quickly, his jaw muscles jumped in irritation before he spoke. 'I doubt you understand the danger of assumption. I can't imagine any play by the Bard would help me comprehend why that bird is currently perched on your shoulder.' His gaze moved from her face to Sir Robin, then continued down in a bold assessment before he stalled at her waist, where her gloveless hands were loosely clasped together. A young lady should never be seen in public without her gloves.

*Neither should she speak to ghosts, control flames, or walk the streets with a raven as her only companion, but that is neither here nor there.*

Heat tingled in her fingers.

Refusing to pull out her gloves and cover her scandalously naked flesh, Clio held his disconcerting stare. 'Because he is my pet.'

Sir Robin ducked his head and nipped Clio's earlobe. He did not appreciate being reduced to a mere pet, but she could hardly tell this stranger that he was her familiar or that they were bound together by mutual choice, magic, and some undetermined plan of the fates.

Clearing his throat, the man stiffened his spine and stretched his wide shoulders. 'Excuse my bluntness, madame, but this is a crime scene. Certainly not the place for a lady and her... pet.' He layered the last word with a heavy coating of sarcasm. 'Which brings me back to my original question: who are you and why are you here?'

'That's two questions,' Clio pointed out. 'And I don't answer queries posed to me by rude men.'

Before he could respond, another gentleman appeared in the open door. His neat coat, high white collar, matching cravat, and crisply pressed trousers were at odds with the wild curl of his hair.

'Ah, Clio. Here already. I was no' sure if your aunt would give you the mornin' off after we met. I know how demanding she can be.' The Scottish burr from Superintendent Lachlan MacDougal's childhood still flavoured his words. 'And good mornin' to you, Sir Robin Goodfellow.' He tipped his top hat to the raven.

'Lollygagger,' the raven replied, prompting a wry smile from Uncle Lachlan.

'I see you've been chatting with Rowan, Sir Robin. Watch out for that one; her tongue is sharper than any sword.'

The bird chirped his agreement.

Clio turned to her uncle and stretched her mouth into a friendly smile. 'Hullo, Uncle Lachlan. Aunt Rowan doesn't need me at the apothecary for a few hours yet.' She wasn't about to tell her uncle that Aunt Rowan had no idea she was even at Viscount Beachley's house, let alone that she was taking on the case. He might not get along with her aunt, but he would never defy the woman when it came to her nieces. Uncle Lachlan cared too much about his own bollocks to risk them so easily. 'I thought I would come and er...' She glanced at the man glowering in the shadows. She could hardly tell her uncle she was here to see if the ghost still lingered. 'Determine if my services will be of use.'

'Uncle? This is your niece?' The man in black swung his focus to Superintendent MacDougal.

Uncle Lachlan was not small – indeed, he stood well over six feet tall – but his companion had several inches on him, though the stranger's frame was lankier. Still, her uncle clapped his hand on the taller man's back in the hard, brutish way men had of showing affection to each other. 'No' by blood, perhaps, but close enough. Allow me to introduce Miss Clio Blair.' He turned to Clio. 'And this is an old friend of mine from our military days. Lieutenant General Grey, son to the Earl of Thornbrook, so mind yer manners, Clio.'

'I always mind my manners,' she hissed through clenched teeth, unaccountably annoyed that her uncle had so easily given up her name when she was determined to thwart him. He now knew who she was, even if he did not yet comprehend why she was at the crime scene.

Cocking her head, she tried to guess his age. She knew Uncle Lachlan was several years older than Aunt Rowan, putting him somewhere just beyond forty. A safe bet would place Lieutenant General Grey in his mid to late thirties, perhaps ten years older than herself. While she was considered a spinster most firmly on the shelf, he was very much in his prime. Not that any of that mattered. She would rather boil her own entrails in bull urine than enter into any binding union with a man.

No man wanted a woman more powerful than himself. It was a truth Clio, Eleanor, and Helena had watched come to fruition with both of their mothers. In direct contrast, Aunt Rowan kept her heart buttoned tight against the insidious lure of love, and she was wealthy, powerful, and content.

Grief, old and worn, blended with anger, fresh and powerful. Clio could never forgive her mother for being such a fool. Using a man to slake one's desires or to bring new life into the world was one thing, but sacrificing one's elemental power for something as weak and paltry as love was sheer lunacy.

The stranger, his silver walking stick clutched in his large fist, recovered once more from his shock at discovering her connection to Uncle Lachlan, and his features hardened. 'If she is known to you, that is even more reason to keep her away from such rough business. This is no place for a gently bred lady.'

'There is nothing gentle about me, Lieutenant General Grey, including my breeding.' Clio gave him a blistering smile.

'Clio, behave. And she canna' stay away from the crime scene if the lass is going to help you find Viscount Beachley's killer, now can she?'

'I am going to help him?' Clio pointed a finger at the man, her abrupt movement disturbing Sir Robin, who hopped off her shoulder and resumed his exploration of the entry.

'She is going to help me?' Lieutenant General Grey spoke at the same time, pointing his walking stick back at Clio.

'Killer,' Sir Robin added helpfully from the corner before pecking at something on the floorboard.

'Exactly.' Uncle Lachlan tucked his fingers in the pocket of his coat and rocked back on his heels, nodding like a teacher whose pupils had just mastered a complicated concept.

'I haven't even decided if I'll take this case, Uncle. And if I do, I will work alone.' Uncle Lachlan must have taken leave of his senses. Clio wished she could use her magic to read his thoughts, but that was Cousin Helena's speciality. Clio could only communicate with the dead. If she had her way, Uncle Lachlan might soon be joining that group. Maybe then she could determine what he was up to with this foolishness. 'We both know a partner will only hinder my progress.' She couldn't very well tap into her magical abilities if some hulking beast of a man was watching her. She glanced over at Lieutenant General Grey, and just as she expected, his gaze seared through her.

'I promised to help you on this case, but I never promised to work with someone else. And certainly not a woman.' Lieutenant General Grey didn't look away from Clio, though his words were directed at Uncle Lachlan.

'Bastard!' Sir Robin interjected with an aggressive caw.

Lieutenant General Grey shifted his glare to the bird. 'Or her foul-mouthed pet.'

Clio desperately wanted to point out his pun, but she feared that would not improve the situation.

The lieutenant general continued, oblivious to his unintended wittiness. 'What help could a silly girl and her ridiculous bird possibly give me?' Disdain dripped from every growled syllable.

*Oh, that does beat all. First, he won't work with me because I'm a woman. Now, he's demoted me to a mere girl.*

Sir Robin Goodfellow flapped back onto Clio's shoulder, sensing she needed his feathered support. Lieutenant General Grey dismissed them both with one blink and returned his focus to Uncle Lachlan.

Sparks tingled on her fingers. She fisted her hand and forced her power to settle.

'I'm hardly a girl, Lieutenant General. Perhaps your objection stems from fear of being outsmarted by a woman. The *only* thing you're right about.' Flame in the glass bulbs flared.

Uncle Lachlan gave her a warning glance, his message clear.

*Remain calm.*

She always had trouble regulating her power over fire when her anger was stoked. Gas-lit flames could be particularly dangerous with such a combustible, hungry fuel.

'We don't have time for arguments.' Uncle Lachlan's quiet voice commanded their attention more effectively than any shout. 'Viscount Beachley's wife is missing. She's our top suspect, and we need to find her quickly. This has already hit the newspapers, and it doesna' look good for Scotland Yard, or for yer dear Uncle Lachlan to have a potential murderess running loose on the streets of London.' Gone was the cheerful uncle who used to sneak Clio sweets when her aunt wasn't looking. In his place was the fearsome

Superintendent MacDougal, who had fought his way from lowly constable to superintendent of district C. One did not argue with Superintendent MacDougal. At least, not publicly.

'Exactly. All the more reason to send this *girl* and her bird back to the playroom and allow me to get on with the investigation.'

*I'd like to see you investigate anything with your trousers in a blaze.*

Uncle Lachlan stepped between them, forestalling the insult burning on her tongue. 'I am confident you'll find her skills far superior to most.' He wasn't suggesting this to Lieutenant General Grey; he was telling him.

Before Clio could gloat, her uncle turned to face her. 'And you will find that Lieutenant General Grey's abilities only enhance yer own.'

She bit her lip to contain her retort. It wasn't wise to be impertinent when Uncle Lachlan used that tone.

He looked from Clio to Lieutenant General Grey and back again. 'You will work together on this case, and you will solve it together.'

*We'll just see about that.*

'May I speak with you privately, Uncle?' Clio spat each word at him like bullets as the heat of power rose in her blood, coalescing in her chest where it burned like a coal. It would only take a flash of intent to turn that coal into a searing flame. She refused to look at Lieutenant General Grey. His scowling face would be the spark to set her temper ablaze.

*Must not call forth the fire and blast Mr Big-and-Surly into ash.*

Even if Uncle Lachlan hadn't been there to remind her, Clio would never harm another. As a family coven of white witches, Clio, Eleanor, Helena, and Aunt Rowan had all taken a blood oath to do no harm. Even if Clio wanted to wield her power and smite her enemies, it wouldn't work without twisting her into a dark, fragmented version of herself. It was a line she would never cross. But sometimes, it seemed a *small* amount of smiting should be allowed. In special circumstances. Like her present one.

Uncle Lachlan exhaled through his nose, his jaw muscles jumping. He nodded. 'Excuse us, Lieutenant General Grey. We won't be but a moment.'

Walking past Clio, Uncle Lachlan strode down the corridor to a door on his left. She refused to acknowledge Lieutenant General Grey as she turned and followed her uncle, Sir Robin balancing effortlessly on her shoulder.

## 2

_____

When Uncle Lachlan held the door open for Clio, she peered into a parlour that, were the day less dreary, would have been lit beautifully from the tall windows gracing the far wall. But the sky outside was battling dark storm clouds, and the gas lighting was losing its fight with the deep shadows claiming the room. Sir Robin clacked his beak in a nervous warning. Clio shivered as she stepped across the threshold.

'Go on, then, Clio. Say what yer thinking.' Uncle Lachlan shut the door behind them. As it clicked closed, Clio pushed aside her disquiet and let the rage bubble over.

'How can I possibly help you with this case if some idiot lieutenant general is watching my every move? You are putting me in an impossible situation, Uncle Lachlan. Witchcraft might not be illegal any more, but that's only because people believe anyone claiming to wield magic is lying. I've no interest in proving how real magic still is when this blackguard sees me conversing with a dead man.'

Uncle Lachlan narrowed his gaze. 'So, Viscount Beachley's ghost is here?'

'Yes, but that's hardly my point.' No longer under Lieutenant

General Grey's sharp gaze, Clio let her power spark and sizzle on her fingertips.

'Tha's excellent news! I need you to speak with the ghost, see if he can tell us where his wife might be hiding, and confirm whether she murdered him.'

Clio shook her head. 'You know that isn't how this works. He must trust me before he'll tell me anything. And I haven't even committed to helping on this case. If you're telling me I have to work with that man, I'm quite certain I won't have the time.' She spoke the word 'man' as if it were a substitute for cockroach or something equally disgusting.

'Is tha' an ultimatum, Clio?'

'It's self-preservation, Uncle. The pompous fools making laws may have decided witchcraft isn't real, but we both know what would happen if someone claimed magic still exists. All it would take is one outstanding member of the peerage – the second son to an earl with military ties and a surly disposition, perhaps – to make a claim. Imagine how quickly the House of Lords could repeal the Witchcraft Act. Witch hunters would be back to throwing people on pyres in less time than it takes to boil a cup of mugwort tea. Or perhaps the good people of Mayfair would take matters into their own hands.' Memories of what happened to Aunt Willow washed through her, faded but still fraught with pain. 'We don't reveal our powers to anyone, Uncle Lachlan. You know this, and you know why.'

Uncle Lachlan swallowed, the flash of grief in his eyes assuring Clio her arrow hit its mark. 'Of course I do. I promised yer aunt I would protect you the day yer mother left you and yer sister on Rowan's doorstep, and again when Helena came. A promise I mean to keep. But we need Lieutenant General Grey's help with this case.'

She blinked, deliberately stretching the moment. 'Then you have a choice to make. Me, or him.'

He ran a hand through his hair, further disrupting the curls. 'I've never seen you back down from a challenge, lass.'

Her laugh was sharper than Sir Robin's beak. 'Don't think you can goad me into this, Uncle.'

The twitch in his lips betrayed him. 'That trick always worked in the past. I forget yer no' a wee lass any more.' His voice softened, his chocolate eyes warming. 'Believe me, Lieutenant General Grey is many things, but he is no' a threat to you. I swear it.'

Clio shook her head. Every particle in her body rejected her uncle's claim. Lieutenant General Grey was setting off a million sparks in her body's alarm system. He was more than just a threat. He was pure danger. Clio knew that with the same certainty she knew Viscount Beachley's ghost still lingered.

'Trust me. I would never put you at risk. Besides, yer aunt would turn me into a toad if any harm came to you, and I much prefer living outside of a mucky swamp.'

She refused to laugh at his ridiculous joke. Aunt Rowan was a powerful witch, but it was superstition of the highest order to think even her formidable magic could transform humans into different forms. If that were the case, Clio would have turned the insufferable Lieutenant General Grey into a squeaking mouse the minute he insulted Sir Robin.

'Aunt Rowan lost both her sisters and took on the responsibility of raising her three nieces alone. I think she has every reason to be protective of us.' No matter what hidden ugliness existed between Aunt Rowan and Uncle Lachlan, Clio wouldn't let him disparage the woman who had become surrogate mother, friend, and mentor to her. 'She won't be happy about this, Uncle Lachlan. After last time, it's going to be hard enough to convince her I'm safe to work with spirits, let alone bringing an outsider into our lives.'

'Let me worry about yer Aunt Rowan.' Uncle Lachlan's eyes hardened. 'You worry about solving this case without getting yerself hurt in the process. If there's any hint of the kind of danger you faced with the last spirit, you'll tell me, and you'll stop. Do you swear it?'

If she took the case, she would see it to completion. Anything less would be failure. Eleanor would say, *Failure is the pathway to success*. But her sister's cheerful mantra only created frustration within Clio.

*Failure is failure. And I refuse to fail.*

But neither would she take on this case if it meant working with an infuriating man, even if he was tall, dark, and delicious.

She couldn't lie to her uncle, so instead, she chose diversion. 'I'll swear one thing to you for certain: I don't need anyone's help, Uncle. Certainly not some blustering bully who thinks I'm nothing more than a silly girl.'

Uncle Lachlan rubbed the back of his neck, ruining his neat cravat. 'That's where you're wrong. We do need his help. The man murdered here was a member of the peerage, Clio. A bloody viscount. While yer powers will be of considerable help when this ghost starts talking, we still need living witnesses to give us evidence tha' we can present to the House of Lords.'

*Blast. He has a point.*

'I can speak to the living just as easily as the dead.' Indeed, the living generally took less convincing to share their secrets. The dead were a cagey group, requiring patience and finesse. Living members of society needed only praise and flattery to grease their jaw hinges. 'I don't need some brooding black rain cloud of a man to scare away potential witnesses.'

Uncle Lachlan's eyes sparked. 'So, you've decided to work this case, then?'

*Sneaky Scotsman!*

She had been so focused on winning the argument, she didn't realise she was fighting for an investigation she hadn't yet agreed to take. 'Not if I'm forced to work with *him*. I don't understand why you think we need his help.'

Her uncle took both her shoulders in his hands and ducked his head to meet her gaze. 'Because he was born into the world of the elite, Clio. He can speak to these pompous arseholes and get them to spill their darkest deeds. You canna' do that, no matter how charming you may be.' He shook her gently and then let go. 'To them, you're a commoner. An outsider. No' to be trusted. The same is true for me. But Lieutenant General Grey is the second son to an earl. He's rubbed shoulders with these men since he was a wee bairn. Went to Eaton with the sons and danced with the daughters at their debutante balls. And unlike most of the blue bloods, I trust Thomas.'

Clio wrinkled her nose. 'What a ridiculously friendly name for such a blustering bully. Thomas.' The syllables filled her mouth like treacle and cream. She wanted to say it again just to sink into the sound.

*Nonsense. I wish to do nothing of the sort.*

'He should be called Clarence or Bartholomew or something equally dreadful to suit his personality.'

Uncle Lachlan snorted. 'Well, he is no'. He is Sir Thomas Grey, and we need him on this case.'

'Wasn't there a poet named Sir Thomas Grey?' She crinkled her brow.

'I do no' know and it does no' matter. Now, will you stop fighting me and get on with the investigation like a good lass?'

Frowning, Clio crossed her arms over her chest.

Sir Robin, who had been dutifully exploring the far corner of the room, stopped his hopping to fluff his feathers in a raven imitation of her posture. 'Good lass,' he cooed before going back to his own private investigations.

'I've never been good at being good, Uncle Lachlan. You know this.'

'Aye, but you're grand at being a persistent, stubborn, wee little termagant who doesn't stop until she's proven to everyone she's right.'

A smile stretched her lips. 'You certainly know how to flatter a woman.' Sobering, she tapped her fingers against her forearm. 'That still leaves us with the issue of keeping my powers hidden.'

'Are you sayin' the challenge is too great? Och. I never thought to hear Clio Blair backing away from a difficult task. Because of a man, of all things. But maybe yer right. Maybe this is too hard for even you to manage.'

He was goading her again. And this time, it was working. Telling Clio she couldn't do something was the quickest way to ensure she did just that.

Huffing out a breath, she tapped her shoulder to call over Sir Robin. 'I can manage that man as easily as I do everything else. The only challenge will be enduring his tedious company. I hope he is smart enough to stay out of my way. We already have one dead peer. I'd hate to add another blue blood to your list of unsolved murders.'

Sir Robin flew to her shoulder, gold glinting in his beak as his wings disturbed a lock of Clio's hair. She twisted her head to see what trinket he had found. Putting out her hand, she gave him a warning tsk. 'Sir Robin, we don't take things that aren't ours. Even if they are shiny and pretty. Drop it.'

The raven shuffled from one foot to the other on her shoulder.

'Now, Sir Robin.' She kept her voice firm, though there was no stopping the twitch of her lips. How could she ever be angry with her mischievous friend?

Sir Robin reluctantly dropped his treasure in her bare hand. A gold locket. As she closed her fingers around the cold metal, the vision came fast and furious.

*Clio reached out a large hand that was not hers and closed strong fingers around a woman's arm. Spinning her, Clio saw Viscountess Beachley's face. She had never met the woman before, but she knew it was Beachley's wife because she wasn't Clio any more. She was someone else.*

*'You must stop yelling. You are frightening sweet Anna, darling.' Clio's voice was the rough register of the viscount. She was part of his memory. He was worried; she could feel the anxious fear thrumming through his veins as if it were happening to her. His heart pounded hard against his chest.*

*'Do not speak to me of our daughter.' Viscountess Beachley was young, not much older than Clio. Her unremarkable features were twisted with rage as she spat the words like poison. A gold locket glinted around her neck, the flash blinding Clio for a moment.*

*'She is sick, Violet. She needs our support more than ever.' Viscount Beachley's voice came from Clio's throat.*

*Ripping her arm free, Violet let her hand fly on the wind to land with a stinging slap against Viscount Beachley's cheek. Clio's head swung to the side from the impact. She reached up with the viscount's hand and pressed it against the stubbled skin.*

*Violet turned and wrenched the door open.*

*'Don't walk away from me, Violet.' Desperation, fierce and frightening, filled Clio. 'Please!'*

*But Violet ignored his plea, her skirts billowing behind her as she disappeared down the darkened hall.*

The vision ended as swiftly as it began. Nausea, familiar and annoying, rolled through Clio's belly in an oily wave. Sir Robin rubbed his sleek head against her hot cheek, clicking his beak in concern. The hard outline of the locket was still pressed into her clenched fist.

Her uncle's face slowly replaced her vision of the past like mist solidifying into sculpture. 'Are you all righ'?' Uncle Lachlan's brow creased.

'I'm fine.' But she knew her skin was already starting to redden from the slap. That was new. Corporeal ghosts could harm her, but never had she experienced a vision so viscerally. And never had people in memories from the past caused her physical harm. Aunt Rowan would not be pleased if she found out about this new development. She would certainly forbid Clio from helping Uncle Lachlan.

*So, I shall keep the secret. For now.*

She could apply a healing balm as soon as she reached the apothecary. By the time she returned home that evening, her cheek would have nary a blemish.

'Did you see something?'

'I think Viscount Beachley wanted to say hello. This belongs to his wife.' She opened her fingers, and when Uncle Lachlan held out his hand, she dropped the locket into his palm. 'One thing is certain: Violet knew how to land a smack.' Her hand shook as she reached into her bag for an aniseed drop mixed with a little something special from Clio's store of herbs and spices. The candy helped to dissipate the sickness brought on by her visions.

'You're hurt.' Uncle Lachlan's voice roughened with concern as he brushed his fingers over her cheek.

She pulled away. 'It's nothing. Sometimes, it happens when a vision is particularly vivid.' If she was going to lie to Aunt Rowan, she might as well practise. 'It will fade in no time.' At least that part was true, with a little magical help.

She knew Uncle Lachlan, much like her aunt, wouldn't let her work the case if he thought she might be hurt. But the opposite was true for Clio. If she had been undecided about whether or not to take the case, Viscountess Beachley's vicious smack sealed the matter. She would find the killer and hold them accountable for their crimes.

Clio didn't take kindly to being attacked, even if it was by the missing wife of a dead viscount. 'Where is Viscount Beachley's daughter?'

Before Uncle Lachlan could answer, Lieutenant General Grey strode down the hall. His all too intelligent eyes stalled on Clio's cheek, then swung to MacDougal. The man's features were striking in repose, but when anger hardened them into sharp angles and hard lines, he was fiercely handsome.

*More like foolishly and rather inconveniently handsome. Blast. How are we going to explain this to him?*

The slap mark was a clear indicator something had happened. It was obvious Lieutenant General Grey assumed Uncle Lachlan hit her. Most men would mind their own business or not care enough to notice, but by the thundering rage rolling in Lieutenant General Grey's eyes, it would seem he wasn't most men. Clio had to give him a smidge of grudging respect. At least he didn't support women being beaten for no good reason.

It was Uncle Lachlan's grand idea to include this man in the investigation. She should leave it to him to create an excuse. But men were hopeless, and based on Uncle Lachlan's panicked look, Clio would need to take the lead.

Before Lieutenant General Grey could say anything, Clio lifted her hand and slapped her uninjured cheek with a cracking smack.

Sir Robin jumped off her shoulder, landing in a disgruntled fluff of feathers by her feet.

*Damnation, that hurt!*

Tears stung her eyes, but she blinked them away and forced her lips into a wide smile as both men – and Sir Robin Goodfellow – looked at her like she might have gone mad.

'Right, well, I must be off to All Things Bright and Beautiful.'

'What the bloody hell is going on here?' Lieutenant General Grey's eyes, greener than a broken bottle and just as sharp, swung from Clio to Uncle Lachlan and back again.

Uncle Lachlan shook his head, equally stunned.

'The price of vanity, I'm sorry to say.' Forcing a giggle, Clio ignored Sir Robin's mocking imitation of her laughter. 'It's all the rage in Paris. Apparently, pinching cheeks is out. Slapping is a far more expedient way to achieve that rosy glow.'

What a load of tripe. But if Clio knew anything, it was men's ignorance of all things relating to female beauty regimes. She spared Uncle Lachlan a glance.

*This is the price I pay to keep my powers hidden, Uncle Lachlan. You owe me for this.*

At least he had the decency to look ashamed.

She turned her focus to Lieutenant General Grey. 'We need to speak with Viscount Beachley's daughter. As Uncle Lachlan believes your connections with the beau monde will be beneficial, I'll leave it up to you to arrange a meeting with the girl. Let me know when and where, please. It was—' She stalled. Clio could hardly say it was lovely to meet him. Nor could she say it was pleasant. Disastrous came to mind. 'Interesting to meet you, Lieutenant General Grey.' Not completely honest, but neither was it a blatant lie.

'Interesting bastard!' Sir Robin blinked his black eyes at the lieutenant general.

'Come along, Sir Robin.' Clio tapped her shoulder, and the raven gave a clack of his beak before flapping his wings and gently landing on her. Tugging on her gloves, she ignored the heat in her reddened cheeks and breezed out of Viscount Beachley's home to her cabriolet, taking the ribbons from her groom. He helped her up the steps and into the hooded carriage before she felt the dip of him hopping onto the bench in the back. She clucked and flicked the reins, directing her horse onto Grosvenor Street and east towards All Things Bright and Beautiful Apothecary on Savile Row.

\* \* \*

Lieutenant General Thomas Grey was rarely confounded. Yet, in the space of a quarter hour, Miss Clio Blair had managed the task with inordinate ease. Her feathered friend certainly helped.

*A woman who keeps a talking raven as a pet. Ridiculous.*

And the things her bird said. Thomas couldn't help but suspect he was being insulted by the bloody creature. Intentionally.

He couldn't shake his encounter with the enigmatic young lady as he sat at a corner table in his club, Boodles, and ignored the looks and whispers emanating from members he once called friends.

It had been eight years since Thomas' shameful scandal made all the newspapers, but still, men he had known since childhood looked at him with a mixture of sympathy and disgust.

*Hang their opinions. They mean nothing to me.*

They meant a great deal too much to him, hence his infrequent visits to the prestigious club where his family had held a membership since its inception. The rooms at Boodles had been more familiar to Thomas than his own drawing room, with shouted invitations calling him to one table or another. He once drank, gambled, and caroused with fellow members of the peerage, confident of his place in society. Now he felt like a stranger in an unwelcoming land. Gentlemen went out of their way to avoid him.

Pushing away the useless anger and awkward awareness of so many eyes locked onto him, Thomas refocused on the man sitting opposite him.

Superintendent MacDougal shifted in his seat, not attempting to hide his discomfort at being in a gentleman's club that would never deign to offer him membership. No doubt the whispered discussions circulating the room were just as focused on MacDougal's presence in the elite club as they were on Thomas' return.

They could all go stuff themselves. Thomas was still a member of the beau monde and still a bloody member of Boodles. If he wanted to invite a lowly street sweeper into the club, he would do it.

Still, it was nice to know he wasn't the only person suffering judgement from the lords, drinking and gambling away their fortunes. Although, unlike Thomas, MacDougal hardly deserved such censure.

*What crime is worse? Being a failed member of the peerage, or not being a member at all?*

A question Thomas didn't dare voice, as there was no satisfactory answer.

MacDougal could face off against an army of enemies, seek out London's worst criminals, and fearlessly lead men into the fray, but this stuffy room full of London's upper crust looked at him like he was a piece of shit on their boots.

*It's ghastly. I don't know why I used to enjoy coming here with these self-important snobs. Probably because I was one of them. A pig rarely notices his own stench.*

But Thomas smelled the stink now. Life had decimated his sense of superiority and educated him on his fallibility. But he was still the Earl of Thornbrook's son, and his place in the upper echelons of London's society had not changed even if he had. It was the reason MacDougal needed him. He was a necessary evil, it would seem.

*Bloody brilliant.*

At least he could do something worthwhile with his useless pedigree. If he must re-enter the fray of the beau monde to solve this case, he would. But he wouldn't suffer alone. MacDougal would endure with him. One more debt he owed the man, and one more reason he couldn't refuse MacDougal's request.

'There is something decidedly strange about your niece.' Not a kind thing for Thomas to say, but their friendship had moved beyond the bounds of polite conversation in the Crimean War when MacDougal carried Thomas' bleeding body through mud, piss, and God knew what else to safety, refusing to abandon him after a skirmish with the Russian troops went disastrously wrong.

MacDougal had been a lowly foot soldier, but the man's tenacity and courage outshone his rank. Despite Thomas' slurred command that MacDougal abandon him and seek his own safety, the stubborn Scotsman refused. He hefted Thomas' substantial weight over his shoulder and wouldn't stop walking until they made it back to the relative safety of their camp. He earned Thomas' unending loyalty and a promise from Thomas to offer help if MacDougal ever had need. A promise he wouldn't have made if he knew MacDougal's need would include a raven-wielding terror of a woman.

*I should have fought harder to be left behind on that battlefield.*

Thomas was sent home to convalesce while MacDougal remained in Sevastopol until the Treaty of Paris was signed. Hard to believe ten years had passed. It seemed like another lifetime. And like yesterday.

'Careful. Another man might take that as an insult.' MacDougal's eyes flashed with warning.

'No offence intended. But she walks around with a bloody bird on her shoulder. You can at least admit she is... eccentric.'

'Clio has always been a singular personality. But every woman in tha' family is unique. And as stubborn as the day is long. Fighting against them is like takin' on the force of a thunderstorm and expectin' to win. It will no' happen. The sooner you accept tha', the less damage she's likely to do to you.'

Thomas shook his head. No woman could out-stubborn him. Certainly not the amber-eyed beauty with hair as sleek as her raven's wings and skin that glowed like a sunrise. He banished the image of her fierce gaze and soft lips from his mind. Her appearance made no difference to him.

*Although her bird would have to peck my eyes out to not notice her beauty. It doesn't mean I am attracted to her. She's at least ten years my junior, and I don't dally with innocent young misses.*

His interest in women was limited to those professionals he could pay to sate his rather particular needs. A simple, mutually beneficial arrangement that guaranteed no messy attachments. Miss Blair certainly did not fit into that category. Everything about her screamed messy.

She might not be a titled lady, but neither was she a light skirt. For God's sake, she was the niece of his friend. A respectable woman. He had nothing to offer a respectable woman. A fact his wife – *no longer* my *wife* – had been so eager to remind him of at the end of their doomed marriage. And why was he thinking about *her* again? Because something about Miss Blair reminded him of the aching desire he once felt, so long ago. It was a whisper in the raging storm of his emotions. One more reason Miss Blair didn't belong on this investigation. She stirred up carefully controlled *feelings*. The bane of any man's existence. She had already taken up too much space in his mind when he should be thinking only of solving the case. The woman was a dangerous distraction.

*It is my own lack of discipline that causes my distraction. I will not place the blame at her feet for that particular failure. It is mine to shoulder.*

One more example of Thomas' ineptitude. But that stopped today. He refused to be diverted from his goal. Even by a woman who defied all reasonable explanation.

'You must admit, it isn't exactly the done thing to include young ladies in this kind of work, MacDougal.'

The frustratingly enigmatic man shrugged. 'She would argue that she's no lady. And why shouldn't we include the fairer sex in criminal investigations? Women are just as intelligent. Just as courageous. Just as capable of solving the puzzles of human behaviour.

Sometimes even more so. Clio and her kin show far more intuition than any man I've worked with, present company included. We are blunt instruments of destruction, but women are the delicate prick of a needle, capable of knitting the fabric of humanity together or stitching us into knots. Maybe both at once, aye?'

Thomas sipped his whisky. 'That is a decidedly progressive view to hold.'

'Do you disagree?'

Tapping his fingers on the crystal glass, Thomas huffed out a breath. 'No. I don't. Women are capable of far greater treachery than we give them credit for.' Thoughts of Lissandra stabbed at his hardened heart, much like the needle MacDougal described.

*She is Lady Ellingsworth now. Happily remarried with a growing brood, and I should be glad for her.*

But it was not joy that filled him. It was a black rage wrapped in shame and tempered with grief. Her new life was a disgraceful reminder of his inadequacy. A failure from which he could never recover.

But today wasn't about the past. It was about paying off a debt and creating a path forward to a future he would endure blessedly alone and free from obligations.

'You've had a rough go, Thomas. I'll no' argue that. But you canna' judge all women by just one example. Lissandra was never right for you, but I'll never understand her choice to destroy your marriage.' Lachlan sipped whisky from a crystal glass.

Thomas pushed back the anger and shame, working hard to keep his voice steady. 'She isn't to blame. The fault lies with me. That was determined in court when they agreed to grant her a divorce.' His smile felt like it might crack his skin and reveal the monster beneath. 'Not an easy thing to do.'

'No' easy or cheap.'

'Yet Lissandra was able to convince the judge of her claim. Infi-

delity and desertion. Serious crimes for which I was found guilty.'
Eight years had dulled the sharp edges of gossip, but nothing would
restore either of their reputations completely. Thomas had been
begrudgingly welcomed back into society's arms, and Lissandra's
speedy remarriage to a wealthy earl from an old and prestigious
title – after stirring up the gossips once more – eventually forced
even the most petty peers to forgive, although they would never
forget. It was something Thomas could not do. Forgive himself. He
did not deserve such grace.

MacDougal pounded his fist on the table, causing raised
eyebrows from several men drinking at a nearby table. 'I can hold
her responsible for lying. And I can hold you responsible for no'
defending yerself. Why didn't you refute her claims? I know you are
many things, but you're no libertine and you certainly did no' desert
her.'

Thomas' chest tightened. MacDougal was one of his few
remaining friends, a man who had proven his loyalty time and
again, but still, Thomas couldn't admit the truth. 'I fucked my way
through most of London and didn't see her for over two years.'

'At her request.'

Thomas shook his head. 'It doesn't matter. What's done is done.
I have no wish to relive it. We have more important matters to
discuss than my failed marriage.'

MacDougal opened his mouth to say something, but clamped it
shut again, to Thomas' relief. There were no words to fix what was
broken within Thomas.

Better to focus on a task he was able to accomplish. Like finding
Violet Beachley.

'Your niece wants to speak with Viscount Beachley's daughter.
The poor girl was in the house when the murder happened, but she
was in the nursery in a sickbed. She is not more than nine years,
correct?'

MacDougal nodded confirmation.

'What possible information could she give us that would warrant me seeking an invitation to speak with her? She wouldn't be privy to the happenings below stairs, and it is indelicate to ask questions of someone so young. Children are just as prone to flights of fancy as women who think they can assist in murder cases.'

Lifting a heavy brow, MacDougal crossed his arms over his barrel chest. 'Or maybe they are just as underestimated, letting important evidence remain undiscovered because we are too arrogant to believe a child – or a woman, for tha' matter – might have eyes in her head or thoughts in her brain.'

Thomas slid his gaze to the side, not ready to admit MacDougal might have a point. 'Where is the girl now?'

'With Beachley's sister. Lady Diana Langley, Duchess of Devon.'

Thomas raised his brows. 'The Duchess of Devon?'

'Surely you've heard of her.'

Leaning back in his chair, Thomas allowed a small smile to tip the corners of his mouth.

MacDougal's gaze sharpened. 'I've seen tha' look. You know something and you're no' telling. Out with it, lad.'

'Her Grace is a close personal friend of my sister's. We don't run in the same circles, but I've met her at a few events my sister hosted.'

MacDougal's face broke into a grin that made him look ten years younger. 'I knew you'd be worth the trouble.'

'Don't say that until you know just how much trouble I am.'

Thomas hated to ask any favours of his sister. She had stood by him through the entire divorce debacle, even when he urged her to step away and preserve her own reputation. Her response to that still brought a smile to his lips.

'I dare any member of the beau monde to disparage you in front of me. I will destroy them before the tea cools.'

A delicate flower, his sister. The last thing he deserved were any more favours from Lady Cynthia Burrows, Marchioness of Kentmore. But his sister was the only person he knew who could grant him an audience with the Duchess of Devon.

'Can you get yer sister to arrange a meeting with the duchess?'

Thomas tapped his fingers on the table in a quick rhythm. 'I'll ask.' Though even if she were able to arrange a meeting, he doubted it would bring any meaningful information to light. MacDougal might think his niece was a crack investigator, but Thomas would need a lot more convincing than the skewed opinion of a fond uncle.

# 3

It had been three days since Clio left Viscount Beachley's home, and she hadn't heard a single word from Uncle Lachlan or the cursed Lieutenant General Grey about a meeting with Miss Anna Beachley to question the girl. Of course, she didn't expect Lieutenant General Grey to be forthcoming with any invitations, but why did Uncle Lachlan want her help on the case if he wasn't going to keep her informed? She would have to work on procuring a means to meet with the young lady herself. But such plans must wait until she completed her work at All Things Bright and Beautiful.

Aunt Rowan was predictably infuriated about her niece choosing to disregard her edict and forge ahead with Uncle Lachlan on a new case despite the danger Clio might face. All the flowers in their house wilted at once as Aunt Rowan pierced Clio's heart with a well-placed arrow disguised as a question.

'Why must you insist on risking yourself? I have already lost my sisters. Don't force me to lose my niece as well. My heart is hard, but even stone can break, Clio.'

And then Uncle Lachlan invited himself for dinner and told Aunt Rowan about Lieutenant General Thomas Grey joining the investigation. Lightning split the sky, and Londoners spoke for days about the sudden storm that flooded the streets.

After the girls were sent to bed, serious negotiations must have taken place because the next morning, Aunt Rowan wouldn't say a word about Clio's part in the investigation, but the fresh milk in the larder had curdled, and the weather remained tumultuous.

Aunt Rowan was clear on two points. The moment Clio experienced another incident of physical harm, she must quit. And Aunt Rowan wouldn't stand for Clio shirking her duties at All Things Bright and Beautiful just to chase down some murderer. If she wanted to risk her life for some imbecile dead viscount and help her feckless uncle on the case, well, she was a grown woman free to make her own choices, but Aunt Rowan wouldn't be saving her from the consequences of those choices. Nor would she expect Clio's sister or cousin to take up any slack at All Things Bright and Beautiful just because Clio had divided her loyalty between her coven and her bloody uncle, who wasn't even real kin.

*Aunt Rowan really handled the whole thing very well.*

And so, instead of heading directly back to Viscount Beachley's home on this rainy morning, Clio did her best to keep her smile genuine as she stood on the business side of the shop's counter and dealt with one of their most challenging customers.

Lady Honoria Pestlewit.

Women like her were exactly why Clio preferred to work in the cellar of the shop. They had converted the cavernous space into a kind of spell room cum laboratory cum storeroom. For Clio, it was a magical oasis. Quiet, calm, and redolent with fresh herbs, dried flowers, and essential oils. Crystals hung from the beams, catching the minimal light and fracturing colours on the stone walls. All of

Clio's carefully procured ingredients waited patiently to be blended into concoctions part-natural, part-mystical, all brimming with healing properties. She could spend countless happy hours instilling her magic into the potions handed down by generations of witches on her mother's side, experimenting with old recipes and adding new ones to the large book kept safely hidden away in a cabinet bespelled to only open for their family coven. It was one of her most favourite places. She would much rather be there than chattering uselessly with London's wealthiest ladies. But today, the fates had conspired against her.

Ellie or Cousin Helena usually worked at the front of the shop, but Helena's fox had taken ill, and she refused to leave his side until he was better. Ellie, who rarely asked favours of anyone, had asked Clio to cover her at the front of the store this morning so she could run a special care package to an ageing baroness – one of Ellie's favourite customers. Ellie was beside herself with worry for the old woman, and Clio could hardly refuse her sister's request. Aunt Rowan managed the books for All Things Bright and Beautiful, but only worked in the front of the store during dire emergencies. Clio doubted her aunt would consider this a dire emergency, especially given her current mood. So, Clio was left alone. With Lady Pestlewit.

*The most insufferable woman in all of London. This is my penance for some terrible crime I must have committed in a past life.*

'I tried your cream, and it hasn't done a thing for my complexion. Look!' Lady Pestlewit leaned closer to Clio, the angry red lesions on her cheek impossible to ignore. 'It's made everything worse! I demand you return my payment. Immediately!'

Exhaling a slow breath, Clio noticed the flames jump in the small hearth warming the shop. 'Have you also been using other products? Madame Rachel's Royal Arabian face elixir, perhaps?'

Lady Pestlewit stepped back abruptly, her eyes darting around the simply decorated salesroom of the apothecary. Aunt Rowan believed in clean surfaces, ample light, elegant displays, and natural materials. It was a drastic contrast to Madame Rachel's shop, where heavy crimson drapes, lattice screens, and Middle Eastern wall hangings created an exotic atmosphere, enhancing her claims of using only the rarest ingredients from Morocco, Arabia, Egypt, and beyond. Of course, what she actually used in her products were chalk, arsenic, lead carbonate, and prussic acid.

'I don't know what you mean.' Lady Pestlewit refused to make eye contact with Clio.

Clio chose to ignore the blatant lie. When dealing with a duchess, it was important to use diplomacy, even if it rankled. 'I've seen this reaction before.'

'I'm sure other ladies have come in with similar complaints after using your poisonous concoction.' Lady Pestlewit shook the pot of cream in her hand like an angry baby shaking its rattle.

'Actually, most of them were suffering ill effects from enamelling.' It was a process Madame Rachel was famous for, though the benefits were short-lived and often resulted in unintended and painful side effects. 'Once the paste and chalk wore off, they were left with lesions of an almost identical nature to your own.'

Sir Robin cawed before muttering something about 'vanity and madness' from his perch in the corner where he looked out a large paned window onto Savile Row.

The woman's already compromised complexion darkened to an alarming crimson. 'How dare you suggest—'

'Of course, a confident lady such as yourself would never stoop to such silly – and ridiculously expensive – methods.'

'Are you implying I don't have the necessary funds to—'

Clio continued speaking. 'Knowing, as you do, the secret to true beauty is far more complex than the smoothness of one's skin.'

Lady Pestlewit swallowed audibly. 'O-of course.' But her voice quavered. Clio felt a twinge of sympathy for the woman. As a matron nearing her fifth decade and pre-disposed to a plump figure and the natural effects of ageing, she would never meet the unattainable beauty standards currently popular in the beau monde. Sir Robin was right, as always. Her vanity would lead to madness if she didn't learn to accept herself.

Clio softened her voice and tempered the sharp flame within her to a warm heat that soothed instead of singed. 'A lady of your calibre understands it is the invisible qualities shining through a woman that make her quite spectacular.'

'Er, yes. Of course. Qualities like...' Lady Pestlewit pursed her lips, waiting for Clio to finish her sentence.

Clio nodded as though Lady Pestlewit had said something remarkably clever. 'Empathy, understanding, love without judgement – especially loving oneself – and a willingness to see the joy in life. To marvel at its wonders. These are the traits that create an unmatchable charm within a woman. Something no cream, oil, wafer, or poultice can ever achieve. But you already know this, Lady Pestlewit.'

Clearing her throat, Lady Pestlewit's lips softened, erasing the harsh lines bracketing her mouth. 'Exactly. It's a shame more women aren't as enlightened as I am about the nature of beauty.'

Clio smiled. 'Thank goodness you have such confidence to share your thoughts with so many.'

Lady Pestlewit fluttered her lashes and returned the pot of cream to her reticule. 'Perhaps this er... reaction I'm having isn't what I thought. I did eat strawberries the other day, and I've heard they can bring on a rash.'

Tapping her finger on her lip thoughtfully, Clio cocked her head to better assess Lady Pestlewit's skin. 'It's possible. I have a poultice I think you'll find works wonderfully. Some have even said its effects are so good, they're magical.' She stepped behind the counter, and Lady Pestlewit followed her down a row of white shelves. 'Ah. Here it is. The Calm and Confidence salve.' She took a clear glass bottle from the shelf. The soothing cream was tinged green from a mixture of aloe vera, distilled cucumber water, and dew collected on the first morning of the spring equinox. It nearly hummed with healing energy. Not that Lady Pestlewit would notice. Those without magic seldom recognised its vibrations.

Lady Pestlewit's brow came down as her grey eyes clouded with confusion. 'Calm and C-confidence?'

Forcing a light-hearted giggle, Clio wrinkled her nose. 'Just one of those silly names we like to give our products.'

*Hardly.*

No potion could change someone's belief, but the magic instilled in the bottle Clio pressed into Lady Pestlewit's hand would give the woman a boost of confidence, which might help her see the intrinsic worth she held far beneath her skin.

'And lucky you, we are running a one-day sale on this cream.' Clio walked back to the counter and wrote the price of the potion minus a 20 per cent deduction into the ledger. She could hardly charge her full price when Lady Pestlewit had doubtlessly been fleeced by Madame Rachel for the enamelling which had left her in such a sorry state. 'Shall I add this to your account, or would you like to pay for it now?'

Lady Pestlewit sniffed and pulled out a crystal-beaded coin purse. 'I shall pay in full. I've had quite enough of debts, I'll tell you.'

Clio made a notation in the ledger and wisely kept her thoughts to herself.

After plunking down the exact change, Lady Pestlewit tapped her gloved finger on the counter, lingering. 'You've heard the dreadful news about Viscount Beachley, I suppose.'

*My reward for giving her a discount: free gossip.*

As it was gossip about the very man Clio was investigating, she found herself unusually interested. Opening her eyes wide, she aimed for a look of shocked innocence. 'Not at all. Has something happened?'

Lady Pestlewit, in addition to being demanding, proud, and entitled, was also one of the biggest chinwaggers in the beau monde. If anyone had information on a potential murderer in Mayfair, it would be her.

'I heard from my lady's maid, who spoke with the viscount's chambermaid, who got it on good authority from the housekeeper that the poor man has been,' Lady Pestlewit paused, looked over each shoulder, then ushered Clio closer, 'murdered!' Her whisper might as well have been a shout. If anyone else had been in the shop, they would have heard everything.

Honing her best attempts at play-acting, Clio leaned back, hand at her throat, and gasped. 'No! Do they have any idea who might be the culprit?'

Lady Pestlewit shrugged, though her keen eyes betrayed her. She might be a vain woman with no confidence, but she could ferret information from a rock. Perhaps Clio should recommend her services to Uncle Lachlan. 'Apparently, his wife has gone missing.'

'Ah. Well. Most murders are committed by someone close to the victim.'

Lady Pestlewit tapped her finger on the counter. 'Or perhaps, there have been *two* murders. My lady's maid said the chambermaid told the laundress, who is a close friend of hers, that the housekeeper never got along with Viscountess Beachley. And according to the footman whose sister works in our kitchen, the housekeeper got into a huge row with the viscount only two days before his...' She shuddered, and before she could say the word again, Sir Robin flapped his wings.

'Murder!' he cried helpfully.

Clio's heartbeat increased. 'Really?'

Lady Pestlewit sent Sir Robin a searing glare before turning back to Clio. 'You'll never guess *who* they were arguing about.'

Clio shook her head, actually breathless to hear Lady Pestlewit's next words.

'Lady Violet Beachley! The missing viscountess herself! Apparently, the viscount knew of his housekeeper's dislike for his wife, and during their fight, the footman overheard him shouting, "You will not disparage Lady Beachley so grievously! How dare you make such accusations!"'

'Accusations about what?' Clio leaned forward on the counter.

'Well, that's just it. My maid doesn't know, no matter how boldly I pressed her. I suppose the footman only heard a few pieces before the viscount stormed out.'

'Shocking.'

Lady Pestlewit shuddered. 'Well, you know how dangerous servants can be.'

'I know how dangerous people can be, regardless of their station.'

Lady Pestlewit nodded as though Clio had agreed with her before continuing. 'I'd wager all my pin money that the housekeeper killed them both.'

*Dear goddess, she is ridiculous.*

*Dear goddess, she could be on to something.*

Viscountess Beachley's disappearance was certainly suspicious, but it wasn't evidence of her guilt, even if the woman was prone to slapping her husband. Could both the husband and wife be victims? Clio didn't sense another spirit in the house, but not all deceased became haunts. Perhaps Lady Beachley was killed and transitioned on her own as most spirits were wont to do, or perhaps her ghost attached itself to a different location. In Clio's experience, spirits were not trapped in the place they died. There were a myriad reasons why a ghost might choose to linger in a certain locale. She had heard spirits could even link themselves to a person, following them wherever they might move. Just because Lady Beachley's ghost wasn't in the Mayfair mansion didn't mean she was still alive.

*Is Lady Beachley the murderer or another victim?*

Before Clio could ask Lady Pestlewit any more questions, Ellie returned from her errand in a flurry of mint-green skirts.

'Lady Pestlewit! How lovely to see you again.' Ellie's soft voice brimmed with honest joy before she quickly grew serious. 'Oh dear. I see you've been suffering the ill effects of Madame Rachel's enamel—'

'Strawberries!' Clio shouted over her sister, causing Ellie's ferret to pop out from her coat pocket and chatter a rebuke at Clio. Ophelia did not appreciate anyone yelling at Ellie.

'Ah. I see you still have that rat.' Lady Pestlewit's lip curled as she glared at Ophelia.

'Ferret, Lady Pestlewit.' Ellie smiled warmly at the woman as her familiar hissed what Clio could only imagine to be a ferret version of some highly inappropriate language. Thank the goddess ferrets didn't mimic like ravens, or they would be in very hot water with Lady Pestlewit.

'It is a rodent, and all rodents are the same. Filthy creatures.'

Where Clio would have been tempted to scorch the woman's hair with a wild spark from the fire, Ellie just laughed.

'Oh, Lady Pestlewit. You say the funniest things.' She was the opposite of Clio in both appearance and temperament. Probably a result of different fathers. Their mother had kept both men for only a night, knowing she wanted children, but had no interest in a husband. If only her disdain for marriage had remained, Aspen might still be with them instead of choosing love and death in equal measures.

Ellie's sunny hair and bright complexion – gifts from an English lord – complemented a disposition that saw a new friend in every stranger, a rainbow in every stormy sky, and a promise of goodness to come in every difficult situation. A direct contrast to Clio's darker colouring and far more pragmatic nature. No one would guess they were sisters except for the shape and clarity of their eyes – though Ellie's were a bright blue to Clio's glowing amber. They also shared an unusual birthmark high on the inner thigh of their opposite limbs. Of course, few people ever saw the star-shaped stain. Their cousin had a similar marking over her breastbone. The ancients would consider it a blessed symbol of the divine feminine. More current opinion would label the wine-red marking a cursed witch mark. Maybe it was just a birthmark shared by many of the women in their family. Whatever caused the shape to form, Clio was grateful they no longer lived in a time where women were stripped naked to search for such sinister evidence of their evildoing.

*Ignorant fools. Most witches want only healing for others, and yet we are painted as the Devil's handmaidens by men threatened because of our knowledge. Why any woman would want to tie herself to such a pompous creature I shall never understand.*

Inexplicably, Lieutenant General Grey popped into her mind as clear as if he were right in front of her.

Without warning, she was sucked into a vivid vision.

*Thomas stood outside a stately country home. His. She knew it, just as she knew this was a memory from his past. But unlike her vision with Viscount Beachley – and every other ghost encounter she'd experienced – she was not inside Thomas' mind. She was watching him from a distance.*

*Her skin tightened in the frigid air. Grief and guilt filled her like ocean water rushing into the hull of a sinking ship. She felt Thomas' black despair as if it were her own. He reached out for the handle of the* large oak door, but his fingers were shaking too much to grip the brass. Whatever or whoever was inside that home created an ache in Thomas that fractured his heart into jagged pieces. Every cell in his body wanted to open the door, but fear kept him frozen. After a moment of hesitation, he turned and walked down the impressive stone stairs, his silver cane tapping a hollow rhythm as he reached a horse being held by a footman.

'Shall I tell her you came?' the footman asked, his eyes never quite reaching Thomas' gaze. It could have been an act of deference, but it felt more like embarrassment. Clio felt Thomas' reaction: shame followed swiftly by anger.

'No. It would only make her hate me more.' In a graceful move that made Clio's belly clench, he mounted the horse, still holding his cane like a sword, then squeezed his impressive thighs, and flew away from the home.

Gravel flew from beneath the animal's hooves as Thomas' black cloak flapped around him like wings in flight. He was running. From someone. Fear blended with impotent rage like ink swirling into water. Clio's hair caught in the rush of air, and an ebony strand broke free, brushing her cheek with the soft caress of someone's fingers. Goosebumps erupted on the back of her neck and over her arms as a charge of energy stroked down her spine.

Sir Robin's call pulled her back to the present. The vision dissipated and the chill with it as the shop's warmth enveloped her.

Ellie's light brows drew down, creating a crease above her nose. She knew something was wrong. 'Lady Pestlewit, is there anything else we can get for you today?' She linked an arm in the woman's, much to Lady Pestlewit's alarm, and deftly walked her to the door.

'No, thank you.' Though her words held no gratitude. 'I've gotten what I came for.'

'Wonderful. I'm sure Clio told you to use that cream twice a day, and you can keep using your Wrinkle's Away cream. They will work

beautifully together to heal your skin. Just try to avoid any more...
er... strawberries.'

Lady Pestlewit pulled free of Ellie and lifted her chin. 'Indeed.'
She swept out of the door in a rustle of yellow lace and crinoline.

Ellie quickly turned, walked through the brightly lit store, and
ducked behind the counter. She put a soothing hand on Clio's arm,
her energy buzzing along Clio's nerves and steadying her. 'What
happened? You look as though you've seen a ghost. Have you?'

Clio shook her head. 'No. I mean, not for a couple of days. I've
just...' She stopped herself. Though she was tied to the past, Clio
never had visions about the living. Her gift of seeing memories was
bound to the lingering dead, except for the two glimpses she'd had
of Lieutenant General Grey's past. What if the first was a premoni-
tion, and this second vision a confirmation the lieutenant general
had met an untimely demise since they parted?

*Screaming Saints! What if he has been killed?*

For inexplicable reasons, the idea of Lieutenant General Grey
dying sat rather ill with Clio. Of course, she wouldn't wish death
upon any soul – with a few minor exceptions – yet imagining Lieutenant General Grey lying cold and lifeless somewhere sent a
strange, desperate fluttering at her pulse points and a chill down
her spine. She needed to find him. Immediately. Uncle Lachlan
would want to know if something had happened to his friend.

*Yes. That is why I'm so unsettled. Uncle Lachlan will be upset if his
friend has met any harm.*

'What is that location charm you're always using to find things?'

Huffing out a breath, Ellie unbuttoned her coat as Ophelia
scampered out of the pocket and onto the counter, her sleek, white
hair begging for Clio to reach out and stroke. It was an invitation
she couldn't refuse. Ophelia hummed happily. She only allowed
those trusted few family members close to Ellie to touch her, and
Clio found comfort in the soft warmth of her fur.

'I don't *always* use it. It isn't as though I'm *constantly* losing things.' Ellie patted the pocket of her coat, then her skirts, then looked around the counter. 'Where the blast did I put those lemon drops?'

Clio would have found the whole thing amusing if she weren't plagued with a sense of unease about Lieutenant General Grey. 'You left them by the True Love's Scent.' A new product Clio developed using rose oil, steamed Anthurium leaf, distilled Hoya Kerri petals, amethyst crushed into a fine powder for clarity, and a bit of heat pulled from the heart of her witchflame to bubble the components into a perfume. The scent changed based on the unique chemistry of the woman wearing it and was designed to help the wearer find deeper appreciation for oneself. Coincidentally, it also seemed to draw men like moths to the flame, making it one of the more popular sellers in the store.

Ellie floated down the far left aisle, finding her abandoned bag of treats and popping one in her mouth. She was addicted to anything saccharine, and though she cursed her plump figure, she wouldn't sacrifice her craving just to fit into a smaller dress size. Clio thought her sister's figure was magnificent, even if she would never achieve the tiny waist so popular in fashion plates. Who wanted to force their body to be any shape other than exactly what it was, at any rate?

*Every corset manufacturer in England and France. And we are the bloody fools who wear them.*

Her distracted thoughts bounced like marbles on a stone bench. Ellie was the scattered one of the two sisters, but Clio couldn't seem to pull herself to rights after the unexpected vision.

She needed to find Lieutenant General Grey and confirm he wasn't dead.

*Unless he is. Damnation.*

'The location charm... what is it?'

Ellie spoke around the lemon drop, causing her to lisp. '"Goddess, Mother, Great Divine, send to me what I cannot find." And then you just visualise the thing you've lost. Did you lose something?'

Clio bit her lip. She hated lying, so she opted for omitting some truths. 'Err, not really. Just, well, do you think the spell works on people as well as it does on bags of gumdrops?'

'Lemon drops. And I've no idea if it works on people. I've never lost a person.' Ellie narrowed her eyes, no doubt seeing the odd fluctuation in Clio's aura. It was one of Ellie's gifts and made it dashed difficult to get away with any falsehoods around her. Ellie once told Clio that when people lied, the colour of their aura shifted, almost like gauze being draped over a lamp. Clio hated to guess what her aura was doing right now.

She called Sir Robin to her shoulder and gave her sister the brightest smile she could muster.

'Have you lost someone?'

'Bastard!' Sir Robin rubbed his head against her cheek.

Clio laughed, the shrill sound making her wince. 'Don't be silly. Lost someone. Really. Who could I possibly lose? Right, well. Now that you are back, I shall go and see if your charm works on helping me find... err... my missing ear bobs.'

'Your favourite amethyst ones? The pair Aunt Rowan got you for your birthday?' Ellie's eyes widened with worry.

Relieved her ploy had worked, Clio nodded emphatically. 'Yes, those.'

'The ear bobs you're wearing... right now?' She pointed helpfully to Clio's earlobe, where the blasted teardrop dangled.

'Umm, no. Not these ones. A different pair,' Clio hedged.

'A different pair of amethyst ear bobs that Aunt Rowan got you for your birthday?' Ellie's sweet smile belied the wicked glint in her eyes.

'Yes. Exactly.'

'Of course. Well, good luck finding whatever it is you've lost. Or *whomever*.'

'Thanks.' Clio didn't try to correct her sister. There was no point as they both knew Ellie was right. And Clio appreciated any luck her sister might wish. She was going to need all of it if she found Lieutenant General Grey dead.

## 4

It had taken Thomas three days to secure a meeting with his sister, and even then, it was only because he agreed to meet with her in the middle of a fitting with her modiste, the infamous and highly sought-after Madame Laurent.

Thomas sat in a delicate wicker chair, surrounded by swatches of lace, silk, cotton, and God only knew what else. His sister stood in the centre of the frilly fitting room on a small, raised dais while a young woman crouched on the floor, measuring the hem of a new ballgown under the watchful – and terrifying – gaze of Madame Laurent. Frankly, he was astounded the shop had any fabric left. Surely most of it must be draping his sister.

'I can't imagine the soldiers in my battalion carried more weight in their armour than you are currently holding up in that skirt.' Thomas looked at his sister in the reflection of a three-panelled looking glass.

'Men 'ave their uniforms, and we ladies 'ave our own.' Madame Laurent purred, her thick accent most assuredly fake. She gave Thomas a heavy-lidded look that dripped with sexual invitation. A hot flush darkened his cheeks.

'So true, Madame Laurent. I warrant a ballroom can be just as deadly a battleground as any foreign fields upon which my brother marched.' Lady Cynthia Burrows gave Thomas a far different glare full of sisterly censure. Her message was clear. *Do not dally with my modiste.*

Hopefully, his wide eyes and subtle head shake allayed her fears. He was confident in his skills as a lover, but he was also quite certain the sultry older woman would eat him alive and spit out his bones if he ever entered her bedchamber.

Cynthia returned her gaze to the mirror. 'A lady never enters the fray without being prepared, Thomas. In my case, that means endless skeins of silk.'

'Indeed. Well, I wish any opponent who tries to best you all the luck in the world. They will need it.' Thomas winked at her.

Lady Cynthia Burrows pinched her cheeks, reminding Thomas of the cracking smack Miss Blair had given herself the day they met. He found the perplexing woman crossed his mind with alarming regularity. He shouldn't be thinking of her at all, and yet her face appeared in his imagination at the oddest times. It rankled him, and he pulled his attention back to his sister with difficulty as she continued their conversation, oblivious to his distraction.

'They most certainly will. Now, what brought you out into the bustling world of the living after hiding away to lick your wounds for so long? And to a dress shop of all places, Thomas. You must really be desperate for my company.'

His cravat felt uncommonly tight. Though the esteemed dress-maker had closed her shop for Cynthia's fitting, allowing only her staff to remain, he still felt on display. His shoulders tensed. 'I have not been licking my wounds.' He had, but he wasn't about to admit such a weakness to his sister and certainly not in front of Madame Laurent and her young assistant.

'You have. But let's not argue.' Seeming to pick up on Thomas' discomfort, Cynthia adjusted her gaze to the modiste. 'Madame Laurent, I think we need some of those divine crystal clusters just here.' She pointed to a spot where the fabric had been gathered and pleated to highlight her small waist and flaring hips. 'I saw them in your showroom as I came in.'

Madame Laurent tilted her head and squinted at the spot. She pursed her lips and nodded. 'Oui. You 'ave such an eye for fashion.'

Thomas guessed it was the depth of his sister's purse, not her sophisticated taste, that Madame Laurent found so appealing, but what did he know of gowns except how to unfasten them?

'Come with me, Sally.' The modiste snapped her fingers.

The assistant jumped to her feet, quickly following Madame Laurent out of the private fitting room and into the main salon, where mannequins showcased various dresses.

Turning to face her brother, Cynthia's concern bled through the mask he knew she had perfected for society. 'What has brought you here?'

'I need to request a favour.' He hated asking for help. It was one of his least favourite things, but not making good on a promise was even worse. Especially when the promise was made to a woman who didn't believe he could deliver.

*Damn Miss Blair for putting me in this predicament. Speaking with Beachley's daughter won't prove a blasted thing, and yet, here I am on a fool's errand.*

'Of course. You know if it is within my power to help you, I will.' Cynthia was a formidable member of the beau monde who could cut down a debutante in seconds, but she was also the best of sisters who would sacrifice her own security to help her brother just as quickly.

'It isn't really for me.' He felt the need to clarify. 'I'm helping Superintendent MacDougal with a case for Scotland Yard.'

Her gaze softened. 'Dear Superintendent MacDougal. How is our friend?'

Cynthia had met MacDougal once when he returned from Crimea. She'd insisted on inviting him to an intimate family dinner to thank him for saving Thomas' life. It had been an awkward affair, with Lachlan never feeling comfortable at the finery of a marquess's table, and Cynthia's husband, the marquess, never quite managing to hide his disdain at hosting a man who didn't even own a proper dinner suit. Lachlan made Thomas promise to never take him to Cynthia's house again, even though she kept extending invitations.

'He is fine. And no. He isn't available to dine this week, or next, or the one after that.'

Cynthia tsked in annoyance. 'I don't understand why we can't all be friendly with one another. The man saved your life. Surely that should matter more than whether or not he carries a title.'

'Such questions are for philosophers and politicians to argue about, not such lowly minds as ours.'

Cynthia raised expertly sculpted brows. 'My mind is of the highest quality.'

'Of course, forgive me. I was only speaking of myself.'

Her brows retreated from their fighting stance. 'Hmmm.'

'MacDougal is currently investigating Viscount Beachley's death and has asked for my help.'

The name caused his sister to press a hand against her throat, her eyes clouding. 'Poor Beachley. I still can't believe it. My dear friend Lady Langley has taken his sweet daughter, Anna into her home. Her Grace was never close to her brother, but when tragedy strikes, family must pull together. With all of the gossip swirling, they've retreated to their country estate to try and protect the darling girl from the worst of it.'

'Damn.' Thomas stood, his irritation making movement necessary.

Cynthia stepped off the dais and approached him, putting her hand on his arm. 'What is it?'

'I was hoping you might prevail upon Lady Langley to allow me to speak with her niece. I know it's unlikely, but the girl might have seen or heard something that will help us locate her mother. That's hardly possible if she is tucked away in the country.'

Cynthia pursed her lips. Thomas could almost see her sharp mind whirring away. 'Unless...' Her eyes lit with what was sure to be a plan.

Before she could explain any further, voices echoed from the front of the dress shop.

'I'm so sorry, the door was open, and I was told Lieutenant General Grey would be here. I really must speak with him...'

The unmistakable caw of a raven had tingles of awareness skating over Thomas' skin.

'Miss Blair,' he hissed.

Cynthia frowned at him. 'Pardon?'

Thomas tugged on his jacket. 'Excuse me for a moment. I must...' He walked towards the door leading to the main salon.

'We do not allow *animals* in the shop.' Madame Laurent's voice was decidedly frosty as she glared at Miss Blair.

*Blazes, she is lovely.*

Thomas blinked, clenched his teeth together, and dispelled the unwanted thought.

*She is not lovely. She is a nuisance. One I should stop staring at like a fool.*

But it was impossible to look away. Miss Blair struck a memorable image standing in the centre of the store in a high-collared, structured black coat. Her wide, sapphire skirts bled colour into the rather grey day, as did the general brightness of her countenance. Thomas was momentarily distracted from her face by the top hat she wore – a masculine design that highlighted her feminine profile and contrasted with the soft mass of black curls twisted into an intricate bun at her nape. His belly tightened, and he was reminded of all the reasons why women could be so very dangerous. The blasted raven, perched nimbly on her shoulder, only added another layer of intrigue and drama to the woman who didn't need any help drawing attention to herself.

'Oh, Sir Robin isn't an animal. He's a raven.' Miss Blair's smile created a spark of fire in her amber eyes.

The modiste held a pair of shears dangerous enough to cause significant bodily damage. Thomas worried she might fling them at Miss Blair like a dagger. 'The door should 'ave been locked. We are conducting a private fitting.' She glanced away from Miss Blair to her assistant. The poor girl would be seeking a new job by teatime if she were responsible for the unlocked door. 'If you wish to make an appointment, Sally can 'elp you. I think there is some space in late August. Next year.' Madame Laurent stood next to a mannequin, scissors hovering near the crystal cluster pinned to the skirt. Her lip curled in obvious disgust at the raven. Or perhaps it was Miss Blair. Likely both of them.

'Oh, no. I've no need for new dresses, though I've heard such wonderful things about your store, Madame Laurent. These gowns are remarkable.' As if the woman hadn't coldly dismissed her, Miss Blair turned to admire a cream and sage ballgown.

'Bastard!' Sir Robin burst out as his black eye caught Thomas.

Madame Laurent sputtered like a teapot at the profanity, and her assistant looked like she might faint. Miss Blair ignored them both, her amber eyes following where her raven's beak pointed. When she saw him, her golden gaze brightened with some unnamed emotion. He felt unexpectedly exposed. A hunter, mesmerised by something rare and wild instead of lining up his shot.

Her chest hitched. She exhaled loudly. If Thomas didn't know any better, he would think she had been holding her breath until the moment she saw him. But that was nonsensical. And he was always sensical.

*Is that even a word?*

Miss Blair flattened her rather beautifully shaped mouth into a hard line, and her raven let out a sharp caw.

'Lieutenant General Grey. There you are. I must speak with you.' Her calm, low voice stroked along his nerves like a caress.

The rustle of silk behind him alerted Thomas to his sister's presence. Of course, she wouldn't be content to stay in the fitting room alone. For reasons he didn't wish to examine, he found the idea of Cynthia meeting Miss Blair to be a terrible one. His sister knew him far too well. She was certain to get... ideas.

*Decidedly misguided ideas.*

'What are you doing here and how did you find me?' His tone was harsh, and his words bordered on rude, but really. The woman had tracked him to a modiste shop on Bond Street. It was completely untoward. And disconcerting. And baffling. Who had given her his location? Who even knew he was at Madame Laurent's outside of his household staff? Even if she knew where he lived, Thomas' butler would never give out his location to a stranger. Especially if that stranger was a young woman with a raven on her shoulder.

'I need to speak with you. About...' She looked past him, no doubt seeing his sister, whose floral scent tickled Thomas' nose. 'Something,' Miss Blair finished lamely. He noticed her cheeks flushed a delicate rose.

'Oh, my. Isn't that intriguing? A young woman, desperate to speak with you about... *something*.' Cynthia stepped from behind him, her gaze sharper than Madame Laurent's scissors. 'Do introduce us, Thomas.'

Miss Blair took a small step backwards, her focus bouncing

between Thomas and his sister. But her display of hesitation only lasted a moment. She dropped into a graceful curtsey, the raven flapping his wings to keep his perch. When she popped back up, her pixie eyes held his sister's gaze with steady confidence. A feat few could manage.

'You must be Marchioness Kentmore.' Miss Blair's smile was remarkably friendly towards his sister in comparison to the frosty glares she sent his way. 'An honour to meet you, your ladyship. Please excuse my interruption, but I need to speak with your brother. By the by, that colour is stunning on you.'

*How the bloody hell does she know my sister?*

'It is rather divine, isn't it?' To Thomas' increasing astonishment, Cynthia batted her eyes and ran a hand over the still unfinished skirt. 'You have me at a disadvantage. You know who I am, but I don't believe I recognise you. And I thought I was well-versed with every young lady in Debrettes.'

'She isn't a member of the peerage.' Thomas sounded like a pompous prig. The approving look he earned from Madame Laurent only made him feel like a bigger arse, but something about Miss Blair provoked him to lash out.

Miss Blair flicked her gaze to him, her gloved hand twitching. The light in Madame Laurent's showroom brightened for a flicker as though all the lamps suddenly flared. His eyes must be playing tricks.

If her slightly trembling lips meant anything, his arrow had hit the mark. Instead of feeling triumph, Thomas felt small and petty. Because he was behaving small and petty.

'Ah. A point in your favour.' Cynthia smiled kindly at Miss Blair. 'There are far too many silly misses making their debuts this year. It would be ghastly if you were among their set.' She covered grandly for him, but it was no excuse for Thomas' rude behaviour.

'Thankfully, I'm old enough to have learned that pedigree does not denote one's worth.' Miss Blair looked pointedly at him. Madame Laurent's indignant exclamation left none of them in doubt as to her feelings on the matter.

'Miss Blair is Superintendent MacDougal's niece.' Thomas tried to soften his tone and failed.

Cynthia's smile grew brighter. She stepped forward, her hand extended to Miss Blair. The young lady's eyes widened as she took his sister's hand and was pulled into a hug. The raven jumped off her shoulder and landed on a nearby mannequin, much to Madame Laurent's outrage.

'Well, any niece of MacDougal's comes from the best pedigree of all and is a friend of our family. We owe your uncle an unpayable debt, my dear.'

'*Merde!* I must insist you take your bird and get out of my store. I cannot 'ave 'im making a mess on my dresses.' Madame Laurent strode to the door in a righteous fluttering of skirts and pushed it open, pointing her bony finger to the street outside as if Miss Blair might not know how to exit a room.

'Messy dresses!' Sir Robin fluffed his feathers, his talons digging deeper into the mannequin.

'Of course, Madame Laurent. I think we should all go. Our alterations are done for today. I shall have someone come and collect the finished gown in a week.' Cynthia smiled at the modiste, then turned back to Miss Blair. 'Thomas can escort you to Gunter's. As soon as I've put myself to rights, I shall meet you both there so we can get better acquainted.'

Thomas stiffened. Alarming tingles jolted through him at the very idea of escorting Miss Blair anywhere. He was reminded of an old feeling from the battlefield. The fear of knowing any moment might be his last, and the consequent thrill of still being alive. Both terrifying and addictively potent. 'I don't think Miss Blair—'

'I would love that.' Miss Blair spoke over him. She turned her golden gaze to him, and the warmth in her eyes cooled considerably. 'Lieutenant General Grey, shall we take my carriage, or do you have your own?'

Once more, Miss Blair had flummoxed him.

*Infuriating woman!*

'I came in a hansom.' It seemed a waste to put his coachman to so much trouble for a quick visit with his sister. Now he cursed himself for being at Miss Blair's mercy. A place he vowed never to be again.

'Marvellous. You can ride with me. Unless you'd rather hail another cab?' She widened her eyes in false innocence. Of course, he wasn't going to hire a cab and ride separately to the same location. But the idea of being trapped with her inside a small carriage tightened the tension thrumming through him.

'It would be my pleasure to join you in your carriage.' He ground out the acceptance with the terse tone of a man demanding a duel.

'Oh, this is going to be such fun.' His sister's slow smile did nothing to alleviate his darkening mood.

\* \* \*

Clio never realised how small her cabriolet was until she had to fit a large, angry man inside with her. It didn't help that the weather had turned into an icy drizzle, forcing them to sit beneath a sturdy wool blanket to avoid ruining their clothes in the half-open carriage. She should have brought the landau, but Clio loved to drive and hated giving that control over to a coachman. Sir Robin Goodfellow didn't help matters. Always insistent on where he sat, the raven preferred to be nearest the window. This forced Clio to sit in the centre of the carriage with Lieutenant General Grey pressed next to her. Why she invited him to go with her at all was a mystery.

*Pride.*

She wanted to show him what a skilled driver she was. It was rare for a woman to be afforded such an opportunity, but Aunt Rowan wouldn't dare restrict her nieces in any endeavour they wished to pursue, regardless of how society might judge them. And so, Clio had insisted on learning how to drive her small, swift carriage and practised until her abilities rivalled any gentleman of the ton. She wanted Lieutenant General Grey to see how formidable she was despite her age and gender. And this was her punishment for caring about his opinion. A mistake she wouldn't make again.

Thank goodness Gunter's was only a short drive down Berkeley Square. Despite their close quarters, it was so delicious to take the lead when Lieutenant General Grey obviously preferred having the upper hand.

*One of the few things we have in common.*

An uncomfortable silence descended. Lieutenant General Grey's emerald eyes were focused on watching the street ahead as Clio seamlessly entered the flow of London traffic.

'I'm surprised your aunt allows you to drive alone. A rather dangerous activity, wouldn't you say?' He gritted out the words, his hand gripping the side of the carriage as she swerved to avoid a wide cart carrying barrels of beer. Clio glanced at him while he kept his gaze on the road. He had a Roman nose, stupidly full lips for such a hard man, high cheekbones, and a strong jaw which clenched rhythmically. The twitch of muscle fascinated her as it hardened his already granite profile. His black hair was almost a perfect match to her own, the fine ends curling just a bit at his neck. She was reminded of her first vision of him. He had been younger. His hair was crisp and perfectly combed, his face softer. But she preferred him now. Hard and a bit wild. She hated to admit it, but he was her ideal version of masculine beauty.

Returning her focus to the road, she tried not to embarrass herself by running them into a post.

*Must not make moon eyes at Mr Dark-and-Surly. Now... what did he say? Ah, yes. Shouldn't women avoid driving? No. But we should certainly avoid men like you.*

'My aunt allows me to make my own choices. Almost as though I might have rational thoughts in my head and enough intelligence to navigate this world as well as any man. I suppose some might find that far more dangerous than driving a cabriolet.'

When she first met Lieutenant General Grey, she hadn't recognised him. It was only later that night, when discussing her investigation with Ellie and Helena, they reminded Clio of his infamous past.

When the scandal broke, Clio had just turned seventeen. Uncle Lachlan forbade the girls from reading about it in the papers, so of course, they became obsessed with the story.

'Good for her!' Helena had declared at the time, and Clio wholeheartedly agreed, cheering on a woman with the courage and determination to free herself from a horrendous marriage.

According to the scandal sheets, Lieutenant General Grey was wildly unfaithful and had abandoned his wife in the country for a full two years while he drank, caroused, and frequented every bawdy house in London.

But that was nearly a decade past, and Clio had almost forgotten about the scandalous lord deemed unfit by the courts to be a husband. Now, she burned with curiosity to know his version of the story.

Watching Lieutenant General Grey grind his molars into dust as she divided her attention between the slowing traffic and her fuming passenger, Clio tried to align this man with the one she read about so long ago in the *Times* and the *Illustrated London News*. The character artist had certainly done an excellent job of capturing his brooding, dark beauty. But nothing else about the man's taciturn nature rang true of the rake described in those news articles. It was a mystery. And Clio found mysteries to be irresistible.

Lieutenant General Grey turned his attention from the road to Clio just as she stole another glance at him. Heat crept up her neck. She quickly turned back to the street ahead. Sir Robin clacked his beak. He hated traffic.

'How did you know it was my sister at Madame Laurent's? And how did you find me there? Your uncle said you were a skilled investigator, but I had no idea your abilities extended to tracking down unsuspecting men.'

*Blast and damn.*

In her haste to determine if Grey was living or deceased, she hadn't thought of a good excuse for finding him. She could hardly say she found him at Madame Laurent's because her sister's location spell worked a treat on irritable military men. Instead, she decided to distract him from the second question by answering the first as she manoeuvred around a portly gentleman selling roasted chestnuts on the street corner. 'Your sister bears a striking resemblance to you.'

His eyes hardened. 'Say that to her, and she will never forgive you. We look nothing alike.'

Clio could never back down from an argument. Especially when she knew she was right. 'Your eyes are different colours, but the same shape. Her mouth is much like yours, though lacking such a sinister sneer, and you both have a mark just here.' She brushed a finger where her jaw met her throat while driving with one hand. 'Though yours is almost hidden by—' Clio stumbled. A woman did not discuss a man's facial hair. Far too intimate.

He rubbed his hand over the spot. Something dangerous and wild flashed in his eyes. 'My valet would blush to hear you criticise his work.'

His valet wasn't the only one. Clio ignored the heat pulsing beneath her skin as she took the reins in both hands again. 'I just mean, it wasn't an act of brilliance. You have striking similarities. Although your sister's personality is far more pleasant.' She shrugged a shoulder. 'In that way, you are nothing alike.'

'But you find us equally appealing in appearance?' He asked his next question before giving her time to respond to the first. Regretfully, that question was the one she had hoped to avoid. 'And how did you find me at Madame Laurent's?'

*Come along, bloody hansom. Gunter's is just down the street.*

But London traffic was doing her no favours as the cab in front of her slowed nearly to a stop. 'I, er, was… shopping.' A wave of inspiration washed through her. 'I saw you entering the modiste's as I was looking for, um, a new bonnet,' she finished triumphantly as she pulled around the cab.

He looked pointedly under the blanket and in the corners of her very small carriage. 'I don't see any packages. Were you unsuccessful in your hunt?'

Clio stretched her neck and avoided his gaze. 'I'm always successful. My purchases are being delivered to my residence, if you must know. But that's hardly important. I needed to speak with you about the investigation and decided intercepting you at Madame Laurent's was the most expedient avenue for reaching my goal.' Distraction was her best chance of derailing his dangerous questions. 'I have important news to share.'

She wondered if he would take the bait, willing him to ask, needing to direct his focus away from her and back to where it belonged: the investigation.

'What news?'

Clio hid her small smile and quickly filled him in on the information Lady Pestlewit had shared. She could see the crowd of people on the street around the tea shop's entrance. They were so close, and then she could escape the confines of her carriage and gain some distance from this far too commanding man.

'So, based on information gleaned from one of the beau monde's most prolific gossips, you think we should focus our investigation on the housekeeper now instead of Beachley's daughter?' His sardonic stare left no question as to his opinion on her evidence.

Fingers tingling with tightly controlled power, a spark jumped between Clio's thumb and forefinger where she clasped the rein. In the gloomy light, it was impossible not to see the bright flash.

Lieutenant General Grey's eyes flicked to her hand. She jerked the ribbon, her horse stalling as the driver behind her shouted an insult.

# 5

---

*Keep talking. Pretend nothing happened.*

'I think we should explore both avenues of inquiry.' Clio's voice sounded shrill to her own ears. 'I still believe his daughter could have important information, but we shouldn't assume his wife is the murderer just because she is missing.'

Tapping his fingers on the blanket covering them, he turned back to the street ahead. Clio's chest loosened. He hadn't seen the spark from her fingers, or he would say something. Lieutenant General Grey was hardly subtle. 'The household staff were all questioned. Nothing suspicious arose from the interviews.'

Clio widened her eyes in false shock. 'You mean the housekeeper didn't confess to killing Viscount Beachley and his wife? Well, that must mean she is innocent. I mean, surely a murderer would just admit the truth and face their certain death rather than stoop to subterfuge.'

Lieutenant General Grey leaned closer to her as she made a quick adjustment. They were almost alongside Gunter's. Starch, soap, and a spice she couldn't name tickled her nose. She forced herself not to shift away from him, even though her heart beat madly in her chest. He would take her retreat as a sign of weakness, and one never showed weakness.

'You are an incredibly difficult woman, Miss Blair.'

Pulling to a stop in front of the crowded tea shop, Clio turned to face him as warmth, unexpected and soothing, washed over her. 'Why, Lieutenant General Grey, what a lovely compliment.'

'It wasn't a compliment,' he growled.

The carriage dipped as the footman hopped down from the back and took the reins from her.

'It most certainly was.' Clio accepted the footman's hand. 'Meet us back here in an hour, John. Thank you kindly.' She tapped her shoulder for Sir Robin to join her on the busy street. Making her way through the crowd to the entrance of Gunter's, she didn't wait to see if Lieutenant General Grey followed her.

Thankfully, Lady Cynthia arrived not long after they were seated, alleviating the need to make awkward conversation. They all ordered: tea for Lady Cynthia, coffee for Lieutenant General Grey, and Gunter's famed hot chocolate for Clio.

'How unexpectedly delightful to make a new friend, Miss Blair. My brother was in the midst of asking me a favour when you arrived at Madame Laurent's.' Cynthia's eyes, hazel to her brother's clear green, sparkled with mischief.

'I'll bet you that iced cake he was asking to meet with the Duchess of Devon.' Clio had done her research on Lieutenant General Grey. Cynthia wasn't the only one who knew how to study Debrett's, but unlike Clio, his entire family was listed.

Cynthia was married to the Marquess of Kentmore, and it was well known among the ladies who frequented All Things Bright and Beautiful that the Marchioness of Kentmore and the Duchess of Devon were intimate friends. The Duchess of Devon was also Viscount Beachley's sister, and Anna's aunt. Uncle Lachlan was right. Grey's connections within the beau monde were helpful even if the man was not.

'Aren't you a clever one. So, this mysterious *something* you wanted to speak with Thomas about is the case he's working on?'

'The case *we* are working on,' Clio corrected. There was no reason to hide her involvement. While ladies were meant to follow strict rules of decorum set forth by their fathers and husbands, Clio had no men controlling her choices. She could move in the world far more freely than the highly esteemed Marchioness of Kentmore.

The marchioness leaned back in her chair; her expertly tinted lips curled in a smile. 'I see.' She glanced at her brother, then back to Clio. 'You might be one of the most interesting women I've ever met. Don't you agree, Thomas?'

Lieutenant General Grey sipped his coffee and kept his – no doubt dim – opinions to himself.

'I'm flattered.' Clio forced a bright smile.

Cynthia leaned forward, her delicate features growing serious. 'And you think it might help to speak with poor Anna?'

'Miss Blair thinks the girl *might* have some insight as to what happened that night.' It was clear he did not agree.

'Unlike your brother, I think it's important to pursue every possible lead.'

'Even if it is a complete waste of our time,' Lieutenant General Grey muttered.

'Or the key that unlocks our entire case,' Clio hissed.

Cynthia gave each of them a curious glance before directing her question to Clio. 'Because you think the viscountess murdered him?' She shook her head, her chestnut hair catching the weak sunlight battling through a stormy sky. 'Violet Beachley hasn't the backbone needed to squash a spider, let alone kill her husband.'

'You know her? What kind of woman is she?' Clio's pulse quickened.

'Admittedly, I don't know her well.' Cynthia spun her cup in a slow circle on the saucer. 'According to her sister-in-law, my dear friend Lady Langley, she doesn't possess the kind of passion needed to commit such a violent crime.'

Clio swirled whipped cream into dark chocolate with her spoon. 'I don't know if the viscountess is a murderer. We don't have any evidence to prove her guilt or innocence. Many people had access to the viscount, which is why we should leave no avenue unexplored.' Clio sent a pointed glare in Lieutenant General Grey's direction before sipping her decadent treat. Her eyes fluttered closed for a moment as she let the warm, rich sweetness of cocoa and cinnamon coat her tongue. She swallowed and opened her eyes to see Lieutenant General Grey's face tighten. She couldn't even drink her chocolate without angering him.

*Well, too bad. It's delicious, and I won't hide my enjoyment because it irritates you. In fact...*

She took another sip, licking her lips and marvelling at the flare of incendiary frustration in the lieutenant general's gaze. Pulling her thoughts back to the case, she refocused on Lady Burrows. 'But finding Viscountess Beachley is of paramount importance, if only to determine that she is alive, and possibly eliminate her as a suspect.'

'You think she might also be... deceased?' Cynthia's eyes widened.

Clio ignored Lieutenant General Grey's exasperated sigh. 'I don't know. She is missing. We need to find her. That is all I know for certain.'

Cynthia picked up an iced cake and nibbled on the edge before her mouth turned down in a small frown. 'Her Grace is incredibly protective of Anna. Especially now. If you are right and both Anna's parents were murdered, she is wise to shield her so fiercely.'

Lieutenant General Grey exhaled. 'Exactly. I would have misgivings myself in her situation.'

'I suppose even a gentleman of the beau monde has limitations on what he can and can't accomplish.' It was a petty barb, but Clio couldn't help herself.

*If he won't procure a meeting with Anna, then I shall use his ineptitude to convince Uncle Lachlan his ties with the beau monde are useless in this investigation.*

Especially if the housekeeper was a suspect. The peerage might have suspicions about speaking to a commoner, but the reverse was true for the serving class. They were far more likely to speak with Clio than the scowling Lieutenant General Grey.

'You've no idea what I can accomplish, Miss Blair.' His rough voice and hard gaze did something strange to Clio's blood, warming it and creating an aching pulse through her system.

'Well, I'm quite certain I know what *I* can accomplish.' Cynthia smiled.

Lieutenant General Grey turned to his sister. His furrowed brow conveyed concern. This worried Clio.

'What are you thinking, Cynthia? You only tap your finger on your chin like that when you're hatching plans.'

'Don't you think a small house party with some of Lady Langley's most intimate friends is exactly what she needs to find strength in such difficulty?'

'No. I don't.' Her brother's implacable tone didn't dissuade Cynthia in the slightest.

'Pish, Thomas. How would you know? As her friend, it's my duty to lend support to Her Grace during this time of mourning. A visit will break up the tedium of such grey months in the dreary country.'

Alarm bells rang in Clio's head. Sir Robin, who had been eyeing the cakes hopefully, clacked his beak. She picked one up, broke it in half, and held it flat on her palm for the bird, who delicately plucked it from her hand. How could a house party help them speak with Anna?

'She has always expressed an interest in getting to know you better, Thomas.' That statement had his Hessian tapping madly on the tile floor. 'And I know she would happily welcome a new friend into the group. A far-flung cousin of ours from the north. I shall write to her today.'

'Cynthia! You can't just invite yourself to a duchess's country estate.'

While Clio generally disagreed with Lieutenant General Grey, in this instance, she was wholeheartedly of the same mind.

Lady Burrows tipped her head back and laughed. 'Of course I'm not inviting myself. I'm inviting all of us. She'll be thrilled for the company.'

'Party!' Sir Robin's gaze stayed on the remaining cake.

*Oh. Dear. Goddess.*

Lady Burrows was suggesting Clio leave London and join her in the country for a house party. In the home of a duchess. With Lieutenant General Grey. It was a terrible idea. She wanted to spend less time with the infuriating man beside her, not more.

*Ideally, I'd like to spend* no *time with him.*

And she could hardly leave Sir Robin. Or the coven. But Lady Cynthia Burrows had one thing in common with her brother: bull-headed determination. The wheels had been set in motion, and Clio feared nothing could stop them from moving forward. Still, she had to try.

'I can't imagine your friend wants a stranger in her house when they are grieving their murdered brother. And I couldn't possibly leave Sir Robin for two weeks. He wouldn't know what to do without me.' More importantly, Clio wouldn't know what to do without the comfort of her familiar, but she wasn't about to admit that.

The woman waved away Clio's very valid points. 'Don't be silly. Lady Langley never liked her brother, though she is devoted to her niece. I'd bet all my pin money she is already chafing at the constraints of mourning. Company will thrill her, and she'll love your darling Sir Robin.'

The raven in question fluffed his feathers at such praise and softly cooed at Cynthia.

*Marvellous. My familiar is flirting with Lieutenant General Grey's sister.*

Cynthia ran a gloved finger over Sir Robin's head as he preened. 'My husband abhors the country, but I doubt he'll care if I am gone for a week or two. This will be such a lark!'

Investigating a peer's murder was hardly what Clio would call a lark. But this did mean she would get to speak with Beachley's daughter. Sometimes, sacrifices had to be made. Aunt Rowan wasn't going to be happy, but it couldn't be helped.

Standing from the table, her tea still steaming, the marchioness effectively ended the discussion before Clio or Lieutenant General Grey could convince her to alter course. It was a skilful strategy that Clio planned to steal.

'I can't simply abscond to the country for a fortnight, Cynthia.' Lieutenant General Grey rose, no doubt his manners forcing him to stand as his sister prepared to depart.

Clio followed suit, regretfully abandoning her hot chocolate. She could hardly stay alone with Lieutenant General Grey after his sister left.

'Why? What pressing social events must you attend in London?' Lady Burrows' scathing comment filled Clio with even greater admiration for the woman.

The glare Lieutenant General Grey sent his sister would wither most, but she just nodded her head at him. 'I thought so. I shall send the letter today and let you know as soon as I hear word from the duchess. Miss Blair, how can I reach you?'

Clio rattled off her address without thinking. She didn't miss the raised brow of Lieutenant General Grey.

*Yes, I live in Mayfair, Mr I'm-so-much-better-than-you. One doesn't need a title to have an esteemed address.*

But that thought was quickly followed by another.

*Blast. I should have told her to contact me through All Things Bright and Beautiful.*

An invisible string running from the back of Clio's neck down her spine tightened. Lieutenant General Grey now knew where she lived. Not that it mattered. He was hardly going to pay her any visits.

'I'm so looking forward to knowing you better, Miss Blair. By the by, shouldn't we dispense with such formalities? If you're pretending to be our cousin, we're practically family. Please call me Cynthia. And I shall call you Clio.'

Heat washed over Clio, colouring her cheeks pink. Family was a sacred thing. Hers was a close-knit group that only included her aunt, sister, cousin, and Uncle Lachlan. She couldn't fathom so easily incorporating a stranger into their tight circle. 'I, um. Yes. Well.'

'She is hardly family. We don't even know her.' Clio was amazed Lieutenant General Grey could enunciate so clearly with his teeth clenched together tighter than a clam holding onto its pearl.

'We'd better get to know her if we plan on convincing Her Grace of this little ruse, Thomas.' Cynthia might have been pointing out that butter was meant to be applied to toast. She deftly wound through the crowd, out the door, and paused on the street as she looked expectantly for her carriage. 'You must come for supper this week, Clio. We'll sort out our false history. And of course, you can't keep referring to my brother as Lieutenant General Grey. Thomas might be too intimate, but certainly Grey should do.'

*Oh my.*

'Cynthia, you go too far.' Fire was Clio's element, but it was Lieutenant General Grey who looked ready to combust.

Lady Burrows' landau pulled up to the kerb. A footman in dark-green livery jumped down to set the step.

'Oh, Thomas. I've only just started.' She pulled Clio in for another hug. Sir Robin bobbed his head happily as Cynthia pressed a kiss against Clio's cheek. 'I'll send an invitation for dinner. Until then, dear cousin, farewell.' She turned to her brother. 'Shall I give you a ride home?'

'I'll hail a cab.'

'Suit yourself.' And with that, Cynthia alighted and waved gaily out of the window as the carriage lurched into London traffic.

\* \* \*

Thomas was quite certain he was in a nightmare. Miss Blair was standing on the crowded street, her raven composed and regal on her shoulder, her amber gaze both steady and disconcerting. If he woke up from this dark dream, she would disappear, and he wouldn't be able to finish the argument they'd started in the carriage. It smouldered between them like a coal. He very much wished to blow on that ember and watch it burn. Almost as much as he wanted to watch her finish her cup of hot chocolate. So he didn't pinch himself awake.

Seeing her savour that drink was the most erotic thing Thomas had ever witnessed. And he had seen a great many erotic things. It was a disconcerting thought he refused to entertain. No matter how easily Miss Blair sparked his desire.

*My only desire is to be rid of her.*

Yet instead of walking away, he stayed. 'You will not call me Grey. Nor will I call you Cousin Clio, no matter what my sister thinks.' He snapped each syllable like crystallised caramel between his teeth.

She blinked slowly. Something bright and hot flashed in his periphery as the streetlamp next to him flared to life.

'I can think of several names far more worthy of you.' Her voice was soft, but her words were harder than steel. 'Blackguard for one. Arrogant prig for another.'

*The nerve of this woman!*

Stepping closer, he leaned down to better hold her fiery gaze. 'Careful, madame. I am a gentleman, but I can still be pushed past my limits.'

Sharp laughter scratched down his spine like a nail, tightening his skin and sparking heat along his nerves. 'What would you do if I gave you one hard shove over that line, *Grey*?' She drew out his name like a curse. Perhaps that explained why it was suddenly hard to breathe.

Miss Blair's carriage rolled up, and the footman hopped out, holding the reins for her.

Thomas moved into her path, blocking her escape. The raven cawed a warning, but she had stoked something within him too hot to control.

'Don't play with fire, Miss Blair. It will singe you.'

She narrowed her gaze, her thick lashes framing golden eyes. 'Fire doesn't frighten me, Grey. Neither do you.'

Lightning cracked, the sky split open, and heavy raindrops fell like a curtain.

'Arrogance and courage are not the same thing. If you come with us on this debacle of a house party, there won't be anywhere to hide.'

She swallowed. 'I have nothing to hide.'

She was lying.

The rain increased in intensity as he sought for her shield's weakness. And then he realised, they were both completely dry.

Looking up, he saw the rain evaporating into steam a foot above their heads. They could be standing in the centre of a bonfire whose heat turned the water into vapour.

Fear, unfamiliar and shocking, thrilled through him.

'What the bloody hell?'

Miss Blair stiffened her spine. Whatever had been protecting them dissolved, the deluge quickly drenching Thomas and dripping down his neck. He hissed air between his teeth at the shockingly cold water.

Stepping past him before he could reach out and catch her arm, Miss Blair took the ribbons from her footman and disappeared into her carriage so swiftly, her raven fluttered his wings to keep his perch.

Thomas was left standing in the frigid rain, watching Miss Blair's carriage as it disappeared into traffic.

'What the bloody hell?' he repeated, but no answer came to him from the bustling crowd scurrying to find shelter from the storm.

He needed to pay a visit to Superintendent MacDougal. Not all was as it seemed with Miss Blair.

Hailing a hack, he gave the directions to Scotland Yard.

## 6

Lachlan's office was just as messy as his wild curls.

4 Whitehall Place had originally been a house before it became the hub of London's Metropolitan Police force. One of the guest rooms on the second floor comprised Superintendent MacDougal's office.

Papers were scattered over the surface of his large desk. A coat dangled haphazardly from the arm of a small settee shoved into the corner of the room. A side table next to the couch was covered with books, a magnifying glass, and something greasy wrapped in wax paper. A meat pie, perhaps.

A flickering lamp illuminated a mahogany bookcase dominating the far wall. Superintendent MacDougal himself stood next to the shelves stuffed with books, thumbing through a tome containing ghastly drawings of decomposing bodies.

'What the blazes are you reading?' Thomas tried not to smile as Lachlan startled. His eyes, the colour of rich earth, lifted from the book to focus on Thomas.

'Thomas! I was just about to send you a message.' Shutting the book, he balanced it precariously on the windowsill next to a battered leather satchel that threatened to spill its innards at any moment. Striding across the room, he shook Thomas' hand and gestured for him to take the seat across from his desk. When he realised the chair was already occupied by yet another stack of books, he picked them up, turned right, left, then shrugged and plopped the tumbling pile next to the settee.

Thomas lowered himself slowly into the chair. 'What about?'

'We got the report back from the coroner on Viscount Beachley. I was going to speak with you and Clio about it together, but you're here now.'

'Yes. I'm here. Now.' Thomas tried to keep his tone calm, but just thinking about Miss Blair set his nerves jangling. He had revisited their interaction in front of Gunter's as his hack crawled along glutted streets to Scotland Yard. And it wasn't just then. Something odd had happened when she was driving them to Gunter's as well. The longer he considered, the more certain he became. Miss Blair was keeping secrets about herself.

'There was a fair amount of blood found on and near Beachley's body.'

Thomas shrugged. 'Blood is to be expected when a man is murdered.'

Lachlan sat in his chair, watching Thomas carefully. 'No' when the cause of death is poison.'

'Poison?'

'Poison,' Lachlan confirmed. 'And he had no lacerations on his body. No evidence of blood in his nasal passages or throat. No reason for there to have been any blood at the scene. Unless it wasn't his.'

It made no sense.

*Blast and damn.*

Was Miss Blair right? Could the blood belong to the viscountess? Were they dealing with two murders?

'I need the addresses of his staff. Have any of them remained at the house?'

Lachlan frowned. 'We spoke with them already.'

'I want to speak with them again.'

'A skeleton staff remains until the new viscount takes over the residence. Beachley's cousin will inherit the title and property. He's already applying pressure for us to move things along as swiftly as possible.'

*A greedy relative waiting in the wings to inherit. Brilliant.*

'I'll start with the remaining staff, then.'

Lachlan took a quill, dipped it in ink, and made a list of names. 'Here.' He handed the parchment to Thomas, who flicked his gaze over it. 'When shall I tell Clio to meet you at Viscount Beachley's?'

Thomas hesitated, unsure of how to broach the question burning in his mind. Because it defied logic. A woman could not create sparks from her hand, cause streetlamps to spontaneously light, or cast an invisible shield against the rain. And yet he saw it all with his own eyes. Parts of him might be irrevocably broken, but there was nothing wrong with his vision.

The echo of an old conversation tickled Thomas' memory.

'Didn't you once tell me you came to London because of some bad business in your village in Scotland?'

Lachlan's body hardened, and Thomas didn't miss the way he shifted in his chair, readying for a fight. 'Aye. But what does this have to do with meeting Clio at Viscount Beachley's?'

Thomas forged ahead even when his survival instincts were screaming for him to retreat. 'I remember now. It was after the battle of Balaclava. What a nightmare that was. Funny what men will share when they're soaking in cheap spirits and convinced their death will arrive on the morrow. Do you recall what you said?'

Lachlan slowly shook his head. 'No.'

'I almost didn't remember myself. Confessions made when staring at the abyss are uncomfortably honest, don't you think?'

'I would no' trust anything I've said after too many drams of whisky. Scotsmen love to tell a tale, and we're no' above embellishing.'

'You told me you fell in love with a woman in your village. You said she had bewitched you. That she held the power of the earth in her hands, and she was an all-powerful sorceress. One of her sisters was murdered, and the other died before her thirtieth year. Both women left daughters she took on as her own. You swore to always protect this witch and her nieces. Such an odd term of endearment. Witch.'

Lachlan pressed his lips together, his eyes flashing dangerously. Thomas knew how deadly his friend could be. He was reasonably certain he wouldn't attack Thomas, but one could never tell. 'It was a long time ago. I barely remember the conversation I had with my secretary this morning.' His voice was strained.

'You said your only regret if you died in Balaclava would be not fulfilling your promise to her. What was her name?' Thomas asked, though he knew Lachlan wouldn't answer. 'Women are named after flowers, but rarely trees. Rowan, wasn't it?'

The small smile creating creases on either side of Lachlan's mouth held no humour. 'What does this story have to do with Clio?'

'Aunt Rowan.'

Lachlan's brow drew down in a question.

'On the first day we met, Miss Blair told you her Aunt Rowan didn't need her at the apothecary until later. Strange for two women you know to share such an unusual name.'

'Strange indeed.' Lachlan leaned back in his chair, the wood creaking under his solid weight. 'Are you asking me if Clio's aunt is a witch? According to the law, witches are no' real, Thomas. Nothing more than superstition.'

'I'm not asking what the law thinks. I'm asking what you think. Do you think witches are real?' Thomas' chest was tight, his ribs frozen as he waited.

'I think only a foolish man pretends to know the mysteries of the universe.'

'That doesn't answer my question.' He couldn't voice his real question. *Is Clio a witch?* Because it was madness. As impossible as sparks flying from a woman's fingers, or rain sizzling into steam on a cold London street.

'Some answers can only be found when you're ready.'

Thomas shook his head. 'You sound like a bloody mystic yourself, Lachlan.'

His friend merely shrugged, then leaned forward. 'Why are you asking me these questions? It's a strange thing to be wondering abou'. Witches and magic.'

This was his opportunity to put forward his suspicions. But he couldn't do it. He would sound like a madman. Or worse. He might be proven right. And then what?

Lachlan waited a beat. When Thomas refused to answer, Lachlan dipped his chin in curt acknowledgement, disappointment clear in his small frown. 'One thing is certain. Accusing a woman of witchcraft is a dangerous thing no' matter what the laws say abou' it. If any man made such a claim abou' my family, it would no' end well for them.' His expression could have been carved from stone and left no doubt: Lachlan's vow to protect Rowan and her nieces still held true.

Tucking the list of Viscount Beachley's servants into his pocket, Thomas stood and nodded. 'My sister is arranging an invitation to Lady Langley's country estate for a house party. Your niece is included, as am I. In such close quarters, secrets won't be easy to keep.'

'The perfect setting for investigating a murder.' Lachlan narrowed his gaze. 'Which is the only mystery you need to solve.'

'Are you certain you still wish for my help?'

Standing, Lachlan tucked his hands in his pockets. 'Are you certain you still want to help?'

And that was the sticking point. He should walk away. This was far more than a murder investigation. If he found the answers he sought – and despite Lachlan's warning, he knew he could not let the mystery of Miss Clio Blair remain unanswered – it might threaten his only remaining friendship and destroy the life of an intriguing woman... who might also be a witch. But discovering Miss Blair's secrets was quickly becoming an obsession. A need, not a want. He was determined to find Viscount Beachley's killer. But he was equally committed to revealing the truth about Clio Blair, no matter the consequences.

'Tell your niece to be at Viscount Beachley's house tomorrow morning, ten o'clock sharp. I'll not wait for her if she is late.'

Lachlan nodded. 'Remember what I said, Thomas.'

He returned the man's frank stare. 'I remember everything you've said, Lachlan.'

Turning, he walked out of Superintendent MacDougal's office, his shoulder blades hitching as if a pistol were aimed at his back.

\* \* \*

Clio was the silliest witch in all the covens. She left Sir Robin at home, a rare occurrence that strained nerves already twanging with anxiety. But after her ridiculous display with Grey outside of the tea shop, she thought it wise to minimise her occult accruement. It might also help to put Viscount Beachley's staff at ease. Sir Robin could have a certain effect on people. It would hardly help her cause if he was shouting, *Murderer*, or, *Bastard* during questioning.

*I don't understand how anyone isn't charmed by him.*

Feeling the absence of her familiar most acutely, she cursed herself for letting Grey provoke her anger. In her need to verbally decimate him at Gunter's, her powers had slipped free unbidden. Which was unacceptable.

The first and most important lesson she learned when her magic first manifested at seven was to *always* maintain control. Anything less was irresponsible at best and deadly at worst. A witch without control was a witch who didn't deserve her magic. Yet whenever she was with the infuriating man, it was like touching a live wire that scrambled her concentration.

The heat shield at Gunter's had been minimal at best, but strong enough to dissolve the rain into mist and certainly noticeable. And more importantly, unintentional. It caught Grey's attention which exceeded carelessness. Her slip was dangerous.

*Stupid, arrogant witch!*

Aunt Rowan would have had a fit of apoplexy had Clio told her about it the night before. So instead of admitting her failures to her aunt, she had kept her whispered confession to Ellie and Helena as they huddled on Clio's bed to gossip before bidding each other goodnight. Her sister and cousin responded exactly as Clio knew they would: with unwavering support. It was one more reason why the three women were irrevocably intertwined.

'He deserved far worse than a heat shield. You should have used your witchfire to burn off his eyebrows!' Helena was the most bloodthirsty of the three. Her copper hair shone in the wavering candlelight.

Ellie's eyes grew wide. 'What if he discovers your powers? Would he report you?'

'To whom? The magistrate? Uncle Lachlan? The House of Lords? He would sound like a mad fool.' But Clio's argument was weak, and they all knew it.

'Did anyone else notice?' Helena's grey eyes darkened with her mood.

'I've no idea. The street was crowded. Perhaps.'

Ophelia scampered out of Ellie's pocket. Her sister was sitting cross-legged on Clio's bed. The simple cotton nightgown Ellie wore created the perfect hammock as it stretched over her knees. Ophelia circled three times before curling into a comfortable ferret ball in the centre of Ellie's skirt and chittered happily.

'I just can't believe you lost control. You are always so careful. We all are.' Ellie's voice was troubled. Her pink lips formed a perfect circle as she sucked in a whoosh of air. 'You don't think this is...? No. Never mind.'

'What are you talking about, Ellie?' Helena ran her hand down her fox's back. Hamlet's rich copper coat perfectly matched Helena's hair. She was sitting opposite Ellie at the foot of Clio's bed. Her fox stretched next to her leg, his gaze on the ferret. They were infatuated with one another. It was the inspiration for their names. Aunt Rowan had suggested Romeo and Juliet, but Helena had strong opinions about Romeo being a milksop, and Ellie always thought Hamlet and Ophelia needed a second chance to find their happy ending.

Ellie's gaze bounced from Helena to Clio. 'A spirit match.' She mouthed the last two words as though voicing them would lend power to the syllables, like a spell.

Clio had rolled her eyes the night before, and she did so again as she briskly walked the few blocks from her house to Viscount Beachley's. But in the grey morning light, every cell in her body hardened into a protective shell at the very thought. Ellie's suggestion was impossible. Clio had been quick to point that out the night before.

'There is no such thing as a spirit match. In all the lore, a person would have to be willing to accept every part of the witch to be a true spirit match, and no man is willing to do that. Our powers are too threatening. They would either use our gifts for their own advantage or force us to reject our magic. We know this. We all saw it happen to our mothers. Those teachings are just silly superstitions. Fairy tales.'

'Our entire existence could be summed up as silly superstitions.' Helena's dry sense of humour wasn't always funny.

'What are the signs?' Ellie was speaking to herself. A habit the others barely noticed any more. 'He provokes your magic.'

'Grey only provokes my anger.'

'You can share your elemental power with him.'

Clio shook her head. 'I can't even share that I'm a witch with him, let alone my witchflame.'

'Your abilities extend to him when they shouldn't. I'm not exactly sure what that means, but...' Ellie looked hopefully at Clio.

*Seeing memories from his past, even when he isn't dead?*

Clio had ended the conversation at that point, blaming her early-morning appointment with Viscount Beachley's staff. She needed to focus on something real: the investigation.

Uncle Lachlan had told her about the coroner's report and Grey's demand for her presence at the unsightly hour of ten in the morning on one of the few precious days Ellie had the morning shift, stealing any chance Clio had of sleeping late. She had a few suspicions as to who the blood belonged to, the viscountess sitting at the top of her list, but couldn't begin to guess who had poisoned the viscount. Poison was thought of as a woman's weapon, but ruling out anyone seemed silly at this point.

She clipped down a drizzly street when she could have been snuggled in her bed and muttered curses on Grey's head. There was no reason they couldn't have conducted their investigations at a much more reasonable hour on her morning off. If he had deigned to enquire as to her schedule.

*The arrogant, insufferable...*

Sparks tingled from her palms to her fingertips. Stopping in the damp morning air, she took a deep breath and let the London chill cool her.

Even if one believed the witch lore about spirit matches – which Clio certainly did not – Ellie was stark raving mad if she thought Clio and Grey could ever be one. They were two opposing forces destined to destroy each other. Whatever allowed Clio to see his memory twice – *the first time hardly counts* – wasn't because of any spiritual connection. It was a ridiculous suggestion by her soft-hearted sister. Ellie's belief in 'true love' was naïve at best, danger-ously delusional at worst.

She shook her head and continued her way to Viscount Beach-ley's. She had more important things to think about than fairy-tale spirit matches or rogue visions about a certain lieutenant general.

*I just need to focus more intently on my control. Seeing his memories was an inconsequential misfiring of magic. It means nothing, and it won't happen again.*

She froze mid-step. Because the inconsequential misfiring of magic was happening again.

Wind blew down the street, catching her skirts and throwing them around her ankles as the vision swept her into another place. Another time.

## 7

*Thomas sat in a large bedroom. Windows on the far wall looked over pastoral views of an endless manicured lawn bordered in the distance by a dark forest. This was his country estate. Clio wasn't aware of how she knew, just that it was so. As before, she wasn't in his head but instead watching the entire scene like a play being performed for her alone.*

*A woman stood in the doorway; her sumptuous rose gown draped beautifully over an hourglass figure. She moved with the practised grace of someone used to wearing miles of silk. Kneeling next to Thomas, her dress pooling around her feet like a waterfall, she took both of his hands in hers and ducked her head to catch his gaze. 'I'm begging you, Thomas. You must leave. I do not want to hate you. You promised you would stay away for the remainder of the year. Perhaps absence will convince me there are still reasons for us to be together, but you can't blame me for how I feel. Even if—'*

*He stood abruptly, pulling her up with him. 'Absence hasn't encouraged your affections thus far. And being with other women hasn't changed anything between us, despite your promise that it would. I never should have agreed to this foolish plan. I haven't seen you in months. If you wish me to leave again, then come with me. We can take a tour of*

*Europe, get away from all of these people.' He spat the last word like it burned his tongue. 'We've been apart for far too long already. You are my wife, and I do not desire to live separate lives. I don't care if our plans must change. I miss you, Lissa.'*

*The woman's lips twisted into a grimace. 'Don't. Call. Me. That. I hate it when you call me that. You may want us to be together, but what about my desires? My wishes? Do they not matter in the shadow of your selfish needs?'*

*Clio felt the sharp ache in Thomas' chest, the desperation to convince Lissa of his plan, the oily guilt of being unfaithful, the hope – more painful than a bullet ripping through his flesh – that she might stay. That she might accept him. That they might reclaim their easy affection. His love for her cut like a sword, and Clio was never more convinced: if this was love, she wanted none of it.*

The cold splash of water from a hansom cab's wheel running through a puddle shocked Clio back to the present.

'Blast.' Her skirts were sodden. Looking left, then right, the quiet neighbourhood street was empty. She spread her fingers wide, her hands hovering over the wet satin, and let her magic heat her palms, steaming away the dirty water. Straightening, she brushed out the emerald skirts patterned with bold black and gold paisley. It was only then she realised the familiar wave of nausea accompanying her visions of the dead was absent. She hadn't felt it after her other visions of Grey either. Stranger and stranger.

Shaking her head, she refused to think about any of it now. If she wanted to make her appointment with the insufferable man, she would need to hurry.

When she arrived at the gate leading to Lord Beachley's front stairs, Grey was already there. He stood large and tall like a sentinel guarding the entrance of Hades with his silver-tipped cane tapping impatiently against the stone path.

'You're late.' His deep baritone resonated in her bones.

Clio made a show of unbuttoning her wool coat, flicking open the pocket of the double-breasted vest she wore in the same material as her skirt, and pulling free a gold watch attached to her with a sparkling chain. It was a daring ensemble that few women would chance, as it played with masculine and feminine silhouettes. Her crisp white shirt with its high collar and starched creases could just as easily have been from Grey's closet as her own, though his would need to be larger to accommodate his thick chest and muscled arms.

Forcing her attention away from Grey's torso and pushing down the heat rising to her cheeks, she studied the face of her clock. 'It would appear I'm bang on ten o'clock, *Grey*.'

He clenched his teeth. She knew she'd annoyed him by foregoing his title.

*Wonderful. Better to keep him frustrated. A frustrated man has no time to question whether or not I have any magical powers.*

Pulling his own watch out, Grey flicked open the gold cover plate and turned it so Clio could see the big hand sitting smugly on five minutes past ten. 'London Time would disagree.'

Every Londoner knew standardising their watches to the railway time was the most accurate measure. Clio hadn't calibrated her watch in several weeks. Damn him for winning this round.

'All good things come to those who wait... Isn't that how the saying goes?' She tipped her chin up, refusing to admit her defeat.

'Where is your bird?' Grey's sharp gaze moved from her shoulder down her body before quickly resettling on her face.

Clio tried to reconcile the hard features of present Grey with her vision of him in the past. That version of Grey had been vulnerable and hurting, instigating a wild need within Clio to protect him from whatever future pain awaited. This man only provoked her ire.

'Sir Robin isn't really a morning person. Er. Bird. And since you didn't give me any influence over our meeting time, I thought it best to leave him to his perch.'

Grey's grunt gave her no inclination as to his opinion on the matter. But neither did she care. 'Shall we?' He pushed open the iron gate with his cane. The plaintive squeal of metal on metal rang mournfully off the cobblestones.

Clio was careful to avoid touching Grey as she moved past him and along the path leading up to Viscount Beachley's stone stairs, but she couldn't escape his enticing scent. Soap. Starch. Spice. Both comforting and disconcerting. A wicked combination.

Physical contact had always increased the intensity of her power. Holding something the dead person treasured, touching the furniture, floor, and walls of where they died. It all helped to focus and increase the flow of power coursing through her, intensifying her connection with the deceased. She couldn't imagine what touching Grey might do, but she guessed it wouldn't be good. Best to make sure she stayed well away from him until she could determine why his memories kept invading her mind. Memories that contradicted her opinions most inconveniently.

What she knew of Grey's past came from newspaper articles, scandal magazines, and whispers of ancient gossip from nearly a decade ago. Those sources described the man as a rakehell who callously abandoned his young and beautiful wife. Nothing like the taciturn gentleman in front of her. Nor did they accurately depict the Grey she saw in his memories. Nothing added up. Clio felt the need to pick at the mystery until it unwound. An inclination she resolutely ignored.

She made her way around the side of the house to the mews. The servants' entrance would be at the back of the residence. She pulled her thoughts together, banishing her incessant curiosity about Grey to the dark recesses of her mind so she could focus instead on what mattered: finding Viscount Beachley's killer.

Gravel crunched behind her, alerting Clio that Grey was following her. The heat of his gaze burned the back of her neck, and she stiffened her shoulders. When she reached the small over-hang of the doorway boasting a small entrance and hallway to the underbelly of Viscount Beachley's home, Clio knocked sharply. Grey stood directly behind her. If she leaned back even a little, her shoulders would bump against his chest.

The door swung open, and a maid, young enough to still be in the schoolroom, stepped back, her eyes widening to round saucers.

'Hello. May we please speak with the butler?' As the head of domestic staff, he would be the person to arrange interviews.

'Mr Chatham, I believe.' The now-familiar growl of Grey's voice was becoming a problem. It vibrated down her spine. Clio's belly clenched.

*It's nothing. I'm merely hungry.*

She should have eaten breakfast, but there simply wasn't time. Thanks to Grey's ridiculous schedule. One more reason to hate the man.

After several seconds of stammering, the girl scurried away, and they waited another fifteen minutes on the stoop before the butler arrived.

The tall man was thin as a reed and stood straighter than a ruler. Grey produced a letter. From the messy penmanship, Clio could only assume it was some kind of directive from Uncle Lachlan. Whatever he wrote worked a treat as the butler's stuffy attitude melted away. He quickly ushered them down the shadowy corridor, through a small office, and into a much larger room with cupboards on three walls, and a long table running down the centre. Clio guessed this was where the staff took their meals.

Freshly baked bread, spiced meat, and something sugary wafted from under a swinging door. The kitchen must be on the other side.

Comforting sounds of cheerful voices, banging pots, and crackling wood confirmed her suspicions.

'If you will stay here, I shall gather the remaining staff and send them to you one at a time. Will that suffice?' The butler spoke to Grey, then glanced at Clio. 'Does your, er, secretary need any supplies? Pen? Parchment?'

Grey's smile only fanned the flames of Clio's indignation.

'I am not his secretary. And I require nothing more than my own wits. If you would take a seat, we shall start with you. As the head of the household, I'm sure you are privy to all manner of information.' Clio knew her tone would do no favours in lowering the butler's defences, but it couldn't be helped. The arch look Grey bestowed upon her intensified the flames licking away her patience.

The butler slowly sat, his spine fairly creaking as he folded himself into the chair. He gave a stilted report of what he remembered from the night Viscount Beachley was murdered. As Grey stood to dismiss him, his information as helpful as spitting on an inferno, Clio cleared her throat.

'How would you describe your relationship with the housekeeper?'

Grey sat down again, twisting to look at her. Though they weren't touching, she could sense the tension in his body. He didn't like her asking the questions.

*Too bad. I don't like you sitting next to me smelling of clean linen, frost, and Christmas. Of all the ridiculous scents!*

'Mrs Coggins?' the butler asked.

Clio stretched her mouth into a friendly smile. 'You no doubt work closely with her. Both heads of your department. Would you say Mrs Coggins enjoyed her position here? That she got along with the staff and Viscount Beachley? That she worked well with his wife?'

The thin man stretched his neck and tugged at his collar. 'I don't see what this has to do with Viscount Beachley's murder.'

Clio just raised her eyebrows. 'You don't? Hmm. Interesting.'

Alarm widened the butler's eyes.

'I think we've gotten the answers we need from Mr Chatham.' Grey's terse words prompted the butler to stand, his sigh of relief leaving no doubt about his feelings.

'If you need nothing else from me?' He spoke to the lieutenant general, avoiding Clio's gaze.

'Thank you. You have been most helpful. Please send in the next staff member.' Grey nodded his dismissal.

'We'd like to speak with Mrs Coggins last.' Clio spoke quietly, but the butler stiffened his spine.

As soon as the man left, Grey turned to her, his green eyes so bright, they almost glowed.

*Anger suits him.*

Not that it mattered.

'What are you on about?'

Clio shrugged, enjoying knowing she'd gotten under his skin. 'The butler will share our questions with the rest of the staff. Mrs Coggins will know we're focusing on her. Nervous people often say things they don't mean to, reveal secrets inadvertently, hide the wrong things. Don't you think?'

'I think nervous people are inclined to make mistakes.'

Triumph swelled her chest. 'Exactly.'

'Which means they might mislead us without meaning to. Perjure themselves, not because they are guilty, but because they are scared.' He turned in his seat to face her. 'Coercing a confession out of a frightened housekeeper is hardly showing investigative skill.'

'Rattling the cage and seeing what creatures scuttle out is exactly the kind of investigative skill that has helped me solve eight cases for Uncle Lachlan over the past three years.' Of course, speaking to dead victims about who killed them didn't hurt. Ghosts could be amazingly helpful witnesses when seeking justice for their deaths.

Before Grey could offer a rejoinder, the door opened, and the cook entered.

Grey pressed his lips together, stood, and gestured to the chair opposite them. 'Please, have a seat.'

The cook's eyes widened. Probably because his offer was closer to an angry command than a polite request. Which was Clio's fault. But she couldn't dredge up an ounce of remorse.

*I'm right, and he knows it.*

They spent the next several hours speaking with every member of Viscount Beachley's remaining staff. Clio asked each one something about the housekeeper. Only one member of staff answered her. Miss Sanders, the young maid who had opened the door for them. When Clio asked her thoughts on Mrs Coggins, the girl burst into tears.

Through halted sobs, she confessed her job was in peril now that the viscountess had gone missing. Apparently, the housekeeper had been threatening to sack Miss Sanders for weeks, but Viscountess Beachley wouldn't allow it. She felt the girl had promise and went toe to toe with the housekeeper about keeping her on despite Mrs Coggins' insistence Miss Sanders was insolent and lazy.

'The viscountess was a right hero, she was. Defending me to that 'orrible witch.'

Clio blinked, her fingers twitching on the table. 'Let's not digress to name-calling, Miss Sanders.'

The girl wiped her nose on her sleeve and sniffed loudly. 'Beggin' your pardon. It's just, I don't know what I'll do if she doesn't come back. Mrs Coggins already warned me I'll get no letter of reference from her. Mother and Father depend on me wages to help with the little 'uns. I can't go back to the workhouse. This was me chance.' She dissolved into loud wails.

Grey frowned at Miss Sanders as though she were a puzzle he couldn't quite solve. 'How long have you been in service?'

She startled, no doubt as terrified of Lieutenant General Grey as she was of Mrs Coggins. 'S-six months on Wednesday next.'

Grey nodded, as if this were good news. 'My housekeeper has been looking for a new maid. She is firm, but fair. She's trained many young women who have gone on to work in grander homes. If circumstances change for you here, there might be a place for you with her for a time. Can you read?'

Miss Sanders' mouth dropped open before she snapped it shut again. 'I knows me letters and numbers, but I'm no good at sums.'

His firm lips twitched. If Clio weren't so filled with astonishment by his unexpected kindness, she would have found room to be shocked by the humour dancing in his eyes. One more incongruent wrinkle in the fabric comprising Lieutenant General Grey. He pulled a card from his pocket and handed it to the maid. 'My address is there. I shall tell Mrs Hughes not to be surprised if she gets a visit from you. But perhaps the viscountess will return, and all will be well.'

Clio rolled her eyes before she could stop herself. Thankfully, Miss Sanders didn't see as she was too busy staring at Grey like he was some kind of guardian angel.

*More like a fallen angel.*

'Well, thank you so much for your help. If you wouldn't mind sending in Mrs Coggins, I believe she is the last person we need to speak with today.' Clio tried to keep her tone kind, but really. Did the girl need to bat her eyes at Grey like some twitterpated fool?

Clio gave him a sidelong glance as Miss Sanders left the room.

'What?' He kept his eyes on the door.

'How fortuitous that you need a maid. Now. The timing is remarkable.'

'I don't. But she needs a steady income and training if she wishes to make any kind of future for herself. My housekeeper excels at teaching new staff how to master their work, and—' He stopped abruptly as if realising he revealed too much. 'I don't need to explain myself to you. Or anyone.'

She snorted. 'Dear goddess, no. One might think you cared what others think, and that couldn't be farther from the truth.'

'Caring about other people's opinions is a waste of time.'

Annoyingly, she happened to agree with him, so she remained silent.

Grey stood from his seat, tugged down his coat, and strode to the end of the room. Tension corded his muscles as he turned to face her. 'For someone who seems convinced the housekeeper is a prime suspect, you were quick to admonish Miss Sanders for insulting the woman. What was it she called her? A witch?'

Her shoulders hitched, and she straightened her spine. He was trying to provoke her. She wouldn't allow it. 'Name-calling benefits no one. My desire for people to be treated respectfully, regardless of their guilt or innocence, has nothing to do with my suspicions regarding Mrs Coggins.'

He walked back and took his chair. 'Hmm. Interesting.' As he mirrored her last words to the butler, Clio realised something.

'I don't like you, Grey.'

'Finally. Something upon which we agree.'

Grey didn't like her either. Fine. Grand.

*Or does he agree with me because he also doesn't like himself?*

A fascinating idea she had no time to ponder as the door opened, and Mrs Coggins entered.

## 8

Grey could say with utmost confidence that Miss Clio Blair knew how to do one thing extraordinarily well: get under someone's skin. This time, he was just glad it wasn't his.

They had been questioning the housekeeper for twenty minutes, asking her to walk them through the final hours of Viscount Beachley's life.

The viscount had been taking afternoon tea with his wife. Mrs Coggins served them both in the front sitting room, then left to oversee the cleaning of the silverware. It was a weekly task that Viscount Beachley preferred she manage to ensure no theft occurred.

'One can't be too trusting. Anyone is capable of deceit if the stakes are high enough.'

'Even you, Mrs Coggins?' Clio's gaze was steady on the housekeeper.

Miss Blair was formidable. Even without her raven.

Mrs Coggins' cheeks grew red. 'That's not what I meant.'

'What did you mean?'

The housekeeper folded and unfolded her hands. 'The viscount knew I would never betray him. I've known him since he was a boy. I worked for his father before Viscount Beachley inherited the title. He trusted me because he knew my loyalty to him and to his family was unwavering.'

'And was his loyalty to you equally constant?'

The housekeeper sniffed. 'He could have turned me out, started new with a fresh household staff when he married. The viscountess wanted him to do just that, but he wouldn't hear a word of it. He appreciated my knowledge and expertise. He was a good man. He didn't deserve what happened to him.' Her eyes filled with tears.

'What about your feelings toward the viscountess? Are they as sanguine?' Clio began tapping her finger in a steady rhythm on the table.

Mrs Coggins shrugged. 'We got on well enough.'

*Tap. Tap. Tap.*

'But you just said she wanted you to be replaced by someone new. Perhaps a housekeeper who wasn't quite so loyal to Viscount Beachley, but deferred to her instead? Surely, that would create some bad feelings between you.'

*Tap. Tap. Tap.*

Shrugging, Mrs Coggins shifted in her chair. 'She was young. Didn't always know what the viscount might want or how to run a household befitting of his status. She needed help, but the prideful woman would never ask a lowly servant like myself. She had a rather high opinion of herself for someone who married above her station.'

*Tap. Tap. Tap.*

'Do you think the viscount was better than his wife?'

The housekeeper's eyes darted to Clio's fingers as she fiddled with an apron frill.

'More esteemed within society, certainly. And his family. His sister is a duchess, you know. She was kind to Lady Beachley, but it was clear Her Grace was disappointed by her brother's choice.'

'Did you agree with Her Grace?'

*Tap. Tap. Tap.*

Clio leaned back in her chair, her finger never missing a beat.

The woman snorted. 'I wouldn't dare disagree with a duchess.'

The tapping stopped.

Clio's smile sent a shiver down Grey's spine. 'So, you didn't like Viscountess Beachley.'

Realising her misstep, Mrs Coggins' face grew red, her eyes popping wide as she looked from Clio to Thomas and back again. 'I didn't say that. I had no issues with the viscountess. We worked well together.'

The tapping started again.

'Except that she had a rather high opinion of herself. Wouldn't ask for your help. Wanted to replace you with someone new...'

Slamming her hand on the table, Mrs Coggins' voice shook. 'I held no ill will towards the woman. But I do now.'

'Why is that?' Clio kept her voice steady and calm.

'Because she killed her husband!' The housekeeper became shrill. 'Make no mistake of that. The nasty witch couldn't wait to be rid of him.'

Clio's body stiffened again. It was the second time she reacted to the insult from two different members of Viscount Beachley's staff. Her tapping paused for a moment as her gaze flicked to Grey.

*Yes. I noticed. I notice everything about you, Clio Blair.*

Turning back to the housekeeper, Clio sat straighter in her chair, her lips pressing into a determined line.

Thomas leaned forward, speaking before Clio could. Her scowl brought him immense joy. 'Did you see something? Hear something to make you believe she might be responsible for his death?'

The housekeeper bit her lip, her brown eyes narrowed. 'It was no secret among the staff the viscountess wasn't fond of her husband. We are trained to understand the needs and desires of our employers. Lady Beachley's desire was clear: to avoid her husband whenever possible. When they were together, the rows they got into were so loud, you could hear them from the attic to the cellar. But that afternoon was different.'

'How—'

'How—'

They spoke together, then stopped. Clio's glare could have singed his eyelashes. He actually felt heat wash over his face like opening a furnace door. It was enough to stall him and let her ask the question.

'How was it different?' Clio returned her focus to Mrs Coggins. The temperature immediately cooled.

*Sparks. Fire. Heat. She is a living flame. Would my fingers burn if I touched her?*

He shifted uncomfortably in his chair and forced his focus back to the housekeeper.

'She was being so pleasant to Lord Beachley. They rarely took tea together, but she asked him to join her. She wanted to speak with him about Miss Anna. That child was the only thing they had in common. Lady Beachley mentioned reading about a new treatment in one of the medical journals she started ordering when Miss Anna fell ill. She was always coming to him with hair-brained treatments to cure her. Lord Beachley wouldn't allow it. He wouldn't let poor Miss Anna suffer, and rightly so.'

Clio pressed her lips together, and Thomas jumped into the small window of silence. 'You told the police that you served them tea, then went to polish the silver.' He wouldn't let Clio commandeer this entire interview.

The housekeeper nodded. 'Yes. That was the last time I saw

Lord Beachley alive.' Her chin quivered, and she covered her mouth with her hand.

Clio's finger began tapping again.

Mrs Coggins' mouth hardened, and her eyes flicked to Clio's hand before she returned her gaze to Thomas as she resumed her tearful story.

*Well played. She got her to break. Mrs Coggins isn't nearly as upset as she wants us to believe.*

He had to give Clio credit. She knew how to turn the screws on a witness. Which was incredibly unfortunate, as credit was the last thing he wanted to give the woman.

'Daisy found her. She's worked in this house for over five years. Daisy is a good maid. Reliable. Respectful. Nothing like who is left now.'

Thomas could only assume she was talking about poor Miss Sanders. His soon-to-be-hired maid. The girl was right; Mrs Coggins did hate her.

'Poor Daisy had to go home to be with her family after she spoke with the constable. The shock was too much for her.' Mrs Coggins shook her head. 'In the space of a moment, everything's changed. It was never meant to be like this.' Her voice caught, and for a brief glimmer, Thomas saw real grief in the woman's eyes.

Clio stopped tapping. 'Like what?'

Looking up from where she had been staring at a spot on the table, Mrs Coggins shook her head, realising she'd mis-stepped again but not knowing how. 'What?'

'You said it was never meant to be like this. What was it meant to be like?'

Mrs Coggins blinked rapidly, sniffed as she swept her knuckle beneath each eye to erase non-existent tears, then cleared her throat. 'I just mean, no man deserves to die at the hands of his own wife. We live in a civilised society. This kind of injustice cannot stand. I hope you find her and make her pay for what she did.'

Clio's fingers tapped again. 'Unless someone has already made her pay.'

Mrs Coggins met her gaze, her features hardening into a mask. 'I wouldn't blame whoever they were if they did. An eye for an eye, Miss Blair. God himself demands no less.'

'I find His demands to be rather contradictory.'

Sucking in her breath, Mrs Coggins covered her throat with a shaky hand. 'That's blasphemy!'

'Only if I believe in your god. And I don't.'

'Thank you, Mrs Coggins.' Thomas stood, walked around the table, and helped the housekeeper stand on shaky legs. He escorted her to the door. Clio had thoroughly scandalised the woman. One thing was certain: they would discover nothing more from Viscount Beachley's staff today.

'We don't have any more questions for you. Thank you for your time and candour.'

'I have one more question.' Clio's voice was calm, but Thomas could feel the anger vibrating from her in waves behind him. He turned from the door to face her. Mrs Coggins mirrored his movements. His gaze flicked to Clio's hands, but no sparks flew from her fingers, though the air shimmered in a heat wave. She was still tapping the table. He wondered how much longer the wood could stand up to the assault without cracking down the centre.

Mrs Coggins cleared her throat. 'Ask it then so I can get back to my work.'

'According to your god, what sin is worse? Blasphemy, lying, or murder?'

Lifting her chin, Mrs Coggins straightened her shoulders. She had a streak of grey hair starting at her temple and disappearing into a severe bun. 'All sin separates us from *our* God.'

'So, in your estimation, all sins are equal?'

'Sin is sin.' Mrs Coggins thrust out her chin.

Clio's finger stilled. 'Then, a liar is no better than a blasphemer. Or a murderer. Hmm. Interesting.'

The housekeeper's cheeks reddened. She turned and nearly slammed her shoulder into Thomas as she opened the door, stalked through, and shut it loudly behind her.

'Well done, Miss Blair.' Thomas walked slowly back to the table, staying on the opposite side. 'You've completely disarmed her. She'll tell us all her secrets now.' He let sarcasm sharpen each syllable.

'She is lying.' Clio stood, brushing her hand down her distractingly well-tailored outfit. No woman should look so bloody enticing in a man's dress shirt and fitted waistcoat. Nor should her scent of bergamot and rosemary fill his head with thoughts of bodies twining together in the dark shadows of an old forest. And yet, it did. She was both wild creature and refined lady, and Thomas couldn't stop imagining how easy it would be to flick open the buttons of her high collar and reveal her throat. Inhale her essence. Press his lips just there, at the hollow of her neck where her pulse beat to an ancient rhythm.

Shocking thoughts. She was too young. Too innocent. Too much his best friend's bloody niece. And possibly a witch.

'Are you even paying attention?' Anger made her golden eyes spark.

No. He was letting his mind conjure images of her naked flesh. But he could hardly admit that. He cleared his throat and organised his thoughts back into some semblance of order. 'What evidence do you have of her lies?'

'None yet. But you know I'm right.'

*That is neither here nor there.*

He crossed his arms over his chest. 'Today has been a waste. We have uncovered no new evidence. We have no new avenues of inquiry to find the viscountess. We have nothing.'

Clio pushed back the chair, knocking his cane from where it balanced against the scarred wooden table and stepped over it as she approached him. She pointed her finger at him like a small dagger. 'Then you really weren't paying attention. We know Viscountess Beachley had a contentious relationship with her housekeeper. We also know she had a change of heart towards her husband the day of his death. We know Mrs Coggins was the last person to see either of them alive, and she served them tea. The last drink Viscount Beachley ever consumed before he died – of poisoning – was given to him by his housekeeper. And we know Mrs Coggins is lying about something.'

'If you think she is lying, then how can we trust any of her testimony? How do we even know Lord Beachley and his wife had a friendly afternoon tea together?'

Clio's smile created a stir in Thomas' chest. 'Because she isn't the only person we spoke with today, or have you forgotten? The butler mentioned that he went to Lord Beachley's study at ten past three to deliver a letter, but he wasn't there. The footman informed him he was in Lady Beachley's sitting room, which he noted was quite odd. Your new maid, Miss Sanders, remembered complimenting Lady Beachley on her dress that day. The viscountess told her it was one of Lord Beachley's favourites and she was wearing it especially for him. And the cook remembers making lemon tarts. A treat she rarely made for Lady Beachley as the woman hated citrus, but one that the viscountess specifically requested for afternoon tea because it was her husband's favourite.'

'And how does this prove the housekeeper killed Viscount Beachley?'

'I never said she killed him. I said she was lying. And she *could* have murdered him. She had the opportunity and the means. What remains to be discovered is whether she had a motive. Unlike some, I like to keep my mind open to *all* possibilities.'

'Are you accusing me of having a closed mind, Miss Blair?'

Her eyes swept from the top of his head to his feet. A strange sensation washed through him. The only women who had been so bold with their gaze on his person were courtesans whom he paid. Yet it was disdain, not lust, he read in her face. 'I'm accusing you of missing the details, Grey. Details that will lead us to the killer.' Turning, she led the way out the door, down the servants' corridor, and outside to the mews. She glanced up to a dreary sky. 'Rain is coming.'

As if conjured by her words, a fat drop landed on his jacket. He adjusted his coat, buttoning it against the angry weather. 'Did you bring your cabriolet?' There were no carriages waiting in the mews save his own.

She began walking to the front of the house and the street beyond. 'I don't live far from here. Good day to you, Grey.'

Catching her arm, he turned her before thinking better of it. She froze, her pupils blowing wide as a jolt of electricity jumped from her body to his. The energy shot up his arm like a lightning bolt. He dropped his hand.

'Damn static electricity,' she muttered.

He clenched his hand in a fist, his fingers tingling with the intensity of whatever had passed between them. 'My sister wanted me to enquire about your availability two nights hence for supper. She has news from the duchess.'

'Oh. Yes. Well.' Clio looked at the pathway leading to the gate that would take her to the street beyond and freedom. She turned back to him, tapping her hand against her skirt. He could imagine her impatience to escape. 'I believe I am free that evening.'

He nodded. 'I shall come for you at seven.'

His words must have caught her off guard. She took a half-step back and swallowed. A thrill ran through him to have taken her by surprise. He doubted many men had achieved such a feat. 'I don't need an escort, Grey. I'm quite able to transport myself to your sister's.'

Unsteadying the woman was becoming a new obsession for Grey. Which was hardly flattering of his character. But it was not an easy task. Knowing he could accomplish something most people could not brought him a small measure of pride, which was more than he'd felt in quite some time.

Taking her hand, to test if another bolt of lightning would strike between them, he wasn't disappointed by a pleasant hum zinging along his nerves. He bowed over her hand, resisting the urge to lift her gloved fingers to his lips. 'Miss Blair, would you allow me the honour of escorting you to my sister's house for dinner?' He straightened to his full height, tightening his grip. As she tilted her chin, sunlight broke free from the clouds, bathing her in brightness. Her bottom lip was fuller than her top. She had a single freckle just beneath her left ear. Her right incisor was ever so slightly crooked.

And she didn't think he noticed details.

He had put her in a difficult position. She could refuse, but it would be uncommonly rude. Not that the woman seemed to care overmuch about social niceties, but it would also mean the idea of riding with him in his carriage bothered her. And he was willing to wager she wouldn't admit such weakness.

Pulling her hand free, dark clouds once more covered the sun. She dismissed him with a single blink. 'No, thank you.'

*Damnation! I've never been a lucky gambler.*

'Good day, Grey.' Not waiting for him to return her goodbye, she turned smartly on her heel and strode down the street.

The sky opened, and rain fell in earnest. Though it was difficult to see through such a heavy curtain of water, he guessed Miss Blair would arrive at her home completely dry.

* * *

Clio didn't immediately return home. She waited for Grey to climb into his carriage before looping back to Viscount Beachley's mansion and knocking smartly on the servants' door.

Miss Sanders answered, her eyes again growing large. Perhaps she needed spectacles. 'Miss Blair. I thought you were done with your interviews.'

Clio nodded. 'Yes. I am. But I wondered if I might take another tour of the house. I wish to examine Lady Beachley's sitting room. The last place they were together before he was found in the main hall.'

The maid's brow lowered in confusion. 'Is Lieutenant Grey not with you?'

'Lieutenant General,' she corrected. Not that it mattered. The maid could call him whatever she liked.

'Er, yes. Well. Is he not—'

'He had other business to attend. I shan't be long, I promise.' Clio stepped inside, forcing the girl to step back. Thank goodness it wasn't the butler or Mrs Coggins who'd answered the door. She would have had a much harder time brushing past them. Nodding to the maid, she quickly made her way up the dark staircase that opened to the entrance of the home. The last time she had been in the house alone, Sir Robin was on her shoulder. She felt oddly vulnerable standing in the entry without his comforting weight. But if she wanted to solve this case, she needed to convince Viscount Beachley that she was here to help him. The only way to do that was finding the ghost. She might not have any other opportunities, so she couldn't squander this one.

'Come on, Clio. Be brave,' she whispered as she walked down the hall to the room where she had her first and only vision of the viscount. Stepping back inside, she looked around. The sitting room was much as it had been before. Walking to the couch covered in a delicate rose print, it was clear this space had been decorated with a feminine view. She sat and ran her hands over the material. Nothing.

Standing, she walked to the corner where an easel was positioned to take advantage of the light from the window behind it. Leaning closer, linseed oil and turpentine tickled her nose. It was a portrait of what had to be Miss Anna. Clio didn't realise the viscountess was such a talented painter. She had completed the eyes and soft curls, but the girl's nose and cheeks were only faint sketches in charcoal.

Before she could reach out to touch the canvas, a vase fell from the mantel, crashing to the floor and shattering. She straightened and focused her gaze on the hearth. In the gloomy, late-morning light, there was a faint shimmer.

'Viscount Beachley. Were you trying to get my attention?' She moved away from the painting, slowly approaching the cold hearth. A thrill ran through her. Something sharper than excitement. 'I was hoping you might pay me a visit.'

The shimmer grew darker, shadows and light playing off it until a hazy image appeared. The viscount was taller than she expected. His eye colour was impossible to discern as every feature was painted in varying hues of silver and grey, but they sparked with intelligence. He had a strong jawline and thin lips. Even in death, his hair was meticulously combed. Phantoms presented themselves the way they wished to be seen in life. Beachley clearly cared about his appearance as every stitch of translucent clothing was pristine and neatly tucked, buttoned, and tied. 'I'm here to help you, Lord Beachley. To find your killer and bring them to justice.'

He reached out a ghostly hand. As Clio extended her own, their fingers brushed. It was like slipping one's hand into a cold, rushing stream. The vision hit harder than she expected.

'I don't want him to come again. He isn't helping her. Anna is getting worse.' Clio's voice was once again the low timbre of Viscount Beachley. Anger and fear rippled through him in equal measure. She was standing in the centre of Lady Beachley's bedroom. The woman sat at her dressing table to Clio's right, a hairbrush in her hand. She wore a nightgown of cotton that buttoned all the way up to her throat. Lamplight illuminated the spacious room decorated in green and gold. Powder and peonies, a sickeningly sweet combination, had Clio's belly roiling in an uneasy wave.

'He's highly regarded in the medical field. I won't send him away because of your baseless accusations.' Violet's voice shook.

Clio strode closer to Lady Beachley, and the woman's knuckles whitened around the silver brush handle. For a moment, Clio feared the viscountess might strike out and hit her husband with the makeshift weapon. It would leave more than just a red mark if she did.

'My accusations come from your blatant disregard of our vows. I know what I saw when I walked into Anna's room.' Fear and anger churned in Clio's belly as Viscount Beachley leaned closer to his wife. He wanted her to hit him. Wanted to feel the sharp bite of the silver brush cracking into his cheek. Because it would remind him what was at stake.

Violet stood, her chest expanding and contracting with rapid breaths. 'You saw a worried mother consulting with a talented physician about the health of her child. Nothing more.'

Viscount Beachley's laugh nearly scorched Clio's throat. 'Do not play me the fool, Violet.'

'Get out.' Violet reached blindly behind her, grabbing a bottle and throwing it at Clio. Viscount Beachley ducked, and the glass shattered against the wall. Powder and peonies flooded the room. 'Get out!' Violet screamed again, this time finding a hatpin and wielding it like a dagger.

Clio stumbled back. Viscount Beachley kept a careful eye on the sharp tip of the hatpin, but his voice was steady. 'He will not come into this house again. I will instruct the staff to bar his entrance. They will inform me if you try to subject our daughter to his dangerous medical experi-

*ments.' Turning, Clio stiffened as the hatpin flew over her shoulder, clattering to the ground.*

'I hate you.'

Violet's words echoed in her head as Clio slumped to the floor, nausea forcing her to curl into a ball.

'Miss Blair!'

*Blast!*

It was the last possible voice she wanted to hear.

*Lieutenant General Grey.*

# 9

Strong hands wrapped around her shoulders, pulling her from the floor and into Lieutenant General Grey's equally strong arms.

Oddly, the nausea eased as his scent surrounded her. He carried her to the settee. She breathed him in, replacing the sickening remnants of cloying summer flowers with clean soap and warm spice. He gently placed her on the couch before kneeling next to her, taking her hand and placing his fingers at the pulse point of her wrist. It took all of her concentration to ensure sparks didn't fly where his bare fingers touched her skin.

'Why are you here?' Her voice was rough, but thankfully no longer the deep timbre of a dead man.

It made no sense for Grey to be back at the house. He was supposed to be on his way to goddess knew where. Purgatory. Hades. Harrods. Anywhere but here.

'I forgot to give the maid my card. She thought I was looking for you and told me you were in the sitting room. It doesn't matter. Your heart is racing. What happened?' Grey's deep voice rippled over her raw nerves.

*I saw Viscount Beachley. He showed me a memory from his past. His wife was having an affair.*

The thoughts almost escaped her like steam.

*What would he say if I told him the truth? All of it?*

Clio knew the answer. If he believed her, he would condemn her. If he did not, he would think her mad and refuse to work with her on this case. Either way, he would never accept her or her power. The very idea was impossible.

Clio pushed aside the rogue desire to be honest with Grey, instead creating a believable lie. 'I wanted to see the sitting room once more. Make sure we didn't miss any clues. I didn't break my fast this morning. When I came in, I felt dizzy. I must have passed out.' Clio couldn't determine if her thoughts were fizzing because of her vision or because Grey was touching her. His fingers gently stroked over the delicate skin of her wrist, no longer seeking her pulse, but something else entirely. Heat and power thrummed in rhythm with her heartbeat. She could feel her magic arcing between them like an electrical flare as her control started to slip.

She pulled free, pushing herself up to sit properly. The world tilted, and she nearly fell from the settee, but he caught her once more in his solid embrace. Her nose brushed against his neck, and she couldn't stop inhaling. She held his scent inside her lungs, letting a small part of him absorb into her bloodstream.

*A woman could get drunk on this man.*

Pushing him away once more, she tried to create distance, but he kept his grip on both her arms. 'You can't walk home like this. I have my carriage. I'll take you.'

Before she could argue, he was lifting her in his arms once more.

'Maybe I wouldn't be dizzy if you didn't keep hauling me from one place to the next.'

Grey didn't respond, but she felt his body flex and shift beneath her as he strode out of the sitting room.

'I can walk.' Her sharp tone should have at least stalled his step, but he kept a steady pace down the empty hall and through the front door. He must be remarkably fit. He moved as easily as if he weren't carrying a fully grown woman. Clio struggled, but he only held her tighter against his solid chest. A dangerous desire to stop fighting and let herself melt into his strength, burrow into his warmth, nearly stole her breath. The buzzing in her ears grew louder.

*I don't want him carrying me. I can carry myself. Er. Walk myself.*

Her thoughts were still jangled from the vision. When Grey stepped up into his carriage, the fluid movement made her belly flip. He settled onto the squabs, but instead of placing her on the seat opposite, he kept her snug on his lap. Fresh linen and the blasted spice she couldn't place beckoned her to lean closer to his cravat and bury her nose in the soft fabric. The carriage lurched forward, and he tightened his hold, once more saving her from a fall.

'Put me down.' She struggled to remove herself from such an inappropriate position, but his arms only grew harder. She might as well be fighting an oak tree.

'No.'

Her futile efforts to escape were creating an odd reaction in Clio. She knew Grey wouldn't hurt her. She knew she could unleash a fireball that would render him helpless. But an awareness of his physical power over her created an inexplicable ache low in her belly.

'Release me this instant.' Even as she spoke the breathless words, she questioned if she really wanted to be free from his arms. Perhaps sharing her body with a man she despised was the best way to explore physical intimacy without worrying about losing her heart. Not that she had spent much time thinking about physical intimacy. Until recently, that is.

Helena had engaged in a wild fling once, telling her cousins about the misadventure. Based on her experience, it seemed too much effort for very little reward. Clio had decided then she would much rather focus her energies on developing her craft. Though there had been a few interested suitors in her younger years, she quickly shut down any men interested in wooing her, and the gossip spread that Clio Blair was a shrew best left alone. Which was fine by Clio. So why was she suddenly wondering what it might feel like to have his fingers trail up her naked spine?

'Not until I know you won't faint again.' He bit out the words, turning so his face was only inches from hers. What she saw burning in his eyes was deeper than frustration. Sharper than fear. Hotter than anger. 'I won't let you go until I know you are safe.'

As a firewitch, she was used to running hotter than most, but her skin felt oddly tight, and the warmth in her belly was nothing like the heat her magic usually conjured. This was something entirely new.

She could see the individual hairs covering Grey's cheeks and jaw. His mouth was pressed tight, creating two creases on either side, and she wondered if she brushed her thumb over his bottom lip, would it soften? She couldn't test her theory because he held her arms tight to her side. Even that was strangely arousing. She was helpless. Unless she chose to unleash her powers and crisp him into ash.

While he had shown no signs of being winded when he carried her from Viscount Beachley's house, Grey's chest now rose and fell with harsh breaths that matched her own. She leaned closer. Her nose brushed his stubbled cheek as she tilted her head.

Clio had been kissed before. Once. An uninvited smash of wet lips that ended with her fist in the would-be suitor's belly. If she didn't already hold a dim view of romance, that kiss confirmed all her suspicions. It certainly wasn't pleasant. But here, now, she wondered. And wondering was a dangerous thing indeed.

'You are not a nice man.' It was her last attempt at denying what she most desperately wanted. And it failed spectacularly.

'I know.'

The depth of grief in his words cracked open something in her heart. Because while she didn't really think he was a bad man, he certainly did. It was his flash of soul-clenching honesty that undid her. She closed the distance between them, pressing her lips against his, tasting mint and surprisingly... pepper.

She didn't think his body could get any harder, but everything did. His chest. His thighs. His arms. His fingers. And his mouth became ravenous.

He released his grip around her only to plunge his fingers into her hair. She had lost her hat somewhere. She would have to return to Viscount Beachley's house to retrieve it. Later.

His strong grip at the base of her neck was the only thing tethering her to the world.

'Tell me to stop. Tell me and I will.' His words were as fierce as his gaze.

She bit her lip and slowly shook her head. A girl born of fire couldn't possibly douse this blaze.

'Damn you,' he growled before pulling her face closer, pressing his lips against the sensitive flesh where her jaw met her neck and sucking hard, nipping in sharp, sweet bites that nearly stole Clio's sanity. Sparks were igniting all over her skin. Lights flickered behind her closed eyes, but when he caught her earlobe between his teeth, biting hard enough to have her gasping, she didn't care if the carriage became engulfed. She wanted more. Pressing her thighs together, she savoured the delicious ache at her apex. A pulsing need demanded friction.

Grey tugged on her hair, the pain creating heat. He kissed along her cheekbone, over one eye, then the other. His hand slipped down to cup her breast, testing her shape against his palm. Her nipples hardened instantly, greedy little things needing more pressure. She desperately wished for fewer layers.

The carriage hit a rut in the road, and Clio was weightless for a moment before bouncing back onto his lap. She could feel the hard ridge of his erection even through the volumes of silk and lace separating them.

*Oh my.*

This could so easily burn out of control. That realisation was enough to crack the haze of lust infusing her.

The air inside the carriage had grown heavy and hot. Like being trapped in a greenhouse or orangery. Pulling back from his drugging kisses, amber clashed with emerald as she held his gaze. His lips were red from her teeth scraping them. His pupils blown wide with untamed need. She knew her face would carry the marks of his shadow beard where he'd scraped his rough cheek against her smooth one, and it created a strange sense of satisfaction to know they had marked each other in such a primitive way.

The carriage pulled to a stop, and Clio didn't miss the slight singe on the edge of the curtain closest to her.

*Blasted damnation. Perhaps he won't notice.*

Of course he would notice. He noticed far too much. This was lunacy of the highest order.

Grey seemed to come out of a trance as the carriage stilled. His eyes shifted from wild passion to bitter regret. 'I should not have... that is. Please forgive me for taking such unforgivable liberties.'

Something about his immediate shame rankled her. 'You didn't take them. I gave them.' Was his attraction to her so disgusting because of her station in life, or her general person? And why was she offended? She didn't want this to happen again. His disgust should be a welcome reason to avoid ever repeating this most obvious mistake. 'And there is nothing to forgive. No crime has been committed.'

'You are at least ten years my junior. And my best friend's niece. An innocent who doesn't deserve to be toyed with by someone like me.'

*Ah. Well. He is trying to be honourable. How damnably lovely.*

But it didn't take the sting out of his rejection. 'I am also a woman well into my adult years and able to make my own choices. Trust me, I have no illusions of a future with you, nor do I want one. This was a moment of madness we shall never repeat.'

That certainly shocked him.

He gritted his teeth. 'Indeed?'

She raised her brows and lifted her chin. 'Indeed.'

Exhaling through his nose, he flexed the hand still wrapped around her waist. She resisted the urge to arch her back in offering. Because she would give nothing to this man. Not her body. Not her heart. Certainly not her magic.

'Good. Because I have no intentions of courting you, Clio.' He spoke her name like a prayer. Or a curse. The intensity of his dark voice wrapping around the syllables nearly drew her back to him, like a moth to a candle. If only the rest of what he said wasn't so insulting.

The irony of him taking offence at her rejection of his rejection was not lost on Clio. She laughed, though it was a sharp sound devoid of mirth. 'And I certainly have no wish to be courted by you, as I just said. Really, Grey. For an investigator, you are terrible at paying attention.' She slipped off his lap and twisted towards the door. Gripping the handle, she glanced over her shoulder. He was ridiculously handsome with his tousled black hair, piercing green eyes, shadowed jaw, and sinful lips, pressed into a hard, disapproving line. He could have been the Devil himself, stern and determined to drag her soul with him into the fiery pit. Something about his dark beauty fuelled her simmering anger. 'Fear not, Grey. I am in no danger of falling in love with you. I would rather burn forever than suffer such a fate.' She smiled at him, a baring of teeth that intensified her cutting words. She pushed open the door and jumped from the cab to the cobblestone street in a splash of muddy water.

*Marvellous.*

Hoping for a dramatic exit, this fell somewhat short. Her boots were already soaked through.

Grey leaned out of the hansom, the wind playing with his hair. 'This will not happen again, Miss Blair.'

She rolled her eyes. 'I already said that. Details, Grey. Start noticing the details,' she hissed before turning and walking down the cobblestone path to her front gate.

\* \* \*

Thomas sat at his at his sister's dining table and, for the 879th time, wished he had never kissed Miss Clio Blair. It was impossible to watch her delicately sample the soup from a silver spoon, nibble the poached turbot, savour the venison, or practically make love to the trifle without remembering every erotic moment they'd shared in his bloody carriage. Tasting her unique flavour was a cataclysmic event in his life upon which everything would be measured as before or after.

*The viscount's murder happened* before *my entire life was turned inside out by the lips of a woman who might also be a witch, and dinner at my sister's happened* after *my entire life was turned inside out by the lips of a woman who might also be a witch.*

Conversely, and infuriatingly, she seemed completely unaffected. She barely even acknowledged his presence throughout dinner. Any time he spoke, she kept her eyes elsewhere. He should have been relieved. The very last thing he needed was a romantic entanglement. He could not walk down that path with any woman, and certainly not with Miss Blair. Yet each time she avoided him, he only became more determined to capture her attention.

'I'm sorry Lord Burrows wasn't able to join us. He had pressing business at his club.' Cynthia's smile was bright as ever, but there was a tension around her eyes. She was upset. And he had been so focused on forcing Miss Blair to look at him, it had taken him nearly all of dinner to notice. He couldn't very well ask her what was wrong in front of Clio, but when they were alone, he would press her to be honest with him. Something he feared she had not been for quite some time when it came to her marriage.

'I can't think of any business important enough to keep me away from this dessert.' Clio's pink tongue darted out, and she licked her spoon clean.

Thomas shifted as his cock, an appendage he was usually able to keep under strict control, hardened.

'The first thing we'll need to work on if you're going to pass as part of the peerage is your table manners, Miss Blair. One does not lick cutlery in public.' His words were harsh, and his glare was no doubt harsher. But really. A man could only endure so much.

'Thomas! Clio's behaviour is far better than yours. A gentleman never speaks so rudely to a lady.'

Clio's cheeks grew pink. She carefully placed her spoon on the dessert plate. Her bloody raven, who had been given his own chair at the table, glared at Thomas.

'Lick my cutlery!' The raven knocked his spoon to the floor with his beak.

Cynthia let out a startled laugh.

'Perhaps this is a terrible mistake.' Clio's low voice stalled something in the vicinity of his chest. 'I could come as your lady's maid

instead of your cousin. I'm fairly decent at dressing hair.' Clio bit
her lip. Thomas hated that he put the glimmer of uncertainty in her
golden eyes. She was confident in everything she did, but
pretending to be a peer was rattling her, and Thomas was making it
worse. Because she aroused him, and he didn't know what to do
about it. So he was being cruel. Which was unacceptable. He might
be a broken man, but despite the raven's opinion, he was not a
bastard.

'My apologies, Miss Blair. I did not mean to imply you were not
capable of playing your part.'

Clio finally deigned to look at him. The sharpness of her gaze
could have cut through the table. 'Of course you did. But I am used
to being underestimated by fools.'

Cynthia covered her mouth to hide her smile.

*Thank you for your loyalty, sister.*

Coughing, she took a sip of her wine. 'Cousin Clio. You must
start calling her that, Thomas, or you'll slip up at Lady Langley's
and then we'll be in quite the pickle.'

He shot his sister a glare, then turned back to Clio. 'My apologies, Cousin Clio,' he ground out her name.

'Much better. And you can't possibly be my maid, Clio. Don't be
ridiculous. You are our dear third cousin twice removed from the
northern countryside, and we are thrilled to introduce you to
London's best society. It's the perfect story because we won't be
expected to know much of each other.'

The remainder of dinner and port thereafter in the sitting room
was spent planning their trip, which was to commence only three
days hence. When the clock struck midnight, Clio rose and tapped
her shoulder for Sir Robin, who had been happily hopping around
the edges of the sitting room, exploring.

'Perhaps Grey could walk me out to my carriage. It is awfully
late, and one never knows who could be lurking in the shadows.'

Clio blinked innocently at his sister, but Thomas' body tightened. The woman might be an enigma, but one thing was certain: she had no fear of the dark. What was she playing at? She couldn't possibly be planning an assignation with him. She made her thoughts on that perfectly clear the day before. Much to Thomas' chagrin. That didn't stop his imagination from painting a wild image of him pressing her body against the side of her cabriolet, exploring her mouth with his tongue. Testing her heat and seeing if they could set the spindly wheels of her carriage alight. Because, though it defied logic, he suspected the singed curtain in his carriage was directly related to their kiss.

*Only one way to test my theory.*

Damn his heart for speeding up at the thought. And damn his cock for growing even harder.

He held out his arm for her, on the opposite side of where her raven perched for fear the bird might try to peck out his eyes if Sir Robin caught him looking where he shouldn't.

Clio's dress was another daring ensemble blending masculine and feminine styles. The skirt and bodice were the colour of ripe cherries with black pinstripes reminiscent of a suit but cut to high-light her feminine curves. She wore a cherry cravat tied intricately around her neck, barring any glimpse of skin and begging Thomas to untie her like a present. If only he were so bold.

Cynthia walked with them to the door and leaned in to kiss Clio's cheek before bidding them both goodnight. Thomas paused in the entrance to collect his coat from the butler and, after Sir Robin hopped to the ground, helped Clio into her own sharply tailored jacket made entirely of black leather.

'You certainly don't shy away from rather risqué fashion, dear cousin,' he murmured near her ear as he helped pull the coat up her arms and settled it onto her shoulders. The scent of leather blending with rosemary and bergamot only further heated his blood.

She stepped away from him, and Sir Robin resumed his place on her shoulder. 'I don't shy away from much, Grey.'

The butler opened the door, waiting dutifully for them to exit.

'And yet you've suddenly developed a great fear of the dark.' Thomas raised a brow and secretly thrilled at the heat flaring in her eyes.

*Good God, anger suits her.*

'I need to speak with you.' She flicked her eyes to the butler, who stood with his back straight, his eyes staring ahead at nothing. 'Come.'

The imperious command should have stoked his anger. But instead, another emotion – just as hot and twice as dangerous – flared deep in his chest as she swept out of the front entrance, down the steps, and into the night. Without thought, he followed her.

Clio's heeled boots crunched over the gravel drive to where her carriage waited, sans footman. Thomas eyed the empty back seat.

'Where is your man?' He attempted to keep his voice level.

She looked around, going so far as to check under the cabriolet. 'Oh dear. I must have misplaced him.' She opened the door and patted the seat for Sir Robin, who happily hopped in and fluffed his feathers.

'Did you drive here alone?' He wasn't trying to keep his voice level any more. It was futile.

Clio's golden eyes flashed with warning, but he cared not. He could withstand her fury. Indeed, he welcomed her fire.

'I didn't feel the need to bring my footman when I knew the carriage would be watched over by your sister's groomsmen. It seemed a waste of poor John's time to sit out here in the cold for hours waiting on me to finish my dinner. I am more than capable of managing the journey from my house to here and back again alone. This is hardly St Giles or Whitechapel.'

Thomas stepped forward, gripping her arm. 'You will do no such thing. It's bad enough you insist on driving yourself, but to come without the protection of a footman is unacceptable. Only a fool would tempt fate so boldly. A lady such as yourself is just as apt to find trouble on the streets of Mayfair as anywhere else.'

The lamps lighting Cynthia's drive flared and popped as Thomas' fingers began to tingle, then burn where he touched her.

'Must I remind you again? I am no lady. If you are so concerned with safety, look to your own. Men issuing commands to someone like me have far more to fear than any woman driving alone.' Clio's arm was hotter than fire, even through the layers of satin and leather. Rosemary and bergamot filled his lungs as her scent intensified with the heat. His hand reacted instinctively, releasing her as quickly as one might pull back from a burning coal.

He looked from his unmarked palm to her covered arm. Heat waves emanated from her body in the wavering lamplight. But it wasn't fear that filled him. It was wonder, and a desperate need to know what in the blazes was going on with this woman.

'You are keeping secrets from me, Clio Blair.'

She narrowed her gaze. 'I could say the same of you, Thomas Grey. You told me you came back to Viscount Beachley's the other day to give the maid your card. That's how you found me in the study. But you gave her your card in the servants' dining room. I watched you hand it to her, and I watched her take it. So, tell me, why did you return to Beachley's after we concluded our interviews with the servants? What were you looking for in the study?'

*Damnation.*

'I was looking for you.' Her anger stoked his own, and he clamped his teeth together, frustrated that he let her provoke him so easily.

Uncertainty showed as she hitched her shoulders. 'Why?'

There were a million reasons why he might look for Clio Blair, but none of them were appropriate to share. 'Has no man ever pursued you before, Miss Blair?'

Lifting her chin a fraction, he noted her error. Her white throat gleamed in the moonlight like a flag waving in the dark, but this was no mark of surrender. This was a warning before the battle began. Thomas wanted to pull her closer, breathe her scent, taste the vulnerable skin behind her ear and make her shiver. Instead, he held himself in check.

'My romantic history is none of your business.'

*Ah. So, you've never been courted.*

If he needed any more proof that men were idiots, this would suffice. Clio was wealthy, beautiful, and intelligent. She should have a bevy of impoverished lords seeking her hand in marriage, yet there were none. And Thomas could guess the reason: her entire person defied anyone who might try to control her fate. No man, titled or not, would be willing to let his wife hold the reins, and Clio wasn't about to give them up willingly.

'I suppose you've never wished to be courted.'

She curled her lip in a sneer. 'I'd rather go swimming in the Thames on a snowy day in January.'

It made sense. She didn't need a man for income or security. She and her female relatives had done an exemplary job of creating a life relying entirely upon their efforts alone. Unlike so many unhappy ladies within the beau monde, she did not need to marry and would never be forced into a union by her aunt. If a man wished to woo Clio Blair, he would have to convince her that what he offered was worth her time. And Thomas guessed no man she met was ever willing to take on such a challenge. Until now.

*Absolutely not. She is not for you. And you certainly have nothing to offer her beyond physical pleasure.*

But even that was impossible, Thomas did not dally with virgins, especially a witchy one with a raven on her shoulder and fire in her eyes.

'No man has ever tempted you before?'

Why was he asking these questions? He didn't want to know her answers. He certainly had no intentions of pursuing her. No matter how enticing the challenge of making her want him might be. Of all the men in London, he was the worst choice for Clio Blair.

'Not a single one.'

*Ouch. That arrow hit its mark.*

Clio shifted her feet, her hand resting on her hip. 'You are trying to distract me, Grey. It won't work. Why were you following me?'

He raked his hand through his hair and grasped at the easiest lie. 'I wanted to ensure you arrived at your home safely.'

She rolled her eyes. 'Please. Neither of us believes my safety ranks high on your list of priorities, no matter how you bluster on about my missing footman.'

She was wrong. Her safety was becoming increasingly more important to him. But he could hardly admit that to her, as he was only just realising it himself. 'Fine. I wanted to determine where you were going after our investigation. Because I don't trust you.' That was also true and put him in a prickly conundrum. 'When you doubled back and re-entered the house, I realised my suspicions about you were justified.'

She blinked, her amber eyes as hot as molten gold. 'What suspicions are those, Grey?'

'You aren't being honest with me, Miss Blair.'

'Who is ever completely honest? We all have our secrets. Even you.' Her pupils dilated. For a terrifying moment, he thought she knew. Had she somehow seen the hidden shame he kept buried in the darkest cellar of his soul? But that was impossible.

She blinked, breaking the odd spell. 'And you shouldn't trust me either. I won't hesitate to cut you down, any chance I get.'

That was an invitation he could accept. The warrior in him flared to life. He might not rise to the challenge of courting her, but he certainly wouldn't back down from fighting her.

'I expect nothing less.' He risked her heat and stepped closer. When she didn't back away, and he didn't instantaneously combust, he took another step. 'I will discover your secrets, Miss Blair, no matter how cunningly you hide them.'

'Careful what you wish for.' She gripped the back of his neck, sudden and shocking, pulling his head down to hers and stopping when their lips almost touched. 'You might discover some truths are best left alone. If you come after me, I'll make sure we burn together.' Instead of closing the distance as he ached for her to do, she pushed him hard. He stumbled back. She was stronger than she looked, and he nearly landed on his arse.

Turning in a swirl of leather and silk, she swept into the driver's seat with the grace of a bird taking flight. Before Thomas could recover from his near fall, the smart little buggy was trundling away. Sir Robin cawed, 'Bastard!' from the window.

*Blast and damn!*

# 10

'Are you certain this is wise?' Aunt Rowan was tapping her foot. Never a good sign.

Clio checked her bags for the seventeenth time. Determining what one should take for a fortnight in the country was challenging. Cynthia had sent a rushed note over the day before to inform her Lady Langley had invited a few more guests to make the visit a real party. Nothing lavish. A simple affair, really. Only ten or fifteen of their closest friends. Clio shouldn't worry.

In Clio's limited experience, nothing simple involved ten or fifteen members of the beau monde. It was rather scandalous of the duchess to propose a house party while she was still in the first month of mourning for her brother, but Clio supposed she and Lady Langley had something in common: neither needed to follow society's expectations. Lady Langley was too far above the purview of the beau monde to care, and Clio was too far below it to merit any notice.

She puffed her cheeks and squashed the fluttering in her belly. She might not rank in the peerage, but that was no reason not to look fabulous. She knew societal armour was very often comprised of silk, lace, and taffeta. Clio would certainly hold her own in a room full of London's bluest bloods with her daring ensembles. It did result in a rather prodigious amount of luggage.

Clio nodded at the footmen who stood waiting to begin loading her cases in the carriage before answering her aunt. 'I'm certain Viscount Beachley's daughter will help our investigation. Both memories he shared with me were about Anna. He wants me to speak to her. I know it.'

Cynthia had booked them tickets on the London and South Western Railway. Lady Langley would send carriages for them at Burnham station when they arrived. All Clio needed to do was get herself and her trunks to the train on time. A feat in peril of failing if she didn't hurry.

Aunt Rowan's chestnut hair gleamed in the watery sunlight filtering through their entry window. 'I'm worried, Clio. You know I rarely have visions, but last night, I dreamed of fire and ash. A tall man with a silver cane stood in the centre of the flames. Your Lieutenant General Grey.'

Clio shook her head. 'He isn't my anything.'

'Are you certain? I fear he is a threat. I should never have allowed your uncle to bring him into your life.'

Clio placed a reassuring hand on her aunt's arm. 'You can't always protect us from harm, Aunt Rowan. We are women, grown. Life is full of danger, but to live in fear is not to live at all.'

'You, Ellie, and Helena are all I have left of my sisters. I swore a blood oath to them that I would protect you.'

'And you have. But you also taught us how to protect ourselves. Trust us, Aunt Rowan. Trust the lessons you provided. If Lieutenant General Grey is a threat, fear not. I will vanquish him. Just as you taught me.' She squeezed her aunt's arm, willing her to understand.

Her aunt's skin was as clear and smooth as Clio's despite the thirteen-year gap in their ages, but it paled as Clio walked to the door and patted her shoulder for Sir Robin. Aunt Rowan was not a demonstrative woman, so Clio was shocked when Aunt Rowan glided swiftly across the room, pulling Clio into a stiff hug. 'I don't like you being so far away. We are a coven. Most powerful when together. If you need us, promise you will send a message.'

'What's wrong? Why are you hugging? Has someone died?' Helena traipsed down the stairs, her fox slinking along, so near to her skirts, he was almost hidden by the forest-green velvet.

'Surely not.' Ellie was close behind, her blonde hair swept into a loose twist, tendrils framing her concerned face.

Aunt Rowan broke the hug and stepped back. 'No one is dead.' Clio nearly missed the muttered, 'Yet.'

'Farewell, Clio.' Her sister rushed up and pulled her into an embrace scented with sage and sugar, an odd combination of sweet and fresh that was so very Ellie. 'You are going to have such a marvellous time. I know it.' She pressed a soft kiss on each of Clio's cheeks before squeezing Clio's hands and stepping back.

'Hurry home, cousin.' Helena's grey gaze was as steady and calm as the woman herself. 'And keep your eye out for trouble on your travels. Fine ladies like the duchess and her friends are far more treacherous than they appear.'

It was a cryptic statement in perfect alignment with Helena's tendency to always expect the worst.

'Thank you, Helena.' Clio gave her cousin a quick hug, looked at the three women who were her closest friends, her kin, and coven. 'I shall miss you all, but I will return in a fortnight with this case solved and one more restless soul eased. I swear it.'

Aunt Rowan opened her mouth to say something, but seemed to think better of it. She bit her lip and held her hands in front of her, fingers laced together. 'Return to us healthy and hale, that is all I care about. Solving MacDougal's case means nothing if you don't come back to us just as you left, Clio.'

'No one returns from a journey just as they left, Aunt. It rather defeats the purpose of an adventure in the first place, wouldn't you say?' Helena raised a copper brow at Aunt Rowan.

'Right. Well. My adventure will end before it begins if the train leaves without me.' Clio gave them each a final smile. 'Blessed be until we are together again.'

'Blessed be.' Aunt Rowan and Helena spoke together.

'Blessed be, sister.' Ellie's clear voice cheered Clio. She turned, walked swiftly down the stairs and into the waiting carriage, laden with trunks, bags, and multiple hat boxes.

When Clio arrived at Waterloo station, Grey was standing on the steps. He wore another one of his long, black coats. His high collar, black top hat, crisp white cravat, and silver cane left no doubt the man came from the peerage, even if he was a second son.

A long liquid pull in Clio's belly had her pressing her thighs together as the memory of their kiss crashed through her system. Aunt Rowan was progressive in her role as matriarch. When the girls asked questions, she didn't shy away from answering them. She explained the details of how two bodies might come together, but she also encouraged them to privately explore on their own. Aunt Rowan reassured them, it was far safer, less messy, and more likely to result in pleasure. Helena's disastrous experience only further proved their aunt's wisdom.

Because of this, Clio knew what the tingling pulse in her core meant, but she had never felt it outside her own breathless explorations in the privacy of her bedroom. Until that kiss.

She might have no wish to be courted, but for the first time in her life, she felt fire sparking between herself and another. Fire she wouldn't mind playing with to see how hot it might burn.

Dallying with a man wasn't strictly forbidden in their household. Indeed, Aunt Rowan told the girls if they ever found themselves unwed and with child, the coven would happily expand to accept the girl, for there was no doubt in her mind any baby brought forth would be female. Only giving one's heart away threatened a witch's magic, and Clio was hardly stupid enough to ever fall in love. But to explore this burgeoning desire with a willing partner... the thought was becoming harder to dismiss the longer she spent in Grey's company. It helped that she hated him. There would never be any danger of letting the fire between them burn out of control.

He tapped the handle of his cane against his palm, and a wild image of him tapping something else with that hard length of wood had heat flooding Clio's cheeks.

*Control yourself! Fantasies are one thing, but turning into a dithering fool is quite another.*

For a woman so devoted to retaining her autonomy, it troubled her to realise her fantasies often involved Grey taking control. It was something she would never allow, and yet, her mind spun out wild, impossible scenarios.

Clio exited the carriage and ascended the stairs towards him. His emerald gaze flicked to the porters rushing to unload her trunks.

'You may not share blood with my sister, but you certainly pack as though you are related. The two of you will leave no room for passengers on the train with so much luggage.' The arousing effect of his growl on her senses was becoming as familiar as it was annoying.

Stiffening her spine, she breezed past him and entered the station. 'It's a marvel they can fit anything onto the train at all with your self-importance taking up so much room.'

Cynthia was easy to find; her travelling gown of bright copper, expertly tailored to show off her trim waist and flared hips, stood out from the dreary black coats around her. She had a smart hat with a veil covering half of her face. The other half beamed in pleasure when she caught sight of Clio.

Throwing her arms out, she rushed forward. 'Cousin Clio! Don't you look marvellous! What a dashing ensemble.' She pulled Clio in for one of her warm hugs and then held her at arm's length. 'I dare say I would never have the courage to wear such a bold outfit, but that tartan looks stunning on you.'

Clio attempted not to preen, but the green and blue tartan travelling costume set off with black leather piping was one of her favourites. The coat was cut to mirror a man's riding jacket, her skirt was narrow, making it easier to manoeuvre through narrow train passages, and the leather boots were both warm and comfortable. The bowler hat she wore included a ribbon of the same tartan as her suit. Sir Robin ducked his head up and down in excitement at seeing Cynthia.

'Oh, and you look as handsome as always, Sir Robin.' Cynthia ran her fingers over Sir Robin's sleek feathers, much to his delight.

'Stunning!' the feathered flirt chirped.

*He'll be sneaking off my shoulder and onto hers by the time this trip is done.*

Grey joined them, and they showed the conductor their first-class tickets before being ushered onto the train, down a short corridor, and into a private carriage. Clio had never ridden in such style. She looked around a room that could have been any esteemed peer's parlour. The furniture was secured to the floor, but it didn't diminish the elegance of the delicately carved chaise, wingback chairs, or low table laden with tea things, plates of iced cakes, cucumber and salmon sandwiches, miniature mince pies, and a bowl of fresh fruit.

'Oh my. We shall be quite comfortable all the way to Buckinghamshire.' Cynthia declared, making herself at home in one of the overstuffed chairs.

Clio decided upon the hunter-green settee, leaving the chaise and a second wingback free for Grey to take, but the infuriating man sat next to her on the couch. She refused to move closer to the side. If he was determined to invade her space, the last thing she would do was grant him more room. In point of fact, she shifted to the centre of the cushion. Let him move out of the way for her. She was not retreating.

Pulling off her leather gloves, she leaned forward to pour herself a dish of tea at the exact moment Grey reached out for a sandwich. Their hands brushed. Small sparks burst brightly between their fingers as the gas lighting in the carriage flickered and flared.

*Damnation.*

It was embarrassing that she kept losing control of her magic around Grey. Ellie's list of indicators for a spirit match echoed through her head.

*'He provokes your magic...'*

*Balderdash! He provokes my anger, and that sparks my magic. This is a test from the goddess to gain greater control over myself. That is all.*

Control she would begin exerting immediately.

Cynthia looked at the lamp nearest her and laughed. 'We must be getting ready to depart. What a miracle of technology to be able to light these carriages with gas. It's a wonder it works at all.'

Grey looked from their hands to Clio. 'A miracle, or magic?'

Her heart thumped painfully.

Did he suspect? And what if he did? Would he burn her at the stake? Turn her in to the magistrate? Demand she be condemned? Or just walk away? Because he certainly wouldn't accept her.

'Some might argue they are the same.' She added milk to her tea, forcing her voice to remain steady and the heat of her power to stay contained in her chest.

'Magic and miracles, the same? I beg to hear your explanation.' Grey placed his sandwich on a plate and leaned closer to her.

She could feel the energy zinging between them, building power, readying to crack into white-hot flame.

Clenching her teeth, she took a deep breath and willed it away, forcing the magic to dissipate like smoke while she concentrated on her argument. 'One man's faith is another man's fallacy. One man's truth is another's delusion. Religious zealots see miracles, mystics see magic, and fools see evil to be feared. The unknowable depths of the universe confound us, so we try to create reason out of chaos. Inventing rules we can play by brings comfort many crave, but accepting life as an unexplainable mystery brings enlightenment few achieve.'

Grey's gaze sharpened. 'Would you consider yourself enlightened, Miss Grey?'

'I consider myself constantly bewildered by life's inconsistencies.' It was a disconcerting truth she hadn't realised until it spilt from her lips.

'And so, you seek control.'

*Dear goddess. I do. I want control because nothing is guaranteed. Mother lost everything. So did Aunt Willow. They gave themselves up for their husbands. Mother abandoned her family and her magic. Aunt Willow allowed her gift to be twisted into something insidious. Both traded autonomy for obedience. Sacrificed control for comfort. And the fates ruined them.*

It was a path Clio refused to walk. But it was also something she would never share with Thomas Grey.

'You believe deeper understanding is found by embracing the unknown, so what might you find if you let go?'

Fear, unfamiliar and profound, flooded her system at the very thought.

*Damn this man for pulling back the veil. Who does he think he is? My bloody spirit guide?*

Or perhaps her spirit match.

*Impossible. Spirit matches are not real.*

Distance was necessary. Clio stood abruptly and moved to the seat opposite Cynthia and farthest from him.

'Trains sometimes make me ill. I would hate to cast up my accounts all over your lovely jacket, Grey.' She was lying. And retreating. Two things she loathed to do, and both because of the vexatious, stupidly intelligent, highly antagonistic man.

Settling in her new seat with a dish of tea she no longer wanted, Clio looked out the window and willed the train to depart. The sooner they left, the sooner they would arrive at Burnham station where she could escape Grey's watchful gaze. He had promised to uncover her secrets.

*Damn the bastard for trying to keep his promise. But he will fail. I will ensure it.*

* * *

The journey through some of England's most beautiful countryside was surprisingly unremarkable. Especially considering Grey was reasonably sure the train held a witch. Who was also a compelling individual with hidden depths he desperately wished to explore. It was a marvel to encounter a woman with no desire to be courted, no wish for a husband or family, but who was clearly attracted to him. Even if she hated him in equal measure.

Might that grant Thomas the freedom to pursue her without fear of making promises he could never keep? Was he living up to her bird's assessment?

*Am I becoming a bastard? Not if she wants what I have to offer. If I am clear about what I can and can't give and she makes her choice, I will respect whatever she decides.*

She might not want a future with him – indeed, it was better that she did not, as he had no future to offer – but she could not deny the desire simmering between them.

*Sparks fly when our hands brush. The curtain in my carriage was singed from our kisses. Even an argument between us creates enough heat to transform rain into steam. What might happen if more of our skin came into contact?*

It was a highly inappropriate and arousing thought. Followed quickly by...

*What might happen if she let go of her control?*

Thankfully, Clio had moved away from him. She refused to spare Thomas a single glance for the entire train ride, and he was glad of it. If she had, it would have been impossible to behave like his entire body wasn't attuned to her.

She plucked at the tightened strings around his chest, causing a residual vibration to thrum through his body. That alone seemed like witchcraft, without considering the literal sparks flying between them.

*But how does one prove a woman is magical? And what would such a discovery mean?*

He had no answers. She believed embracing the unknown brought greater understanding. Might it also bring a tortured soul some measure of peace? It wasn't fair to seek out her secrets without also revealing his own. Thomas was many terrible things, but he had always striven to be fair.

*If I uncover her truths and never reveal my own, then I am a bastard.*

The last thing he wished was for harm to befall Clio Blair. Perhaps she was right. Mayhap Thomas should accept the mystery of her without delving any deeper into her shadowy corners. But the question would not stop spinning in his mind like a mad whirling dervish. Was she truly a witch?

He certainly wasn't going to tie her up and throw her in a river to find out. Nor would he prick her skin to determine if she bled.

Those barbaric methods were nothing more than ways to torture women and call it a holy war. While he relished fighting with Clio, he had no wish to defeat her in that kind of battle.

But his suspicions had been aroused. His need to uncover Clio's secrets burned far more brightly than his desire to solve this case. Which was a problem. A man had been murdered. That should be his only focus. But he couldn't stop his thoughts from returning to the enigmatic woman carelessly sipping tea and chatting with his sister while her raven hopped around the carriage, no doubt muttering insults directed at Thomas.

More troubling than how to determine if she was a witch was what to do if his suspicions were true. He was a man of logic, but he had experienced things with Clio he could not explain. Perhaps that was the problem. She was right. Men feared what they did not understand. Was she right about everything else?

Thomas believed in justice. Protecting the innocent. Finding those who harmed others and stopping them. While Clio Blair might be many things, she was not corrupt. Nor did she threaten the innocent or harm others. Indeed. In every interaction he had with her, she sought truth. She was stubborn, quick to leap into danger for a just cause, and uncompromising in her beliefs. In a man, those were worthy traits. Why was it any different for a woman?

*Or a witch?*

If she truly was magical, maybe the way forward would be to accept her abilities instead of assuming her power might strip him of his own. But she would never trust him enough to let him try. The risk was too great.

A rogue thought took hold.

Instead of hunting down her secrets, maybe he could convince her to reveal herself. She showed her power every time he drew close to her. He could feel her heat, see sparks, watch whatever might burn around him flare in unison with her emotions. What if he found ways to touch more of her? To draw closer? To provoke those emotions when they were the only two people in a room? What might she reveal to him in the sanctity of those moments? Could he earn her trust? Was he worthy of it? It had been so long since he felt worthy of anything.

Courting Clio Blair was out of the question and something neither of them wanted. But seducing her, easing her out of the shadows and into the light... that might be a challenge worth facing.

Thomas spent the remainder of the journey creating a plan to woo a witch.

## 11

When the train steamed into the station and their small group departed, Lady Langley didn't just send a carriage for them; she met them at the station in all her glory. Her hair was piled in an extravagant arrangement, highlighting the pure white strands she was famous for popularising among her set. She wore dark shades of mourning, but it was impossible to miss the crimson underskirt peeking from layers of ebony silk and lace. The colour matched the rubies dripping from her wrists and ears. While the duchess was entering into her fifth decade, she still had a youthful figure with a waist cinched so tight, Grey cringed as Lady Langley swept across the platform towards them.

She pulled Cynthia into a tight hug, hardly decorous, but when one was as wealthy and well-titled as Lady Langley, one did as they wished. Her loud exclamations drew the eye of every traveller exiting the steaming train.

'Oh, my dearest Cynthia! Thank goodness you have finally arrived! You have no idea how trying this time has been for me!' Every word from her mouth was an exclamation, and Thomas noticed his shoulders tighten as she became more shrill. 'Arthur getting himself murdered with no consideration at all for my nerves. And poor Anna. The lost little lamb. She spends all day in the nursery in tears. The sound of crying is so distressing. I haven't been past the third floor since we arrived.'

Before Cynthia could offer any words of condolence, the duchess turned to Grey.

Her voice lowered into a throaty purr as the tears retreated and something far more predatory emerged. 'You grow more handsome by the day, Lieutenant General Grey. You'll have an old lady like me swooning before we even exit the station.' She tilted her head so the waning sunlight caught her in a yellow beam as she batted her charcoal-stained lashes coquettishly.

Alarm winged through him, and he took a half-step back. He had never considered himself prey; however, it was apparent who the apex predator was as Lady Langley swiftly moved him into her crosshairs. He needed an escape. 'You flatter me, Your Grace.'

The duchess's keen eyes flicked from Grey to land on Clio as she disembarked the train. An odd desire to step in front of Clio, shielding her from view, had him shifting to his left. Lady Langley misinterpreted his movement, winking before leaning to her right to squint at Clio.

'Is that a crow on the girl's shoulder?' The duchess's shrill voice had all heads swivelling to follow where she pointed her fan.

Clio must have felt the weight of such sudden regard. She lifted her gaze from where she had been watching a young girl and her mother exiting the train to confront the stares of more than a dozen remaining passengers milling on the platform. Instead of blushing or looking for somewhere to hide, she threw back her shoulders, taking time to look each passenger in the eye until, one at a time, they all turned away.

The last person she stared down was Thomas. He was at least a dozen yards away from her, yet he felt the same arc of electricity that buzzed through him every time she was near zing down his spine and tighten his bollocks. Unlike the other people on the platform, he didn't look away. He held her gaze.

'Miller, go and rescue that poor young thing before the wild crow claws out her eyes.'

Before the footman escorting Lady Langley could follow her orders, Grey grabbed his arm, halting him. 'I wouldn't.' He turned to the duchess. 'That isn't a crow, Your Grace. It is Sir Robin.'

'Stuff of nonsense! That thing is nothing like a robin.'

Thomas' lips twitched. 'Yes, of course, you are correct. It is a raven named Sir Robin.'

'That is the most ridiculous thing I've ever heard.'

Thomas had thought the same when he first met Clio, but he found a need to defend both the bird and the woman as Clio drew closer. 'He is our dear cousin's pet.' He delivered the last few words with a charming smile for Clio, whose eyes widened for a fraction before quickly narrowing in suspicion.

*Ah. You have no idea how charming I can be when motivated. But you are going to find out.*

'Bastard!'

The duchess turned her head sharply, looking for whoever had been so rude as to shout a profanity in public, but no one was near enough to be the culprit.

Clio stopped at the edge of their group and delivered a rather exemplary curtsey as Sir Robin fluffed his feathers.

Grey lifted a brow and didn't miss the scowl she directed at him before returning her focus to Lady Langley and tipping her lips in a demure smile.

*You aren't fooling me, Clio. There is nothing reserved about you.*

Cynthia put her hand on Clio's arm. Thomas didn't miss the squeeze of reassurance his sister gave. 'Allow me to introduce Lady Clio Blair of Stirling and her darling pet raven.'

Sir Robin Goodfellow clacked his beak and whistled. The glint in his black eye had Thomas wondering if he didn't dislike being referred to as a pet.

*Nonsense! He can't understand us, let alone have any opinions about what we are saying.*

Sir Robin tilted his head at Thomas. 'Blunder head!'

*Well, at least he didn't say, 'Bastard.' Surely I'm rising in his esteem.*

Or he was wise enough not to get caught swearing by the duchess.

Lady Langley burst into laughter. 'What a clever trick. Can he say anything else?'

Clio's smile was sharper than carved glass. Before she could answer, the raven turned and readjusted his perch on Clio's shoulder. 'Fancy girl,' he quipped.

Cynthia slapped her hand over her mouth at the euphemism, and Thomas clenched his jaw.

*Not so wise, after all.*

Lady Langley would hardly allow such a well-aimed insult at her fidelity. No one called a duchess a whore. Not even a raven. If Sir Robin wasn't careful, he would soon find himself baked into a pie.

Clio shook her head and laughed, and Thomas wondered if she might find herself in the same pie as her raven.

'Well, I never!' Lady Langley pressed a hand against her throat.

'He thinks you are rather beautiful, Lady Langley.'

The duchess's eyes widened as she froze mid-exclamation. 'Pardon?'

'My uncle taught him that word every time Aunt Rowan came

into the room to annoy her. My aunt is quite stunning. She is Sir Robin's favourite. He only uses that word to describe her. It is a real honour, Your Grace.'

'Stunning,' Sir Robin chirped. 'Fancy girl. Stunning.'

Lady Langley lifted her chin, looking from Clio to Sir Robin and back again. Her cheeks darkened to rose as her lips curled in a slow smile. 'Stunning, you say?'

Sir Robin clacked his beak.

The duchess turned to Cynthia. 'I must say, you have the most interesting relatives. We certainly shan't have a dull time while you're here.'

Both Thomas and Cynthia exhaled in tandem. Thomas shook out his hand, which had inadvertently tightened into a fist.

'Come along. Everyone's waiting at Blackthorn Manor. Cook has outdone himself, even if he is French.' Lady Langley said the last as if the word tasted of bitter hemlock. Looping her arm in Cynthia's on one side, and Clio's on the other, the duchess pulled them along with Thomas trailing behind.

Sir Robin turned his head, catching Thomas in his obsidian gaze. He could have sworn the bird winked. Which was impossible.

*Or magic.*

* * *

Clio's afternoon had been an endless lesson in opulence, starting with their arrival at Blackthorn Manor.

The gravelled drive they rolled over was lighted by gilded lamps set five feet apart, reminding Clio of enchanted fairy orbs leading her into another land. As they passed through a stone archway, the gate of black iron was pulled aside by two groomsmen whose only job seemed to be waiting for carriages to arrive and depart.

Lady Langley had an affinity for the French Renaissance

building style. Her palatial home sported spiked gables too numerous to count, rising into a sky painted red and purple by the setting sun. It was breathtaking, and Clio worked hard to school her expression into one of polite interest instead of absolute awe.

The manor sat in the centre of a velvet green lawn dotted by topiaries, statues, and expertly pruned gardens that would be an assault of colour and scent in the summer but were dormant so early in the year. A master sculptor created a fountain of satyrs in fearful pursuit of cavorting nymphs. It stood in front of a large lake with mute swans, as white as purity and as graceful as ballerinas, gliding in lovers' pairs.

On the other side of the lake, the drive led directly to the recessed entry of the house. It was framed by elaborately carved columns reaching four stories from the stone entry to a turreted roof. The entire staff, dressed in smart black and white uniforms, with green and gold livery for the footmen, lined either side of the entry.

Clio was no stranger to the finer things in life. While her youth had been spent in a modest cottage in the Scottish midlands, when Aunt Rowan brought them to London, wealth had found them quickly. It wasn't long before she forgot the exact smell of peat once permeating every dress she owned. Bathing in the brook near the village seemed like a story told by someone else as she soaked in her Parisian tub full of steaming, scented water. The gnawing ache of an empty belly or the numbing pain of frozen fingers and toes were mist and memory. But she never completely forgot the fear of it. She knew she was blessed, and she thanked the goddess for it each day.

But sitting in Lady Langley's carriage and viewing Blackthorn Manor in all its glory made it very clear, Clio might not have known absolute poverty, but neither had she ever experienced true luxury.

'Oh my,' she breathed.

Grey shifted closer to her. She glanced at him, hoping he hadn't noticed her awe. His green eyes glinted in the waning light, and heat crept up her neck to flood her cheeks.

*Of course he noticed. The man notices entirely too much.*

'It's quite spectacular. But don't forget, *dear cousin*, it's made of the same stones and wood as every other home, including yours. The grand and common are not so dissimilar at the core.' The small smile, curling higher on his left side than his right, only fanned the flames of her ire.

She tightened her spine. 'Are you calling me common, Grey?' She spoke in a whisper, but there was no mistaking the warning in her tone.

'Only a fool would believe there is anything common about you.' His gaze flicked to her lips, and Clio felt a corresponding tingle. Which was completely unacceptable. Something had changed over the duration of their train journey, and she didn't trust this new, charming version of Lieutenant General Grey any more than the brooding, taciturn Grey she knew in London. He was up to something, that was certain, but she would not be duped by him. She found *nothing* about Grey appealing in the least. In point of fact, every aspect of the man inspired disdain.

Sir Robin, who had dozed off during the ride with his sleek head tucked under his wing, was roused from his slumber, hopping from the seat to her lap. She absently ran her fingers over his smooth feathers, taking comfort from his weight.

'Only a fool would believe a line delivered with such obvious practice. Lady Langley seems to think you are no rogue, but I have my doubts. Whatever you are playing at, desist immediately.'

'You wound me, dear cousin.'

'Not yet, Grey.' Her words were harsh, but instead of pushing him away, he drew closer.

'How would you come for me? With daggers and guns, or some-thing else? Something far more devilish?'

'With flame and fury.' Her voice lowered into a husky rasp she barely recognised.

*Dear goddess. Are we fighting or lollygagging?*

If only Grey wasn't so damnably handsome with his black hair, hard jaw, full mouth, and brooding brows.

*Oh, for the goddess's sake. Brooding brows. Ridiculous. Scowling brows, perhaps. Ominous, most certainly. One might even say menacing. No need to wax poetical about the imbecile's eyebrows.*

It mattered little that it was Clio behaving like an imbecile, not Grey. She still needed to work with the smouldering man without letting him unsettle her. But whatever he was trying to achieve with this slightly more charming version of himself had thrown her off balance. She should be thanking the goddess for her change in fates. But she didn't trust him. That was the sticking point. Nor did she trust his new behaviour.

Maybe it was the way her belly flipped every time his name fell from her lips. Or perhaps it was that her magic became chaotic and unpredictable when they touched. Whatever the reason for her reaction to Grey, one thing was certain: her lack of control over the one thing she could *always* control boded ill.

*Pity I don't have a spell to banish unwanted lieutenant generals.*

'I suppose I shall have to be very careful with such a fearsome creature as you.' Grey raised a sardonic brow, his low voice barely discernible against the lively conversation between Cynthia and Lady Langley.

*First brooding, now sardonic.*

Before she could invent a witty rejoinder, gravel crunched as one of the six footmen who accompanied Lady Langley jumped from the carriage and swiftly set the step. The other five men rushed to their places, the most handsome of them standing by the door and holding out his hand to help the duchess manage the step with her voluminous skirts.

Cynthia followed Lady Langley. As Grey was closest to the door, he descended and then turned, blocking the footman and holding out his hand to assist her instead.

*He is trying to unnerve me.*

Much to Clio's disgust, it was working. Thankfully, her gloves were firmly in place, though she wished they were thicker. Even with the shield of her kid leather and his sturdier deerskin, there was no denying the thrill of power running through her fingers and into his, or perhaps it was the opposite. Maybe she was stealing his potent energy as it raced through her, leaving sparks in its wake from her fingertips to her toes. Her very hair felt charged.

His pupils blew wide, and she knew the same electric pulse raced through him.

Pulling her hand free, she looked to the darkening sky. 'A storm must be coming. You can feel it in the air.' If only she had Aunt Rowan's gift to harness the weather. But the goddess must owe her a favour because no sooner had she glanced upward than deafening thunder cracked through the sky.

'Hurry!' Cynthia called at the same time Lady Langley let out a shrill cry and nearly leapt into the handsome footman's startled arms.

'Carry me to safety, you fool!'

The wide-eyed young man stumbled forward. Thankfully, the entrance was only a few feet away. Servants covered their heads as the heavens opened and rain came in a sudden, drenching torrent.

Sir Robin, seeing no need to brave the weather, flew from Clio's shoulder and swept into the open door just as Grey grabbed her hand. His long strides ate up the ground, and she ran to keep apace as they caught up to Cynthia and Lady Langley at the entrance. The group tumbled through the door and onto the marble floor in a splatter of wet shoes, flapping feathers, and – on the part of the footman – gasping breaths.

She was ushered up the stairs and to her rather frilly guest room while Lady Langley took Cynthia for a private tête-à-tête in the greenhouse, and Grey reacquainted himself with the duke and several of his cronies smoking cigars and drinking port in the drawing room.

After her trunks were unpacked, a copper tub was brought up for her to wash off the dust from her travels. Clio sighed in relief as the hot water enveloped her body. She closed her eyes, leaning her head against a towel that had been folded and placed on the edge of the tub.

Without warning, she was swept once more into the past.

*Steam from a tub that wasn't Clio's clouded a tiled bathroom. Thomas' scent of soap and spice surrounded her. The moist air billowed in a draft and parted to reveal Thomas, naked and glorious, reclining in a tub much larger than the one Clio had been enjoying. His muscled arms spread wide on the edges of the bath. His legs were bent, the water doing little to hide his member, stiff and long and proud. Clio's cheeks heated. Her nipples grew tight and aching. She should look away. This was an intimate moment, not meant for her, but she couldn't. She watched in fascination as his erection, much larger than she would have imagined, pulsed and bobbed in the water. Her own channel clenched as a wave of need washed through her. She forced her gaze back to his face. Joy lit his green eyes. He smiled as a woman, the same from before, his wife, walked across the floor. She was just as nude as her husband, and Clio fought a wave of jealousy. The woman's breasts were high and pert, her legs long, her waist narrow. Golden hair fell down her shoulders in curling ropes, and a darker thatch glinted between her thighs. She reminded Clio of Botticelli's Venus. She felt Thomas' desire for his wife swell in his chest. But it was more than just lust. Love filled him, bursting out of his pores like sunlight.*

*'My darling wife. Have you come to wash me clean of all my sins?'*

*The woman's smile only increased her beauty. She was radiant.*
*'Hardly, Thomas. I've come to see how wicked we can be.'*

Clio was pulled back from the vision in a violent rush. Her breath came in ragged gasps. She curled her legs up and hugged them to her chest as arousal and an unaccountable anger warred within her. But once again, the nausea always accompanying her foresight was absent. What had happened to that young couple? How did her first vision of Thomas align with this picture of two people desperately in love? What changed to so completely alter them? None of it made sense.

Clio emerged from the water, now gone cold, shivering and numb. She waved a hand at the hearth in her room, the fire blazing to life.

A young maid came to help her change into her dinner dress – a forest-green gown with a daring outer corset in black leather. While the gauzy underlayer buttoned to her throat, the corset left no doubt about Clio's feminine curves, so different from the woman in her vision. Though not prone to insecurity, Clio wondered what Thomas would think of her much fuller breasts, wider hips, and rounder bottom. Would he look at her with the same desire he once felt for his wife, or would he turn away from her? Did pleasure change shape and form to fit the object of one's affection, or was it always the same sensation?

The clever maid piled Clio's shining black hair into an intricate arrangement held together by no less than three thousand pins. Sir Robin watched the entire affair with a certain amount of judgement. No doubt the bird thought all this fuss to be futile. He certainly felt no need to dress up his feathers.

Clio patted her shoulder for the raven and when he had settled, she descended the curving staircase to the second level, following a footman to the drawing room where at least twenty guests milled about in groups clustered around the fire, near the settee, at tables set up for whist, or in the centre of the room where they could garner the most attention. Lady Langley positioned herself there, with Cynthia at her side.

Clio didn't miss the wave of heat washing over her as Grey watched from across the room. She tried and failed to dismiss the image of him naked in a tub of steaming water. How fascinating to have glimpsed the hard and raw man hidden beneath a finely tailored suit and expertly tied cravat.

As soon as Cynthia saw Clio, she squeezed the duchess's hand and extricated herself from the group of fawning debutantes and rakes to join Clio near a beautiful portrait of a much younger Lady Langley and her brother. Clio squinted at the painting, trying to superimpose the ghostly Viscount Beachley with the boy in the picture. It was far more challenging than imagining Grey naked. A scandalous thought and one that brought colour to her cheeks.

'You look positively marvellous! What a daring dress.' Cynthia leaned closer. 'I'm so sorry I wasn't able to help you settle in. I know you are investigating a murder, but the only one at risk of an untimely death here is me. I forgot how singularly demanding Lady Langley can be. I do love her, but the woman can suck all the air out of a room.'

Before Clio could reply, a staid gentleman in black and white entered the parlour and announced dinner was ready.

Grey joined his sister and Clio with Lady Langley at his side.

'I hate that painting.' Lady Langley frowned at the portrait. 'Cynthia, darling, you simply must sit next to me at dinner.' The sly woman turned her eye to Grey. 'You can sit on my left, but mind your feet, sir. I won't have you trying to seduce me with your toe delving beneath my skirts.' She winked, leaving no one in doubt of exactly what she hoped he might manage. Thankfully, the duke was nowhere near the quartet. He looked deep in conversation with a portly gentleman on the opposite side of the crowded room, though Clio wondered if he would care about who hitched his wife's skirts as long as it was not him.

Grey's cheeks darkened, and he clenched his jaw before executing a perfect bow. 'I would never dare take such liberties, Your Grace.'

She pursed her lips and shrugged. 'More's the pity for me.' Sighing heavily, she took Cynthia's arm and led them into the opulent dining room.

'May I?' Grey moved closer to escort Clio to dinner. Not seeing any way to avoid the offer without being extremely rude, Clio nodded. But she refused to touch his bare skin. She ignored his expectant hand, instead claiming the crook of his arm. The brushed wool of his dinner jacket was rough and warm against her tingling fingers.

'You look rather well this evening.' His words were mild, but his growled tone made her toes curl in her heeled slippers. 'I never realised women could wear corsets quite like that. What a revelation.'

'Women can wear whatever they like, however they like it.' Clio kept her gaze forward.

'Lady Godiva would wholeheartedly agree.' Grey leaned closer, the heat of his body seeping through her gown.

Clio did turn then, because he so effortlessly stoked her fire. Of course, he would compare her to a blonde beauty who held no resemblance to Clio whatsoever. Not that it mattered. She didn't want Grey picturing her naked any more than she wanted to see him bare and glistening in firelight.

*Damnation!*

Her mind was relentlessly clever at remembering details. She'd never had cause to despise that gift until now.

'Lady Godiva was willing to set aside her own modesty to fight for her townspeople. If her husband hadn't been such a greedy tyrant, perhaps she would not have been forced to such drastic measures.'

'I wholeheartedly agree. Although her methods seem to reward rather than discourage such behaviour, wouldn't you say?'

'As the only tyrant I know, you would be a better judge of that than I.'

Grey paused next to her chair and pulled it out. 'First, your bird claims I'm a bastard, now you call me a tyrant? I won't challenge Sir Robin, but I will call you out, madame.' He whispered the threat into the shell of her ear.

Clio shivered. Not from fear. From anticipation. Which was far more unsettling.

'Name the time and place, sir. Pistols or swords?' They were back to flirting when she should have been fighting him. How did he so easily blur the lines between conflict and seduction?

She sat before he could answer. When he took his seat next to her, he dropped his napkin and used the excuse of retrieving it to lean closer.

'Tonight. The library. Once everyone is abed. Bring only your wits.'

Clio couldn't stop the rush of desire flooding through her veins, made all the more potent by her vision of him. The candles on the table flared in unison.

'There must be a draught,' Lady Langley declared before waving over a footman. 'Check all the windows, Geoffrey.' Her hand lingered on the servant's arm, his neck reddening as she whispered something. Straightening abruptly, the poor boy nodded quickly and made a show of checking all the windows. Not an easy feat in such a large room.

'I say, we weren't introduced.' The man who had been talking to the duke sat on Clio's right and winked at her. 'Viscount Beachley.

The new one, not the dead one.' He guffawed loudly. 'Poor Arthur. Always had the rottenest luck. In cards and in wives, it would seem.'

*Ah. The cousin set to inherit. What a delightful man.*

Clio glanced at Lady Langley to see how she would react to such an insult against her deceased brother. The duchess was too interested in pinching the bottom of yet another young footman as he served her the creamed onion soup.

'I am so sorry for your loss.'

Before Clio could say any more, the new viscount waved her words away with a soup-coated spoon and narrowly missed spraying the woman to his left with the first course.

'Bah. We were never close. Though I feel sorry for the poor little nipper he left behind. Her father dead. Her mother, God only knows where. Without Lady Langley, the urchin would be bound for the orphanage. Lucky little thing to have such well-appointed relatives.'

It seemed a waste of time to point out the glaring contradictions in his speech. Thankfully, the new Viscount Beachley was far more interested in hearing himself talk than listening to anything Clio might have to say. The only benefit to his incessant chatter was having an excuse to keep her back turned to Grey. While the topic of his many accomplishments spun out endlessly over the seven-course meal, Clio kept returning to Grey's proposition.

*Hardly! There was no offer. Only a demand.*

One she felt compelled to meet. What battle of wits might he devise? And what stakes would they be playing for? Her nipples tightened beneath her corset as her face grew warm.

'I see you are as passionate about swine as I am. It is so rare to find a female whose mind is capable of grasping such concepts.'

'Oh, I assure you, I am well acquainted with all manner of pigs, Viscount Beachley.'

'Fat, dirty pig!' Sir Robin, who had perched himself on the back of Clio's chair, fluffed his feathers. Viscount Beachley nearly choked on his dessert.

Grey coughed loudly beside Clio as Lady Langley looked up from her custard-covered plum pudding. 'Clever boy!' she called over the hum of conversation. 'Do you know who would love that bird? Anna. It would be just the thing to cheer the poor cherub up.'

Clio's heart raced. She schooled her expression to remain calm. This was the perfect opportunity to interview the girl. 'I would be more than happy to introduce Sir Robin to her if you think it might help. He's wonderful with children.'

'You can see her tomorrow. I'll inform her nurse to expect you. The girl wakes at ghastly hours. Far too early for me. But I'm sure you'll be fine.'

Clio had to bite her lip to stop the wide grin. The fates must have taken pity on her. With any luck, she'd have enough information to find the killer by noon on the morrow. She could leave this house party before teatime and never see Grey again. Which should have filled her with relief. Unaccountably, it did not.

'Don't be ridiculous, Lady Langley.' The new Viscount Beachley glared at Sir Robin, who merely clacked his beak. 'The girl's family is dead. A feathered rat isn't about to help her forget that.'

Before Sir Robin could retaliate against the insult, Clio twisted in her seat, reaching up to stroke his sleek feathers and willing him to remain calm. 'I must disagree. Sir Robin has been an endless comfort to me during difficult times.'

The viscount's pudgy cheeks reddened as his eyes narrowed. He did not react well to being contradicted by a woman. 'That only proves how feather-brained you are, silly girl.'

Sparks flared in her belly as her power spiked.

'Or perhaps she is highlighting your lack of education in animal therapy, Viscount Beachley. My cousin has spent several years studying with Florence Nightingale. Her opinions on the therapeutic benefits of animals are widely respected in the medical community. Are you suggesting Florence Nightingale is wrong?' Grey leaned over to better skewer Viscount Beachley with a stare rivalling the most terrifying devil. 'Or are you merely insulting my cousin's intelligence?'

The viscount's mouth dropped open as the table grew quiet.

'I-I merely suggested... that is... I would never think to—'

Grey cut in, his green eyes flashing dangerously. 'No. I should hope not. I would hate for your new title to pass on so quickly to the next in line.'

Silence descended in the dining room as tension pulled tight between Grey and the new Viscount Beachley, whose face had turned an unhealthy shade of crimson as he spluttered.

Cynthia burst into a gale of shrill laughter. 'Oh, brother. You do have such a funny sense of humour.'

Lady Langley looked from Grey to Viscount Beachley, her eyes gleaming with hunger for more drama.

Cynthia dropped her spoon with a clatter, reclaiming some attention from the rest of the table. 'I say, is it time for the men to smoke their smelly cigars? I, for one, am dying to play a game of whist. Lady Langley, I haven't forgotten what a card shark you are, but you won't beat me this time. I swear it.' She stood, forcing the men at the table to join her or risk their reputations as well-bred gentlemen.

Clio spared Grey a wide-eyed glance as he rose. Why on earth would he risk so much to come to her defence against a stupid comment by an even stupider man? If Viscount Beachley weren't such a blustering coward, Grey could have found himself in a real duel.

Lady Langley, seeming to think the fireworks were over for the present, stood as well. 'Of course! We'll leave the men to their whisky and whisperings while we ladies partake of far more civilised entertainment. Do mind you don't start any wars in my drawing room, Lieutenant General Grey. Save that for when you join us in the parlour.'

Tittering from the ladies and laughter from the men dissolved the simmering promise of violence as the guests began moving to their separate rooms. Clio waited until only she and Grey remained in the dining room. She stood and gripped Grey's wrist, ignoring the current passing between them as her bare fingers touched his pulse. 'Don't do anything rash. He's not worth the effort,' she murmured.

'You are worth the effort.' The words fairly singed her as he pressed his lips together, his eyes holding her captive for a breathless moment. She would bet her share in All Things Bright and Beautiful he hadn't meant to say that.

*I'm not. I can give you nothing. I want nothing from you.*

But it wasn't true. She wanted a great deal from Thomas Grey. More than she was willing to admit.

'I can take care of myself, Thomas.' His name came out unbidden.

Something hungry flashed in his eyes.

'I know.' He turned his hand to capture her fingers and brought them to his lips, pressing a kiss against her palm as sparks danced in the space between them. If any of the guests remained in the dining room, they would have wondered at the marvel. 'You are a clever witch, Clio.'

Sir Robin hopped from the chair to Clio's shoulder. 'Bastard!'

Clio blinked as the spell weaving around them shattered. Had he just called her a witch? She pulled her hand free and turned, pausing at the door. 'Don't be a fool, Grey. I told you not to trust me. I meant it.'

'And I told you I would uncover your secrets. Are you brave

enough to show me, Clio? Are you like Lady Godiva or will you slink into the shadows?'

She certainly wasn't going to strip bare and ride through the town naked. Although the idea of removing her shields and showing Thomas her true self was alarmingly tempting and terribly frightening. No. She didn't think she was courageous enough. Not by half. So, she turned and walked away.

## 12

Thomas had a new suspect to add to their list. The living Viscount Beachley. Lord Bartholomew Cuthbert. Berty to his friends, of which Thomas was very much not a member. The fat little toad of a man stood in a cloud of cigar smoke, the Duke of Devon on one side of him, and the Earl of Plinth on the other. While he was all bluster and no blast at the dinner table, once surrounded by his cronies, Berty found false bravado as he sent Thomas yet another blistering glare.

Thomas was alone by the hearth, watching the fire lick hungrily over a large piece of pine. The flames mesmerised him, but he still felt Berty's angry regard and heard the comments rising from the corner of the room. The pompous fool became bolder with each tumbler of whisky.

'You heard the rumours. The bounder couldn't even keep his marriage together. What kind of bastard deserts his wife? And he fucked his way through every whore house in London. No wonder the courts saw fit to grant the poor woman an escape.' Berty spoke loud enough for half the room to hear him. There was no question who he spoke about, even though he wasn't quite soused enough to name Thomas.

'Lower your voice, man. He nearly called you out before. You keep this up, and you'll be facing him at dawn with pistols. I, for one, will not be your second. It's bad enough my brother-in-law was murdered. I won't have any more scandalous deaths tied to my name.' The duke kept shooting worried looks at Thomas. But Thomas remained focused on the flames, pretending not to hear.

'There's another bastard for you.' Berty's guttural voice rose above the murmuring of gentlemen. The crack and pop of fire hitting sap nearly drowned out his next words. 'His death was the best thing to happen for all of us.'

The duke hissed something before calling over a footman. 'Kindly escort Lord Cuthbert to his rooms.'

'I'm not tired,' Berty slurred, nearly toppling over as the footman rushed to take his arm and support him. 'This is no way to treat a viscount!' He raised his fist, forgetting he still held a glass of whisky in his pudgy fingers. The amber liquid arced through the air, landing in a splatter on the rug.

'This way, my Lord.' The footman, apparently used to escorting inebriated guests, deftly steered the portly lord out of the door towards the stairs.

'Shall we join our fair companions in the drawing room?' Lord Langley exuded false cheer as he addressed the room at large. He walked over to Thomas and clapped him hard on the back. 'Don't mind Berty. He's never held his drink well.'

Thomas forced a smile. 'Oh, I don't mind the opinions of men like Berty.'

But the fool had opened up raw wounds. It was infuriating to be reminded of every way Thomas had failed his wife. Every way he would fail another woman if she were unlucky enough to find herself bound to him.

As he walked with the duke into the drawing room, Clio looked up from where she was playing whist with Lady Langley and his sister. A forbidden image of her as naked as the famed Godiva they discussed flashed in his mind, so vivid, he sucked in a harsh breath.

The duke followed his line of sight, seeing Lady Langley at the table. 'She's a wanton creature, my wife. She thinks I'm too addled to notice her liaisons, but I'm just too tired to care any more. A rake like you is exactly what she's looking for, Grey. Don't worry yourself on my account, but a word to the wise. Use a French letter with that one.' The duke had mistaken his reaction, thinking it was Lady Langley who had caught his eye. Before Thomas could correct the man's misunderstanding, the duke was pulled into a heated conversation by two gentlemen discussing a new proposal being brought to the House of Lords.

Lady Langley caught his eye and licked her bottom lip. Thomas' belly tightened, not in desire, but in preparation to flee. He turned and found a trio of gentlemen sipping port and discussing horse breeding. A far more enticing option than the lascivious lady of the house.

If he could not pursue the one woman claiming all of his attention, perhaps he could instead apply himself to the investigation and pursue the next suspect on his list: Lord Bartholomew Cuthbert.

Thomas joined the group of equine enthusiasts and deftly led the conversation in a different direction. After fifteen minutes, he knew Berty held a grudge against his deceased cousin for a land deal that had not ended in Berty's favour. A plot of lush farmland that, because of the former Viscount Beachley's death, now belonged to Berty. Interestingly, the Duke of Devon also seemed to hold no love for the unfortunate Arthur Beachley. Though nothing was said outright, it seemed the deceased viscount had few friends among his family. Considering his relations, Thomas was reasonably confident that was a mark in the dead man's favour.

The gentlemen changed topics once more and spent the remainder of the evening discussing their favourite bawdy houses in London. Thomas' reputation as an established rake had them looking to him for his expert opinion. An opinion he was disinclined to give.

He excused himself from the group and found his sister blessedly free from Lady Langley's company. The duchess was flirting outrageously with a young earl who looked a bit like a hare caught in a trap.

'What a ghastly group.' He inclined his head to his sister by way of greeting and turned so his back was nearest the fire behind him.

'I forgot how dreadful Lady Langley's set of friends are. In truth, I forgot how tedious she can be when she's on the hunt for a new paramour.' Cynthia spared her friend a withering glance before returning her focus to Thomas. 'You were certainly in fine form at dinner. Showing such filial loyalty to our dear cousin nearly brought a tear to my eye.' Her smile took some sting out of the sarcasm.

'The new Viscount Beachley tempts any man to shut him up. I was merely the closest to his vicinity at the time.'

Cynthia raised a knowing brow. 'Really? I can't recall you being so swift to defend the honour of a lady since... well, since I'm not sure when.'

'That hardly paints me in a flattering light, sweet sister.' Grey forced his tone to remain flippant.

'I just mean it's been an age since you've shown interest in anything, Thomas. But something has changed. It's like watching a flower come back to life after a long winter.'

'First I'm a cad who doesn't defend ladies, now I'm a wilted flower? You certainly know how to boost a man's confidence, Cynthia.'

She looked away from him to survey the crowd. 'Yes, well. Mayhap that is why my husband prefers it when I'm away.'

It was the perfect opening for Thomas to ask the question he had been too scared to broach. But before he could form the words, she turned back to him, her hazel eyes pinning him in place. 'Is it the investigation or Clio?'

His mouth went dry. 'P-pardon?'

'Which has brought you back to life? The case, or the woman? I rather think it's the woman.'

*Damn you for knowing me too well.*

And knowing if she did not change the subject, she might be forced to share details about her marriage she did not wish to divulge. Cynthia was always far cleverer than anyone gave her credit, including Thomas. He forgot how quickly she could pivot a conversation away from any topic she wished to avoid. 'You know I have nothing to give a woman, Cynthia. Certainly not a woman like Clio.'

'And what exactly is she like? Do tell.'

He clamped his jaw shut, and Cynthia's eyes lit with humour.

'I'll tell you what I think,' she continued.

'As if I could stop you,' Thomas muttered.

'I think Clio is an independent woman who isn't looking for marriage – which obviously terrifies you – and isn't hampered by the rules of decorum some of us must bend to no matter how we wish to break free. And you like her, Thomas. Don't try to deny it because you know I'm right. What danger is there in exploring your interest in Clio if she is willing?' Both of their gazes travelled together to the woman under discussion. She was standing on the edge of the drawing room, Sir Robin on her shoulder. As if she felt their twin regard, she lifted her chin and met Thomas' gaze. A spark of something incendiary flashed in her amber eyes.

'Everything about her is dangerous.' As he spoke, Clio drifted through the crowd like smoke over water towards them.

'You've never been frightened of danger. Quite the opposite. It seems to draw you into its flame.'

'What about her? I can't offer her any future.'

Cynthia shrugged. 'Perhaps she isn't looking to you for a future. I dare say she can find that on her own. And who can ever offer anything more than this moment? The future is as much a fantasy as the past is a prison. Don't stay trapped in either, brother. Life is here. Now. You might want to try living it.' Turning away from him, she extended her arms to Clio as she approached and drew her into a brief hug. 'How are you enjoying your first night?'

Clio rolled her eyes. 'Blue bloods leave much to be desired.'

Cynthia laughed. 'Well, hopefully not *all* of us.'

'Not you, at least.' Clio's smile was brief and brilliant, dying instantly as she turned towards him. 'I hope you've not issued any more threats, Grey. It's dashedly difficult to get information out of people when they're terrified.'

'I'd wager you terrify people on a daily basis with your fearsome feathered companion and wicked wit.'

She fluttered her lashes. 'Flattery will get you nowhere with me, sir.'

'Oh dear. Lady Langley has given up on the earl and is headed our way. You better dash before she sets her sights on you, Thomas. I shall head her off.' Cynthia waved gaily at the duchess who was making a determined beeline towards them. She was as good as her word, leaving Thomas with Clio to intercept Lady Langley before she reached them.

Thomas leaned closer to Clio, her scent wrapping around him like a forbidden embrace. 'The library. Later. Will you come?'

Sir Robin chirped, tilting his head, his gaze disconcertingly knowing. But damn Thomas if he would be intimidated by a bloody bird. No matter how sharp his beak looked in the wavering candlelight.

Clio bit her lip, and Thomas nearly groaned as his cock grew impossibly hard.

'Unless you are worried I might win our little battle of wits.' He couldn't help himself. He was a bastard for bullying her, but she was a fearsome warrior. He was confident she could handle whatever taunts he might throw.

'I'm worried I will leave a bloodied mess the maids will have to clean before morning.'

Thomas thrilled at her answer. 'Until later, then.' He nearly leaned closer. Nearly brushed his lips against her cheek just to see if her skin was as soft as it looked. Nearly let his heart crack. Just a little. Just enough to know he could still bleed. But Cynthia's efforts to distract Lady Langley had failed. He could see the duchess approaching with Cynthia in tow. If he wished to escape the drawing room, now was his only chance.

Stepping away from Clio, he nodded his head in an abbreviated bow, abandoning her to the company of the duchess as he swiftly found the nearest exit.

\* \* \*

*Of all the ridiculous, silly, ill-advised things I could be doing right now...*

Clio froze as a creaking board further down the hall had her heart leaping into her throat. Her magic could do many things, but it couldn't make her invisible. After a long stretch of silence where she determined the house was settling instead of a rogue footman wandering the halls at three in the morning, she continued her mad, sneaking journey to the library.

She should never have let Grey provoke her into meeting him. Alone. And like a fool, she hadn't even brought Sir Robin. The poor raven had found himself a comfortable perch on a sturdy lamp in the corner of her frilly guest room, head tucked under his wing. He showed no signs of waking when she slipped out of the door in her nightgown and thick, woollen shawl. She had debated keeping her dress on, but when the maid came to help her get ready for bed, Clio worried gossip might stir if she sent her away still fully dressed.

Pushing the door to the library open, Clio couldn't decide if she was disappointed or relieved that the room was dark and empty. Perhaps Thomas had already come and gone. Maybe he was snoring away in his room, oblivious to their missed meeting. Or he was toying with her. And like an untried fool, she had fallen for his ploy.

'Or I might be early.'

*Damn.*

That was troubling. What if he hadn't arrived yet and she left? She would be toying with him. The power would be realigned in Clio's favour, which should have filled her with satisfaction. But instead, she felt... deflated. Like a child who, on Christmas morning, finds nothing but coal in her stocking.

Something glimmered near the smouldering hearth deep in the recesses of the room. She was drawn to the flash of light as much as the lingering heat from the banked fire. The closer she drew, the clearer the image became.

The viscount solidified.

'Lord Beachley.' Clio tried to hide her surprise. She supposed it wasn't impossible for a ghost to travel so far. Spirits were insubstantial creatures after all, and the rules of physics wouldn't apply, but she had never worked with a phantasm who manifested in such diverse locations. 'Have you come to see your daughter? Or perhaps to haunt your sister... She seems to hold little love for you.'

'Anna.' The echoing timbre of his voice whispered over her nerves as gooseflesh broke out over her neck and arms.

It was the first time he spoke to her, and a huge step forward in her investigation. She wished Uncle Lachlan were here so she could share the triumph with him.

Nerves spiked. If she pushed the ghost too hard, he could disappear. But she might not get another chance to communicate with him. She couldn't let this opportunity pass. 'Who took you away from Anna, Lord Beachley? Who did this to you?'

Pewter eyes, which once held colour but were now opaque orbs in an ashen face, filled with silver tears. 'I lost everything. Everything!'

'I'm going to help you. I promise.' Her heart ached for the man. To be taken away from his daughter, his life, it seemed immensely cruel.

He drifted closer to Clio, and something shifted. The lines of his face hardened in a rictus of rage. He wasn't looking at her, but rather through her. He wrapped bony fingers around her neck before she could react. 'Murderer!' The silent scream echoed in her head. Spots flashed in her vision as Viscount Beachley squeezed. His face transformed from fearsome rage to heartbreaking grief. Tears once more filled his pewter eyes but his fingers only tightened.

She struggled against him, power pooling in her belly as panic fought with logic.

*I must stop him. He does not mean to hurt me.*

But he was choking the breath from her. Magic built, rising within her like lava. 'I am not your enemy, Lord Beachley. I'm here to help,' she rasped the words as he increased pressure on her throat. A silver tear tracked down his face. Soon, she wouldn't be able to breathe.

Heat from her witchflame pulsed out of her like a wave,

escaping from every pore in a white flash of concentrated power. Viscount Beachley flew back, swirling and spinning like a dust mote until he disappeared completely.

Clio's breath came in rasping gasps as she touched her bruised neck. Nausea swept through her on an oily wave.

'What the fucking hell was that?' A dark growl dispelled her queasiness and filled her with something far worse: fear.

She turned to the open door. Light from the hall silhouetted a powerful form.

*Grey.*

He promised to uncover her secrets. And the damnable man was true to his word.

She had been discovered.

## 13

Reason fled. There was no logical explanation for what Thomas saw. Clio was being strangled by some invisible force. Fear hit him, visceral and raw. He crossed the threshold of the library, determined to save her, but before he went more than three steps, she became a human flame. The white glow started in her sternum, bleeding through her nightgown and robe, lighting her like a bloody lantern. It spread over her entire torso, down her arms and legs, until in a sudden and brilliant flash of light and heat, the power pulsed from her in a wave, knocking him several paces back. If he ever questioned whether she was a witch, that query was answered the moment she ignited.

But it wasn't fear that filled him. It was awe. She was magnificent. The most incredible force he'd ever witnessed.

In the afterglow of her supernova, he saw the faint glimmer of a form spinning backwards and dissolving like ash in the wind.

'What the fucking hell was that?'

Clio had her hand over her throat, but fear only came when she turned and saw him. Even in his shock, it cracked something inside his chest. Fury washed through him. That some unknown enemy would attack Clio, and instead of looking to him for support, she saw him as another threat.

'What did you see?' She closed her eyes and scrunched her face, shaking her head back and forth like a child refusing to take medicine. 'It doesn't matter.' She opened her eyes and pointed her finger at him. 'Whatever you think you saw, you are wrong. It was nothing.'

If she were trying to cast a spell to repel him, she was failing miserably. Because he was only drawn inextricably closer.

His feet followed his heart as he crossed the space between them and gripped her arms, tilting his head to better see her neck.

'Are you well?' It was all that mattered. Once he knew she was safe, he could kill her for lying to him.

Amber eyes widened as fear softened into confusion. She blinked, pulling her shields up and gathering her formidable wits.

*Dear God, she is a wonder.*

'I am hale and hearty, Grey. I certainly don't need you fussing over me.'

His hand skated up to her neck, but he didn't touch her, worried he might further damage her bruising skin. Instead, his fingers tangled in her silky hair, no longer bound by the loose braid. He pulled the midnight strands away from her injury. 'You're hurt. And I am not fussing.'

She stepped back, and he reluctantly let her go. 'Yes, you are. It's only bruising.'

'Who bruised you, Clio? What happened?' He couldn't exhale. If he let the air out of his lungs, he would lose the tenuous control he had on his temper. He needed to punish whoever had hurt her.

The image of her neck, tight as a bow string, held by an invisible hand, played through his mind. To watch her fight a foe he couldn't even see was a poignant reminder of his uselessness. Even in this.

Thomas was a warrior. He might lack in certain areas, but he had always been able to fight. If the enemy was stronger, he was smarter. If they were faster, he was more determined. But with Clio, even that skill was stripped from him. How could he fight an invisible foe?

'No one bruised me. Nothing happened.'

Her blatant lies fuelled his anger.

'No one did this?' He did touch her then, his rough fingers brushing softly over her delicate throat as sparks cascaded. 'And what of these?' He let his hand trail down her neck, staring intently at the sparkling embers that followed his fingers to the hollow of her throat. While they should have burned his flesh, he only felt the thrilling tingle of awareness. The banked fire behind her roared to life. 'Is this also nothing?' He spoke through clenched teeth, willing himself to remain calm.

Clio's lip trembled, but she nodded. 'Exactly. Nothing.'

Three things were instantly clear. One: 'nothing' translated into 'a mammoth pile of something'. Two: his suspicions about Clio were correct. Three: she wasn't going to admit to any of it. Because she didn't trust him.

Incredibly inconvenient, because he was quickly discovering a fourth revelation: he very much wanted Clio to trust him.

Which was a terrible idea. Trusting led to wanting. Wanting easily became needing. And he had already made that mistake with Lissa. It nearly destroyed them both.

Unfortunately, he'd never been good at learning lessons.

'I saw you, Clio. You turned into a human pyre. Don't tell me that was nothing.'

She changed tacks, narrowing her gaze, readying to attack. 'What exactly are you implying, Grey?'

'I'm not implying anything. I'm asking. What the bloody hell is going on?'

'Whatever you suspect, no one will believe you. Your reputation is already ruined. Every member of beau monde thinks you are a rakehell who abandoned his wife. If you start spouting off about some girl being a witch, they'll know you're a lunatic as well as a bounder.'

She was lashing out, attempting to divert his attention. Damn her for being so effective. She swiped at his vulnerable underbelly, and he retaliated. Just as she wanted. 'Maybe I am a rakehell, but I'm no liar.' Thomas leaned closer. 'And I never called you a witch.'

She took a ragged breath. He had her.

'Those were your words. And that is exactly what you are. Try to deny it. It will do no good.' He should have stopped there, but her accusations poured acid into old wounds already broken open by Berty and his drunken insults. 'You are a witch. And I am nothing but a feckless rake. Isn't that what you think?'

She pulled her shoulders back. In her struggle with the invisible bastard who hurt her, the thick woollen wrapper she wore had fallen open. The firelight illuminated her thin cotton nightgown. Arousal hit him harder than a punch. He had no right to feel such a potent need and yet he did. His helpless desire only fed his rage.

'I don't know what I think.'

Laughter tore at his throat like claws. 'When have you ever not known your own mind, Clio Blair? I've called you a witch; now it's your turn. Call me a blackguard.'

He knew he'd stoked her anger when her eyes glowed like golden lanterns. 'Pay attention, Grey. I don't make assumptions without evidence. And the evidence about you puzzles me exceedingly. Your actions do not match your reputation. A selfish lord who abandons his wife but dotes on his sister. A renowned rake who is rumoured to have endless paramours, but damns himself for stealing kisses from a common girl? The pieces don't add up. Who is the real Thomas Grey?' She had masterfully twisted the conversation from focusing on her being a witch to him being a libertine. Not that it mattered, as both were true.

His mind snagged on the way she described herself. A 'common girl'. Nothing about her was common. She was the most extraordinary woman he'd ever known. And he wanted to prove he was worthy of her. Worse, she was giving him a chance to do just that. Which meant she might see something of worth within him.

*But that is a lie. Which is why I can't do this. She needs to leave.*

Pushing her away was the last thing he wanted. And the one thing he needed to do.

She wanted to make a logical decision based on reason and fact. Thomas could give her reasons and facts that would prove he was the last man she should be meeting in libraries at three in the morning. What had he been thinking? He allowed himself to be swept away, but no more. Providing Clio the evidence she demanded was the fastest way to ensure she walked away from him. And the fastest way to remind himself he deserved to be alone.

'Perhaps I can shed some light on the matter. Provide you with enough facts to reach a decisive conclusion.' He leaned closer. Drawn to her even as he knew she would consume him. 'I fucked any willing woman.'

He threw the words like daggers. But she didn't pull away. She wasn't disgusted. Quite the opposite, in fact. His coarse language caused an entirely different reaction. A million gossamer threads of energy connecting them suddenly tightened.

Clio's chest rose and fell in shallow inhalations as rosemary and bergamot infiltrated his senses. Dark nipples peaked against her thin cotton nightgown. She wasn't afraid. She was aroused.

*Not the reaction I needed. Let me try again.*

Thomas went further. Testing her. Testing himself. He backed her against the wall, placing his hand over her shoulder and leaning down to whisper in her ear, his voice a rough rasp in the dark room where only the crack and pop of the now-blazing fire punctuated his words.

'I spread a widow's thighs in the middle of a masked ball.'

She hissed air between her teeth.

'A celebrated soprano begged me to turn her bottom red with my bare hand.'

A barely audible moan.

'The bordello beauties took turns letting me tie them up until their needs twisted into my own.' Her hair tickled the tip of his nose as he inhaled her like opium. 'Bored wives. Sophisticated debutantes. Talented actresses. If they wanted me, they could have me.'

Her body tensed. Not in fear, not in preparation for escape. But in anticipation.

'There is your evidence. I am the worst of men.' Sparks sizzled along her exposed skin, washing up her throat like a blush, hot sparkles kissing his jaw and lips.

Whatever incendiary magic smouldered between them wasn't his imagination. She was the cause. Her mysteries intoxicated him.

'Do I not disgust you, Clio?'

She swallowed and slowly shook her head.

Fine. He would try a different approach. 'Did you choose to be a witch?'

A wrinkle formed between her brow at the abrupt change in topic. She shook her head. 'Of course not. It's not something one chooses.'

He couldn't stop the small smile. 'Ah.'

Fury flared in her golden gaze. He'd tricked her into admitting her secret. Which she hated. Which was the point.

Instead of backpedalling, she jutted her chin out, defiance in her eyes. 'Fine. I'm a witch.'

'I know.'

Pressing a hand against his chest, he thought she would shove him away, but she kept it there, splayed over his heart. He could feel each finger like an individual brand, burning into him, leaving an indelible mark. 'What will you do with my secret, Grey?'

'Protect it. Protect you.' He gave the answer before he considered what it meant. Before he could think of a response. Because it was the only answer to give. Ensuring her safety was the only thing that mattered. Even if he must protect her from himself.

She shook her head, not ready to believe him. Grand. Her mistrust would help his cause and keep her at arm's length. Because if he pulled her closer, he would not be able to let go. And that was a fate no woman deserved. Certainly not one as important as Clio.

'Men say all manner of things. But they don't mean them.'

'I mean this: you are a miracle, not a monster. You did not choose to be a witch, but I chose to be a faithless bastard. Of the two, I am far more evil than you, Clio. I am everything you've heard and worse. I will burn in the fires of hell for my sins.'

'What if I want to burn with you?' Her words were air on coals, breathing heat into his already blazing arousal and destroying his reason. No matter what his goal, she seemed determined to work against him. Only in this, a hopelessly optimistic part of himself was thrilled.

*Because what if. What if we burned together?*

The idea was impossible to dismiss even when he knew one taste of Clio would never be enough. She was innocent and inexperienced, but she also knew what she wanted and wasn't shy about voicing those desires. Lissa hid her hatred of Thomas for so long, when he finally realised she despised him, he couldn't argue. He hated himself just as vehemently. But Clio wore her feelings for Thomas on her leather sleeve. Her disdain and desire were as bright and contradictory as her colourful dresses. It was refreshing. He knew exactly where he stood with her. And he wanted her. More desperately than any other woman.

*She doesn't really want me. Only the fire between us. Which means I can't hurt her by having nothing more to give than this.*

He was playing a dangerous game. Justifying what he wanted against what he knew he should do. An honourable man would walk away. But Sir Robin was right; he was a bastard. If he was destined to spend eternity in hell, he might as well enjoy the heat.

'Be careful what you ask for. Some deals, once struck, can't be taken back. Are you sure you want to take this path?'

*Do you want me? Even if it is only for this moment?*

She bit her lip, and his already swollen cock turned granite. 'Yes. I mean, perhaps. It depends.'

For a woman who fearlessly leapt when others might flee, he found her hesitation desperately sweet. 'On what?'

'What do you expect?'

*To walk away from this irrevocably altered. To fall deeper than I want and not nearly far enough. To become bewitched by a sorceress and hope the spell is never broken.*

'Just this. Here. Now. You control where we go. When it's over, it's over.' *I don't think this will ever be over for me.* But he told her what she wanted to hear, because he couldn't tell her the truth.

Clio swallowed. Her bruised throat contracted, reminding Thomas of all she had faced this evening. All he still did not know. But he would find out. Whoever had attacked his wicked witch would pay. He was going to hunt down the enigma and wreak holy hell. Later. First, he was going to seduce Clio.

'What if I don't want to control where we go? What if I'm tired of always being in control?' She looked away from him, her gaze drawn to the windows at his back where the reflection of the flames danced in the glass. 'What if I want someone else to lead?'

It was a staggering admission. For her to admit such a shocking desire. And it cost her. He knew by the way her body trembled.

*She is bewitching me. Each word from her mouth a spell binding me to her. And I am longing to be entranced. She is far more dangerous than I ever guessed. And me, the fool who always loved a bit of danger.*

*Damnation.*

\* \* \*

*Dear goddess. What have I done?*

It must have been the interaction with Viscount Beachley. Clio was still shaken. Perhaps the spectre had stolen her wits entirely.

She didn't think the ghost wanted to hurt her. Indeed, she wasn't even sure he saw Clio when he wrapped his hand around her throat. He had been attacking his murderer. But it didn't stop the violence from shaking her to the core. Whatever Viscount Beachley faced in his final moments, Clio did not envy him. And she was more determined than ever to help him. The whole encounter had been disastrous. Then the worst had happened. Grey saw her.

He knew the truth.

But instead of reacting the way she expected, hurling accusations, condemning her, holding her to the flame, he'd stepped into the blaze himself and admitted his own damning secrets. It was unaccountable.

*'You are a miracle, not a monster.'*

Words Clio never expected to hear, and certainly not from Lieutenant General Grey.

The rest of what he shared, the things he had done with other women, was as illuminating as it was incendiary. She wanted to understand the why. But the what had stolen her reason. The images he conjured! She nearly swooned. And Clio never swooned.

In any of the silly discussions she had with Ellie and Helena about potential romantic entailments, Ellie spoke of everlasting love. Helena wanted anonymous, passionate liaisons. And Clio

imagined a simple man she could instruct based on her own explorations and then discard with little fuss.

But there was nothing simple about Grey. She couldn't possibly
instruct him. The man was a bloody expert in an area she had
almost no knowledge. And she certainly couldn't discard him
without a great deal of fuss. Not after the things he'd seen. And the
things he'd said.

*Sweet goddess!*

It awakened a need in her. To let go of everything. To let
someone else – Grey – take responsibility for something she had
given far too little time to in her life: pleasure. What a wondrous
and terrifying thought.

While her magic was empowering, it also isolated her from
anyone outside her family. Taking on the investigation was fascinating, but she bore the duty of helping poor Viscount Beachley
find peace. Every person, living and dead, who needed something
from her was a precious burden, and the weight sometimes over-
whelmed. The constant pressure to keep her most authentic self
hidden. Always wielding her shield against anyone who dared
come close. It was exhausting. She wanted to burn everything
away until nothing remained. Except sensation. Simple, hot, clean
need that she didn't have to think about or control. Only
experience.

But to admit such dark desires to Grey – a man who could so
easily overpower her if she gave him an opportunity – was madness.

*A madness I wish to welcome. Just for one night.*

And why not? She did not risk her heart with him. She would
not lose any part of herself if she indulged in one night of lust.

*But what if my fire burns him? I lose all control when he touches me.
He might not harm me, but what if I hurt him?*

Sparks had covered them both, but he hadn't experienced any
burns. It was unaccountable, but somehow he was as immune to

her witchfire as she was herself. Something she would have to ponder. Later.

She held no allusions as to his desires. He wanted her physically, but he would never ask more than that. And if he did, she would refuse.

*Liar.*

The sharp whisper almost convinced her to step back. Step away. Escape to the safety and solitude of her room. Almost.

But she didn't want to be alone. And if she did not indulge in this hunger now, then when? This man had seen her wielding her craft, and he hadn't run. He hadn't shouted accusations or threats. He had offered instead a piece of his own darkness. And for the first time in her twenty-five years, she wanted someone. She wanted Thomas Grey.

She gathered her courage and forced herself to look at him. His brooding beauty nearly levelled her. But she was made of sterner stuff. Aunt Rowan didn't teach her the skills of sorcery and witchcraft, passed on by generations of women, to have Clio tremble in the face of a green-eyed devil.

He watched her carefully. 'I won't claim to know you well, but I do know you are loath to surrender your power in any situation.'

That was true. But what might happen if she did? The thought was equal parts tantalising and terrifying.

'I'm loath to suffer fools, and in my experience, most men fall into that category. But you are a most unusual man.' That was putting things mildly. No other man haunted her visions. At least, no living man. And he was certainly the only person to inspire such an acute ache within her. 'Could you handle the flame of my desire, Grey? If I gave you temporary control of what happens tonight, and only tonight?' It was a dangerous proposition, but Clio suspected he was the one man who could stand in her fire and not turn to ash.

He lifted his large hand and traced a rough finger from the

middle of her forehead, along her hairline, following the edge of her jaw until he held her chin, tipping her head up, making it impossible to look away. 'What exactly do you wish to happen tonight?'

A blush washed over her, painting her skin a deep rose. Because something he confessed had sparked an image in her mind. A desire she'd never imagined until he gave it life. But how to tell him? She shrugged.

Thomas tsked, shaking his head. 'That won't do. For a woman who doesn't like people to assume, if you want me to form an accurate conclusion, you must explain the facts to me, Clio. Details are so important, didn't you say?'

He was provoking her on purpose. The anger helped, damn him. 'You are capable of listening? Astonishing.'

'You'll find I'm capable of a great many things.'

She narrowed her gaze. 'Actions speak louder than words, Grey.'

'And what actions would you like me to take, Clio?'

She swallowed, suddenly nervous. She had never let fear stop her in the past. She wasn't about to start now. 'You spoke of tying women.' As soon as she said the words, embarrassment threatened to eclipse her burgeoning desire. But then his eyes flared, and every line of his body somehow hardened.

He put his other hand on the wall, caging her body.

'Dear God, you will be the death of me. Yes. I tied women.' His voice lowered to a rumble. 'Would you like me to tie you? Do you wish to be bound and helpless?'

'I am never helpless.' She thrust out her chin, daring him to contradict her.

'Not even to your desires?' He tilted his head, his eyes dipping to the swell of her breasts. She felt his gaze like a brand.

'You are not a nice man, Thomas Grey.'

'You don't want a nice man, Clio Blair. But tell me what you do want. To submit to the pleasure I bring you? Because I *will* bring you pleasure. I swear it.'

And he kept his promises.

All of the air was sucked from the room. She felt hot in the oddest places. The back of her neck. The crease of her thigh. The base of her spine.

'Yes,' she managed.

## 14

He leaned closer and nipped her earlobe. The sharp bite resonated in her nipples, tightening her belly, creating a divine spark in her clitoris.

'Then there must be ground rules. I will not risk going further than you want.' His voice vibrated along the tiny hairs in her ear canal.

*Oh my. Since when did rules become an aphrodisiac?*

She inhaled through her nose, buying time. But it backfired. Her lungs were full of soap and spice, and her thoughts scattered. She pulled them back into order with extreme effort. Because he was right; rules were necessary to ensure she didn't lose her head. Or her heart. And she would never risk that.

'Rules. Yes. Good. Three, I think.'

He raised his brow. 'Three? All right. The first?'

'No penetration.' She might be innocent, but she wasn't an ignorant fool. She had no interest in one night of exploration ending in a lifetime of responsibility. Certain herbs could be brewed in such a way to discourage a man's seed from taking root, but there was no method to completely guarantee a woman would not conceive. She didn't have access to her herbs and potions, but even if she had, she wouldn't risk falling pregnant. A moment of madness was allowed, but not if it altered her life's trajectory.

He gave a silent nod of acknowledgement. 'The second?'

She hadn't thought that far. He ran his nose up her neck to her temple, burying it in her hair.

His lips tickled her ear. 'Think, little witch. What is the second rule?'

*Not helping!*

'I... um... h-honesty.'

He pulled back, quirking his head. 'What do you mean?'

This was more embarrassing than the first time she practised spells with Aunt Rowan and accidentally caught the kitchen curtains on fire. 'If I do something wrong, you'll tell me.' She hated the idea of failing at this. She didn't know what she was doing, so missteps were inevitable. But she would be damned if she didn't learn. And get better.

Something melted in his eyes. 'Impossible. Nothing you do between us could ever be wrong.'

She narrowed her gaze. 'What if I singed your bollocks? Or accidentally incinerated your willy? Would that be wrong?'

He swallowed. 'Point taken.'

'Brilliant. I won't have you pretending something is good if it isn't. You'll tell me if I do anything you don't like.'

'And you will tell me the same. Before you resort to blasting me with hellfire.'

'Witchfire.'

His brows drew down in a question.

She couldn't hold his gaze. 'That is my gift. Witchfire.'

'Ah. You truly are a wonder.' He grazed his thumb over her lip, and she had an impulse to bite him. Taste the salt of his skin. 'All right. Honesty. And what is the third rule?' His voice was burning brimstone.

'If I tell you to stop...'

'I will stop.'

She knew beyond a question he would hold true to his word. Which gave her enough courage to step into the unknown. 'Then we have an accord. Tonight, I give you the reins, Grey.'

'Thomas.'

*No.*

Names held power. If she used his name, he would cease to be her enemy. He would become more. Far too much more. She pulled free of his grip on her chin, shaking her head. 'I think not.'

He opened his mouth to dissent, but she pushed up on her toes and closed the space between them, claiming his lips and stealing his argument. He tasted of whisky and pepper and smoke in the forest.

He froze for a moment and then came alive. Taking over the kiss, he licked her mouth, his teeth scraping over her lips, his hard hands insistent as they ran down the length of her arms, encircling her wrists, lifting them above her head so her breasts thrust against his hard chest. She only wore a thin cotton nightgown, but he was still dressed in his dinner jacket, vest, shirt, and cravat.

He pulled away, holding her wrists tight in one hand as he untied his cravat.

'You gave me the reins tonight, Clio. And I want you to call me Thomas.'

She lost all logical thought as he jerked his cravat free in tight movements, whipping the white silk away from his neck and snapping it. He looked above her head, searching for something. When his lips curled into a wicked smile, anticipation warred with apprehension. What had she gotten herself into?

*I can ask him to stop. He will honour my command.*

She knew this was true.

*And if he does not, I will simply incinerate him.*

Also true.

The fire cracked, sparks flying out of the hearth. He glanced over his shoulder as the embers flared from red to black before landing in sooty specks on the wood floor. He turned back to her, his black brow raised in censure. 'Is this going to be a problem?'

She didn't know. Her powers had never been so unpredictable. 'No?'

'If you burn down Blackthorn Manor with your witchfire before Lady Langley can seduce her footman, she will be most displeased.'

A giggle burst free before she could stop it. This man was a wonder. He could infuriate her, arouse her, terrify her, and amuse her all in the course of one evening.

'Heaven forbid.' She pressed her lips together to keep the laughter within.

'Heaven has nothing to do with this.' Grey let her wrist go and captured one hand, tugging her several paces to her right before positioning her once more against the wall.

'What are you doing?' Her unexpected burst of joy spun into something headier.

'Do you trust me?' He held the cravat up, then looked at her wrists.

'In this?'

'Just this.'

She nodded.

'Then give me your hand.'

She hesitated. Could she do this? Give him her hand? Let him tie her? She had asked for this. Did she actually want it?

*Yes.*

When she held her hand out, something dark and hungry flashed in his eyes. Slowly, carefully, as though her wrists were made of glass and not flesh and blood, he wrapped first one, then the other. It was obvious he knew what he was about, and that caused a rogue wave of hot, wet need to wash through her.

His knots were loose enough they wouldn't constrict her blood flow, but as he lifted her bound hands over her head, she realised what had caused his smile and why he shifted her to the left. An iron wall sconce with an empty candelabra wasn't lighting the room, but Grey had found a better use for it. The decorative swirls were perfect for hooking his cravat, and it was high enough to force Clio onto her toes.

'These older homes are so sturdy.' Grey pulled experimentally on the sconce before securing her arms over her head and stepping back. Clio felt like a painting on the wall as Grey's emerald gaze lit small fires wherever it touched her. Throat, breasts, belly, legs, and the shadowy patch between her thighs. 'I should strip you naked.' His tongue made a lazy swipe over his top lip as he assessed her. 'Would you like that? To be on display for my eyes alone?'

An errant thought of Lissa flashed through her mind. Would he compare her with his wife? But as soon as it came, she pushed it back into the depths. Tonight was about Clio and Grey. No one else. She nodded her head in jerky movements. The heat building in her sternum licked over her skin. She knew she would be glowing in the dark room, but she couldn't stop the power washing over her, reaching out in swirling reds and blues.

Grey's eyes widened, but he didn't step back. 'Call me Thomas.'

She bit her lip and shook her head.

'Do you know what happens when you refuse to follow my lead?'

'Generally, things work out in a much more satisfactory fashion.'

Humour glimmered before he shut it down. He pressed his lips together in a firm line. 'Outside of this night, perhaps. But tonight, when you refuse to follow my commands, you must suffer the consequences, Clio.'

She had never been good at following orders. But never before had the repercussions seemed quite so enticing.

'And what are my consequences, *Grey*?' She couldn't stop her rebellious smile.

His jaw muscles jumped as he stepped closer. The heat of his hand seeped through her thin cotton shift as it hovered just over her left breast. Her nipple hardened painfully, and she inhaled, waiting for the inevitable pressure of his palm. The sharp sweetness of his fingers. The pain that spun into pleasure.

'Do you want me to touch you, Clio?'

Of course he would make her say it. But she was too lost in desire to deny him. 'Yes.'

'Then tell me, what is my name?'

Realisation dawned. This was what he meant by consequences.

'Bastard,' she hissed.

He lifted his hand to the lace edge just above her collarbone. His finger slid over her skin in a silken glide, tracing the scooped neck. But it wasn't what she needed. It wasn't even close. And he knew it.

'No. That isn't it, although Sir Robin thinks otherwise.' He leaned closer, his hard chest almost pressing against her aching breasts. His lips hovered near her ear. 'Say my name, Clio. Say my name and I'll rip this nightgown off you and suck those sweet nipples until you scream.'

*Sweet goddess!*

Flames wrapped around them both, holding them in the moment.

She turned her head, trying to catch his mouth, bite his lip, force him to bend to her will, but he was too quick, leaning away from her. She narrowed her gaze. 'Sir Robin is a very intelligent bird. If he calls you a bastard, it's probably because that is exactly what you are.' Her breath was coming hard and fast. The shift of cotton against the sensitive buds of her breasts only made her need worse.

Grey's eyes glittered as he smiled. 'Balancing on the precipice of pleasure can bring with it a unique pain. Only a true bastard would do that to someone.' He let his hand slip lower, circling her right nipple with his thumb over the thin cotton until it peaked against the material, but he never touched the tip. It hardened so tight, her skin tingled. A corresponding spike of sensation exploded in the cluster of nerves hidden in her sex. 'Mayhap Sir Robin is right.'

Without warning, he gripped the neckline of her gown in both hands and in one violent jerk, ripped the cotton down the centre.

*Yes. Please.*

She wanted him to strip her bare. To do all the things he spoke about. A small burst of pleasure fired low in her belly. But he didn't pull aside the material. Disappointment flared. She wanted him to see her. Naked. Real. Raw. Instead, he trailed a finger from her throat, between her breasts, grown heavy and aching with need, over her sternum to her belly. Her muscles clenched as he tickled her navel.

'Women, in my experience, are amazingly soft, and deceptively strong.' His insidious finger dipped lower, tangling in her maiden-hair before he softly brushed where no hands other than her own had ever ventured. Every nerve in her body fired at once. But when she would have burned the earth to cinders for friction, he brought his finger back up, dipping beneath the cotton to trail along the underside of her right breast.

'Damnation! Grey. Touch me, please.' She pulled against the cravat to lean closer to him, but he only stepped back, capturing her gaze.

'What is my name, Clio?'

'Lieutenant General.' She wouldn't give in. Not yet.

Bending his head, he brought his mouth to her left breast, so close she could feel the heat of his breath. But he didn't draw the puckered tip into his mouth and suck as she so desperately wanted. Instead, he blew a stream of air over her sensitised flesh, his finger resuming its devastating circles around her right nipple. His other hand trekked lower again, palming her pussy, pressing his hard palm over her slick flesh, but pulling back before she could grind her hips against him.

'You intoxicate me, Clio. Say my name.'

'You infuriate me... Thomas.' The word escaped, and she couldn't regret her choice.

'Thank God!' He gripped both of her legs, wrapping them around his hips. She could feel the hard ridge of his erection through his breeches. The rough cotton created delicious friction as he rubbed his length against her.

He palmed her breast, but this time, strong fingers pinched and plucked. Ducking his head, he licked her nipple before nipping and sucking.

She wanted to wrap her arms around him, strip him bare, feel the glory of his naked skin against her own. But she could only absorb the sensations as his hand returned to her core, fingers sliding through her wet folds until he found the tight bundle hidden there. As his tongue swirled around her nipple, his finger circled her nub. Soft. Hard. Fast. Slow. Flames of pure pleasure burned through her systems. When he bit the tip of her breast, Clio's world was consumed in fire as an orgasm ripped through her.

She cried out his name, his finger never stopping. Heat coalesced in her palms. The cravat smoked, smouldered, then incinerated, raining ash around them. Her hands fell from the sconce, and she landed heavily on the floor, nearly losing her balance. Thomas gripped her around her waist, steadying her.

For a moment, they stood that way. Both breathing as though they'd run, far and fast. Almost embracing. But not quite.

'That was...' There were no words. She had experienced a climax before. Many times, from her own efforts. But it had never been like this.

'Are you well?' The concern in his voice shifted something in her chest. It was the second time he'd asked her that question this evening. This time, her answer was honest.

'I'm marvellous.'

He raised his dark brows, mischief dancing in his emerald eyes. 'I suppose cravats are no match for witchy magic.' Did her powers unsettle him? Because his powers certainly unsettled Clio. He stepped back but kept his hand on her hips.

'I suppose we'll have to use stronger binding next time.' She tried to keep her voice light and steady.

Grey's hands fell from her waist. He smiled with all the smug confidence of a cat who caught the canary. 'I thought you said this was just for tonight.'

*Blast!*

She had said this deal between them was only for one night. But now she knew a little of what magic they could make together, and she didn't want to stop. Not yet. She wanted more. Far too much more for a woman determined to maintain her independence. Even affairs – hot, passionate, complicated things – could trap a woman into commitments she neither wanted nor could sustain.

'I just meant, if there was a next time.'

'Will there be one?' It was impossible to ignore the hope in his voice. In the end, that's what won her over. Fragile faith from a man who seemed to have lost it somewhere along the way.

She wrapped the woollen robe over her ruined nightgown. 'That depends. Did you bring anything sturdier than silk cravats?'

He shook his head. 'You are trouble.'

'Double, double toil and trouble.' She walked to the library door and turned. 'Fire burn and cauldron bubble.' With a flick of her gaze, the fire flared, then burned down to nothing but coals.

'Something wicked this way comes, Clio.'

'Yes. And his name is Thomas Grey.' She turned and walked down the hall to her room as his dark laughter echoed in the shadows.

## 15

Thomas woke early after a night of tossing and turning as fantasies spun out in his dreams. He never should have done those things to Clio. She was innocent.

*At least, inexperienced.*

Because no one was truly innocent. His actions should have scandalised her. She should have told him to stop. And he would have done it. But she had loved it. More than he expected. He half-hoped his sexual inclinations would have frightened her off. Then he wouldn't be rolling around on damp sheets wishing for something that could never come to fruition. Not just one more night with Clio, but every night with her.

When he had first expressed to Lissa his desires for darker play, they had been married for over six months, and she was already looking for something more. With so much out of his control, he wanted to claim power over something. Anything. He knew he wasn't satisfying Lissa and hoped his desire for more daring bed sport might meet both their needs. For a time, it had. A very short time. Because it didn't change what he could not give her.

When it became obvious how broken their marriage had

become, and Lissa was demanding they both seek satisfaction outside of their vows to each other, the women he pursued were all experienced with dominance and submission in different measures. It was something Thomas knew excited them, and he sought those women out, avoiding any lady who might find his needs depraved. That Clio, such an independent and powerful woman, was so interested in submission, surprised Grey exceedingly. Although perhaps it also made some kind of sense. He felt out of control in his daily life, therefore craved that power in the bedroom. She was always in control, always driving decisions in her daily life, so desired a moment of reprieve where she didn't need to make any choices. They were perfectly matched.

*What a goddamned lie! I could never be her perfect match. Certainly not in anything outside of the deal we made last night.*

A deal that had at least brought Clio pleasure. And hopefully a brief escape from the burdens she carried so effortlessly. The power she wielded was difficult for Thomas to comprehend, but he imagined, as with all power, it required an immense measure of responsibility.

And wasn't that a wonder? Witches were meant to be evil mistresses of the Devil, but nothing about Clio was evil. Of the two, he was far more devilish than she could ever be. In truth, her magic wasn't nearly as concerning to him as her stubborn independence. The woman would throw herself into danger without a second thought. Because she was far more capable of protecting herself than Thomas ever could. Which jabbed in vulnerable places.

The one thing outside of pleasure he might have to offer a woman was protection. Clio could manage that quite well on her own.

*If I can't offer her safety, and I can't provide a future, then all I can give is desire. So that is what I shall do.*

He rolled out of bed and padded over to the wall where a

bellpull hung. Yanking on the decorative rope to summon a valet, he moved to the small basin and water jug sitting on a beautifully carved desk. The valet entered as Thomas towelled soapy water from his face.

Best prepare for the day ahead. If his suspicions were correct, Clio might already be making her way to the nursery to interview Miss Anna, and he wasn't about to miss their conversation. The investigation still needed to take priority, although any excuse to be in Clio's presence would also work towards his more insistent goal: to show her a different kind of magic. A powerful fire they could conjure together.

The valet was excellent at his job. Thomas was shaved, combed, and neatly attired in less time than it would have taken him to find his smalls. He thanked the man and enquired as to where the nursery was located. The servant furrowed his brow in confusion but gave Thomas clear directions regarding a set of side stairs at the end of the northern wing that would take him to the third floor. From there, he could traverse the entire length of the upper level to the southern side, where the nursery was located. There was no central staircase from the third floor to the rest of the house. It could only be accessed from stairs on the northern guest and southern family wings, which allowed the children to be more easily kept separate from the public parts of the house. A safety measure, and also practical for a duchess who seemingly had no interest in regular contact with any children, even her orphaned niece.

He dismissed the young man, gave himself a final glance in the mirror, then opened his door, intent on hunting down Clio.

The fates were smiling on Thomas, because as he stepped out of his own room, the unmistakable click of another latch sounded across the hall. Awareness, hot and spiky, had his hair raising and his gut clenching. He knew it was Clio seconds before she opened the door.

Her gaze found his immediately, and she froze. Sir Robin, perched resolutely on her shoulder, cocked his head and blinked an obsidian eye at Thomas. 'Bastard!'

'And a lovely morning to you, Sir Robin.'

The bird ruffled his feathers, and if a raven could have harrumphed, Thomas suspected that is what Sir Robin did.

He shifted his focus to Clio. Her morning dress was a graphic affair of crimson with large black silhouetted flowers splashed over it. The colour enhanced her cherry lips and the slight flush painting her high cheeks. The bodice was cut with clean lines, lacking any frills. The simplicity drew attention to her luscious figure. A flash of her the night before, hands tied over her head, hair tumbling down in a cascade of midnight silk, breasts thrust forward, shielded only by the thin gauze of her cotton gown, had his cock hardening and his mouth watering for a single taste of her.

*One taste will never be enough.*

Fear flared. Is this what it felt like to fall under a witch's spell? Because this was nothing like falling in love with Lissa. Even in the height of their happiness, he never craved her the way he did Clio. But Lissa had never been completely honest with him. Not from the beginning. It was something Thomas was only starting to realise. She told Thomas what he wanted to hear, not what she truly felt.

Clio couldn't be more opposite. She was happy to explain exactly what she wanted from Thomas, and it wasn't forever. It was now. And only now.

A part of him found the entire thing ironically amusing. He was seducing the perfect woman. Someone who had no interest in anything lasting. Which meant Thomas couldn't hurt her when their liaison came to an end. And if he found himself more attached than he wanted, it would be his pain to bear when they broke ties with one another. He could live with that.

'Grey.' Her terse morning greeting belied the spark and sizzle of heat between them. 'I wasn't aware Lady Langley had placed us in such close proximity.' Clio shut the door behind her with a definitive click. She looked down the hall. 'Is your sister on this wing as well?'

Thomas raised an eyebrow. 'I've no idea. I would guess not. Lady Langley likes to keep her friends close and her potential paramours at a distance. I suppose she wouldn't want me seeing who was coming in and out of her bedroom for fear it might deter my interest.' He couldn't stop the wicked smile.

Clio raised a brow. 'Are you?'

'Interested in Lady Langley?' He let the silence tighten between them before slowly shaking his head. 'I thought I made my intentions clear last night.'

Shrugging, Clio turned to walk towards the centre staircase. 'I only meant, we didn't discuss the particulars of our agreement.'

Thomas lengthened his step to catch her, deftly placing his hand around her waist to settle on her opposite hip. He applied pressure, guiding her in a tight pivot.

Sir Robin fluttered his wings to keep his perch and cawed his objection to such an abrupt change in direction.

'What are you doing?' Clio turned to face him. If she were taller, her mouth would have been close enough to claim as he kept her at his side. He nearly bent down but held himself in check.

'You are going the wrong way. And I recall us talking specifically of rules. No penetration, honesty, and I stop when you ask.' He ticked them off his fingers, then stopped them both. 'In the spirit of honesty, I must say I'm relieved your neck has healed so well.'

She reached up to cover her throat. No doubt her magic potions had been employed the night before. He was glad of it. But she clearly didn't think he would notice, or perhaps she assumed he would reject such a display of her powers. Defying her expectations was becoming one of his new favourite things.

'You are a remarkably beautiful woman, Clio Blair.'

Before she could respond to that particular piece of honesty, he turned and continued down the corridor. He had her off balance as they walked deeper into the shadows.

With no windows in the hall and the candles extinguished from the night before, the morning light couldn't pierce the gloom as they came closer to the northern stairs.

'Would you like to add another rule to our list?' He asked the question lightly, but his heart pounded.

'What do you suggest?' Her voice held a breathless quality that tightened his belly.

'We do not dally with others during our time together.'

Clio stopped walking. 'Where are you taking me?' She was avoiding his question.

'To the nursery. Of course. Did you wish to go elsewhere?'

Anger brightened her amber eyes. 'How do you know this leads us to the nursery?'

She didn't like being in the dark. A creature of fire and light never would. Pity for her, the dark was Thomas' favourite place.

'Because I asked. Just as I am asking you now, would you like to amend our rules?'

'It was only meant to be one night.' Clio raised an eyebrow. She was baiting him, the tricksy woman.

'It can only be one night, if that is your wish. We never need talk of this again.' He shrugged as if her answer couldn't so easily shatter something inside him. If she didn't want more, he wasn't sure he could stay across the hall from her. He would need to abandon the investigation. Escape to London. Avoid Lachlan and anything else that reminded him of Clio. Parks would be out of the question. Too many crows that looked like ravens. But he would do it. He would walk away if she did not want him.

She pulled free but continued down the hall. 'We shall amend the rules. But when this investigation ends, so does our arrangement.' Looking over her shoulder, her amber eyes glowed in the gloom. 'Agreed?'

*Absolutely not. Unless you break this spell you have over me.*

'Of course.' Thomas schooled his features into stern lines to hide his lie.

'And I shall take the lead when we interview Anna.' It wasn't a question, but he responded regardless.

'I expected nothing less.'

'Exactly.' She paused at the stairs leading up. The dim light faded into total blackness. Holding her hand in front of her, a single flame, tall and unwavering, glowed to life in the centre of her palm. She looked at him, golden flickers spilling over her features. There was a challenge in her eyes. And pride. And a glimmer of fear. She could have been a fairy. Or a goddess. Or a witch. His witch. 'Are you with me?'

She wasn't asking about the stairs. He felt the weight of her question, but it didn't crush him. It grounded him.

*Always.*

'Lead on, my lady.'

'I'm not your lady,' she muttered before turning and stalking up the steps, her bottom swaying enticingly.

*But what magic that would be. To claim a woman like Clio Blair as my own. To have her claim me as hers. Such sweet sorcery.*

Because how could any man not lose himself in such a woman? Certainly not Thomas.

\* \* \*

She was showing off. With her magic. In front of someone outside her coven and kin. It was unaccountable. But also a strange miracle. To be able to reveal such a visceral and sacred part of herself to someone, and instead of experiencing fear or rejection, he looked at her like she was something immeasurably valuable. A woman could become addicted to that kind of regard. Which was a rather large problem.

When Clio reached the top of the stairs, she clasped her hand in a fist, extinguishing the witchfire. She needed to focus less on impressing Thomas and more on solving this investigation. So that it would end. And she could leave. Because that is what she wanted. To return to her home and her life before Lieutenant General Thomas Grey came into her world and turned everything upside down.

Topsy-turvy moments were exciting, and new, and all good and well, but they couldn't last forever. Nor did she want that. Because it would mean sacrificing an integral piece of herself. At least, she always thought so. But with Thomas, new questions formed. Was it possible to find a partner who accepted every piece of her and didn't ask her to change? What an astounding thought. One she would need to ponder. Later.

'Where do we go from here?' It irritated her that she had to ask him. Based on his smug little smile, he was very aware of her frustration. And why did that cause a clenching awareness low in her belly? Since when did his arrogance inspire her arousal?

'On the southern side. Over the family wing.'

Clio nodded as Sir Robin's claws dug into her shoulder. He clacked his beak before rubbing his head against her cheek. 'It's all right, Sir Robin.'

But something felt very wrong. She hastened her steps along the corridor, passing too many closed doors to count. Grey's quiet footfalls behind her assured Clio he was staying close. A girl's voice echoed in the stillness. A corresponding murmur from the nanny sounded before a door opened, light spilling far down the hall as a woman exited the nursery.

Clio froze. What would they do if she turned towards them? How would they explain their presence? Lady Langley had given permission the night before, but Clio doubted the woman had time to explain the plan to the nanny. She was far too busy chasing footmen. And Grey. And any other man on the short side of forty. The very idea of Grey doing any of the things he described to her the night before with Lady Langley inspired a sharp, unfamiliar emotion in her chest.

Jealousy.

She did not like it. Jealousy indicated some kind of proprietorship between herself and Grey. While they may have amended their agreement to include fidelity within the bounds of their fortnight together, it hardly signified any lasting commitment. Nor did she wish for that. She could not keep Grey. He might seem to accept her powers, but this was only a dalliance for him. A man as dominant as Grey would never accept such an affront to his authority in a marriage. That which he found exciting and unusual about Clio would quickly become threatening when facing a lifetime together. It was the same for her mother. And when her lover demanded she abandon her powers, she did so without hesitation. Such was the curse of love. A curse Clio would never cast upon herself.

Her mother gave up more than just her witchcraft. She gave up her daughters. Their futures. Everything that should matter most. And when her husband caught the fever, she had no power to save him. He died, and Aspen welcomed the illness when it came to her as a way to reunite with him. Aunt Rowan tried to help her. She went to their dirty little cottage, stinking of decay and despair, but Aspen would not let Rowan past the entrance. She had become so twisted by the views of her husband, she believed her magic was the

Devil's work. A sin from which her husband saved her. Aspen accused her own sister of being Lucifer's handmaiden, trying to seduce her back into the darkness. Her own daughters, flesh of her flesh and blood of her blood, were spawns of men unworthy of God's love, or Aspen's. She would rather die than welcome evil back into her heart. And so, she did.

Clio would never give a man such control of her thoughts. Her powers. Her very self. Not even a man like Grey. The risk was too great.

His fingers wrapped around her arm and squeezed gently, bringing her back to the present. 'It is all right. She has taken the far stairs to the family wing. Come, we should hurry. There is no telling when she might return.'

He misunderstood her hesitation. Which was best. As he was also correct. They needed to move swiftly.

Gliding on silent feet, she paused at the door to listen. No sound emerged, so Clio held her breath and twisted the handle, hoping Anna wasn't prone to screams.

The nursery was exactly what one might expect. It was painted in soft pinks and dewy greens. Large windows let in the wintry morning light. A fire crackled in a hearth on the far side of the large open space, and lamps had been lit to bring false cheer to the room. Lemon oil and fresh linen lent the air a comforting cleanliness.

Clio's eyes stalled on a young girl sitting in a bay window, a book on her lap and a doll leaning drunkenly against the girl's side. She was dressed in a beautiful white lace affair that heightened the sense of fragile innocence surrounding her. She looked very much like the half-finished painting Clio had found in Lord Beachley's home. Her dark-blonde hair lay around her shoulders in perfect ringlets. Huge, brown eyes only grew larger in a face that was porcelain-doll pale. Anna's pink lips opened in a silent, 'Oh.'

Before she could make a sound, Clio moved swiftly to where

Anna sat and crouched so she was at the same level as the girl. She smiled kindly, and Sir Robin cooed a gentle, melodic whistle.

Anna's gaze moved from Clio to the bird and back again. 'W-who are you?'

'Hullo, Anna. I'm Clio. A friend of your aunt's.' She turned to look over her shoulder at Thomas. 'And this is Lieutenant General Grey.'

*Goddess, he is handsome. And looks as sinister as the Devil on Samhain. The poor girl will be terrified.*

She turned back to gauge the child's reaction. Instead of screaming or jumping from her seat and attempting escape, Anna turned to Sir Robin. 'Is that a raven?' She pointed her finger at the bird.

Sir Robin fluffed his feathers, clearly pleased the clever girl had correctly identified him. He stretched his neck forward, and the young girl bravely extended her hand, running chubby fingers over his sleek head.

'Yes. Your aunt thought you might like to meet him.'

'He is very beautiful.' Anna's gaze remained locked onto Sir Robin.

'Beautiful!' Sir Robin chirped. Anna's face broke into a delighted grin, the book falling from her lap as she clapped her hands and giggled.

'He talks! A bird who really talks!'

Clio couldn't stop her own smile. The girl's joy was infectious. While she knew Anna had been very sick, she seemed to be moving towards recovery. Her cheeks held the faint blush of health, her eyes were bright and flashed with intelligence, and there was a glow about her that defied any lingering illness.

'Sometimes, he talks entirely too much.' Grey's rough voice stroked over Clio's senses, but she refused to be distracted.

'Mother told me not to speak to strangers. She said I must

always be very careful. Even now. But a bird can't possibly be a stranger.' The girl's brows drew down in confusion as she looked from Clio to Thomas. 'But you are strangers. Mother wouldn't want you here. Are you going to take me to my father?'

Clio's heart stalled.

Dear goddess. Did the girl not realise her mother was missing, and her father was dead? Had grief pulled her into madness?

'He said a woman would come with black hair and a bird. But Mother told me to stay away from him.' Tears filled Anna's eyes, and Clio tried to follow her skipping logic. Who told her they would be coming?

Sir Robin hopped onto the girl's lap, tucking his head under her chin and leaning his body against her narrow chest, chirping in his version of a soothing murmur.

Anna's eyes flew wide for a moment before she lifted her hand and stroked his wing. 'You're such a lovely raven. I don't think Mother would tell me to stay away from you, Sir Robin.'

A cold ball of dread formed in Clio's belly.

'How did you know his name?' She asked the question in tandem with Thomas, but fear eclipsed any annoyance she might feel at Thomas for stepping into her investigation.

Anna blinked owlish eyes at Clio, then over her shoulder at Thomas. Shrugging, she resumed stroking Sir Robin's midnight feathers. 'Father told me, silly. When he said you would come to visit.'

## 16

Clio looked back at Thomas, her mouth going dry as her thoughts raced. His worried gaze communicated everything she felt. Carefully relaxing her features to be neutral, she turned back to the child.

'Anna, when did your father tell you that?'

'A few days ago. Mother told me not to listen. She said Father is full of lies, but he said a girl would come with a raven, and look. Here you are.'

*Damnation. Can she see the dead?*

Witches weren't the only ones who had strange powers. Clio had heard of others, mages and mediums who could commune with the dead, but she'd never met one who wasn't a cheap charlatan.

Perhaps it was because Anna was so young. Children lived closer to the veil separating life from death. If her father had reached across the void, maybe his connection to Anna, their shared love, created some kind of temporary avenue of communication. Whatever the reason, she needed to know.

'Anna, your father is dead, dear.'

She quirked her brow at Clio as if she were the stupidest creature in the world. 'Of course he is. I was there when it happened. Although Mother made me promise I wouldn't leave my room. I usually didn't feel well enough, but I was having a good day. Mother promised I would start feeling better and better, but I had to stay in my room. She was having a very important discussion with Father and they couldn't be interrupted. Only I did sneak down to the kitchens. Cook makes the yummiest treacle cookies. Do you like treacle cookies?' Her stream of thought was too difficult to process so quickly.

'Y-yes, of course,' Clio answered, still scrambling to understand.

'So do I. But I hadn't wanted one in ages. I was always so sick. But that day, I wanted one for the first time in forever and the nurse wasn't in my room, so I thought I would just sneak down to the kitchen and see if Cook had any in the white jar on the little shelf by her office. That's where she always kept them. But on my way, I bumped into Uncle Berty. Only I didn't know he had come to visit. No one tells me anything. Mother knows I hate him, so maybe that's why. He was so angry when I saw him in the kitchen talking to our housekeeper.' She clapped her hand over her mouth. Speaking through her fingers, her words were slightly garbled. 'But I wasn't supposed to say. He made me promise. They both did.'

*Blundering Beelzebub.*

Clio's head was spinning. How much of what Anna said was true, and how much was this the fancy of a young, traumatised child?

Thomas shifted next to Clio, kneeling to be closer to Anna's height. 'What happened after that, Anna?'

'He told me I had to go to bed and stay there. That I must promise not to come down again, or he would thrash me.' Her eyes filled with tears again. 'Mrs Coggins told me if I said anything to Mother or Father, she would make sure I stayed in my room forever.

I ran upstairs and hid in my bed. I don't remember anything else until Nanny Francine came and told me something terrible had happened.' A single tear tracked down her cheek. 'They said I would never see Father again. That I might not see Mother either. Aunt Diana sent a carriage for me... but they were wrong. All of them.'

'Why were they wrong, Anna?' Clio wasn't sure she wanted to hear the answer.

'I see them all the time.' The girl continued to pet Sir Robin's head.

The nursery door opened with a loud creak. A maid stood in the archway, her eyes widening to round saucers as she looked at Thomas, then Clio, then Sir Robin sitting on Anna's lap. Anna might not have screamed when she first saw Clio and Thomas, but the maid certainly did. Long and loud and frantic.

* * *

It had taken the better part of an hour to explain what Clio and Thomas had been doing in the nursery with Anna. The nurse had run pell-mell down the stairs, found a burly footman exiting Lady Langley's room, his uniform dishevelled and his hair a mess, and dragged him to the nursery where fisticuffs almost ensued between Thomas and the servant.

Lady Langley, hearing the commotion outside of her room, had raced upstairs in her satin negligee, not bothering with a robe, only to loudly forbid the men from fighting over her while her eyes sparkled with undisguised glee that they might do exactly that.

Cynthia, who had indeed been placed in a room adjoining Lady Langley, followed the sounds of commotion instead of going to breakfast as she had originally planned. When her gaze fell upon Thomas, it was clear she had questions. Many questions.

Clio, with quick thinking and admirable calm, was able to explain that they were only in the nursery to introduce Anna to Sir Robin based on Lady Langley's invitation the day before.

Anna was immeasurably helpful as she stated the raven was her favourite pet in the whole wide world.

Sir Robin, confirming Thomas' suspicion that he did not appreciate being called 'pet', hopped from Anna's lap to Clio's shoulder, much to the girl's tearful disappointment.

Her emotional reaction prompted Lady Langley to usher the entire group downstairs for breakfast.

'We'll let the poor little lamb rest. Her nanny is ill today, but I'll send Mary up to sit with her.'

This only resulted in louder cries from Anna, who claimed she wanted Nanny Francine.

'We'll come back with Sir Robin soon, Anna. I promise.' Clio spoke over her shoulder as Lady Langley rushed them out of the door, claiming that Anna's cries were bringing on a megrim and they must all leave immediately.

The remainder of the day was spent in a host of organised activities precluding any privacy for Clio and Thomas to discuss the information Anna had presented. It wasn't until they were given time to dress for dinner that Thomas saw his opportunity. He dismissed the valet, and walked across the hall to Clio's room, knocking loudly on the door.

The maid assigned to Clio opened the door, whereupon he demanded to see his cousin on a matter of grave importance.

Clio emerged from behind the maid in another shocking gown, this one with a bodice comprised entirely of black leather. The royal-blue skirt beneath was a waterfall of silk. Clio's hair still hung loose in midnight waves around her shoulders. Thomas suddenly forgot how to breathe.

'I haven't dressed her ladyship's hair yet.' The maid looked worriedly from Clio to Thomas.

Clio waved the girl's concerns away. 'You've done a wonderful job helping me with this gown. I can manage my hair tonight. Thank you, Sarah.'

With no other choice, the maid bobbed a curtsy and left the room.

Sir Robin, who perched on the headboard, cawed loudly, but at least he refrained from calling Thomas a bastard. That felt like progress.

'You are lucky we are family, or this little tête-à-tête would prove quite scandalous.' Clio's censure lacked heat. She was no doubt just as anxious to discuss their interview with Anna as Thomas. 'Come, sit while I finish getting ready.'

Lady Langley spared no expense in the fittings of her guest rooms. Clio had a small sitting area complete with a couch, two wingback chairs, and a low table in front of a hearth glowing with a crackling fire. To the left was a vanity with an oval mirror and a beautifully upholstered chair upon which a lady could sit and ready herself. A scattering of bottles, pots, powders, and varying brushes, powder puffs, combs, and hairpins littered the tabletop. She took a seat in front of the vanity and gestured for Thomas to shift a footstool closer.

'Anna certainly had much to say.' Thomas settled himself and watched with growing interest as Clio began twisting and clipping her hair into an intricate coiffure he couldn't begin to recreate.

Clio had a hairpin clamped between her teeth. She spoke around it, drawing Thomas' attention to her lips. 'What is unclear is whether she reported fact or the fancy of a troubled child.'

'How could any of it be true? She said she speaks to her parents. Her father is dead, and her mother is missing. How could Anna be talking to either of them?'

Clio set a rather winsome curl next to her crown and secured it in place with the clip from her mouth. She paused in her activity to catch Thomas' gaze in the mirror. The air grew heavy as the fire popped and flared behind Thomas, warming his back. She was considering something in that clever mind of hers. Determining whether she would trust Thomas. He held his breath, willing her to take the step and knowing anything he said could shatter the fragile spell weaving between them.

'I can speak to the dead.' Clio's amber eyes glowed, and her lips trembled.

Thomas knew his response would either open a new door of connection between them or destroy every chance of knowing Clio better.

He refused to look away even as nerves thrummed through him. He believed Clio. And that was the trouble. Speaking to the dead was akin to the Devil's work. And yet, he didn't know why that would be true. Only that it was told to him since he was a child by his elders, his spiritual leaders, the lawmakers. But if he reacted in fear, he would never understand. And he desperately wanted to understand.

'Is that part of your...'

'Craft. Yes. My power is tied to fire, as all witches are connected to one of the earth's elements, but it is also tied to the past. I can see memories and speak to those no longer here. If they wish it.'

Thomas furrowed his brow. 'You can see memories of dead people?'

Clio pressed her lips together and nodded.

'What about other people?'

She blinked and looked away. 'My powers are centred on those who have already passed.'

She was avoiding a direct answer. Which was interesting. And something he would investigate more thoroughly later.

'Have you spoken with Viscount Beachley?'

Clio returned her focus to dressing her hair, coiling a long strand and twisting it in an intricate swirl. How did women learn to do such creative things? Men spent most of their time shooting guns, riding horses, and hitting each other with padded fists. Women's endeavours were far more imaginative and resulted in beautiful creations rather than bloody destruction.

'I have seen the viscount. And some of his memories. He hasn't spoken with me yet. Well, not really. But ghosts usually won't unless they trust me first.'

That explained what she had been doing when he found her in Beachley's house after their interviews with the staff. She must have been poking into the viscount's past.

'You've seen his memories? Can you not just look at the night he was murdered? See what happened?' The case could be solved in mere moments. And then his time with Clio would be at an end. He almost bit his tongue for suggesting such a simple and expedient solution.

Clio raised a censorious brow as she secured the last strand of hair into place. 'Oh, yes. I could have done that ages ago. I just thought it would be so much fun to drag out the investigation.'

*Right. Of course. If she could have seen the memory of Viscount Beachley's death, she would have done so. Imbecile.*

'I can only see the memories shown to me by the departed. I don't get to choose. I'm not sure they even have a choice. At any rate, Anna claiming to have spoken to her father isn't necessarily a lie. Aunt Rowan has spoken of other witches through the ages who could speak to the departed.'

'Do you think she's a witch?' How did one know they were a witch? There was so much about Clio that remained a mystery. It could take Thomas his whole life to discover every facet that comprised her. A life that suddenly seemed far more interesting and enjoyable than any solitary future he had imagined for himself. Which was probably due to whatever spell she cast on him. Certainly not because of true feelings he might be developing for her. That was sheer madness.

'No. At least, it's unlikely. A witch's power is passed down from her mother's line. It isn't impossible that the viscountess was a descendant of witches, but we don't come into our power until... well, it begins in our seventh year, gains power in our fourteenth, and is fully manifested by our twenty-first.'

'Three sets of seven?'

'Yes. A witch in her forty-second year experiences another wave of magic, sometimes gaining new powers, or enhancing what she already has, and then again at sixty-three and eighty-four.'

'So presumably, your abilities will only continue to increase as you age?'

Clio's smile could have frozen him in place. 'Exactly. It makes sense that men would fear a witch ageing into her fullest potential when all others lose their strength. No wonder so many of us were killed before we reached our forty-second year.'

Thomas felt the punch of her words. The craze of witch hunts in the sixteenth and seventeenth centuries was not unknown to him, but he'd never thought about what that meant. It was just boring facts in dusty history books. Not actual women being tortured, burned, and killed. All for something they could not control. Yet that is exactly the heritage from whence Clio came. It was no wonder she kept her gifts hidden so carefully.

'I am so sorry, Clio.'

She shrugged. 'It wasn't you who did it.'

'But it could have been.' He stood and walked to where she sat, knelt and gripped the chair, turning it so Clio faced him. Her eyes widened. It was a heavy chair, but he was rather strong. A fact he wanted her to notice. Which was silly and prideful, but also true.

He took both her hands in his and squeezed softly. 'I swear to you, Clio, on my family name, on the blood in my veins, on all that I hold dear, I will protect your secrets. Your truth is safe with me. *You* are safe with me. No matter how long our arrangement lasts. This promise is for now and always.'

Clio's eyes brightened. Her chest rose and fell as rosemary and bergamot surrounded them. The glow started in her sternum, pulsing through the leather, changing the black to heated red as it spread out like fire. When it reached her hands, Thomas felt the electric current passing through her to him. He watched in amazement as his own hands began to glow, the heat moving up his arms, over his chest, like a soothing bath or warm sunlight after a particularly cold winter.

Clio blinked, seeming to realise her power had seeped into him. She pulled her hands from his, breaking the contact and extinguishing the light as quickly as one might snuff a candle.

'What—?'

She stood, walking swiftly to Sir Robin and tapping her shoulder. 'We should head down to dinner. We wouldn't want to keep Lady Langley waiting. I'm sure she's hoping you'll escort her to the table.'

Whatever just happened between them had frightened Clio. Thomas was certain of her fear. But it had done more than that for him. It shook his very foundations. Whatever magic Clio possessed had transferred into him for the briefest moment. And it was pure light.

'Clio, we need to talk about this.'

'About Anna? We will. After dinner. But we don't want to arrive late; it's likely to stir up gossip.'

*Not about Anna. About us.*

But she wouldn't. He knew this. And pushing her on the matter wouldn't change anything. Whatever had occurred, whatever it meant to Clio, she needed time to process it. He would give her time. But he wouldn't give her forever.

'All right. Tonight. After everyone has gone to bed. I'll come to you.'

Clio shook her head. 'No. I shall come to your room.'

A week ago, Thomas would have assumed she was trying to exert her power by controlling where they met. It would have infuriated him. But now, he knew differently. She needed to direct their meeting place because she wasn't in control of whatever was happening. And Clio was always in control. That had an entirely different effect on him.

'As you wish. Shall we?' He extended his arm to her. Clio hesitated before she walked to him and gently placed her fingers on his sleeve. The corresponding snap of flames in the hearth brought a smile to his lips and a scowl to hers.

\* \* \*

Clio spent most of dinner trying to ignore Thomas. She was feigning interest in the lord next to her as he discussed the merits of pipe tobacco, while desperately trying to untangle what the bloody hell was happening with her magic whenever Thomas was near. One thing was certain: it wasn't a bloody spirit match. No matter how unequivocally the evidence aligned with the blasted witch lore.

*It's a fairy tale. Only romantic fools like Ellie believe in such nonsense.*

And Clio was no romantic fool. The obvious solution was to separate from Thomas. Which meant solving this case. Quickly. She turned her thoughts to their conversation with Anna. As she reviewed Anna's version of events, several facts emerged.

The first: Anna was speaking to both of her parents.

The second: if she was able to speak to the dead, and it was becoming increasingly likely this was true, then it was also reasonable to assume the viscountess couldn't be found because she was no longer living.

The third: if Viscountess Beachley was deceased, she couldn't be a perpetrator of murder, but rather a victim.

Most importantly, the fourth: Clio had a new suspect.

Berty.

He was noticeably absent from dinner that night. Clio would very much like to ask him what conversation he had with Mrs Coggins in the kitchen before Anna interrupted them. But she could hardly throw the question out over a game of charades in the parlour.

Even without the details of their conversation, his presence at Viscount Beachley's Mayfair home meant he could easily have poisoned the man's drink. He had motive and means. She needed to discuss this with Thomas. As much as she hated to admit it, he was sharper than a rapier and just as quick. She needed his help.

Which brought her scattered thoughts back to the man sitting across from her. She had been avoiding looking at him all night for fear of what her magic might do, but her gaze inadvertently flicked over the table, and she froze. He was staring at her. Not just looking but eating her up with his eyes. It was incendiary and sparked a resonating hunger within her. She rubbed her hand over her wrist, and his fork clattered onto the table. She couldn't forget the bite of his silk cravat as it cut into her flesh. Gas lights flared before she could look away.

'Blast! We must have someone look at the lines,' the duke called from his end of the table. 'These damnable old houses weren't built for modern conveniences.'

The duchess merely waved her wine glass at him in what one could only assume was agreement. Crimson liquid splashed onto the white tablecloth. She whispered something to Cynthia, then threw her head back in a gale of laughter. Cynthia shot Clio a look. Poor woman. They were only on their second night of this house party, and it was clear Cynthia was rethinking her clever plan.

As dessert was cleared away and the party separated to allow the gentlemen time for smoking and manly discussions of horses, hunting, and politics, Clio made sure to find herself in Lady Langley's circle of ladies in the parlour.

Cynthia reached out a hand and pulled Clio into a tight embrace. 'Save me. I cannot endure another evening of her salacious confidences alone,' she whispered before releasing Clio and pasting a bright smile on her perfectly stained lips.

Clio squeezed her hand in a silent promise to remain near. 'She is rather insatiable. I suppose one must admire her stamina.'

Cynthia's dry laugh held sharp edges. 'It's been so long, I hardly remember.'

Clio wasn't sure how to respond. Luckily, Lady Langley saved her by joining their duo. 'There you are! I must say, Cynthia, your brother's reputation is far more scandalous than the man himself. I dare say I'm disappointed.'

Cynthia's eyes hardened. 'Don't tell me you believe the gossips. They'll say any manner of lies to keep their sycophants titillated.'

'Hardly lies when every widow, harlot, and actress south of Cambridge had a tale to tell of their wild nights with Lieutenant General Grey once upon a time.'

'There are a million justifiable reasons why a man might turn from his marriage bed to seek comfort in the arms of another, Diana. Of all people, you should understand that.' It was a sharp barb, and Clio's respect for Cynthia grew.

'His wife might have a different view.' Lady Langley's tone turned frigid.

'Wife no longer, and I am glad of it. I will not discuss *that* woman.'

Lady Langley raised a brow as her eyes narrowed like a hound scenting blood. 'The court certainly agreed with *that* woman. They felt your brother's behaviour beyond the pale.'

Unexpected rage welled in Clio. How dare a woman as wanton as the duchess cast judgement upon anyone? A spark from the fire popped, landing on Lady Langley's skirt. The duchess screeched, knocking the ember free, but not before it singed her gown.

Cynthia's hand shook as she helped swat the smouldering silk.

'Beyond the pale!' Sir Robin blinked at Clio, but try as she might, she couldn't feel guilty. She didn't know why Thomas sought out other women during his marriage, but whatever the reason, she wanted to understand. Lady Langley was right about his reputation, but it did not align with the man she knew. And she would not judge him without knowing the details.

'Let me help you with your gown.' Clio could see the effort it took Cynthia to keep her voice pleasant as she attempted to assist Lady Langley.

The duchess pulled away from her. 'I have many close friends, Cynthia. I don't need help from those not willing to give it freely.' She turned in a rustle of silk and lace to join a tittering group of ladies on the far side of the room.

'Blast! I shall have to make it up to her somehow.' Cynthia turned to Clio, a false smile on her lips as tears of frustration shone in her eyes.

'Why? In the little I've observed of your friendship, it does not seem the duchess brings much to the table.'

Cynthia burst into laughter. 'One of the wealthiest, most highly titled women in the beau monde isn't doing her fair share in our friendship?' She shook her head, her joy dying as quickly as it appeared. 'Not all of us are free to flout society's rules, Clio. Some must bend their will to husbands, duchesses, and all manner of ugliness.' Her harsh words were softened by a small smile. 'But not you. I admire you, Clio. And I'm honest enough to admit I also envy you.'

The men rejoined the party, and Thomas walked across the floor to join Clio and Cynthia.

Cynthia deftly changed subjects, her pleasant mask back in place. 'How was your interview with poor little Anna?'

Clio wished she could have responded to Cynthia. She wished she could have told her that she respected her immensely for standing tall when so much weighed her down. But the moment had passed. 'Informative,' she said instead.

'Confounding,' Thomas countered as he stood closer to Clio than was entirely polite. But Lady Langley's guests were far too deep in their cups to notice.

Cynthia looked from one to the other. 'Marvellous. So, the investigation is going well.' She didn't attempt to hide her smile.

'It would be better if I could talk to Berty alone. Flatter him a bit while he's soused. There's a world of information a man will share if he's properly motivated.'

'Absolutely not.' Thomas' growl had the fine hairs on her arms raising as her inner muscles clenched.

Cynthia looked from Clio to Thomas and back again. 'I think I shall just... err... make amends with Lady Langley. An unpleasant task is best handled immediately.' She glided across the parlour floor, leaving only Clio and Thomas.

'I know you prefer to take charge, but we are a team, Clio. I won't have you alone with that disgusting man.'

Clio lifted her chin and kept her eyes on Lady Langley. As soon as Cynthia approached her, she flitted to a different group, forcing Cynthia to chase her like a lap dog looking for a treat. Clio wished she had flung a larger coal, one that singed more than just Lady Langley's skirts.

'That woman is a harridan.'

He followed her gaze. 'What's going on?'

Clio shook her head. 'The duchess made some unsavoury comments. When Cynthia disagreed, she left in a huff.'

'Unsavoury comments about what? Or given the duchess, who?' *Bugger.*

She couldn't very well repeat what the duchess said about Grey. Instead, she shook her head. 'It doesn't matter.'

He turned to face her, gripping her elbow and forcing her to mirror his movements. 'It matters a great deal if she has upset my sister.'

'I come from a very loyal family. We protect each other. Your sister is cut from the same cloth, I believe.'

His eyes hardened as his fingers tightened. 'Ah. So she was discussing me. Cynthia should not have wasted her efforts.'

Clio couldn't stop the well of righteous anger at his easy dismissal of such loathsome insults against him. 'Whyever not? Are you not just as worthy of her protection as she is of yours?'

He held her trapped in his gaze. 'No. I am not.'

'Why do you say that?' She held her breath, thinking he wouldn't answer. That he would turn and walk away. But he surprised her with honesty.

'Because my secrets are far more damning than the gossip surrounding me.'

She sucked in air and with it, his scent of starch and spice. 'What secrets do you have, Thomas Grey?'

His eyes flashed, enigmatic and impossible to read. But he did not share whatever darkness lingered there.

She cursed him for refusing to answer her question. And then it dawned on her. While he and Berty had many differences, there was one way all men were similar: they would do almost anything to get what they wanted. And Thomas wanted her.

She subtly shifted her stance, cocking her hip and letting seduction smoulder in her gaze. 'I was thinking about that cravat last night. It occurred to me, leather is far more difficult to burn than cloth or rope.'

Her abrupt change in conversation wasn't the reason his jaw clenched, or his pupils blew wide. 'Fascinating.' He ground the word from his lips like crushing stone. 'I happen to have a few lengths of leather strapping in my room. Excellent for keeping a razor sharp. Or tying up certain ladies who tend to run hotter than most.'

Clio's nipples hardened against her corset, and she tightened her thighs as a hollow ache bloomed in her centre. 'Really?' She tried for nonchalance but failed miserably. Sir Robin's mocking caw confirmed her suspicions.

'Shall I show you?'

All of the air was suddenly sucked out of Lady Langley's parlour. She was supposed to be seducing him, but the damnable man had flipped the coin. Clio swallowed, trying to align her thoughts. 'Where?' Such a proposition should have scandalised her, but she was well beyond that now.

'Later. In your room. Or we can discuss the case, and each retire to our separate beds. The choice is yours.'

But this was her chance to discover what he kept so carefully hidden.

She let out a gusty sigh. 'I suppose we could test your theory. For scientific purposes. Of course.'

'Excellent. Until later, Clio.' He wandered away from her, leaving Clio to lean against the wall and think of glaciers. Icy rain. Cold bath water. Anything to cool the inferno raging through her system.

# 17

Thomas knocked on Clio's door, the leather straps coiled loosely in his left hand. His heart raced. It took all his willpower to remain calm as she opened the door and let him into her room. She was wearing another white nightgown. This time, her robe was green velvet tied tightly at her waist.

'Come in.' Clio's cheeks grew pink, and it was breathtaking to see such a strong, confident woman turn shy.

Thomas still wore his breeches from dinner, though he left his coat, cravat, and vest in his room and wore only a linen shirt. Clio watched him enter with eyes as luminous as a jungle cat. He didn't miss how they froze on the V of skin exposed by his unbuttoned shirt. She licked her lips, and he wondered if she wanted to taste him as badly as he wished to savour her.

Looking around the room, a certain raven was noticeably absent.

'Where is Sir Robin?'

Clio's blush deepened. 'I put his perch behind the screen.' She gestured to a darkened corner. 'The last thing we need is for him to start repeating what is said between us. He could accidentally expose the entire investigation.'

Thomas highly doubted it was the investigation she was worried about exposing. But he wasn't going to argue. The evening would progress much more pleasantly without Sir Robin's piercing, 'Bastard!'

'Please, sit. We should discuss the case before—' Clio seemed to have walked herself up to a verbal cliff.

'Before I tie you to that bed over there?' The gothic headboard was helpfully adorned with carved filigrees and swirls, providing ample choices to anchor someone.

Clio swallowed. 'You really are committed to that second rule.'

'In this kind of situation, honesty is best. It leaves no room for misunderstanding.'

'Ah.' She narrowed her gaze. 'Yet you still hide the truth from me, don't you, Thomas?'

He clenched the straps, letting the bite of leather centre him. Because it would be so easy to tell her everything. His deepest shame. And then she would leave. And he would never have another chance to taste her. To feel her supple skin beneath his hands. To hear his name ripping from her throat. And he wasn't ready to let her go. Not yet.

*Not ever.*

But that was impossible.

'Do you still wish me to take command of our bed sport, Clio?'

She pressed her lips together, inhaled a deep breath, and nodded.

'Then stop asking me questions, or I won't tie you to that bed tonight. I won't strip you bare. Suck those pretty nipples until you burn. I certainly won't spread your beautiful legs and finally taste what I've been craving. Do you understand?'

Her chest rose and fell in a ragged rhythm. Every word he spoke increased the flush covering her neck and cheeks. Her skin began to glow, her power pulsing from her sternum. His body hardened in response.

'Yes.' She threw the word at him like a dagger. He knew she wanted to uncover his secrets. But it seemed she wanted the pleasure he could bring even more.

'Thank the bloody saints for that.'

She thrust out her chin, obviously unwilling to give him the upper hand just yet. Not when he had refused her something she wanted. 'Don't thank them just yet. Before we do all that,' she flapped her hand at the bed, 'we must discuss the case.'

Keeping his need chained, he sucked air through clenched teeth. 'Yes. The blasted case. How could I forget?' With a Herculean effort, he walked to one of the wingback chairs next to the hearth and carefully sat, mindful of the raging erection pressing painfully against his falls.

Clio took the opposite chair and pulled her legs up, wrapping her arms around her knees.

'I've thought over what Anna told us, and I have reached several conclusions.'

She spent the next few minutes detailing her thoughts. With each new explanation, Thomas found himself increasingly more impressed with her quick mind.

'So, you believe Anna is seeing both of her parents because they are both dead?'

Clio nodded, her black hair spilling over her shoulder. 'I think I should try to reach out to them, together. If I can get into the nursery when Anna isn't there, I might be able to convince them to speak to me. They both want to protect their daughter. Maybe I can use that as leverage to get them to trust me.'

Thomas shook his head. 'The last time you spoke to the

viscount, he strangled you. I saw the bruises, Clio, no matter what kind of magic you used to heal them.'

Clio shook her head. 'He didn't mean to do that. He wasn't seeing me. He was seeing the murderer.'

'I don't care what he was seeing. I won't have you putting yourself in danger. Not with the current Viscount Beachley, and certainly not with the deceased one. I can't protect you against a spirit.'

She narrowed her gaze. 'You don't need to protect me. I can protect myself.'

The truth of her statement rubbed salt into old wounds. Because it meant he wasn't necessary.

Thomas tried a different tactic. 'I don't doubt your skills in self-preservation. But what if you scare them away? You said that could happen, and then what? We must speak with Mrs Coggins again. She knows why Berty was there. Your suspicions of her are entirely supported by Anna's testimony.' No one was immune to flattery. He hoped. 'And unlike your ghostly friends, if she attacks you, I can help beat her back.'

'Trust me, if she so much as tried, I would have her hair smouldering to cinders.'

He shook his head. 'Wicked witch. Attacking a woman's hair.'

'I should have thought of that with the duchess.'

Thomas held back a laugh and tried to remember they were arguing, and he was quite possibly losing. 'It hardly seems sporting.'

'This isn't a sport. It's murder. And we don't need to go back to the horrid housekeeper. I still think I could get Berty to talk.'

'Not unless I'm with you.' The very idea of Berty putting his sweaty hands on her body was enough to provoke a jealousy he hadn't felt since Lissa.

'You don't trust me to contain all my lusty desire with a gentleman as debonair as Berty?'

He was being ridiculous. Berty was disgusting. And even if he had been a dashing duke ripe for marriage, Clio was nothing like Lissa. She would never betray his trust.

*But would she accept me if she knew everything?*

He shut down such dangerous thoughts. The very idea was madness. And what kind of selfish bastard would he be if he let her sacrifice her future to be with him?

She squared her shoulders, always ready to meet him in a challenge. 'Does it matter? You'll have to trust me with this.'

'Trust. It's a funny thing. So difficult to give, and so easy to break.'

Tension pulled tight between them.

'I'm trusting you tonight. I wish you would trust me with whatever it is haunting you. I'm good with ghosts, you know.'

Thomas shook his head. 'That sounds dangerously close to a question you promised not ask. I think we are done discussing the investigation. It's time to move on to the second reason we are here.'

She lifted her chin, always so defiant. 'What is that?'

'Pleasure.'

Her throat hollowed as she sucked in a breath. 'Perhaps I would gain pleasure from hearing about your past.'

Thomas' eyes hardened into emerald shards. 'You would not.' He pushed down the panic and shame conjured by her words and focused on what he could control. Her desire. And his own. 'But you will gain a great deal of satisfaction from what I have planned, Clio. I promise to fan your witchfire into a conflagration that will consume us both if you follow my instructions.'

She narrowed her gaze. He knew everything in her wanted to challenge him. But he also knew she wanted to let go. The lights flared as sparks gathered in her palms. The glow covering her skin was an eloquent expression of her desire. 'You really are an impossible man, Thomas Grey.'

'It lends me a certain charm, don't you think?' He lifted his brow. 'Stand up and take off your robe, Clio.'

It was a test. If she refused, then she was not ready. Whether she knew it or not. And he would need to rethink his plan. Because the goal was still the same. Bringing her pleasure so bright, so hot, their time together would stay with her for all her days. He would be seared into her memory. A brand she could never erase. After their first night together, he knew he would spend the rest of his life craving her. Maybe she had bewitched him. Perhaps he was under her spell, but one good charm deserved another, and he was determined to weave his own enchantment over Clio. He might not have her power. He might not have any magic. He might not hold value to Lissa, the beau monde, or himself. But he would do something worthy for Clio. He would bring her beauty or blaze like a dying star in the attempt.

She pushed to her feet, straightened her shoulders, and lifted a shaky hand to the tie around her robe. When she paused, he held his breath. Waiting. Yearning. Needing her more than the next beat of his heart.

She slipped the tie loose, her heavy robe falling open to reveal a nightgown of nearly sheer cotton. With a slow shrug, the velvet slipped to the carpet.

Thomas couldn't stop his gaze slipping down her body. There was something undeniably erotic about seeing the hint of her nipples, the shadow of her mons, but still not knowing her exact taste. 'Good girl.'

'I hardly think a good girl would stand in her unmentionables in front of a gentleman, but isn't that the point?' Her lips curled in a devilish smile, and Thomas felt his cock grow heavy and hard. He was supposed to be in control, but she summoned his arousal as easily as she conjured her flame.

Not able to stay still, he stood, prowling around her, watching as the pulse in her throat quickened. He walked behind her, and when she turned her head, he tsked. 'Face forward, Clio.'

She clenched her jaw, mutiny flashing in her eyes, but did as he asked.

'I told you I would strip you bare. I meant what I said.' He stood close enough, their bodies almost touched. Heat pulsed off her in waves so powerful, the air shimmered between them. Before he could reach for her nightgown, it began to smoke, the cotton flared like a lantern wick, then turned ashy grey and fell from her body like burned paper. Sooty dust lay around her feet in a ring on the carpet.

He whistled low, stepping back to admire her generously curved arse. 'That was a wicked little trick, my sweet witch.'

'Wicked witches have the best tricks and the most fun.' Clio didn't move, but he knew she was smiling.

He took a single finger and traced it down the pearls of her spine. She hissed in a breath. Pulling her hair to drape over her shoulder, Thomas forced himself to remain focused. It would be so easy to get lost in the silky tresses. But there was so much more to discover. He leaned forward, pressing his lips where her shoulder met her neck.

'A bastard like me couldn't possibly resist a witch like you.'

Clio swayed, and he gripped her arm, holding her steady as he sank his teeth into the skin he had just kissed. Her body tightened, and a jolt of electric current bolted through her and into Thomas.

*Fucking hell. She will ruin me.*

Never before had a woman affected him on such a visceral level. Her power poured into him, enhancing every sensation. He forced himself to step back, refusing to lose control before they had even started. He was as randy as a schoolboy and just as likely to unman himself.

*Do not spend before you've even gotten her onto the bed!*

'Go and lie down. On your back.'

She hesitated. 'W-what are you going to do?'

'Watch you.'

'Oh.' She glanced over her shoulder before slowly padding her way to the bed, her bottom swaying like a metronome counting the rhythm of his heart. He saw the flash of strawberry high on her inner thigh as she climbed onto the tall bed.

*A birthmark.*

He couldn't wait to trace it with his tongue.

She flipped to face him. Finally, he could look his fill of her, gloriously naked. His gaze caught on glossy pink scars swiping over her abdomen and right arm like slashes from a beast with razor-sharp talons. They were healed, but she must have sustained them within the last year.

Anger raged through him, sweeping away his desire. He strode to the bed, climbed onto the feather mattress, and ran his fingers over her smooth skin.

'Who did this to you?'

Clio froze. She tried to scoot away from him and cover the marks. He caught her wrist, then the other, pinning her hands over her head. When she bucked her hips, he held her in place with his own.

'Tell me, Clio. Who did this to you? Give me the name of the blackguard so I can hunt him down and kill him.'

She shook her head, her amber eyes gone wide. 'You can't. She's already dead.'

Realisation dawned, and with it fear. 'A ghost did this to you?'

'Such things rarely happen.' Clio swallowed, drawing his gaze to the delicate column of her throat. A throat he had seen darken with bruises from a different spectre.

'What about being choked? Was that also rare?'

Her delectable mouth hardened. 'I told you, he didn't mean to hurt me.'

Thomas nodded, his own sense of helplessness transforming fear into cold determination. 'I don't want you speaking to any more ghosts.'

Clio's jagged laughter cut through his tightly reined control. Her wrists grew warmer beneath his fingers as a blast of heat engulfed him. 'I gave you leave to command me in seduction, but you will not control my actions anywhere else. If you can't agree to that, this ends now.'

The very idea of some insubstantial spirit leaving such horrible scars on his woman tore at Thomas' already ravaged soul.

*But she isn't my woman. She has no wish to be my woman. And if she were mine, I still could not control her choices.*

A brutal lesson he learned during his doomed marriage and one he couldn't afford to forget. If he pushed Clio on this, she would make him leave. What would he gain other than aching bollocks and a wall separating him from her? If she was determined to put herself in harm's way, his best chance of protecting her was to ensure he stood beside her. And to do that, he would need to agree to her demands, even if it countered every instinct in his body.

'Will you at least promise not to conjure the viscount and his wife unless I'm with you?'

She exhaled through her nose in a delicate expression of frustration. 'I can't control when a ghost will appear. But I promise to include you when I go to the nursery to seek them out. Will that suffice?'

*Not even close.*

But it was the best offer he was likely to get from Clio.

'And you will call for me if they come to you when you're alone? Or send Sir Robin. Surely he'll put aside his dislike for me if you're in danger.'

Clio's smile stole his breath. 'He doesn't dislike you. He just likes provoking you.'

'A trait you both share.'

Her amber eyes danced with mischief. 'Perhaps. Now will you hold to your promise? You spoke of conflagration, but I am not burning yet.'

Damn her for being so impossible to resist.

'I have always prided myself on being a man of my word.' He let go of her wrists and pushed himself up. Slowly, with lazy intent, he dragged his hands down her body, caressing the curve of her breasts without letting himself play with her nipples. Not yet. He bumped over her ribs and feathered over the slashes on her abdomen, willing her body to feel pleasure where once she endured pain. He enjoyed the flare of her hips before pausing as his thumb reached the birthmark on her inner thigh.

'What have we here?'

Clio clamped her legs together instinctively.

'Show me.' He forced command into his voice.

Hesitation created a crease between her brows. Slowly, she relaxed her legs and let them fall open, showing him more than just the strawberry-coloured star high on her inner thigh. Pink lips peeked from the nest of black maidenhair, wet and glistening.

'Beautiful.' The word couldn't possibly encompass the fullness of her magnificence, but it was all he could manage.

She arched her back, a silent offering of something more precious than all the Queen's vast riches. He pushed off the bed, needing distance if he was going to maintain his control. Stepping back, he tried to memorise her in this moment, an image he could take with him always.

Clio's breasts were full and delightfully belled. Her creamy skin contrasted against dark cherry nipples. His cock pulsed painfully as she pulled herself further back on the bed, her breasts jostling with the movement. This must be a new level of self-torture, and he was ready to revel in it until the pain became pleasure.

'Do you like what you see?' Her low voice nearly broke him.

'You are perfect.'

Pale skin flushed rose.

He still had the leather straps in his hand. He smacked them hard against his thigh, needing the sharp bite of pain to help him focus. Clio jumped at the loud thwack, her eyes growing wide as she focused on his leg.

'One day, perhaps we can experiment with spanking. I bet your bottom would turn such a delicious shade of rose.'

Clio bit her lip as the candle next to her flared.

'Would you like that?'

She inhaled, her ribs pressing delicately against her skin, and then nodded. 'Does that make me wanton?'

His lips curled in a knowing smile. 'No. It makes you undeniably, irrevocably, and absolutely wicked. But I recently learned wicked women have the best tricks and the most fun.'

Her breathy laughter eased some of the tension growing between them.

'But I don't think we'll explore that today.'

Thomas didn't miss the flash of disappointment before she nodded in agreement.

*Dear God. Her tastes run as dark as my own. A miracle. And a tragedy.*

It was a cruel twist of fate to give him such a perfect partner when there was no way to take their relationship any further than the fortnight they shared at Blackthorn Manor. But he would not think of that now. The only moment that mattered was this one. If he only had these fleeting fragments of time with Clio, he would not waste any of them on regrets. He had the rest of his bleak life for that.

'Hands over your head.'

Clio complied, the movement doing fascinating things to her breasts. Thomas walked to the bed, running his hand along the sensitive underside of her arm, over the crease of her elbow, to her wrist. He focused on his task, wrapping one length of the leather around her and quickly tying it to the headboard. He moved to the other side, mirroring his actions with her left wrist. As he tested the knot, he trailed his hand back down her arm. When his fingers brushed over the soft hair at her armpit, she tightened, trying to pull away.

'Ahhhh. You're ticklish.' A bubble of joy burst in his belly.

'I am not!'

He tickled again, with more intent and was rewarded with her breasts swaying as she tried to squirm away. But the ties held firm.

'Not fair!' Clio gasped.

Thomas stopped, pulling back. Her words struck a chord within him. 'So much of life isn't fair, is it?'

Clio's giggles died. Her eyes were locked onto his, and Thomas knew she saw far more than he wanted. Far more than anyone before her ever had and anyone after ever would.

'How have the fates wronged you, Thomas?'

Temptation swelled once more. To open up the poorly healed scars hiding his rotten soul and let the poison pour out of him. Seep into her. Destroy whatever was starting between them. A courageous man would do just that. End this now. It was the kindest thing he could do. Because anything between them was doomed. But he was too selfish to destroy this moment, not before he tasted her. Not before she screamed his name in ecstasy.

'Tonight is not a night for confessions.'

'What if I want your confessions?'

Thomas forced a smile. 'You gave me the reins, remember? Such an important detail. Or did you change your mind? We can stop now. Whenever you say.'

Anger, familiar and beautiful, painted a new flush over her skin as her scent blended with burning ozone. 'I don't wish to stop.'

'Then stop asking questions. I have a better use for that pretty mouth.'

Watching her desire war with her need to understand him was enthralling. But desire must have won as she slowly parted her lips and licked them. Thomas walked to the end of the bed, needing to complete this quickly. He made fast work of one ankle, then the next, and finally, let his gaze trail up her calf, over her knee, along the pearl skin of her inner thigh where her birthmark begged to be licked, and paused where she glistened with liquid need. Her midnight maidenhair only intensified the innocent pink of her swollen lips. His mouth watered. He didn't want to taste her. He *needed* to taste her. To lick, and suck, and savour every single drop.

'Fucking hell. You are stunning.'

Clio squirmed. 'You can't possibly think I am beautiful... there.'

'You are beautiful everywhere.' He ran a finger over the sole of her foot, delighting as her body tightened. 'Even the bottom of your feet.'

Clio scrunched her nose and shook her head in dismissal.

Thomas bent down to press a kiss against the top of her foot, then her ankle. He nipped her calf and nuzzled behind her knee.

'What are you doing?' Clio's voice was ragged.

'I'm kissing your pretty parts.' He climbed on the bed, moving to her inner thigh where he swiped his tongue over her star and sucked the skin into his mouth. He pulled back and marvelled at the change in colour from strawberry to plum. Alternating soft kisses with sucking bites that would leave marks by morning, he slowly devoured every inch of her body. The idea of leaving little love nibbles thrilled him. She would look at herself and remember what he did to her. How her body melted under his ministrations. How the very mark she had been born with was altered because of him.

'Thomas...'

He was inching closer and closer to her core. His fingers played over the jutting bone of her hip, then gripped to keep her steady.

'Yes, Clio?' His mouth nearly brushed her soft petals. He knew she felt his breath against her most sensitive flesh.

'Don't.'

He froze. His lips hovering over her wet pussy. His body was harder than steel. He would pull back. If she asked, he would stop. Even if it destroyed him.

'Stop.'

*Fucking blasted hell and damnation.*

'Don't stop, Thomas.'

Relief rushed through him.

'I wouldn't dare, sweet Clio.'

## 18

Clio had completely forgotten why she was supposed to seduce him. Something about discovering his secrets. But secrets didn't matter when she was drowning in delicious need. Power pooled in her core, liquid and molten and beyond her control. The silken glide of Thomas' velvet tongue swiped over her slit, and she cried out.

'So fucking delicious.' His words vibrated against raw nerve endings, scattering a million sparks through her veins.

He delved deeper, so close to the cluster of nerves where ecstasy waited. And then in a fiery swipe, he found her secret centre, and she burned in an inferno.

'Goddess... yes!' She writhed, wanting to bury her fingers in his hair, needing to push him harder against her, desperate to ride him, wrap her body around his like a siren pulling him into her depths. But she couldn't do any of that. The leather ties cut into her wrist, and the bite was as delicious as his teeth scraping her clitoris. She could do nothing but feel. It was glorious. It was torture. It was everything.

He flicked and nipped. Sucked and licked. Wet need washed through her, soaking into her soul.

She felt the hard penetration of his thick finger, pushing past swollen flesh into her tight cove. His sweet invasion only heightened the tension coiling inside, heating like glass, ready to shatter.

He sucked her clitoris harder, his finger curling as her channel clenched in aching spasms. Her world imploded into a supernova as she screamed his name.

* * *

Clio came back to herself in slow degrees. The bed hadn't burned into charred cinders, so that was a relief. One of her legs fell free as Thomas untied her, then the other. When he unbound her right wrist, he rubbed it gently, then leaned over her to release the last leather strap. Before he could pull away, she caught him, wrapping her arms around his chest and pulling him against her. His linen shirt scratched against her naked flesh.

'Hold me.' It wasn't a request. It was a command.

Thomas' rough chuckle unwound some of the tension still coiled within her. The solid weight of him held her steady, reminding Clio she was flesh and bones, not just flames and ash.

She could feel the hard ridge of his desire. The poor man had tended to her needs without seeking his own relief. A problem she would happily remedy.

'Are you well?' His deep voice rumbled against her ear.

'I am... remarkably well.' She gave in to temptation, her fingers tangling in his thick hair as his flat chest pressed against hers. Heartbeat against heartbeat.

And then the vision took her.

* * *

*She was in a room. Not a bedroom. A sitting room. It was a bright summer day, and the windows had been opened to relieve the staggering heat. Thomas sat on a settee in cream breeches, a blue coat, and white shirt. He looked young, and handsome, and devastated. His elbows were braced on his knees, and he held his head in his hands.*

*'What the bloody hell is this?'*

*Clio turned to her right as alarm, bright and sharp, zinged through her. Because Thomas also stood next to her. Not the memory, the reality. Older. Harder. Far more devastating to her heart.*

*Clio parted her lips but couldn't speak. He was in her vision. With her. Standing on the edges of his own memory as it played out before them. It was impossible.*

*Lissa walked in front of them, her sprigged muslin gown almost brushing over Clio's bare feet. 'I'm sorry, Thomas. I know you didn't want things to be this way, but I won't be denied a family because of your failing.' She stopped in front of where Past-Thomas sat on the couch.*

*Clio realised she was still naked and crossed her arms over her chest, horribly exposed in front of Lissa and two Thomases, even if only one Thomas could see her.*

*Real-Thomas turned to Clio, his eyes darting over her naked body. Gone was any hint of desire. In its place was fear and quickly growing anger. He whipped his shirt over his head and handed it to her. After she donned it, grateful for some kind of shield, he grabbed her arm. 'Whatever sorcery this is, you must stop it. Now, Clio.' His rage dissolved into unhinged panic. 'I beg you.' His voice broke on the last word as he darted his gaze to his other self sitting on the settee.*

*Clio's heart cracked. Because she would have pulled them from this private moment if she could. It wasn't hers to witness. But she had never been able to control when her visions came, or when they ended. 'I can't. It must play itself out...'*

*Past-Thomas looked up at Lissa. Tears streaked down his face, and his lips trembled before he pressed them tightly together. 'You are...' He cleared his throat, wiping the wetness from his cheeks with the back of his hand. 'You are certain?'*

*Lissa nodded, her bright hair catching the sun and shining like a halo. 'It's been three months since my last courses. And there are other... signs. I'm pregnant, Thomas.' Though her voice was serious, it was impossible to miss the joy shining in her eyes. The glow of love suffusing her skin. 'I'm going to be a mother. Finally.'*

*Past-Thomas stood. He pulled down his vest and straightened his shoulders like a soldier preparing to enter the fray. 'And you've gone to the courts?'*

*She put her hand on his sleeve, but he jerked away as though her touch burned him. 'It's the only way. How is any other option fair to me? I am not at fault here, Thomas. I don't deserve to be punished because of you.'*

*Anger washed through Clio. She stepped forward, sparks tingling in her palm. She'd never tried to push her power at the memory of a person. Not until this moment. Lifting her hand, the embers turned into a fireball of blue and white. 'How dare you!' she hissed.*

*Lissa's gaze remained steady on Past-Thomas. Because she couldn't see Clio. Nor could Clio's power have any effect on a woman encapsulated in a memory. But that was no reason not to try. Clio pulled back her arm and, like cracking a whip, she threw her magic at Lissa.*

The room disappeared in a swirl of colour, and the sweet scent of summer roses dissolved into the acrid smoke of burning paint. Clio stumbled back, blinked several times, and realised the screen protecting Sir Robin was on fire.

'Damnation!' she screamed, rushing for the pitcher of water next to a washstand by the bed. Sir Robin screeched in alarm, flapping his wings, feeding the flames with the wind he created as he flew over the burning silk and wooden frame, landing in a flutter of feathers on Thomas' shoulder.

Clio tossed the pitcher onto the screen, muttering a spell to triple the water and douse the flames.

Thomas, seemingly unaware of the heavy raven perched on his shoulder, looked from Clio to the charred screen and back again.

Clio wiped a strand of hair from her forehead. 'I—'

'What just happened?' His voice was tightly controlled.

Clio's belly flipped nervously. She was *never* nervous. But a host of thoughts were trapped in Thomas' head, and she guessed several of them were about her. Likely, they were not good thoughts.

She had always been comfortable with who she was, what she wanted, and how she planned on getting it. If other people had opinions about her, she didn't give a fig. Unless they were her family.

But now... she gave quite a few figs. An entire orchard's worth, actually. Never had someone been a part of her magic outside of her coven. Until Thomas. And now she risked losing him.

In the most exposing, vulnerable, violating way possible, she had somehow pulled him into her sphere. He hadn't given her permission to see his memories. He hadn't asked to share in her abilities. But it had happened. And he was understandably upset. She couldn't forget what she'd seen. Or how it felt to stand with him in his memory. It had brought a sense of comfort to know she wasn't alone. Clio doubted it felt the same to him.

'Thomas, I'm so sorry.'

He shook his head, his high cheekbones flushing with anger. 'Save your sorrow. What happened, Clio? That was my past we just saw. My memories. How?'

She felt the sting of tears before a hot drop rolled down her cheek. 'I don't know. I mean, I have always been able to see the memories of those departed, but never the past of someone living. And no one has ever been in the vision with me.'

'How, Clio?' He was almost shouting now, and Clio was grateful they were the only two guests on this side of the manor.

She took a deep breath and tried to make sense of things. 'It's unheard of, unless you believe in the silly fantasy of spirit matches. A witch's magic is hers alone. And I've only ever had visions of the dead until I met you and started seeing your memories.'

His head cocked to the side a second before she realised her mistake. He prowled towards her. 'Memories? You've had other visions about me?'

*Holy Hecate. I've really spilt the potion now.*

But the least she could offer him was some truth. 'Yes.'

Thomas strode to her in two powerful steps. Sir Robin flapped his wings to keep his perch on Thomas' wide shoulder. He reached up and put his hand over her throat, his fingers gentle even when his gaze was fierce enough to shred her soul to ribbons. 'And you didn't tell me?'

Her eyes widened, and she swallowed, but her voice remained steady. 'The first time, I barely knew you. I could hardly tell you I saw your past. You would have thought me mad.'

'What did you see, Clio?' His words were dangerously soft.

Her mind worked furiously but she couldn't focus as he stroked over her pulse point.

'I fucked my way through half of London. Did you see that?'

She shook her head. 'No. Just you and... her. Or you alone, but thinking about her.'

His brows raised. 'You can hear my thoughts?'

'No, not normally.' She was quick to reassure him. That wasn't her gift. It was Helena's. Though it didn't seem the time to talk about the powers of her coven. 'But when I have my visions, it's like I'm in your head. I hear your thoughts, feel your emotions.'

He leaned closer. 'If only you could feel my emotions now, Clio. You would run from this place and never return.' He drew his hand down her neck, over the hollow of her throat, down her chest to her sternum, before he stepped away.

'What happened between the two of you, Thomas? I know you loved her very much. Why did you agree to seek your pleasure with other women?'

'Haven't you put the pieces together yet, my clever Clio?'

She swallowed and shook her head.

'Still looking for all your precious evidence before you form a conclusion. All right. I shall give you some. When Lissa and I first married, it was a love match. We were mad for each other. Couldn't keep ourselves from the bedroom. Lissa wanted children, and I was happy to oblige. But as the months passed, and her courses came without fail, our passion dwindled along with our hopes. We saw doctors. She worried that perhaps the injuries I sustained in the war damaged me. But all the doctors said the same thing. I could engage in sexual relations. So, the fault must lie with Lissa. She was devastated. Then she became angry. She insisted we seek out other bed partners.'

Clio shook her head. 'But why?'

'She told me if I could get a bastard on some other woman, she would take the child. Raise it as her own. As ours. And so, I did as she asked. Even though it nearly killed me. I fucked any willing woman trying to prove that I was worthy. I gave those women my soul. My honour. My dignity. But do you know what I never gave them? Not a single. Fucking. One?'

'Bastard!' Sir Robin's timing couldn't have been worse. For the first time, Clio wished her familiar was anything other than a raven.

Thomas' green eyes grew bright with pain even as he stretched his lips into a smile. He reached up, offering his forearm to the raven, who obliged. 'Exactly, Sir Robin. I couldn't give them a bastard. And so instead, I became one.' With exquisite care, he held the bird to Clio's shoulder, and Sir Robin hopped to his favourite perch.

The raven rubbed his head against her cheek, but she gained no comfort from her familiar. 'And she fell pregnant with another man's child?'

'She did.'

'Thomas. I'm so sorry.' But her words were not enough. Not nearly enough.

He swallowed as tears glistened in his beautiful green eyes. One fell, and she reached up to catch it, but he pulled away. 'Don't.' He sniffed, cleared his throat, and took another step backwards. 'She was right. After so many years of being told she was the problem, Lissa proved that it wasn't her failure. It was mine.' The words ripped out of him like shattered pieces of his soul. Clio's heart bled with him. 'I could never provide her a future. I have nothing to give, Clio. Except for the one thing she asked of me. The only thing I have left to offer. Freedom.' He backed up another step, only a few feet from the door.

He was going to walk away. He was going to leave Clio, just as he left Lissa. But she wouldn't let him.

She moved to block his path. 'That's not true. Freedom isn't fear. And that is why you're leaving. You're afraid.'

He smiled then, a cold expression threatening to freeze her fire. His jaw could have been granite, his body stone, and his heart, cold steel. 'Maybe I am. Maybe I'm scared of a witch who steals the secrets from my soul. I think our games here are at an end.' He stepped around her, walked to the door, and twisted the knob before Clio could process what was happening.

'You can't leave.'

Thomas turned, his face in profile, refusing to look directly at Clio. 'You might control everything else, but you don't control me. I cannot stay here with you. I *will* not.'

He stepped out of the door as Clio's world erupted into flames.

## 19

Thomas had never felt so empty. Not even after Lissa left him. His darkest shame had been exposed by Clio's bright flame, and nothing but charred chunks of coal remained. She was a mystical creature who controlled the elements, and he was a fool to think there could ever be anything more for them than a few heated moments of pleasure. He had to leave. He would not be able to stay away from her if he remained. And seeing her look of pity or disgust after she had time to process his last memory with Lissa would break him. Shame tasted of ash and smoke on this tongue and burned like brimstone in his soul.

He packed his few belongings that night and woke early, asking the coachman to take him to the station. Catching the early-morning train, he was back in London by eleven. Instead of returning to his home, he caught a hack directly to Scotland Yard. At the very least, he needed to tell Lachlan he had abandoned the case.

The train journey had given him ample time to torture himself with memories of Clio. From their first meeting when she stood in Viscount Beachley's entryway, a raven on her shoulder and fire in her gaze, to last night, naked and bound on the bed. She bewitched him. His needs were perfectly mirrored by her own. But it wasn't her body that claimed his soul. It was the woman herself. Her stubborn spirit. Her sharp mind. Her fearless courage. Each facet of her personality was a perfect foil to his own. He could spend a lifetime between her thighs, or standing next to her in a parlour as they puzzled out a murder, or sitting by her side as she drove her carriage to their next adventure. Their future spun out like a silvery spell, as strong and stunning as a spider's web. And he was caught like a fly in his own trap. Because it could never be anything more than a fatal fantasy.

He would never damn her to a future where he could offer nothing more than himself. She deserved more than Thomas. She deserved everything. He loved her, so he would stay far away.

His mind stuttered as the carriage bumped over a rut in the pitted road.

*Dear God. I love her. I love fighting with her, I love solving mysteries together, I love making her burn with desire. I'm even fond of her foulmouthed raven. I haven't been bewitched by her. The only spell I've fallen under is Cupid's.*

It was a devastating realisation. Because it meant he couldn't possibly see her again. Ever.

*She is magic, but I am a curse.*

When she pulled him into her vision, or he fell into it, or the cosmos, in a cruel twist of fate, decided to test his mettle by taking them to the moment that shattered every hope he had of a future with any woman, it became clear he must leave. And now he could admit why. Not to avoid her reaction, but to save her from himself.

In the end, she would thank him for running away.

He shook his head, fisted his hand, and slammed it into the squabs as the carriage came to a stop. He climbed the steps to 4

Whitehall Place, his heart a black hole sucking any hope into its endless darkness.

'What are you doin' back already?' Lachlan looked up from his mess of a desk, his eyes clouding with confusion. 'Is Clio with you?'

Not even caring that the settee was covered in a host of detritus ranging from case files to shackles to a pickled herring sandwich, Thomas sank onto the cushions. 'No. She is not.' And that was his problem.

Lachlan leaned back in his chair. 'Is she well?'

'Better than me, that is for certain. She's still with my sister at Blackthorn Manor. Given Clio's... unique skills, I thought she might do better without me in her way.'

Quirking a brow, Lachlan inhaled a long breath. 'So, you know.' His oldest friend stood, walked around his desk, avoiding the pile of tumbled books, and stopped in front of the bookshelf. Pulling out a large tome, he reached behind it and withdrew a bottle. Scotch. Of course. 'Did she tell you, or did you puzzle it out on yer own?'

'A bit of both. You spoke of a witch who claimed your heart?'

Lachlan tipped his chin in acknowledgement.

'I understand exactly what you mean.'

Bringing the bottle to Thomas, Lachlan pulled the stopper free and offered it.

'Drink?'

Thomas looked up at Lachlan and took the bottle. The liquid burning down his throat brought a measure of comfort. Oddly, the heat reminded him of Clio.

'It is a strange thing to recognise one's limitations. Especially when that revelation comes at the hands of a beautiful woman whose power so easily eclipses your own.' Lachlan took the bottle back from Thomas and took a healthy swig.

'Rowan.'

'Aye. Rowan. And I'll tell you, her nieces are cut from a similar cloth. I hope you aren't as stupid as I was.'

Before Thomas could answer, Lachlan handed back the bottle.

'What happened with Clio?'

Thomas took another swallow, exhaled as the warmth in his belly turned into fire, and was about to tell Lachlan everything when the door behind him banged open. Both Thomas and Lachlan turned as one.

A tall woman with chestnut hair piled in a heap of curls and braids, her grey eyes flashing dangerously, the cut and style of her dress confidently declaring her wealth, stood in the doorway. She glared first at Thomas, then Lachlan. Striding into his office, she carried herself with the grace of a queen.

'You promised me she would be safe, Lachlan MacDougal. You lied!' She advanced on Lachlan, and Thomas had to give the man credit. He had the courage of a Celtic warrior not to shrink away from the woman. She might be slight and delicate, but the power rolling off her in waves was palpable. Thunder cracked, and Thomas glanced at the window. Though it had been a rare sunny day when he arrived at Scotland Yard not fifteen minutes earlier, black clouds now roiled in the sky as lightning streaked across it in a jagged spear of white light.

Thomas rose from the couch. Feeling very much like a soldier once more on a suicide mission, he stepped between Lachlan and the advancing woman. 'Aunt Rowan. How lovely to meet you.' Because she had to be Clio's aunt.

She swivelled her head and narrowed her gaze at Thomas, who immediately regretted his decision. He should have hidden behind the settee, not put himself in the middle of imminent danger.

'I will deal with you later.' She flicked her wrist, and Thomas was pushed back onto the couch by an unseen force. When he tried to move, he realised his arms and legs were frozen. Fear licked up his spine.

Rowan turned her focus back to Lachlan, who paled, but straightened his shoulders and firmed his jaw. 'Calm down, Rowan. Your anger helps no one.'

This was not good. Even Thomas knew telling a woman like Rowan to calm down would only end in murder. Lachlan's murder. Thomas would probably be next for witnessing the event.

Thunder cracked again, so loud, it shook papers off Lachlan's desk, as if the storm were in the room with them. And perhaps it was.

'Tell me to calm down again, Lachlan, and those will be the very last words you ever speak. Ellie saw what is to come. Clio will not escape her fate. Her coven can't help her. She is alone.' Rowan turned to glare at Thomas. He felt the weight of her accusations like an anvil crushing his sternum. 'And in far more peril than she knows.'

Lachlan's face flushed, and Thomas recognised the signs of anger in his friend. 'I don't know what you are talking about, Rowan.'

But Thomas understood with blinding clarity.

*I left her alone. And now she is in danger.*

Thomas couldn't move, but he could speak. 'You must release me. I need to get back to her. I should never have left.'

Rowan turned to him. She cocked her head, and Thomas felt stripped bare.

*My God. She knows. She knows everything.*

She nodded, and he felt the impact of her power like a physical blow. 'If you wish to help, tell me everything from the moment she left until now.' Rowan wasn't asking.

As quickly and succinctly as he could manage, Thomas

recounted everything that had happened, save the intimate moments he shared with Clio.

Lachlan took a healthy draught of his own medicine. 'You believe both the viscount and the viscountess are dead?'

Thomas nodded.

Rowan waved away Lachlan's question. 'He left marks on Clio?' Her anger was dissolving into something far more troubling: fear.

'Yes. I didn't see the ghost, but I saw what he was doing to Clio. Her neck was bruised.'

Lachlan's cheeks paled. 'It isn't the first time. She had a vision in the viscount's house on the first day. The viscountess slapped him in the vision, but Clio came out of it with a mark on her cheek.'

*Of course.*

Clio's behaviour that day had never made sense to Thomas. But it made sense now.

'And you didn't think to tell me?' Rowan might as well have eviscerated Lachlan with a butter knife.

'Clio told me all was well.' Lachlan's voice was strained.

'Oh yes. It's perfectly grand a spirit left marks on my niece.' The next crack of thunder shook the foundations of Scotland Yard.

'She swore the ghost wasn't trying to hurt her.' Thomas shook his head, trying desperately to understand the rules of this new world. 'She said he mistook her for the murderer. Is she in danger from the ghost?'

Rowan shook her head. 'I don't know. Perhaps if someone had thought to tell me what the bloody hell was going on before my niece left her coven to fight some murderer *alone*, I might have more insight.'

Lachlan ran his hand through his hair, tugging hard on the wild curls. 'You are always so protective of them, Rowan. You can't keep them locked away forever. They must live their lives.'

'They cannot live their lives if they are dead.' Her words dripped with barely contained violence as fear punched Thomas in the gut.

Rowan paced from one end of the small office to the other. 'Ellie couldn't see what form the threat took, whether it was a living man or spectre.' She turned her focus to Thomas. 'Do you believe this Berty is the one who killed Viscount Beachley?'

Thomas tried to think clearly through the fear that plucked at his wits. Clio was in danger. And he was half a day's travel away. He was such a fool for leaving her. 'He has motive. He had the means, and according to Anna, he was there the day her father died.'

Rowan tapped her finger against her blue skirt. 'As a rule, I am generally more worried about the living than the dead. If he suspects she knows, Clio has more to fear from Berty than Viscount Beachley's ghost. Especially as the person most capable of protecting her from a violent man ran back to London with his tail between his legs.'

He opened his mouth to argue, but she narrowed her gaze and kept talking.

'When things got messy, you left. Hardly helpful.'

His rebuttal died because she was right.

'You said she pulled you into one of her visions? Was the viscount there? Or the viscountess?'

Thomas hadn't given any specifics about the vision. Rowan might know the truth, but he wasn't ready to share it aloud. He certainly didn't want Lachlan to hear the shameful secret he had guarded for so long. 'No. It wasn't about them. It was... a memory from my past.'

Rowan's mouth parted and her grey eyes darkened to the blue of a stormy sea. 'I see.'

Thomas wished he could say the same. It obviously meant something that Clio was able to see his memories, but while Rowan seemed to know, he didn't think she would share any information with him.

She began pacing again. A sickly plant in the corner of the room swayed towards her every time she drew near it, like a sunflower following the arc of the sun. Noticing, she paused and spared Lachlan a scathing look. 'Why have plants if you aren't going to take care of them?' She reached out and touched the wilted spider plant. Instantly, it turned from yellow to lush green, the fronds plumping before their eyes.

Lachlan brushed aside her criticism. 'Rowan, what are you thinking? What did Ellie see?'

Rowan paused, and Thomas would have grabbed the woman by the shoulders and shaken the answers from her if he could have done more than twitch his pinkie. If Clio's life was at risk, Thomas would tear the bloody ghosts out of the ether where they hid and destroy them with his own hands before he would let them hurt Clio.

'Nothing was clear to Ellie. Perhaps her closeness to Clio inhibits her sight. But she knew Clio was in danger. No doubt from this Berty. And her destiny, whatever that might be, is inescapable. I nearly had to cast a binding spell to keep Ellie and Helena in the house. They were determined to find Clio. But fighting against fate only guarantees failure.' She speared Lachlan with a heavy gaze.

Thomas shook his head. 'I have to go back. I never should have left her. I was running when I should have stayed.' He stood, belatedly realising he had been released from whatever power had held him. Rowan grabbed his arm, halting him.

The world stopped spinning on its axis as everything went perfectly still. Lachlan was frozen by his desk. A fly hung in midflight. Thomas felt the strain of the universe as it flexed to be free.

Rowan's voice deepened and vibrated in the marrow of his

bones. 'You are part of it, Thomas Grey. For good or bad, I cannot say. But you have a role to play in this.'

When Clio touched him, his skin flamed, but with Rowan, everything went still. His heart barely beat. Air slowly seeped from his lungs. He started to pull away, but she held firm.

'Whatever you think ails you cannot be cured. You are not broken, therefore you can't be fixed.'

Anger pulsed through him, bringing with it strength. Rowan was tearing away his shields and poking the raw flesh beneath. Clio didn't have control when she was pulled into his memories and saw beyond the shield he so carefully erected, but her aunt knew exactly what she was doing. He ripped his arm free. Heat and life slammed through his system once more as time restarted.

'I'm leaving now.'

He spared Lachlan a glance before quickly walking out of the office, racing through the narrow corridors, down the stairs, and out the back to Scotland Yard where he hired a hack to take him to the train station.

*I am coming, Clio. You have a long and happy future ahead of you. And I'll be damned if anyone tries to take that away.*

Himself included. Rowan's words wrapped like chains around his heart, squeezing tight. He hated that she spoke what he already knew. What was broken within him could not be fixed. And he would never damn Clio to such a life. But neither would he step aside and let anyone hurt the woman he loved.

\* \* \*

Clio did not expect to see Thomas in the morning room as many of the guests gathered for a late breakfast. But neither did she think he would slink away in the middle of the night like a thief. She was shocked when Cynthia approached her, sympathy rife in her frank gaze.

She pulled Clio close and murmured gently in her ear. 'He left early this morning. He asked me to beg forgiveness of Lady Langley and tell her he was needed urgently in London for an unavoidable business commitment.'

'Balderdash! The cowardly bastard,' Clio hissed, uncaring if her coarse words shocked Cynthia.

On the contrary, the woman leaned back and looked long and hard at Clio. She might not have magical abilities, but Cynthia had the discerning intuition of a sister, and that could be just as power-ful. 'Something is going on between the two of you. You like him. Admit it!'

Clio opened her mouth to deny such an outlandish accusation, but she couldn't. Because Cynthia was right. Damn her. 'I have no interest in tying myself to any man,' she hedged. It was an unfortu-nate choice of words. She might not tie herself to Thomas, but she'd certainly let him tie her to any number of things. And now she was thinking about those leather straps holding her helpless while Thomas ravaged her with his mouth.

*Oh dear.*

The fire that had been lit to ward off the morning chill crackled and popped ominously.

Cynthia's eyes lit with mischief. 'Really? Then I suppose you wouldn't care to know that he is smitten with you.'

'Exactly. I mean, no, I don't care. Wait, what?'

Cynthia's eyes sparkled. 'He has fallen so hard, he doesn't know it yet. But he will realise soon.'

Clio blinked, but the room didn't disappear. This wasn't a dream. And Cynthia's words effortlessly dismantled her shields. She exhaled a long breath as her confusion gave way to something hollow and aching. 'He can't possibly...' But she couldn't say the word pulsing through her spirit with a resonant beat. Because she couldn't sacrifice her magic for love. Even if it was the bright, stunning, breathtaking kind of love written about in the silly romance books Ellie sometimes read aloud to them. Even if it was for a man full of courage and honour whose dark desires could make her melt and whose gravelled voice resounded in her soul. She wouldn't turn her back on her birthright just because she was stupid enough to fall in love with Thomas Grey. Her eyes widened as realisation dawned.

'Oh, dear goddess. I'm in love with him.'

'I know, darling.' Cynthia's smug smile did nothing to help.

Fear and joy were an odd combination, but both emotions filled her in equal measure. How could she have let herself fall? How could he have fallen just as swiftly?

*How could we have done anything else?*

It was as inevitable as the tide crashing against the shore, the wind whipping through the woods, the sun rising in the morning sky and setting in a blaze of colour.

Would he ask her to give up her craft? Would he twist her gifts into something he could use for his own gain?

*Never.*

The answer came unbidden, but powerful enough to cause a corresponding pulse of magic in her blood.

'You really are the perfect match for him, Clio. And now I get to hope my false cousin becomes my true sister.' Cynthia took both of Clio's hands and squeezed them as Lady Langley entered the room and spied them near the buffet table. 'Do not fret. His absence only proves how much he cares for you. He doesn't believe he's worthy, and so he thinks to spare you by leaving. But, if I know my brother, he also won't be able to stay away. He shall return. I dare say before the day is over.' She pressed her lips together as Lady Langley joined them, preventing Clio from asking Cynthia if she knew the truth. The real reason Lissa had divorced her brother.

*Oh, Thomas.*

But that thought was quickly followed by another.

*Selfish bastard!*

To leave without giving Clio a chance to process what she'd learned. Assuming she wouldn't want him because they couldn't have children together was arrogant and asinine... and completely understandable. Most women were raised to believe their one purpose was to provide their husbands with heirs. But Clio wasn't most women. She had been raised to believe her value was far more varied and complex. She was meant to create magic. To help others. To learn the facets of her own power and determine how best to use the gifts she'd been given for the good of all. Children were a far-flung idea that held no charm for Clio.

Her aunt never brought forth any offspring from her body, and yet, her home and her heart were overflowing with Clio, Ellie, and Helena. If one was meant to be a mother, nothing could stop that. And if one were not, the world was full of so many adventures, challenges, and meaning, surely a singular aspect of human existence could not contain the fullness of a person's worth.

Clio had spent most of the night searching her soul. She could only imagine how devastating it must be for Thomas to know he would never have children of his own, and she ached for his loss. But Clio did not want him to provide her with a family. She wanted him to *be* her family. What came from their union was a mystery she hoped they could unravel for many years to come. If only the stupid fool would realise, he brought so much more to her than just the promise of progeny. He brought the hope of embracing a partner without losing an integral part of herself.

*He is the only man I could ever tie myself to, body and soul.*

And he was gone.

*So, I must solve this case and go back to London to find the idiot.*

Lady Langley pulled her from her spinning thoughts. 'Cynthia, Clio. Have you heard the terrible news? Poor Thomas had to leave our jolly party for something as dreary and dreadful as business.' She rolled her eyes. 'Never mind. We shan't let his rotten luck ruin our day. Today promises sunny skies. Isn't that marvellous? The duke is determined to take the gentleman hunting, so I've organised a picnic. It will be such a lark! Once they're done shooting their guns at the poor deer, we can all eat al fresco!'

The rest of the morning was spent in a loud and lengthy breakfast, then watching the men ride off on their horses while the ladies returned to their rooms to ready themselves for what promised to be a bright, but frightfully cold, outing. One Clio had no intention of joining.

The entire house would be empty, save for the servants and Miss Anna. It was the perfect opportunity for Clio to reach out to the two ghosts haunting the manor.

A half-hour before the women were set to depart, Clio sent a note to their host explaining that she had been afflicted with a sudden megrim and, begging forgiveness, would need to remain in her room.

Not five minutes passed before Cynthia arrived.

'Lady Langley sent me to check on you. Are you well? Is this because Thomas left? Please don't let it worry you. He will be back. I swear it.'

Clio did her best to look pale and tragic. 'Not at all. I'm sure it's just all the excitement of the past few days. I shall stay here and rest. I'll be feeling much better by dinner.'

Cynthia frowned, clearly unconvinced.

'Balderdash!' Sir Robin supplied helpfully from Clio's shoulder.

Raising a brow at the bird, Cynthia nodded. 'My thoughts exactly.' She gave Clio a long, rather assessing look. It was a shame she hadn't been born with magic in her blood. Cynthia had all the qualities necessary to be a powerful witch. 'I shall come and check on you the moment we return.' She leaned over where Clio was reclining on the settee next to her window. Giving her a fragrant hug, she pressed a kiss to Clio's cheek and ran a finger over Sir Robin's sleek head, then was gone.

Clio scowled at Sir Robin. 'You are *my* familiar. Need I remind you? You side with me.'

He clacked his beak in a silent rebuttal, fluffed his feathers, and hopped to the edge of the settee.

She watched until the ladies all trundled down the gravel drive. The weather was turning, and the bright sun that greeted them at breakfast now played hide-and-seek with clouds promising mid-winter snow. Clio wondered if the picnic was going to be cut short because surely Lady Langley wouldn't subject herself to such indignities as chapped fingers and a red nose.

She made haste as the skies darkened. Patting her shoulder, Sir Robin accepted her invitation. 'Come, Sir Robin. We have some ghosts to interview.'

Taking the northern stairs, she ascended to the third floor. The hall had no windows, and the lamps had not been lit. With a wave of her hand, Clio solved that problem. Not wanting to disturb Anna, but feeling the closer she was to the girl, the better chance Clio had of convincing the ghosts to speak with her, she walked slowly down the corridor, reaching out with her magic.

The door to her right creaked open. It was pitch-black inside with all the shutters closed.

She paused as her skin tingled and sparked. Calling forth her witchflame, she held her palm in front of her and peered inside the empty room. Three desks sat in the centre with a blackboard attached to the far wall. It was a schoolroom, but it looked abandoned. Miss Anna's education must not be on Lady Langley's list of priorities.

As Clio turned in a slow circle, inhaling dust and the musty smell of unused furniture, chalk scratched over slate, drawing her attention to the board. Letters were being carefully written by an invisible hand.

*M. U. R. D. E. R.*

Clio exhaled and rolled her eyes. 'Yes. I know you were murdered. This is no time to be dramatic. It's hardly productive. Show yourself. I am here to help, but you must be willing to speak with me.'

Dust motes shimmered in the blue flame flickering on her palm. Slowly, a now-familiar image appeared: Viscount Beachley, his silvery eyes full of such sadness. Clio's fire sputtered in the suddenly frigid air as he solidified into a corporeal form.

'Who did this to you?'

'Blasted Berty and his damned selfishness.' His voice was a rasping whisper, common with most ghosts, and his eyes looked through her at a vision she couldn't see. The surprise of hearing him talk was quickly replaced with greater shock at what he said.

Dear God. Did he just tell her the name of the killer?

Clio took a step closer. 'Did Berty kill you? Did he kill the viscountess as well?'

The viscount had a long face. It twisted and contorted as rage replaced his sorrow. He moved faster than she could track. One moment, he was by the blackboard. The next, he was in front of her, screaming. He reached for her, and she stumbled back.

Sir Robin flapped his wings, his talons striking at the ghost, who threw up ashen arms to protect himself from the raven's attack.

'Clio!'

The dark growl could only belong to one man. Thomas had returned.

The heat within her grew molten as her witchflame flared.

Falling back, tears streaked down the ghost's cheeks like silver drops.

Thomas came to her side and reached for her hand. His eyes locked onto the viscount as he shimmered and faded into the shadows.

## 20

Thomas blinked several times, but it didn't change the fact he'd just seen a dead man's spirit. He turned to Clio, his hand squeezing hers tight.

Her amber eyes glowed in the dark room. She still held the witchflame in her free hand, and it washed them both in indigo.

'Are you well?' It was the question he seemed to always be asking her. The question that hounded him on his trip back to Blackthorn Manor. The only question that really mattered.

Clio swallowed, then nodded her head.

'When I arrived and the footman told me the guests were all gone, save you, I knew you must be up here.'

'You may have abandoned the case, but I still have a murder to solve.'

It was a deliberate jab, and he deserved it. But that didn't stop him from wanting to engage in battle. 'Is this case worth risking your life? I've seen what that ghost can do to you, Clio.'

'He is not the one we need to fear. He is angry and confused, but he isn't guilty of murder. And he just told me who is.' Her eyes flashed with excitement and the thrill of the hunt. Thomas was inti-

mately acquainted with that exact emotion. He felt it every time he
looked at Clio.

'Who?'

'Berty.' She spoke triumphantly. 'And with everyone gone, this is
the perfect time to search his rooms.' As she spoke, sleet lashed
against the window. 'But we must hurry. I can't imagine Lady
Langley will suffer through a frozen luncheon. My guess is the party
will be returning sooner than planned.'

There were several other things Thomas would much rather
search while they had a moment of privacy. The inside of Clio's
mouth with his tongue. The soft skin at the hollow of her throat.
The depths of her soul. The edges of her heart. The distance
between now and forever with her by his side for the entire
adventure.

But she was right. This was the best chance they had of poking
around Berty's room and seeing what kind of creatures scuttled out
from the shadows.

*Surely, there is time for one kiss?*

He leaned closer, and when she did not pull away, he pressed
his lips against hers. His tongue sought the seam of her mouth. She
opened, granting him access, and triumph swelled. He groaned as
she wrapped her hand around his neck and pulled him harder
against her. She was just as desperate for him as he was for her.
Thank God.

She nipped his bottom lip with sharp teeth. He gripped her
bottom, his fingers digging into the fleshy globes. He loved how she
overfilled his palms.

'I should never have left.' He pressed kisses down the side of her
neck, inhaling rosemary and bergamot. The scent of home to
him now.

'No. You shouldn't have.' Clio's angry words contradicted her
questing fingers as she tugged his cravat free, then began unbut-

toning his shirt. 'And I am very cross with you.' She pressed an open-mouth kiss against his throat, and Thomas was certain his soul caught fire.

Pushing her backwards until her bottom hit the desk, he sank to his knees, needing to taste the spice of her desire. He reached under her gown, his hands sliding up her legs and parting them. The crisp tangle of curls at her apex guided him to her slick folds beneath. He slid his finger into her tight channel, and she arched like an electric current ran through her body.

'You are so wet for me, Clio.'

She furrowed her brow. 'Is that good?'

When he touched her, she burned so hot, he forgot she was still innocent in so many ways. He let his hand slip from under her skirt, and he sucked her sweetness from his finger. The flare of arousal in her eyes nearly undid him. He wanted nothing more than to bury his mouth between her thighs and feast. But he wouldn't be able to stop at just his mouth on her slick flesh. He wanted more. He wanted everything. And he wasn't sure Clio was ready to give him her maidenhead. Certainly not in a dusty schoolroom, bent over a child's desk. Not when there was still so much to say between them. Not until he was certain she understood what he could give her, and more importantly, what he could not. He stood and took three large, painful steps away from her. 'We must talk.'

She looked from his chest to his eyes. 'Later.'

A smile curled his lips. So stubborn. So confident in her desires. She was a wonder. 'Now. Will you come to my room?'

Clio huffed out a breath. Sir Robin, who had settled on a chair near the chalkboard, cawed. Clio resettled her skirts and patted her shoulder for the bird to resume his perch. 'No.'

Hope, bright and fragile, cracked in his chest, cutting his heart with its sharp edges.

Clio's smile was so earnest, so beautiful, even in the midst of his pain, he couldn't breathe. 'First, we must search Berty's room. Then I shall come to your room, and we can talk. I have things to say to you too, Thomas Grey.'

\* \* \*

Clio and Thomas learned several things about Berty. He kept a deck of cards with crudely drawn naked women next to his bed. His clothing had all been newly purchased, no doubt when he received an influx of wealth from his inheritance. And he had a penchant for peppermint drops. He kept bags of them everywhere. But they could not find any evidence pointing to the fact he murdered his cousin.

As bad luck would have it, the shivering picnickers arrived back at the manor just as Clio and Thomas were exiting Berty's room. Not far behind them were the gentlemen, who had been unlucky in their hunt and were far more interested in warming their outsides by the fireplace and their insides with whisky and port than staying in the winter weather.

Lady Langley declared the entire day a disaster that could only be remedied with parlour games for the ladies and billiards for the men as angry sleet turned to soft snow falling in delicate flurries.

Seeing no polite way to excuse herself, Clio accepted she would have to wait until the guests were dressing for dinner to sneak into Thomas' room. He seemed equally frustrated and gave her a smouldering look before following the duke, Berty, and the rest of the gentlemen into the billiards room. Perhaps he would get a chance to speak with Berty. The man might inadvertently reveal something that could help their investigation, though Clio hated that she couldn't lead the conversation herself.

Her bad luck continued when, after the games had concluded and the guests were returning to their rooms to prepare for dinner,

Lady Langley caught her arm and insisted she join Cynthia and herself in the duchess' suite.

'My lady's maid is so talented with hair. I can't wait to see what she will do with all of yours!'

*Drat! Now our conversation must wait until after dinner.*

As it turned out, Lady Langley wasn't wrong. Clio sat and watched in fascination as the clever young woman with fingers as nimble as a nymph sculpted her long, black tresses into a masterpiece.

'I told you, Penelope is so clever. Now, tell me, Clio, have you set your cap for any of the gentlemen here? I know my cousin isn't as young and handsome as your own, but he certainly comes with a large fortune and would make a profitable match, if not an altogether pleasant one. He really is a dreary man. Poor Arthur is probably rolling in his grave knowing his title and fortunes have gone to the one person he despised above all others.' Lady Langley sipped from a goblet of wine that a maid had been keeping full since they arrived in the duchess' room. Clio would guess the poor girl had been given strict instructions by Lady Langley to ensure her glass never emptied. But if that loosened the duchess' already lax lips, who was Clio to argue?

Cynthia gave Clio a look in the glass as her own maid brushed out her mahogany locks until they shone.

'I wonder why your brother had such a dislike for the man.' Clio tried to keep her tone careless and light.

The duchess looked at Clio and tapped the side of her nose with a gloved finger. 'It's hardly done to speak ill of the dead.'

She held her breath, waiting. Because clearly, Lady Langley was eager to do just that.

'Arthur came to me, not long before his... untimely demise. We had all gathered for a Yuletide feast. Here, as I recall. One of those dreadful family affairs so regrettably unavoidable at Christmas.

Berty was here as well. He came slinking into my room, wanting money of all things.' Lady Langley shook her head as her cheeks flushed from either wine or indignation at being asked for such a gauche favour.

Cynthia turned her head sharply. 'Berty asked you for money?'

Lady Langley threw back her head and laughed. 'No, not Berty, silly. Arthur. I told him in no uncertain terms, any financial decisions were made by my husband, the duke, and he would have to go to him.'

'Did he?' Clio watched the duchess carefully in the looking glass, not wanting to miss any slight tell.

Lady Langley lifted her chin. 'I wouldn't know. The duke and I do not speak of such things.'

*I doubt you speak of anything with the poor man.*

Deflated, Clio would have slumped back in her seat, but the maid tugged insistently on her hair, so Clio stiffened her spine.

A small, haughty smile tilted the duchess' wine-stained lips. 'But Berty isn't quite so reserved. You might have seen how he can be when he's in his cups. Lush of a man.' As she said this, she gestured with her wine glass, slopping crimson over the cushion of her chair.

The maid in charge of keeping her cup full rushed forward to dab at the stain. Lady Langley waved her away.

'He was livid that night. Drank far too much whisky and nearly came to fisticuffs with Arthur. The viscountess packed up her things, and she and Anna left that very night. She said she wouldn't subject her child to such violence.' Lady Langley sniffed. 'She was never a pleasant woman, but she was devoted to poor Anna. I was shocked they came at all, as the dear girl was so sick. But then, I'm sure my brother insisted. The viscountess spent nearly the entire time in the nursery with Anna. I told her she should come down and enjoy herself, let the poor little lamb rest, but she wouldn't hear of it. That's how I know she is no longer with us. Nothing would keep her away from that girl except the Devil himself.' Lady Langley blinked a few times, then turned to Clio, her eyes bright. 'Your hair is divine. I shan't get any attention tonight.' Her face soured as if realising the flaw in her plan. 'We shall sit you at the end of the table.' She brightened once more. 'Come, ladies.'

Clio's head was spinning with the information Lady Langley sloshed around as easily as her wine. She needed to speak with Thomas about more than just their relationship, or what she hoped might become a relationship.

As she descended to dinner in a peacock-blue evening gown with black fleur-de-lis embroidered over the skirt and bodice in a bold pattern, Thomas caught her in his emerald gaze. Every inch of her exposed skin heated.

Lady Langley stepped away from her. 'Goodness! I must speak with someone about opening a few windows. It's sweltering.' The enterprising duchess spied Thomas as he made his way towards them and intercepted him before he could reach Clio.

'You've been a very naughty boy, leaving today without telling any of us. But as you've returned so quickly, I shall forgive you by allowing you to escort me to dinner.' Lady Langley swiftly secured Thomas' arm. True to her word, she made sure Clio sat at the opposite side of the room, and the duchess managed to keep Thomas engaged for the rest of dinner. When the men joined the ladies after their port and cigars, Berty and the duke trapped Thomas on the far side of the room in a conversation she could only hope was revealing much of Berty's intent to kill his doomed cousin. Clio, not generally a patient woman, had to content herself with Cynthia's company until the evening's festivities ended and she could escape.

She sent the maid away, assuring the girl she could manage her own toilet that night and making sure Sir Robin was settled behind a newly procured screen after explaining how she'd stupidly placed the screen far too close to the fire and it had caught alight. She had important matters to discuss with Thomas and decided it best to do so fully clothed. But as she listened at her door for the sound of him moving down the hall and into his room, a chill descended.

A glowing shimmer at her shoulder quickly brightened into the hazy image of Viscount Beachley.

'Please. You must come quickly. It's Anna.' Viscount Beachley's raspy whisper was a desperate plea. His ghostly face disappeared as the flickering light played beneath the crack in her door. He was waiting for her in the deserted hall as she slipped out of her room. The wooden floor was cold on her stockinged feet. She almost turned back to retrieve her slippers, wake Sir Robin from his feathery dreams, and hopefully dally long enough for Thomas to join them, but Viscount Beachley already began floating towards the eastern staircase.

'Please. Hurry.' His smoky words echoed down the hall.

Clio had no choice but to follow him, fear for Anna tightening her chest. Would Berty try to hurt the girl? Anna could place him at her home the night her parents were murdered. Eliminating her as a witness would ensure Berty's safety. Perhaps even now, he was making his way up the southern staircase in the family wing, intent on eliminating the last witness to his dastardly crimes. Clio hastened her steps, flying up the stairs and across the third floor until Viscount Beachley hovered at the nursery door.

Not waiting for him, Clio opened the door, stepped inside the room, and froze.

Violet Beachley, was helping Anna put on a child's winter coat. The viscountess was very much alive as both she and her daughter turned with twin expressions of horror to stare at Clio and the ghost.

## 21

Lifting a grey arm and pointing his charcoal finger at the viscountess, the ghost screamed.

'Murderer!'

Anna cowered behind her mother, her eyes wide with fear. 'I told you, Mother! I told you Papa wouldn't let us leave.'

Violet's face whitened with fear, but she pushed Anna behind her and straightened her shoulders. 'You can't hurt us any more, Arthur. I killed you once. I can do it again.'

The ghost's laughter was a cold and terrifying thing. Chills skated up Clio's spine as gooseflesh broke out over her arms and legs.

'You can't punish the dead. We are already suffering for our crimes.' Arthur turned to Clio, grabbed her wrist, and held her tight enough to leave a bruise. 'Kill her. You must avenge me. You promised to help. She murdered me! Make her face judgement.'

Clio tried to pull free, but his grip was too powerful.

'I won't.' She kept her voice strong and steady. 'Murdering her will not help you find peace.'

'I don't want peace. I want revenge,' he rasped, yanking hard on her wrist, pulling her close and gripping her throat with his other hand. As he began to squeeze, Clio saw stars. His silver gaze held her in thrall. Her magic stalled in her chest, the flame flickering, starved of oxygen as her lungs began to scream for air. She could barely hear him over her pounding heart. 'I can't touch her. But I can hurt you. I can kill you. And I will do it if you don't follow my command.' His harsh promise seeped into her like frigid water, bringing with it the icy guarantee of being forever trapped as a spectre. Not of this world, but not able to leave.

'I don't follow anyone's command but my own,' Clio gasped. *And Thomas' on very special occasions.* The mere thought of him pitched her into a panic. What if she never saw him again? What if she died tonight and he never knew how much she loved him? Her heart beat madly as she tried to think. She should have told him sooner. The moment he arrived, she should have put aside her fear and made him see how very much she adored him, just as he was, with no changes. She closed her eyes and imagined his face. If she were going to die this night, she wanted the last thing she saw to be him.

'Let her go!' Thomas' deep voice resonated in her imagination. It felt so real. As if she'd conjured him from thin air.

The unmistakable caw of Sir Robin pulled her from the edge of darkness. She forced her eyes open, and Arthur was no longer looking at her. His deathly grip fell away as he covered his head, protecting himself from the talons of her raven as Sir Robin once more attacked. Perhaps it was his connection to Clio as her familiar, or some mystical blessing from the fates, but whatever the cause, Sir Robin was able to pierce the viscount's ghostly skin. Viscount Beachley swung his arm blindly, hitting the bird as Sir Robin descended. Feathers flew. Sir Robin careened wildly across the room. He landed with a thunk near Anna's skirts. The girl screamed.

But the bird was only stunned. He hopped to his feet, blinking rapidly and fluffing his feathers, his head cocked to the side.

Clio felt a moment of relief before the viscount reclaimed her attention. He lowered his arms, and silver dripped from his face where black claw marks marred his once-perfect skin.

'I will kill you both. You first, witch.' He moved with inhuman speed, but before he could reach her, Thomas was at her side, gripping her hand in his.

The heat from his palm seeped into her as she took a ragged breath. She filled her lungs, and with it, her flame renewed, heating her chest. A dome of light surrounded them. As the viscount slammed into it, he was thrown backwards, his face twisting in rage.

'No!' He turned to Violet and Anna, moving towards them. 'This is all because of you!' He pointed a grey finger at his wife, the hatred in him creating a pulse of energy that struck out like a bolt, striking near Violet's feet and leaving a charred scar on the wooden floor. The viscount's eyes lit with surprise, then a manic kind of joy. He flung his rage once more, this bolt striking Violet in the belly. She cried out and doubled over.

'Oh, dear goddess.' Clio watched in horror as the viscount laughed in glee. He was somehow able to channel his fury into power. She'd never seen anything like this before. But she'd never encountered a ghost with such malevolent energy pulsing through his spirit.

'You couldn't just let me kill her.' The viscount threw another bolt of energy, this one barely missing Anna. 'I'll finish what I started. And then I'll bring you to this side, Violet. I'll make you pay for what you did for all eternity. You'll never escape me.'

'What is happening?' Thomas jolted forward, but Clio tightened her grip. She didn't know how to defeat the viscount, but she knew they needed to stay together.

She lifted her free hand, their combined power lighting a blue flame in the centre of her palm. Furrowing her brow, she changed the flame's form into an arrow. With a flick of her eyes, it flew, embedding itself into the viscount before he could launch another attack on his wife and daughter.

He howled a chilling scream and turned, the arrow flickering and then dissolving. But it achieved her goal of claiming the ghost's attention.

His silver gaze narrowed on Clio. 'I thought you could help me. But I don't need you to avenge me. Not any more.' The viscount threw a ball of black, roiling rage that crashed into Clio's shield, shattering the dome.

She couldn't destroy the viscount. Her oath to do no harm held true for all, even the poisonous spirit of a dead madman. But she could contain him.

She'd never attempted such powerful magic alone. Thomas tightened his grip, squeezing her fingers and reminding her he was right there with her. She didn't have her coven, but she had him, and he was somehow fuelling her magic.

'Thomas, we are going to bind him.' She needed something to hold the ghost. A vessel to contain his soul. Her eyes caught on the doll clutched in Anna's arm.

Sir Robin needed no instructions. He hopped over to the girl, grasping the doll in his claws and winging towards the ceiling. Anna's eyes widened as her arms fell limply to her side. In a flurry of black feathers, Sir Robin returned to Clio, dropping the doll at her feet. She picked it up, letting her magic fill the doll with a blinding light.

Resuming his position on her shoulder, Sir Robin clacked his beak. 'Bastard!' But this time, he wasn't talking about Thomas.

'By air, earth, water, and fire, I bind Arthur's spirit to this doll.' Clio's voice rang like a bell, resonant with power.

The viscount snarled. His chest expanded as he pulled darkness from the shadows of the room.

'By air, earth, water, and fire, I bind you here to do no harm.'

Muttering his own curse, the viscount held out his hands, and the air between them began to bubble and boil like heated tar.

'By air, earth, water, and fire, in this doll, you shall remain until you choose to leave this plane.' She pushed her power into the spell, willing the words to wind around him like ivy.

Arthur lifted his hands, the sphere of black power hovering. 'You will die screaming, witch.'

Clio repeated the spell, Thomas joining her. His deep voice lent power to her own as the viscount threw his vicious wrath in a jagged sphere of rage.

Clio countered his attack, launching her own blue spear of power that flew true and straight through the ball and into his stomach.

Arthur's volley was aimed at her chest. Her spear did not stop the ball's trajectory, but she hoped it might lessen the blow.

Thomas stepped in front of her, absorbing the orb. His body arced as if electrified. His hoarse cry ripped something in Clio.

Thomas fell to his knees.

The viscount pulled the spear free; it disappeared in his hands. He began muttering once more, weak but intent on his mission.

Fear and love amalgamated in the crucible of Clio's heart. She needed to help Thomas, but the viscount had turned to his wife and Anna. He knew his time was running short, but he would kill them both before Clio could stop him.

'Finish this,' Thomas rasped, sinking to the floor, his body deathly still.

Fear for Thomas transformed into a clear purpose: contain the enemy. Save her love. Live happily ever after.

She lifted her head, narrowing her gaze on the viscount and

calling forth another column of fire that she transformed into a whip. 'You will not hurt them!' Cracking her power, she flung the whip's sparking tongue at the viscount, wrapping the flame around him. 'By air, earth, water, and fire, I bind you, Arthur Beachley.' She repeated the chant; the whip tightened.

The viscount screamed. He tried to claw at the band of fire holding him captive, but the flames surged, blackening his ghostly skin.

Anna covered her ears, curling into a ball as her mother shielded her daughter with her body.

'Now!' she called to Sir Robin, flinging the doll up. The raven flew after it, catching it in mid-air and dropping it into the blaze engulfing the viscount. Swirling flame and smoke spiralled around the ghost until he became part of the inferno, his spirit dissolving into the fire that spun and crackled, sucking into the heart of the doll, a storm of power and fury imploding into the fluff-stuffed toy.

The doll dropped to the floor, spinning to a slow halt and pulsing brightly before it dulled back to worn cotton and wool.

Clio collapsed next to Thomas, her hands cradling his head. He was so still. His eyes were closed, and she couldn't tell if his chest was expanding with breath.

She pushed her heat into his cold body and willed his eyes to open. 'Don't you leave me. I just found you. Don't you dare die on me.'

Hot tears streamed down her face. She pressed a kiss to his mouth, willing him to respond. When he didn't, she buried her head in his chest, pounding his solid muscle with her fists.

'You come back to me. Right now. You come back!' This man had become her world. She refused to let the fates take him. He was hers, and she was his. They were destined for each other. 'I love you, Thomas Grey.'

His chest shifted beneath her. The resounding thud of his heart vibrated through her body as if it were her own as his lungs filled with air.

'Yes, that's it. Breathe.'

'Always so bossy.' His rough voice was the most beautiful sound Clio had ever heard. 'But how could I refuse the command of such a powerful witch?'

She pulled back, wiping the tears from her cheek with the back of her hand. She must look a mess, but she didn't care. Thomas was alive.

His mouth curled in a wry smile as he tried to sit up. 'I had much different plans for us this evening.'

She leaned forward, her hand flattening on his chest, feeling the steady beat of his heart. A heart she knew was now inextricably linked with her own. She just needed to convince him of this truth. 'Bloody ghosts. Always ruining plans.'

He buried his hand in her tangled mass of hair and pulled her to him. 'Are you well?'

She couldn't stop the burst of laughter. 'It is I who should be asking you that.'

'You are with me. How could I be anything else?'

She pressed her lips against his, not caring that the viscountess and Anna saw.

\* \* \*

After fortifying Thomas with one of Clio's tonics and a healthy splash of whisky, fetching tea for Violet and a slice of seed cake for Anna, and settling the girl in bed with a special cup of hot chocolate Clio had infused with a dash of calming lavender oil and a little something extra, it was time to hear what really happened the night Viscount Beachley died.

Violet refused to leave her daughter's side, so they waited until

Anna fell asleep, aided by Clio's magic. Sir Robin perched on the headboard, faithfully watching over the girl as Violet stroked her wispy, blonde hair with a shaky hand.

'I never believed in ghost stories. Or anything I couldn't see. There's enough evil in the world without needing to invent new forms of it.' A tear streaked down Violet's cheek.

'Will you tell us what happened?' Thomas' deep voice was a gentle rumble, soothing Clio's frayed nerves.

Violet looked from the tea to Clio. 'I killed him.'

Clio forced her face to remain neutral. Judgement would only silence Violet. Besides, she needed all the facts before she concluded guilt or innocence. 'All right. Can you walk us through that evening?'

'Are you not appalled? Disgusted? At least shocked?' Violet's lip trembled as her thumb rubbed rapidly up and down the delicate handle of her teacup.

'Of all the astounding things that have occurred tonight, surely this revelation is the most banal of the lot. You have not hurled accusations at me yet for what you have seen me do. I would like to extend the same courtesy to you and better understand the why of it all.' Clio was all too aware that she had revealed her powers to yet another person not of her kin or coven. Given the circumstances, it would be difficult for the viscountess to make claims against Clio, but Clio still appreciated Violet's seeming willingness to accept Clio's powers.

'So, if I don't accuse you of being a witch, you won't accuse me of being a murderess... even though that is exactly what we are?'

Clio nodded. 'Exactly.'

Violet waited, as though testing Clio's resolve. When Clio remained silent, Violet seemed to reach a decision. She sipped her tea. 'All right. I shall tell you, though I don't expect mercy.'

'We all need a little mercy.' Thomas spoke quietly.

Violet turned her gaze to him, then back to Clio. 'You are the strangest investigators I've ever met.'

'Strange bastard!' Sir Robin interjected helpfully.

'All three of you.' Violet eyed Sir Robin before settling into her tale. 'I knew when I married Arthur that he needed my dowry far more than my affections.'

Clio reached out to squeeze Violet's cold fingers. It wasn't just witches who needed protection from bad marriages. It was all women.

Violet cleared her throat and continued. 'When I became pregnant, I focused on our daughter and let him do as he pleased. Which, unbeknownst to me, was to continue gambling all our money away. I knew he was using Mrs Coggins to pawn the silver, paintings, anything he thought might hold value, but I had no idea how dire our situation truly was, or perhaps I just chose to remain ignorant because that was easier. I took to hiding my personal jewellery to try and keep it out of Mrs Coggins' grubby fingers.'

An image of the golden locket Sir Robin found flashed in Clio's mind.

'Then Anna became ill. When the specialist I hired told me he suspected arsenic poisoning, I didn't believe him. Who would want to poison our sweet Anna?'

'Surely not her father?' Thomas' emerald eyes widened in disbelief. 'How could a father even think of doing that to his child?'

Clio fell a little further in love with him. Something she predicted would continue to happen for the remainder of their days together.

Violet narrowed her gaze, her voice growing hard as the tea cooled. 'I thought the same. I suspected Mrs Coggins, in some effort to destroy our marriage, was going after Anna, but even that seemed incomprehensible. Then our solicitor stopped by when Arthur was out carousing at his club. He left papers for me to give to

Arthur. I thought they might be letters of debt, but it was something else entirely. Life-insurance policies for myself and Anna. I was confounded. Anna was ill, but surely, he didn't believe she would die.'

'He was going to cash in on the insurance policy?' Nausea, similar to when she had one of her visions, swirled in Clio's belly.

Violet caught Clio's gaze and held it. 'Berty came to collect on his debts, and I realised how deeply ruined we were. Arthur's motives became clear. He'd always cared more about his title and his comforts than his wife and child. Anna was a girl, after all. She couldn't carry on his name, so what use did she have other than to burden him with the need of a dowry? Killing us both was an easy solution. He could claim the insurance policies and stave off Berty, then remarry another poor, rich debutante who might be more easily cowed by Mrs Coggins. She was happy to help him in the task.'

Bile rose in Clio's throat. 'That is monstrous.'

'He was a monster.'

'So, you used his own weapon against him?' A hint of respect seeped through Thomas' careful question.

'I knew I needed to work quickly. He had to be stopped before Anna suffered any more harm. I thought cyanide would be faster than arsenic, though I wasn't sure about the dose. There was a large amount of it in the larder to rid us of rats, so I took some, knowing it wouldn't be missed.

'I told Arthur I wanted to apologise properly for fighting with him about Anna. That I was ready to accept her illness might not be curable. When Mrs Coggins brought the tea, I sent her away, telling her I would pour so we could have privacy. The way she looked at me.' A small smile curled the corners of Violet's mouth. 'I thought she'd kill me right then. But she nodded her head and walked away. I dosed his tea. I thought it would take a few hours, that he might die in his sleep, but the effects were almost immediate. And when he realised what I had done, he came after me.' She unbuttoned the high neck of her gown and pulled the material aside to show an angry scar.

'Dear goddess. He stabbed you?'

Violet rebuttoned her gown with shaky fingers. 'He tried. The cyanide stopped him before he completely succeeded. I ran, too terrified to think, knowing if they found us like that, my conviction would be certain. I was going to return for Anna, but the cut became infected. I found a doctor near the docks, though I doubt he ever went to medical school. He sewed me up as best he could, and I paid him for his service and his silence. I spent the next few weeks in a rented room, sure I would die of fever. I thought God was punishing me for my crimes.'

Thomas shook his head. 'Protecting your daughter and yourself from a man intent on killing you is hardly a crime.'

Violet laughed, but there was no joy in the sound. 'I doubt the House of Lords will agree with your reasoning, sir.'

'They won't ever hear this tale,' Clio said, looking at Thomas for confirmation. When he nodded, she continued with a daring plan. 'We will go to Mrs Coggins and tell her what we know. Either she admits to "accidentally" poisoning Viscount Beachley's tea and thieving from the family, or we make the case that she was poisoning Anna, then killed Viscount Beachley outright when he discovered her crimes.'

Violet shook her head. 'She'll never do it.'

Clio smiled. 'She will if she wishes to avoid the hangman's noose.'

'But I killed Arthur. I deserve to pay for my crime.'

Thomas shook his head. 'In war, soldiers fight for many reasons. To claim more territory. To protect what is theirs. To find glory on the battlefield. But there is no cause more honourable than fighting to protect your child. You were in a battle, Lady Beachley. And you fought with courage and valour. How would it be justice to see you hang for protecting Anna?'

Violet opened her mouth, then closed it again. Tears glistened in her eyes as she inhaled a shaky breath.

*Holy Hecate. I shall fall forever if he keeps saying such lovely things.*

Clio pulled her thoughts back to the crisis at hand. 'Mrs Coggins would have killed you and Anna for far less worthy motives. You did what you had to do to protect your daughter, Violet. Now, let us protect you.'

Violet exhaled a shaky breath. 'All right. I put my fate into your hands.'

\* \* \*

It took the rest of the night and early evening to devise a plan. Though she nearly refused to leave Anna, they were able to convince Violet to return to London with Thomas as her escort and report directly to Superintendent MacDougal.

Violet would give him all the evidence he needed against Mrs Coggins and return to Lady Langley's post haste once arrests had been made. They would tell the papers that Superintendent MacDougal had been keeping her in protective custody the entire time to ensure her safety while seeking the evidence they needed to prove Mrs Coggins' guilt.

She only agreed if Clio promised to keep a close eye on her daughter while she was gone. A task imminently more pleasant than spending any more time with Lady Langley. Especially when the duchess learned Thomas had once more been called back to London on business.

It was an interminable six days, seven hours and thirteen minutes until Thomas and Violet were able to rejoin the house party. By that time, the scandal had blazed throughout England. Lady Langley was salivating to hear all the gory details while loudly proclaiming she never trusted the horrible Mrs Coggins, and Anna had completely won over Sir Robin.

Clio had just left Anna after a day of reading fairy tales, practising to be ravens – except for Sir Robin, who was already an expert – and pretending the floor was burning brimstone while needing to get from one side of the room to the other without touching it.

Clio needed to get ready for dinner, and Anna only let her go because Sir Robin stayed to watch over Anna. Clio's familiar understood the gravity of his assignment, and while Clio was sure he missed the treats Cynthia snuck him from the table, he was willing to make the sacrifice until Anna's mother returned.

She had just finished dressing and dismissed her maid when the door creaked open.

Thomas stood with the hallway light behind him. He still wore his greatcoat, and his boots were dusty with travel. He tapped his silver-tipped cane on the floor. She was reminded of the first time she saw him in Viscount Beachley's home. He was just as breathtakingly handsome as that fateful day, but far more dear to her heart.

'Finally,' she breathed before rushing across the room and claiming his mouth.

He sucked on her bottom lip, his teeth scraping over her skin as his fingers tugged deliciously at her hair.

It would be so easy to sink into the sensations. Lose herself in the heat of his touch. But after so many days, she still needed to speak with him first. She couldn't cross this threshold without making her intentions clear.

'Stop.' She pushed against his chest, and her heart melted when he immediately did as she asked, pulling back when it was clear everything in him wanted to push forward. This was why she would give him her heart. He was a man she could love without losing herself.

He was breathing heavily; his dark brow lifted in a silent question.

'I love you, Thomas Grey.' The words escaped before she knew she was going to say them. But every syllable resonated in her soul. No matter what happened this night, or every night in her future, she needed him to know that her admission days before hadn't been said out of desperation. Her love for him would endure when all else faded.

'I love you too, Clio. No matter what happens between us. You must know. I would tear the gods from their heavens, vanquish every ghost, destroy any devil who dared to hurt you.'

'I am so sorry you will never be able to have children.' A well of grief sprang up within her. Not for herself, but for Thomas.

His eyes grew glassy with unshed tears, and his throat bobbed as he swallowed. She didn't need Helena's gift to read his mind. Doubt dwelled there. And fear that she wouldn't want to be with him, no matter how much they might love each other.

She pressed on, needing him to hear her truth. 'But I am not sorry the fates have put us together.'

She watched expressions shift over him like a sunset. Surprise. Disbelief. Finally, tentative hope. 'You don't believe they have cursed you by having you waste your love on me?'

She laughed only to stop the tears. He had no idea how much she treasured him. But he was about to find out. 'Love is never wasted, Thomas. Have I ever told you what happened to my mother?'

It was an abrupt topic change. Thomas' mouth turned down as his gaze clouded with confusion.

'No.'

'She fell in love. When I was six and Ellie was only three.'

'Did your father know?'

Clio laughed. 'My father only knew my mother for a night. The same is true for Ellie's father. My mother knew she wanted children, but she never wanted a husband. So, she found men who could give her offspring and nothing more. Until she met Sebastian McClure.'

Thomas exhaled slowly. 'Was she happy with this man?'

'For a spell. She would leave us at Aunt Rowan's for days at a time to be with him. At first, I was happy because she was happy. But Aunt Rowan never approved. I heard them arguing about it the last time she left us. He wanted her to renounce her powers and leave us with Aunt Rowan. Start a new life with him in a different village.'

'So, she left you?'

The pain of her mother's rejection still burned in her chest. She never told anyone this story because those closest to her already knew and all others didn't deserve to know. Something about putting her deepest shame into words made it fresh again. But Thomas had welcomed her into the darkest corners of his heart. She owed him the same honesty.

Clio shifted her gaze away from his too-assessing stare. Despite what she said, the man was remarkably good at noticing details. 'She left me. And Ellie.'

'Clio...' Thomas' deep voice was so full of anguish for her, it was an unexpected balm for her aching soul.

She shook her head, knowing if she didn't tell the whole thing at once, she would never get the words out. 'That wasn't the worst of it. She rejected us, but she also rejected her magic. Her power. The pieces of herself that made Mother who she truly was. She told Aunt Rowan she would never practise her craft again. She used blood magic to bind her powers.'

'I don't understand.'

'Blood magic is ancient and results in the most powerful spells.

It requires sacrifice. She chose to sacrifice herself. To amputate her powers to be with Sebastian McClure. When I realised what she had done, I ran out to try and stop her. I grabbed onto her dress and begged her not to leave. She took my hands in her own, crouched down and told me, "True love demands yielding every part of yourself to the one you love". She said, one day, I would understand. And then she left.'

A hot tear tracked down Clio's face. Thomas brushed it away and she caught his hand, holding it against her cheek.

'I knew she was wrong. I knew it in the very marrow of my bones. And I swore that day, if love meant compromising myself, I would never fall in love.'

'But you've fallen in love with me. And now you must sacrifice any dream you had of children.' The hope in his eyes glimmered and died. 'I can't ask that of you. I won't.'

Taking his hand in her own, she offered a kiss to his palm. 'You don't understand. I didn't tell you about my mother because I feel like I'm surrendering a part of myself to be with you. I told you about her because I want something to be very clear between us.' Clio took a deep breath, pulling the heat from the room into her core and letting it strengthen her resolve before she exhaled slowly. 'I can't change that I am a witch. I won't give up my powers for you, or for anyone. If you asked it of me, I would walk away. I would *have* to walk away, because it is who I am.'

He blinked, quirked his head, then shook it as he processed what she said. 'I would never ask that of you. I love your magic because it is part of you.'

Joy swelled as Clio smiled. 'And that is why I can give you my heart. That is why we can create a future together. Because you aren't asking me to change who I am. And I am not asking you to change either, Thomas. I love every single part of you. The parts you're proud to show the world, like your stern frown,' she traced his lips, 'and your sharp mind,' her finger trailed up the side of his face to lightly brush over his forehead. 'And the parts you would rather keep in the shadows.' She rested her palm over his heart as her magic sizzled and sparked between them. 'No one part of you is less or more than the other. They are all important pieces of the man I find endlessly fascinating.'

He placed his hand over hers. 'You would make a life with me, knowing we could never have children of our own?'

'I will make a life with you, knowing that we will create a family. No matter what that family looks like or how many people... or ravens... it includes.'

He pulled her into his arms and held her tight against him. Her heart beat in tandem with his, their breaths aligned, and her fire flowed into him until they both glowed with pure light.

'Will you make love to me, Thomas? Will you claim me as your own and let me claim you as mine?'

'Always.'

In a move of strength that had her heart fluttering, Thomas swept her into his arms and walked to the bed. He set her down and layer by layer, stripped away her dress, corset, stays, and chemise, all the pieces that had been so carefully assembled, until she stood naked in front of him.

'I do believe we'll be late for dinner.' Clio couldn't stop her mischievous grin.

'With the to-do Violet's arrival caused, I doubt anyone will notice.' Thomas' smile was equally full of glorious wickedness.

Turning, she realised he was still in his coat while she stood naked in front of him. She shivered as her nipples grew hard with need. 'While I love you in this coat...' She pushed it off him and started on his buttons. 'I want you naked.' She was dexterous with preparing herbs and creating potions, but the intricacies of male fashion seemed to confound her. Thomas lent a helping hand as they undressed him together.

When Thomas pushed down his smalls, she couldn't stop herself from staring. He was just as large as he had been in her vision. Only now, he was looking at her. Fear glimmered. She understood the mechanics of what they were about to do. Aunt Rowan made sure the girls were well educated. But knowing the recipe for a potion was very different from bubbling it in the cauldron.

'Touch me.' His commanding tone helped. She didn't have to determine what to do. She only needed to follow his instructions.

Putting her flat palm against his ridged stomach, she marvelled at how different they were.

He took her wrist, guiding her hand lower. 'Touch all of me.'

She paused, and he let her go, giving her the power to explore at her own pace. Slowly, she ran a single finger from the thick root of his erection to the bulging head. His skin was softer than silk, hot and hard.

'Wrap your hand around me, Clio.'

She did as he asked, fascinated by the weight and heft. 'This is meant to fit inside me?' Doubt laced her voice with hesitation.

'When you are ready.'

She looked at him and bit her lip. Aunt Rowan said there could be pain the first time. Clio wasn't afraid of pain. She was afraid of losing this moment.

'Tell me what to do.'

# 22

Thomas had been thrust into a magical world where every dream he'd ever had was coming true. After what seemed an eternity apart, finally Clio stood in front of him, her creamy skin glowing. His fantasies of the past few days didn't compare to the headiness of this reality. Her lush body on display for him to watch, touch, pleasure, and claim. Because she already possessed him. Heart, body, and soul. That was certain. And this fiercely independent, powerful woman was asking him to lead her down a road that would irrevocably bind them together.

'Climb on the bed and lie on your back.'

Clio didn't hesitate. She followed his orders without question.

He joined her.

'If you want me to stop, tell me.'

Her eyes had grown heavy-lidded with desire. 'I don't want you to stop.'

Thomas smiled, her hungry gaze feeding his own needs. 'If you like something, tell me. If you don't like what I'm doing...'

'I will tell you. Honesty. Always.'

'Good girl.'

Something flared in her eyes. Arousal. Rebellion. She didn't want to be a good girl. Luckily, he liked her wicked.

'You have the most beautiful breasts.' He ran the back of his fingers over her nipple. The skin puckered into a point he knew tingled with burning need for more friction. She arched her back, wordlessly begging for something harder. 'What do you want me to do to these pretty nipples?' He leaned closer. 'Kiss them?' Saying the words against her tightening skin, he pressed his lips softly over one nipple, then the other.

'Yes,' Clio hissed. She squirmed beneath him.

'Suck them?' He followed his own advice, swirling his tongue over the ruched bud, sucking hard enough to make her cry out.

'Yes,' she demanded.

'Bite them?' He nibbled, then nipped as heat shimmered around them. Her body tightened like a string. He didn't need to touch her folds to know she was dripping. That her intimate muscles were clenching around nothing when they wanted to tighten around him.

'Tell me, where are you aching for me, Clio?'

She opened her beautiful mouth, but no words came out. Perhaps she didn't know them.

'Here?' he asked, trailing his fingers through her curls and teasing her entrance. 'In your sweet pussy?'

'Yes.'

'Tell me.'

'I want you in me...' She faltered.

He nipped her shoulder hard enough for her to hiss.

'That won't do. Tell me where.' His voice grew hard.

'In my pussy.'

Hearing the coarse word from her beautiful mouth had a surge of need sweeping through him. He ground his teeth together, willing his body to remain under control. He wanted to feel her fall apart before he let himself spend inside her.

'Soon. But first, I want you screaming my name, Clio.' He went to work, teasing her with soft kisses on her throat, rough hands on her breasts, gentle caresses over her sweetly curved belly, nips along her hip bones. 'Hold on to the headboard.'

When she quickly complied, he was rocked. To know such a fierce, independent woman so willingly followed his lead humbled him.

'Dear God, I will never cease worshipping you, Clio.'

He was determined to make her first time something she could treasure. And every time after this.

'Spread your legs.'

She glanced at him, her amber eyes flashing with wicked intention as she deliberately tightened her thighs.

Thomas lifted a brow and tsked. His witch wanted to play. He would give her what she wanted. Always.

Gripping her hip, he tilted her to get access to her luscious arse. Swatting her hard enough to sting, she arched. Sparks skittered over her skin like stars glittering in a midnight sky. Good God. Never before had it been easier to judge a woman's pleasure.

'Spread your fucking thighs, Clio.' One day, he would spank her properly until her pale skin turned pink with pleasure. But as she followed his instruction, his concentration broke. Her sweet lips were swollen and pink and dripping. His mouth watered for a taste. He gripped each thigh, making room for his shoulder as he licked a long, delicious swipe.

Pleasure burned at the base of his spine. His bollocks tightened as his cock grew even harder. Feasting on her, he speared her channel with his tongue before finding the sweet nub holding Clio's secrets. He nibbled and sucked, licked and laved until heat poured off Clio like a furnace. He knew she was close. Pushing one finger into her clenching channel, he continued to work her clitoris. She was so tight around him, he feared he might hurt her. Slowly, he fit a second finger, plunging in rhythm with his tongue. When he curled his fingers, coaxing her to climax, she writhed.

'Thomas!'

Her orgasm drenched his fingers and tongue, and need took over.

* * *

Clio was burning and she called forth the heart of her flame, wanting more, wanting everything.

'I want you, Thomas. Now. Please.' As someone who never begged for anything, Clio would have been appalled at her desperate plea if she wasn't so consumed with need.

'Tell me if you need me to stop.' He rose over her like a god, his body hard and chiselled, his mouth glistening with her pleasure, and his cock a steel length between them. But she didn't care if it hurt. She didn't care if he split her in two, separating her body from her soul; she just wanted him inside her, a part of her, fused together.

'I need you. All of you. Now.' It was her turn to command him. If he did not follow her orders, she would consume them both with her fire. And wasn't that a marvel. To know he could withstand her witch flame without burning. That it became part of him just as he became part of her.

He knocked her legs wider with his own, gripping her hips and tipping her pelvis. Her body still hummed from the blinding orgasm he delivered with his tongue and fingers. The head of his cock nudged her swollen entrance, and he paused.

She held his gaze, nodding as he pushed in slowly, stretching untried muscles. The burn was almost painful, but Clio was born from flame, and she welcomed him into her depths. Sweat dripped from his forehead, landing on her hip, searing her as he continued his slow, deliberate, determined assault on her senses. She clenched her muscles around him, her body pulling him deeper. Until he hit her barrier. He pulled out, just as slowly as he entered, scraping over raw nerves. A fresh rush of wet heat eased his movements.

'Are you sure?' His words were gravel, his eyes burning with need and fear and love.

'Yes,' she willed him to move. To make her his as he was already hers.

In one hard thrust, he breached her final barrier.

The pain blended with a blinding pleasure that sparked in her core, her nipples, the sensitive skin behind her knees, her clitoris. He filled her then held still. It was glorious and overwhelming and more than she could ever imagine. She tried to move, wanting more, wanting everything, but his body pinned her to the mattress.

'Wait, love. Let your body adjust.'

He pressed a soft kiss to her temple and like magic, her tight muscles slowly melted around his pulsing cock, acclimating to his size as they breathed each other's air in heavy gasps.

Brushing a palm over her breast, he kneaded the sensitive flesh. The sweet sensations echoed where her body embraced him. He dipped his head to suck on the tender tip, creating new sparks of need cascading through her body. With heartbreaking tenderness, he pulled out, dragging his heavy cock through her aching flesh and pushing back in, harder. With each thrust, pain ebbed, and pleasure flowed.

'Yes.' She changed the rhythm as he lunged deeper, tilting her hips to meet him, her legs wrapping around his waist, pulling him tighter.

He slammed harder, hitting a place that flashed white light through her body.

Her power pulsed and glowed beneath her skin, seeping into Thomas until they were twin flames, intermingled, separate and the same, feeding one another and growing hotter as she began to shatter around him.

'Come with me,' she demanded, letting go of the headboard, wrapping her arms around his neck and pulling him down, needing his weight to hold her steady.

His hips moved like a piston as he plunged deeper. Harder. His engorged flesh dragging against her swollen clitoris as he splintered her into a million pieces. But she didn't break alone. He fractured with her, melding together in a crucible of acceptance and desire.

'Clio!' His hoarse cry filled her as he froze, his cock growing harder within her, pulsing out his essence. She took what he gave her, giving him all of herself in return.

\* \* \*

Clio's spirit was floating somewhere in the ether. Slowly, it descended like a cloud as she became aware of Thomas' delicious weight on top of her. She buried her nose in his neck and inhaled soap, spice, and salt.

His low grumble vibrated against her chest. 'My God.'

A spark of joy fizzed within her.

'My goddess.' She snuggled closer, wanting to cocoon herself within his arms until she was ready to emerge, a new creature.

'Yes. You are. My goddess.' He pulled away, and she felt the loss of his heat. Standing, he padded naked to the bowl of water and pitcher set on her nightstand.

'What are you doing?' She quirked a brow and enjoyed the view of his powerful, naked body in the moonlight. His skin still glowing.

*I did that. We did that.*

Ellie's words came back to her: *'He provokes your magic. You can share your elemental power with him. Your abilities extend to him when they shouldn't.'*

Thomas provoked more than just Clio's magic. He provoked her trust. Her love. Her respect. She shared more than just her fire with him. She shared her body. Her heart. Her essence. And tonight, her power filled him just as he filled her.

*Spirit match. She will be impossible to live with when she finds out. But he is my match in every way. Heart, body, soul.*

When he came back to the bed, his emerald gaze burned into hers. 'Lay back and let me tend to you, Clio.'

How could she refuse such a charming request? She did as he asked, leaning back against the soft pillows as he gently spread her legs. He wiped the cloth over her thighs, starting with her star birthmark, cleaning the blood away. Her blood.

'We created magic between us. A blood oath,' Clio mused. 'The most powerful spell of all.'

Thomas paused in his ministrations. 'You said blood oaths aren't to be taken lightly.'

Clio bit her lip as he resumed cleaning her. The cloth was both cool and comforting on her heated flesh as Thomas wiped her intimate folds in gentle strokes. Echoes of the pleasure they shared rippled through her. 'They are not.'

'Lasting magic that once crafted, cannot be unravelled.'

'Yes.' She was finding it harder to speak as he pressed the linen against her with firm pressure. His gaze drifted lazily from where he worked, up her body like a caress, to finally meet hers. She'd never seen an emerald burn until now.

'What was woven together between us tonight is forever, Clio.'

Her heart was too full. The emotions overflowed and spilled out in salty tears. 'I am yours and you are mine. Whatever challenges we face, we face as one. Whatever burdens we bear, we carry together. And the joy we create will be ours alone.'

He gripped her hips and rolled them together, so she was on top of him. Clio's world spun as she felt him begin to grow hard beneath her. 'What of our pleasure? Can you take me again?' He raised a wicked brow.

She moved her hips, testing this new position. Her clitoris rubbed in a slow, wet slide over the ridge of his cock. It was heady to control their passion. She liked it. 'Can you take me again, Thomas Grey?'

Lifting her up, he positioned himself at her entrance and waited. 'I will take you forever.'

Clio sank down, impaling herself and revelling in the glory. She rocked slowly at first. His eyes locked on her breasts. She watched with him as they swayed with her movements. He covered them both with his large hands, kneading and pinching and increasing the sharp, sweet burn growing inside her. Her hips moved with greater purpose as she changed the angle. Just there. That incandescent spot that made her body sing. She found it again. And again. Grinding her hips in a slow circle, Thomas clenched his jaw, his gaze locked onto hers, his pupils blown wide. His hand slid from her breast to her waist, aiding her. She tilted her hips, nearly pulled completely off, then slammed down hard, crying out his name as sparks cascaded over her body and onto his. He held her tight against him, their worlds exploding together as he chanted her name like a spell. A love spell that would never break.

\* \* \*

*Two weeks later*

Thomas tugged on his cravat. He didn't remember his valet tying it quite so tight, and yet he could barely breathe. He was quite certain he might swoon in Rowan's front parlour, which would not do. He could hardly faint in the middle of asking Clio's aunt for permission to marry her niece. He was a Lieutenant General in Her Majesty's army, after all. The second son to an earl. By all accounts, a formidable gentleman.

A formidable gentleman who was seconds away from casting up his accounts on the Aubusson rug gracing Rowan's well-appointed front parlour.

'Sit. You look green around the gills, Lieutenant General Grey.'

He tried for a smile but was fairly certain it came out closer to a grimace. 'I am quite well, madame. I assure you.'

'Well enough to ask me for my niece's hand in marriage, I assume. For I can't think of any other reason for you to request an audience with me.' Rowan raised a chestnut brow at him, her grey eyes flashing ominously.

'Give the lad a moment to breathe, Rowan.' Lachlan sat next to the intimidating woman. The look she shot him was sharp enough to fell an Alderwood, but Lachlan only winked at her.

'You are absolutely right. I am here to ask for your permission to marry your niece.'

Rowan leaned forward, and a potted palm in the corner shivered. 'Do you love her?'

'Absolutely.' It was an easy answer.

'Do you accept her just as she is?'

'I accept that she is far more than I'll ever understand. And the only woman I'll ever want in this life.'

Rowan leaned back and the palm seemed to relax its leaves in a rustling sigh. 'Excellent answer, Grey. I can see why she is so enamoured.'

He couldn't stop the flush of heat across his cheek. 'Before you give me your answer, you must know, I will always provide Clio with a home, my love, my protection—'

'I'm quite certain she can protect herself.' Rowan crossed her arms, tapping a long finger irritably. 'Didn't she prove that not two weeks ago at the house party you both attended?'

Thomas inclined his head in acknowledgement. 'Indeed, she did. Yet, even if she does not need my protection, she shall still have it.'

'We don't question yer willingness to fight for the lass, Thomas. I've shared a battlefield with you, and I've met few men as fierce and determined as yerself.' Lachlan raised his snifter of whisky to his friend in a toast. But Thomas couldn't return his friend's gesture. Not until they understood exactly what he was offering, and what he could never provide.

'You must understand, while I would give Clio everything I have, there are certain things I cannot.' He held Rowan's gaze. Clio loved him despite knowing they could never create children together. Her willingness to accept him was like a healing balm spread over his soul, but still the scar tissue pulled. 'You told me that you cannot fix what is broken within me. So, you may already know that I will never be able to provide Clio with a family.' He didn't miss Lachlan's sharp exclamation at his revelation, but he couldn't look at his oldest friend. Not until this was settled. 'If that is a problem for you, it is something you should come to terms with now. Because I won't give her up, Rowan. No matter how you might protest our union.'

Rowan's smile showed off a slightly crooked incisor. 'I told you that I could not heal you because you were not broken. What is meant for you can never be taken, Grey. And I believe Clio is meant for you. Together, you will create a family that is also meant for you, no matter what that might look like, or how it might come about.'

As if her aunt's words conjured her from thin air, Clio pushed open the door and breezed into the room, Sir Robin perched nimbly on her shoulder. She was closely followed by her sister and her cousin.

Clio was a vision in sea-foam green with a bold, black checkerboard pattern pressed onto her skirts. She wore a fitted vest in black with green squares in an oppositional reflection of her skirt. A crisp white shirt and high collar completed her ensemble. Thomas wished for nothing more than to unbutton her and reveal the woman beneath. But now was hardly the time for such lascivious thoughts.

'So, it is decided? I think a summer wedding would be best, don't you?' She held her aunt's gaze as she stood next to Thomas, her hand resting gently on his shoulder. Dear God, was it possible to love someone so deeply, you forgot to breathe?

'Three months to plan a wedding?' Rowan seemed scandalised, which was a feat Thomas never expected to witness. Then she raised an elegant shoulder in a shrug. 'You have decided, and that is really all that matters.' Rowan's sharp tone caused the palm in the corner to begin shivering once more. 'But I suppose summer is always a lovely time for a wedding.' Her expression softened and Thomas didn't miss the slight flush painted over Lachlan's high cheekbones.

'I can't believe you found your spirit match.' Ellie's blue eyes were bright with joy for her sister. The two women could not be more opposite, but Thomas appreciated her guilelessness. He wasn't just gaining Clio in this union; Ellie had welcomed him into their family, and he would forever be grateful for her easy acceptance.

'I can't believe you haven't burned each other to a crisp yet.' Helena stroked the fox who sat at her feet.

He was still working on Helena.

'I think Sir Robin would appreciate some fresh air. Thomas, would you accompany me outside?' Clio's heavily lidded gaze had Thomas thinking of all the delicious ways he could use his cravat and whether or not there were any sturdy benches tucked away in hidden alcoves of Clio's back garden.

'I would be honoured, my lady.'

They excused themselves and as they walked down the hall, Clio pulled a letter from her pocket. 'I received correspondence from Violet.'

Thomas tried to keep his eyes level with her own and not let them dip down to the enticing V of her open collar. 'Are she and Anna well and readying for their trip to America?'

'They are. Anna's health is vastly improved, and Violet is excited to start a new life for them both in New York.'

Clio led Thomas through the house to the dining room. The French doors opened onto a small terrace that led down to the gardens. Winter still held London in its thrall, but a bright sun touched her face with fragile warmth.

Thomas allowed himself a moment to watch the woman who would soon become his bride. Her black hair shone nearly blue, pale cheeks brightening in the cold air. She was stunning. But more than that, she was a beacon of goodness in a world seemingly full of ugliness and evil. Taking her arm, they walked together down the stairs and onto the garden path.

Clio stopped by a stone bench tucked behind a rather large elm tree. Sir Robin hopped from her shoulder to a branch of the tree. 'Imagine if the doctor Violet hired hadn't discovered the true reason for Anna's illness. No wonder Arthur tried to accuse Violet of having an affair. I'm sure he wanted the man to stay well away from poor Anna. And if he had, the viscount's plan would have come to fruition. Violet would never have taken the poison and used it against her husband. He would still be alive, and we would never have met.'

Thomas stepped closer, backing Clio up to the tree and putting a hand on the ancient bark, leaning closer, needing to feel her heat, let it seep through his clothes and warm his heart.

'Do you think we are evil? For letting Violet get away with murder?' He ran his nose along her cheek, inhaling her into his lungs.

'I think what you said was true. She held a man accountable for unspeakable crimes. There is a certain poetic justice to it all.' Clio tilted her head, giving Thomas access to the delicate column of her throat.

Thomas pressed an open-mouth kiss to her fragrant skin, sucking hard enough to make Clio moan. 'I think we are done discussing this case.'

'Is that a command?' Desire flared in Clio's amber gaze.

He circled both of her wrists, lifting them over her head and pinning her against the smooth bark. 'Do you wish it to be?'

'Yes.'

One word, and he was instantly hard.

'My wicked witch.'

'My darling fiancé.' Clio leaned forward, nipping his jaw as sparks crackled between them.

'Bastard,' Sir Robin cooed in the branches above their heads.

\* \* \*

## MORE FROM DARCY McGUIRE

Another bewitching tale from Darcy McGuire, *The Hexing Miss Helena*, is available to order now here:

https://mybook.to/HexingMissHelena

# ACKNOWLEDGEMENTS

To my amazing Boldwood team, Megan, Emily, Niamh, Wendy, and the countless others who work so hard to make these words shine. To my talented agent, Katie Reed, for all her support. To my family for being so understanding. And always to the readers. You bring life to the characters and build worlds out of words. I'm forever grateful for your time, passion, and dedication to a well-told tale – or at least my attempt at one.

# ABOUT THE AUTHOR

**Darcy McGuire** is a high school counsellor who grew up in the wilds of New Zealand but happily settled in the Pacific Northwest. In between dodging territorial geese, gathering duck eggs, taking the dog for long walks, Darcy loves writing about fierce female protagonists who may dodge daggers and bullets but never seem to escape Cupid's Arrow.

Download your exclusive bonus content from Darcy McGuire here.

Follow Darcy on social media here:

facebook.com/AuthorDarcyMcGuire

instagram.com/authordarcymcguire

# ALSO BY DARCY MCGUIRE

You're cordially invited to

*The Scandal Sheet*

The home of swoon-worthy historical romance from the Regency to the Victorian era!

Warning: may contain spice

Sign up to the newsletter

https://bit.ly/thescandalsheet

# Boldw⊙⊙d

Boldwood Books is an award-winning fiction publishing company seeking out the best stories from around the world.

**Find out more at www.boldwoodbooks.com**

Join our reader community for brilliant books, competitions and offers!

Follow us
@BoldwoodBooks
@TheBoldBookClub

Sign up to our weekly deals newsletter

https://bit.ly/BoldwoodBNewsletter

Made in United States
Cleveland, OH
02 March 2026

33695205R10178